# REX

## BETH MICHELE

# TABLE OF CONTENTS

# DEDICATION

*To Rex, for demanding that your story be told. I hope I did it justice.*

"Love recognizes no barriers. It jumps hurdles, leaps fences, penetrates walls to arrive at its destination, full of hope."

—Maya Angelou

# PROLOGUE

## SEVENTEEN YEARS OLD

Hunter dragged me through the dark wooden doors—doors no seventeen-year-old should ever have to walk through—seeing things a seventeen-year-old should never have to see.

Yet there we were.

And it was all my fault.

Actually, I take that back. The woman that sat there, with the perfect hair, black pants and black jacket, as fake tears fell from her eyes? The one who didn't deserve to be called Mother?

Yeah, it was her fucking fault, too.

The smell of something awful distracted me. I never realized death had a smell. But it did, and I'd never forget it as long as I lived. I wasn't even sure how to explain it. Thick, stale air mixed with nothingness? That didn't begin to describe the scent that filled my lungs, constricting my airways and making me want to hold my breath and vomit at the same time. My knees were like lead, yet still I felt like I might collapse. Hunter grabbed onto my elbow tighter as we entered together.

"I don't fucking want to be here."

He peered down at me with a scowl and in a hushed whisper, said, "Watch your mouth, Rex."

His lips looked weird, like two straight lines. His eyes were glossy and sad, and even though anger burned a hole through my outsides, my insides felt the same.

We traipsed by rows of people, and I watched them, pity falling from their eyes onto our faces, but that was the last thing I deserved. No. I deserved to take the poison that would lead to a slow death. Because that's what it would be like from there on out. Living with it—the guilt that would tear apart my insides, shredding me until there was nothing left.

And still, that wouldn't be enough.

We walked by her, that woman who called herself my mother, and she reached out for me. A seething hatred that had been building for quite some time nearly exploded. But it wasn't the time or the place. As I felt her vile hand on my arm, I yanked out of her grasp, holding myself back from spitting on her, because that wouldn't be *appropriate*.

Thankfully, Hunter pulled me toward the front of the room, but I froze when I saw the small casket. I couldn't do it.

"Don't make me go up there, Hunter. Fuck. I can't."

When my feet came to a halt, Hunter turned and crouched down on the rug in front of me like I was a small child, looking up into my eyes. "He'd want to know you're here, want to see you one last time."

I nodded because that was all I had left, the tough kid I knew myself to be was crumbling. So I let Hunter go first, and my hands began to shake when I heard his quiet sobs as he softly spoke to Tyler. I wanted to tell him it was too late. But I didn't want to spoil his moment.

He stepped to the side, and I inhaled a deep breath before I took the three paces up to Tyler. In that moment, I was very thankful the casket was closed. I couldn't have looked at someone who no longer resembled my brother.

I placed my trembling palm flat on the shiny wood, closing my eyes and dragging in a deep breath. "I'm so sorry," I whispered to Tyler. "I'll never forgive myself. You know how special you were to me." A tear dripped from my eye. "I love you, buddy. I hope wherever you're going they have lots of that mint chocolate chip ice cream that you like, and baseball games so you can show them how you play a mean first base. I know there will be lots of music so you'll be able to play your guitar." My voice cracked. "I'll look for you when I chase the moon."

There was nothing more to say. I couldn't form any more words anyway. Hands were wrapping around my throat and the sensation of being choked forced me to let out a pained howl. It wasn't pretty. It was repulsive and loud, attracting glances from everyone in the room.

I turned around and bolted for the door. Hunter followed, catching up to me and clutching my wrist, making me stumble back.

"Where are you going?" he asked, that wrinkle he always got when he was confused came out on his forehead.

"I want to go chase the moon," I said, huffing out heavy breaths.

"It's daytime, Rex."

I shrugged. It didn't matter. I'd never catch it anyway.

# CHAPTER ONE

## PRESENT—TEN YEARS LATER

## LOVE SUCKS

The door to the shop jingles as I'm cleaning up my station in the back, organizing the inks and disposing of needles. I'm getting ready to get the hell out of here. I've been here since the crack of dawn, and I'm bone tired.

Zeek pokes his head in, nodding toward the door. "It looks like we've got a walk-in and I've gotta zip. Going to see my babe."

"Come the fuck on, Zeek." I grit my teeth, exhaustion bringing out the monster in me. "I'm fucking tired."

"Listen," he grins, "you've seen Tabitha's wrath. You're more than welcome to bear the brunt when I tell her you forced me to stay," he eyes the front desk area, "and tattoo some ridiculously hot chick with a great rack."

My ears, among other things, perk up at his words. He knows my resistance is next to nothing when it comes to women. Plus, tits are my weakness. "All right. Get out of here. I'll see you tomorrow."

Zack Reeker, better known as Zeek, manages this shop. He's the one who hired me six months ago when I moved from Boston back to New York City, in desperate need of a gig. I'd been staying with my brother, Hunter, at first. That lasted all of about a month. While he wasn't pushing me out, we were starting to grate on each others' nerves. The irony is that I actually moved back to the city to be closer to him. He's pretty much all I have. My father died of a heart attack when I was twelve and my mother is still alive. But as far as I'm concerned, she's dead to me.

For at least a month, I pounded the pavement, portfolio in hand, showing examples of my work to anyone who was willing. I was like a fucking puppy dog with my tail wagging, waiting for someone to throw me a bone, give me a chance. Zeek took an instant liking to my work, and I took an instant liking to him. He doesn't mess around. He's honest, no-nonsense, and talented as hell.

"Thanks, man. Enjoy." He winks, his cackling an echo in my ears as he heads out.

"I'll be right with you," I yell, and huff out a breath, the only thought on my brain is collapsing onto my bed and zoning for a good eight hours.

I scrape a hand through my hair, bypassing a couple of stations before making it to the front. The first thing I see is a curtain of blonde streaks hanging down over her face as she checks out one of the tattoo books.

"Hey. What can I do for you?"

Her head lifts slowly, hair falling away to reveal a face comprised of porcelain skin, sharp cheekbones, and eyes framed by thick, lush lashes. I'm trying to catch wind of the color from here—pale blue, maybe grey.

"Hi." She stands up, her lips pencil straight like she's nervous or scared, maybe even uptight. That's when I get a good look at the rest of her. My eyes roam lower from the full, round tits amplified by her tank top, to her skirt, baring legs that seem to go on for miles.

What I could do with those legs.

"I want to get a tattoo." Her voice is bland, shoulders completely rigid.

"Okay. Do you already have something in mind?" I turn my head, nodding in the direction of my station. "I can bring you back and you can look through some of my designs, get some ideas."

"I already know what I want," she retorts, and there's a sudden chill in the air. I can't say that tattooing her is going to be all that much fun. She seems like a fucking iceberg, and I'm internally cursing Zeek for handing this one off.

"Sure. Let's sit down, you can fill me in and then I can sketch it out for you."

I take a seat next to her and lean back in the chair, angling my body in her direction. She turns to me, and that's when I get a good look at her eyes. They're a blue-gray, really pretty. But they're cold and sad. For a second, I wonder what that's about.

"I'm looking for something simple." She points her index finger to her upper arm. "I just want it to say, *love sucks*."

I repeat it as if I didn't hear her correctly. "You want it to say, 'love sucks'?"

"Yeah."

As a tattoo artist, it's not my job to argue what art someone wants on their body, but for some reason this doesn't sit right with me. "You do realize this is permanent, right?"

She cocks her head, narrowing her eyes at me. "Yes, of course. I'm well-versed in what a tattoo is, thank you."

And Jesus, she's feisty.

"Okay, but...." I shake my head from side to side. "What happens when love doesn't suck anymore? What happens when it's pretty fucking amazing?" Where that came from, I don't have a fucking clue. That's one four letter word I know nothing about. "I mean, if you were seventy, sure, but you're young, gorgeous...."

Her lips twitch at the corners, but fall flat again. "Listen, are you going to do the tattoo for me or not?" she hisses. This one's got a serious bite on her. Somebody fucked her up bad.

"Well—"

"You know what?" She jumps up, heading for the door. "Just forget it. I'll find someone who'll do it without interrogating me." She storms out the door as quickly as she blew in, kicking up a trail of dust in her wake.

What the fuck was that?

# CHAPTER TWO

## THE BITCH GENE

*Vanessa*

All I wanted was a tattoo—two simple words—yet he refused to do it for me. Isn't that against the law of tattooing or something? That they can question you? They're getting paid to do whatever you want. Now I have to find another shop, but it's late and I'm tired.

I lift a finger to wipe away the wetness on my cheek. I hate to admit it, but his words got to me. What if someday love doesn't suck for me like it sucks for my divorced parents?

I watched them day after day, week after week, year after year, keeping up a facade. Never once did I see the soft brush of a cheek, that simple touch of the lips that says so much more than words. There was no hand holding, nor were there stolen kisses and glances when they thought no one was watching. Tender hugs were nonexistent. Instead, my ears rang from the relentless arguing, doors slamming when they thought I was asleep. The flannel blanket and pillow that were often on the sofa when I came downstairs for breakfast, followed by lame excuses of not being able to sleep. Even then I knew better.

I duck under a store awning, squeezing my eyes shut, trying to force back things I don't want to remember. But they come anyway.

*I got under my blue sheets and pulled the blankets over my head... again. The brown eyes of my teddy bear stared back at me. Even he knew what was happening. And while I was probably too old to hug a stuffed animal, he was all I ever had, so I pulled him close and scrunched my face up tight when I heard the first noise that hurt my ears.*

*"You're a fucking asshole," Mom shouted, and I wanted to laugh at the fact that I was always told in school never to say those words, yet somehow it was okay for them. I didn't understand why they were always saying such mean things to one another.*

*"Maybe I wouldn't be an asshole if you weren't such a bitch."*

*I kept shaking my head, talking to my teddy bear under my breath, but more bad words came.*

*"I saw the way you were fucking staring at those men tonight," Dad said. "I think you forget that you're my wife and that we're married. You're supposed to love me."*

*"Oh, is that what this is?" Mom laughed, but she didn't sound happy at all, and her voice got even louder. "Because that is absurd. This, as fucked up as it is, is a partnership of sorts. You and I both know that. It serves a purpose, plain and simple. Just like Vanessa did, didn't she, Alex?" she snarled, and I pushed off the blanket and sat up straighter in my bed when she said my name, wondering what that meant, listening for anything else that would give me a clue. But the only thing I heard was more cursing from my father before doors slammed and hinges rattled, sending me the same message over and over.*

*Love was cruel and I didn't ever want any part of it.*

"Excuse me, miss," a middle-aged woman with gentle eyes and a cane apologizes after she bumps into me, jarring me from a place I didn't want to be anyway, reminding me where I am. Reminding me *who* I am. Am I a seventy-year-old woman? No, far from it. I'm only twenty-seven. But do I have hope for love? No. I do, however, have hope for sex. Because that's what feels good.

Sometimes in the heat of the moment, I close my eyes, trying to imagine what it would be like if I loved that person, and they loved me. Maybe my heart would beat a little faster or a flutter would make my stomach tingle. But I'll never know—because I'm empty. I don't have love to give. I don't even think I know what the word means.

I walk up a few blocks, spotting a bar on the corner. It just happens to be the one my friend, Ryder Callahan, owns. Being in the event planning business gives me an opportunity to meet a lot of great people. Ryder is one of them. He and I met at an event I organized about six years ago. We got to know each other and even dated on and off, but then he moved to Colorado for three years and we parted as friends. I'm glad he came back, though. Aside from my best friend Olivia Redmond, he's the only other person I feel close to.

The bar is packed when I walk in, but Ryder waves me over the moment he sees me. "Hey, Vanessa, what's up, darlin'? Hey, Jim." He waves his hand in a sideways motion. "Move over so my friend here can sit down."

Jim's bald head does a quick shake before he takes his beer and slides over, his eyes going back to a baseball game on the television overhead.

Ryder pushes the peanuts at me, then leans his elbows on the counter of the bar. "So, what brings you in so late tonight?"

"It's a long story," I reply, popping some nuts in my mouth.

"I'm listening. *After* you finish chewing. I really don't feel like seeing your food." He chuckles and I flick his arm.

"Well, I decided I wanted to get a tattoo, and I went down to Intricate Ink to—"

He cuts me off. "Yeah, I know those guys. They're cool and they do great work."

"Well, as I was saying before I was rudely interrupted," I smile, "I wanted to get a tattoo but the asshole in there wouldn't do it. He was questioning me like what I wanted was stupid."

"The asshole didn't say it was stupid," a voice calls out from behind me, and I whip my head around. "He wanted to make sure you wouldn't regret it."

My cheeks burnish a deep red before I stiffen my spine. "And now you've added eavesdropping onto your list of offenses."

"Listen, Blondie," he says, making my eyes thin, "I came in here to get a beer. Ryder, can I have a beer, please?"

"Sure, Rex, coming right up." Ryder moves down to the far end of the bar while I continue to give this guy Rex the evil eye. He's pretty tall, maybe six feet, so I have to lift my chin to reach his gaze.

"Hey." He holds his hands up in defeat. "I'm not here for you. I just came in to get a beer on my way home."

"Here you go." Ryder flicks the cap off and hands him the bottle.

"Thanks, man." He tips the neck of the bottle to his full lips that I'm trying not to notice, before plodding over to a table, giving me a chance to check out his ass. But that's not what draws my attention. What pulls my eyes in is the hint of a tattoo on the back of his neck. I can't quite make out what it is, but I'm a sucker for ink. It's very hot, and so is he. Well, that is, until he opens his mouth.

"You know," Ryder says when I turn back around, "I don't know what happened at the shop, but Rex is a good guy, and if he didn't tattoo you, I'm sure he had good reason. In other words," he edges forward, whispering, "don't be a bitch."

My lips kick up into a grin, because he's right. I have the bitch gene. I inherited it from my mom. Maybe that's why my father often slept on the couch. Maybe that's why they just got divorced. Maybe that's why there's no hope for me. I huff out a sigh, then pick my bitchy ass up from the chair, crossing the bar to Rex's table. He's watching the ball game and I clear my throat to get his attention.

He doesn't even give me a chance to speak because he instantly chimes in, "If you think I'm going to tattoo you, you're out of your gorgeous mind. So I hope that's not why you came over here." He cracks a smile, circling the rim of the bottle with his thumb.

That's the second time he's called me gorgeous, but the first time I'm noticing the dimple in his right cheek and the beautiful, rich brown of his eyes. He's still a jerk, though. They all are.

He kicks the chair out, motioning with his chin for me to sit. "You want to join me? I promise I'm harmless. Well," he chuckles, "kind of." My lips purse, but curve into a smile as I drop my bag on the table and sit down.

"So, you do know how to smile," he jokes, leaning back in his chair. "You should do it more often. It suits you a lot better than that scowl you were sporting in the shop."

"Well," I challenge, swinging my hair over my shoulder, "maybe you should try to be more accommodating."

His eyebrows jump, a devilish grin spreading across his face. "Oh, I can be *very* accommodating. What did you have in mind?"

I shake my head at his off-color remark. Of course it's about sex. It always is.

My eyes do a quick roll before I remember why I came over here in the first place. "I actually just wanted to apologize. I didn't mean to jump down your throat."

"Okay, that's cool. So, do you come here often?" He smiles, knocking back more of his beer before setting it down on the table.

I shift a hand to my hip, cocking my head to the side. "You did not seriously just ask me if I come here often? That is the lamest pick-up line in the book."

"Whoa, there. Who said anything about trying to pick you up? Someone's got an awfully big head. I was only asking if you frequent Ryder's place a lot, that's all."

"Oh, sorry." I tug at the corner of my lip, feeling like a complete idiot. "Yeah, I do. Ryder's a good friend of mine. Anyway, I should go." With that, I push back my chair, making my way to the door.

"Wait a second," he shouts out above the roar of the customers. "That's it?"

"Yeah, that's it." I don't even know if he hears me and I really don't care. I keep walking until I'm outside, the air warm though a sudden chill has me pulling my jacket tighter around my shoulders.

Because what else is there?

# CHAPTER THREE

## MR. CURIOSITY

Wow, and I thought I was fucked up. I think I may have met my match. She's got anger, bitterness, and pain written all over her. Wears it like a badge. She doesn't need to ink her skin. It seeps from her pores, leaks out into the atmosphere, probably infecting everyone around her.

After she walks out the door, I polish off my beer and take a seat back at the bar. I tap on the counter with my index finger, signaling for another drink and information.

I want information.

Ryder sets another beer down in front of me before continuing to serve other customers. I should be home in bed. But instead, I'm sitting here, waiting to get Ryder's attention—because I'm curious. Even though curiosity ends up killing the cat.

My hand darts out to grab his arm when he finally makes his way over. "Hey, you gotta sec?"

"Sure, let me just get the gal over there her drink." He walks away and my gaze follows to the brunette bombshell sitting on the last chair. Ringlet curls frame her face, green eyes, and as I go lower, lead me to cleavage that suddenly makes me forget what I'm doing here.

I hop off the stool and rake a hand through my hair, making my way toward her. With a subtle shove, I squeeze my way in-between her and the guy attempting to sidle up next to her. Leaning an elbow on the bar, I take a lazy stroll over her body before coming back to her eyes. "Can I buy you a drink, beautiful?"

She fingers a curl, twirling it around seductively, my mouth watering in response. She's got plump lips that would fit perfectly around my cock—and she looks like she's interested.

"Sure. I'm drinking a gin and tonic," she says, my dick twitching when her tongue skips across her lower lip.

"Hey, Ryder," I shout, "when you get a chance, another gin and tonic for the lady."

"Lady," she scoffs, "that makes me feel old. And, believe me," her fingers toy with the buttons on her blouse, "there's nothing about me that's old." She edges forward, shimmying her breasts in front of me, and I raise an interested brow.

"How about you tell me your name?" I ask, forcing my eyes back up to her face.

"I'm Diane, and you are—"

No longer interested.

Diane is the name of the woman I despise most in this world, so she basically just poured a bucket of ice water all over me and my hard-on. It's a done deal. There's no way I'm screwing someone named Diane. Not gonna happen.

"You know," I tap my watch a few times, "I just remembered I have somewhere I need to be. Sorry, beautiful," I apologize, giving her a quick kiss on the cheek so I don't offend her. I throw some money on the bar. "Later, Ryder."

"See ya, man."

The slight chill in the air outside only adds to the pure hatred brewing inside of me. My mother. She's never far away. I can never distance myself enough from her. Reminders lurk around every corner—of what she did, of who she is. What kind of a woman cheats on their husband repeatedly, or isn't tuned in to the fact that her nine-year-old son is being molested. My fists clench at my sides while my feet kick up dirt on the sidewalk. She should have known. She should have been there. Instead, my brother is dead at the hands of pills that he took from *her* medicine cabinet.

She sickens me and I'll never forgive her.

I'm fucking pissed by the time I make it to my apartment. Not only am I angry, I'm horny. And now I'm screwed, and definitely not in the way I was hoping for tonight.

The door slams shut behind me and I toss my keys on the coffee table. My apartment is small—a one bedroom with a living room, bathroom, and galley kitchen. This place is definitely nothing to write home about, but it's what I can afford right now and works for me. It's nothing like Hunter's penthouse on the Upper West Side. But then again, I'm not the owner of a hundred million dollar software company either.

Plodding into the bedroom, I shuck off my shoes, jeans, and t-shirt. I literally collapse onto the mattress, exhaustion overtaking me, yet I'm restless. I'm never gonna be able to sleep when I'm this worked up and my dick is hard. Fuck.

I could call Aileen, who used to work at the shop. We've hooked up before, but it's been a while and she tends to get attached. Attachments don't work for me. Straight, uncomplicated sex does. But tonight, it looks like I'm on my own.

My hand travels down to the waistband of my boxers and I reach inside, gripping my shaft that's now hard as freaking steel. One look at the brunette's tits and I was a goner. I stroke my cock while visions of ripping her shirt open invade my mind, licking and sucking her nipples until the tips harden and she's whimpering like crazy. I can almost smell her pussy, completely soaked as she climbs over me, riding my face. Her slick juices cover my mouth, my tongue, my cheeks, until I can't get enough.

My hand speeds up as I imagine her pinching her nipples, moaning, my tongue delving further into her wetness. Her lustful gaze bears down on me, watching, as I lick her clean. I groan, my eyes clamping shut, hips bucking off the bed, breathing completely out of control as my orgasm tears through me. And then I open them, startled, realizing the eyes staring back at me didn't belong to her.

They belong to Blondie.

# CHAPTER FOUR

## GOTTA HAVE FRIENDS

# *Vanessa*

"So, how's the event business going?" Olivia asks me as we sit in a booth inside Heavenly Lattes. Coffee is something neither of us can get through the day without and is pretty much on par with air. Trent, the owner of the shop, brings over something on the house every time we're here. That's because we've been customers for eight years.

This is where Olivia and I met. It was my first day in Manhattan, and I was desperate as always for coffee. We literally bumped into one another. Once we started chatting, we discovered an instant connection and have been attached at the hip ever since. She knows everything about me and is so much more than just a friend. She's like the family I always wanted but never had.

"It's very busy. I have six events next month, and then the following month I'm traveling to Portland. I haven't been there but have heard good things about it so I'm excited."

Fisting a hand on her hip, she tilts her head to the side, scrutinizing me with those deep, blue eyes. "What is it? What's wrong?"

I shake my head and smile. "You know, it's rather irritating that I can't pull anything over on you. You're like my own personal lie detector test."

"Yup, and the clock's ticking, so what's going on?" she asks, her fingers rapping lightly on the table.

"I've been thinking about the last conversation I had with my dad, a little over two months ago. He was his ice-cold self on the phone, as usual, and it was the same useless discussion we always have. But, when he brought up my mother and the divorce, do you know what popped into my head?" Tension in my jaw makes its way to my whole face and I blanch. "I was thinking about when my mother sat me down, I don't even remember how old I was, maybe seven, and told me there was no Santa Claus. She said she didn't want me forming unnecessary emotional attachments and having expectations for something that wasn't real." I let out a laugh, but there's no smile to go along with it. "I guess she didn't want me forming emotional attachments to real people either."

Olivia gives my hand a sympathetic squeeze, offering me the courage to continue. "I don't know. Something in his voice gave me the sense that he's upset about the divorce. Go figure." I curl the straw wrapper around my finger, trying to sort out my feelings. "I honestly thought there was no love lost between them. But I guess he still loves her, as twisted as that sounds. Anyway," I exhale a breath, "love sucks."

"So that's your new mantra now, huh?" She lifts her fork to her mouth, savoring the taste of the chocolate. "Well, I have a solution that will lift your spirits," she says, a garbled mouthful of frosting obstructing her next words.

"I'm sorry, come again, I couldn't quite understand you." I laugh. "You're enjoying that cake a little too much."

She sets her fork down gently on her plate. "Okay, so Hunter and I are going to the club tonight, and I want you to come."

My head falls back against the booth. "What, so I can sit alone at the bar while you two are dancing the night away? No thanks."

"Nope." She pops her lips together, grinning mischievously, and I know I'm in trouble.

I sit up straight, eyes pinching together. "I sense a scheme of sorts. What have you got up your sleeve?"

"Well...." She scoots closer, clasping her hands together on the table as if she's about to deliver mind-blowing information. "Remember I told you Hunter's brother moved to the city. He's going to invite him along tonight. I think you'll have fun. He's seriously hot," she says with that same Cheshire grin, "and he's got tattoos. You like them twisted, and he's definitely not run of the mill."

I cringe, remembering her last attempt to set me up and how badly it ended. "Liv, I appreciate it, but remember when you tried to hook me up with Victor, that guy from the salon you go to—"

She interrupts, placing a sympathetic hand on my shoulder. "I know, but how was I supposed to know he wasn't into women. I promise you," she makes an *X* with her finger across her chest, "his brother is *not* gay. Plus, I'm not setting you up. He's not relationship material anyway. It's just to hang out for one night and have fun. Besides," she winks, "he's nice to look at."

"Okay, I'll think about it. Oh," I snap my fingers in front of me, "get this. So after that call with my dad and this whole divorce thing, I started thinking a lot about maybe getting a tattoo. And last night, for whatever reason, it hit me, and I decided to be spontaneous. So, I went to this tattoo shop and the asshole there wouldn't tattoo me."

"What do you mean? Why not?"

"He didn't like the idea of my tattoo," I reply, even though I'll never admit a part of me is grateful. He was probably right. It was a shitty idea.

"What was it?" She stares at me over the rim of her cup, blue eyes steeped in curiosity.

"Well, I told him I wanted *love sucks*." I spit out the words, waiting for the impending lecture, but it never comes. Instead, she starts laughing.

"You told him you wanted *what*?" Her eyes grow wide, shoulders shaking with laughter, and now I'm getting irritated.

"What's so funny?" I hiss.

She rolls her eyes, lips quirking at the corners. "That's ridiculous. I don't blame him for not tattooing you. You want that on your skin permanently, V? What happens when you fall in love?" she asks, still looking at me like I've grown two heads.

Obviously, this isn't a fight I'm going to win so I might as well play along. "Well, then I'll cross it out and put *love's grand*."

"Oh, V," she says, patting my hand. "You really need a night out."

# CHAPTER FIVE

## WHAT'S YOUR STORY?

"Zeek, that tattoo is brilliant." I've been watching him do a tattoo on the arm of a guy whose son is returning home from war, and the man is a freaking genius. The resemblance to the picture is spot on: shaggy hair, bold green eyes, cleft indent in his chin, bright smile.

I listened as Michael told Zeek his story. His son, Jed, the class clown and sports enthusiast with aspirations to become a professional baseball player, instead went off to fight for our country. And when he said goodbye to his only son, he wasn't sure if he'd ever see him again. But now Jed's finally coming home.

Michael stands up, examining the tattoo running from his shoulder partway to his elbow. His face completely transforms, the tough exterior peeled away, only a man with a grateful heart left behind. A tear pools in the corner of his eye and he roughly wipes it away. Then he turns around, immediately embracing Zeek and slapping him on the back.

"Thanks, man," he says with the utmost respect before Zeek covers his tattoo with a bandage.

Everyone that comes into this shop has a story. Day after day, I'm privileged to get a tiny glimpse into someone's life, to see through a window, one that remains closed to the outside world.

I may not make a lot of money tattooing, but there's no way on earth I'd want to do anything else. My mother always told me this was a crap profession, but again, she never had a clue about what really mattered. The people here matter. Their stories matter. What we imprint on their skin *matters*.

"What's the plan for tonight?" Zeek asks as he cleans up his station. "Tabitha and I are going to maybe head out later and meet some friends, if you want to join us. I think Stevie and Jaden are coming too."

My cell phone chirps and I pull it from my back pocket. "Hold that thought." I slide the screen, seeing Hunter's number. "Hey, bro, what's up?"

"I called to see if you wanted to hang out with Olivia and me tonight? We're going to a club."

"What, and be a third wheel while you guys are eye-fucking each other?" I say with my usual edge, watching Zeek, Stevie, and Jaden laugh.

He lets out a loud sigh. "No, wiseass, she's bringing a friend. I think you'll like her. She's got the same kind of attitude as you," he adds, chuckling through the phone.

"But tits, how are her tits?" I ask, and I know he's shaking his head on the other end of the line. "All right, all right, what the hell. What time?"

"I'll pick you up at eight," he says. "They're going to meet us there."

"Okay, see you then."

I hope she's got a great rack.

"Jesus, Rex." Hunter scans the apartment, eyeing the clothes and beer bottles spread around the living room. "You need a female touch."

"There's only one female touch I need." I grab my dick before snagging my keys from the table.

"Yes, and might I point out," he waves his hand in the direction of my crotch, "that little gesture right there is one of the reasons you don't have one."

"Funny. Now let's go. I need to get laid tonight," I joke, well, half-joke, just to get under his skin a bit more.

"And yet another reason." He chuckles, shaking his head as he trudges down the stairs in front of me.

"So, where are we going anyway?" I ask as we head outside, waiting for his lead in terms of direction.

"We're gonna take a taxi uptown to the Open Door Lounge." He leans over the curb with his finger in the air, attempting to hail a cab as they speed by us. Of course, they're all full.

"Why are we taking a cab anyway? Why didn't you just have your driver wait for us?" If we have a chance to travel in style, I don't understand why my brother consistently turns that down.

A cab finally screeches to a halt in front of us, and he holds the door open for me to climb in first. "You know, Rex, I don't know if you'll understand this or not, but sometimes I just want to feel like a normal person."

"Whatever, bro, but I feel like a normal person all the time, so for me it would be a nice change of pace." I laugh, and he smiles, shutting the door behind us.

"So, how are things with you and the porn queen?" I tease, his lips flattening into a straight line. The driver speeds off, both of us thrown back against the seat.

Gotta love New York City taxis.

"I wish you wouldn't call her that. You know that's not what she does," he replies, annoyed. But as far as I'm concerned, Hunter hit the jackpot—falling for an erotic romance author. I should only be so lucky.

"Well, it's close enough." I pull a pack of gum from my pocket and peel the wrapper open, holding a piece out to Hunter. "Gum?"

He pushes it away with his hand before responding to my wiseass remark. "She doesn't act in porn, she writes erotic novels. There *is* a difference."

"Whatever you say, bro, whatever you say."

The line to get into the club is wrapped around the block when we arrive. "Do you see them?" I ask, and he steps out of line to check for Olivia and her friend.

"No, but I'm going to text her. They're probably already inside." He plucks his cell phone from his jeans and slides open the screen. After a minute, a grin spreads clear across his face. "Yeah, they're inside," he says, and I'm not even going to ask what that's about. "Sit tight, I'm going to see what I can do about bypassing this line."

Music filters out from the club and I tap a lazy foot against the sidewalk as I wait for Hunter. My eyes roll over all the hot females. There are some real lookers here, and I'm keeping every body part crossed that Olivia's friend is my type. If she's anything like my brother's girl, I'll have hit the motherload.

Not more than five minutes later, Hunter is walking toward me with a satisfied smile. "We're in. Let's go."

"What'd you do?" I follow behind him. "Slip him some cash?"

"Something like that," he mumbles, weaving through a now irritated hoard of people. Someone curses at us as we walk by, but I ignore it. Being Hunter's brother has certain advantages. This just happens to be one of them.

"Normal guy, my ass." I chuckle, and he raises a shameless brow.

The music is thumping when we step inside, the smell of smoke and sweat assaulting my senses, and I breathe it in, instantly relaxing. Bright blasts of multi-colored light mix with blackness, illuminating drunken faces and clinking glasses. My shoes stick to the floor, the beat pulsing thunderously under my feet as we push our way through the crowd.

Hunter raises a hand in the air and smiles, obviously catching sight of Olivia. I'm not really one for being soft, but she's really good for him and a welcome change from the women he's been with over the years—money-hungry, spoiled, self-serving brats.

As we get closer, my eyes rove over the long blonde waves of the chick sitting next to her. A sexy, exposed back also draws my attention. That must be my date for the evening. As long as her name isn't Diane, I'm all in.

Hunter grabs Olivia, smacking his lips against hers as if he hasn't seen her for a month. It makes me want to gag. "Hi, sweetheart." He kisses her again, this time with his tongue before grasping her ass.

"Okay, why don't you guys get a room," I suggest, and Olivia grins, while Hunter tosses me a death stare. The girl next to her pivots around on the stool and the world is suddenly spinning on its axis. "You've got to be shitting me?" I exclaim. "Blondie?"

"You're kidding me?" She turns away, scowling, clearly not happy about her new nickname. A second later, her gaze falls back on Olivia. "*This* is Hunter's brother? This is the guy I was telling you about at the café."

I grin, pleased that I was a topic of conversation. "You were talking about me?" I wink, and she frowns, the tension in her jaw palpable.

Hunter's eyes dart back and forth from me to her, and I realize I don't even know her name. "Wait a minute, you two know one another?" He rubs his chin, his brows taking a dive.

"Kind of." I stare at the grimace on her face. "She came into the shop last night."

Olivia breaks out into laughter, but she and I are the only ones who seem to find this situation funny. Blondie is eyeing her like she wants to rip her hair out. She's almost scary.

"Come on, Hunter." Olivia pulls him toward the dance floor. "Let them duke it out. I want to dance with you." He willingly follows behind, leaving the two of us alone.

"So?" She drops her hands to her sides, mouth still pulling down on that pretty face of hers.

"So?" I mimic, letting my eyes travel the length of her body. The dress she's wearing molds to her in just the way that I like—revealing everything: the smooth angle of her hips, firm breasts, and long, toned legs. I smile, thinking about getting off last night, those pale blue eyes boring into me.

"What's so funny?" she asks, her gaze narrowed. If looks could kill, I'd be a dead man.

"Nothing. Can I buy you a drink, Blondie?"

With fire in her eyes, she fists her hands on her hips, staring me down. God, she's sexy as hell when she's angry. "My *name* is Vanessa. Are you going to stop calling me Blondie?"

"I don't know, Blondie." I grin wickedly. "Are you going to let me buy you a drink?"

And finally a smile.

"You know...." I step closer to her, itching to tangle my hands in those golden strands. I don't touch her, but get close enough to inhale the fresh scent of her perfume. She smells fucking good. "Being a bitch doesn't suit you."

"*Excuse* me? You don't know the first thing about me," she snaps, and I'm near enough that I can feel her breath blowing on my lips, so close I could probably kiss her. Not a good idea though since she might sprout claws any minute.

"It's not who you are, it's a mask you hide behind, to hide whatever's cut you so deep. How do I know that? Because I do the same God damn thing."

And then I take a step back.

What the hell is wrong with me? I slipped. I'm not *that* guy—the cuddly, sharing type. But I see myself when I look at her, and for some reason, I want her to know that I understand.

There's a flicker in her eyes, maybe surprise that I can read her so well. A small smile tugs at her lips as she glances downward and something inside me feels victorious, as if I've chipped away at a tiny piece of her armor.

"Okay," she submits, finally. "I'll have a rum and coke."

I nod, and sandwich my way between two customers at the bar, ordering her drink and a beer for myself. I've never been a heavy drinker and I don't do hard liquor. Probably because I saw the damage it did to my mother, and I don't want to end up like her.

Turning around, I grab our drinks and gesture toward a table in the corner. I let Blondie go ahead of me, taking in the slope of her back in that low-cut dress that fits like it was made for her.

"I can feel you staring at me."

There's not a hint of defensiveness in her response. In fact, I think it's quite the opposite. She takes a seat, a subtle smile playing on her lips as I place our drinks on the table.

"Well," I reply, "you're a stunner. There's a lot to stare at." Her cheeks flush pink in response and she quickly lifts her drink to her mouth. "So... you left Ryder's bar last night pretty abruptly."

She shrugs, setting her drink down and swirling the ice around with her finger. "There wasn't anything else to say."

"Oh, I don't know about that." I take a long pull of my beer. "There's always more to say. What's your story?"

She raises her eyes to mine in question. "My story?"

"Yeah, your story. Everyone's got one. As a tattoo artist, I hear people's stories every day. So, what's yours?" I lean back in the chair, arms folded across my chest.

"I don't have a story." She casts her gaze to a group of people at a nearby table.

"Bullshit." I scrutinize her as if she's a specimen I'm trying to dissect. "Your eyes say something completely different."

She's quiet for a few minutes before her gaze settles on me again and she heaves out a hard sigh. "The bitch thing is hereditary."

"Ah, from your dad," I tease, and she actually laughs. It's light and airy, carefree, the total opposite of how she presents herself.

"Yeah, when he wore dresses it came out the most." She smiles, and that's when I notice the way one side of her mouth lifts a tiny bit higher than the other as she does.

Her gleam fades and she pauses, staring into her glass before continuing. "My mom is a first-class bitch. So let's just say I learned from the best. She's one of the hardest women I've ever met: cold, condescending, judgmental."

"I've got one of those, too. And you want to know the irony?" I shake my head on a laugh. "She writes bestselling romance novels, sappy, happy ending shit. Yet she's as cold as ice."

Raising the drink to her lips, she swallows it down hard. "I'm sorry to hear that."

"Likewise." I clink my bottle against her glass just before she polishes it off, slamming it on the table. "To shitty mothers," I salute, picking her glass back up, the ice clinking around at the bottom. "You want another?"

"Are you trying to get me drunk?" she asks, but she's smiling when she says it.

"Oh, believe me, I want you sober." My gaze sails down to her tits, then lower, to discover her thighs shifting on the chair. She's affected by me.

Good to know.

I move my chair closer, our arms nearly touching. "So, how do you know Ryder?"

Her eyes rake over my face and land on my lips. They linger a beat before returning to my stare. "Um, we've been friends for several years. I'm a manager for an event company and we ended up meeting at a charity ball I organized years ago. Ryder has the warehouse also, so he supplies liquor for the events. He's been a really good friend to me."

"So, you're from New York then?" I ask, and something shifts in her eyes again.

"No, I'm originally from Seattle but moved here eight years ago. What about you?" Her stare once again wanders to my mouth then slides back up.

"I'm from Harrison, a suburb just outside of New York City, but moved to Boston to go to college and ended up staying there until six months ago when I moved back." My gaze drops to her full lips, and I can't help wondering what she tastes like. I bet she's so fucking sweet.

And now I'm done with the small talk.

"Do you want to dance?" I hold out my hand hoping she'll take it, and I've won yet another battle when she does.

As she slips her hand into mine, my thumb involuntarily skims across the top of it, skin bristling at how smooth she is. I bet she's smooth everywhere and my dick jumps at the thought. I'd love to see how smooth her thighs are as I'm spreading her open on my bed.

We plow through the crowd to the dance floor that's packed with people gyrating, rubbing against one another shamelessly. I snake my arms around Vanessa's waist and she loops hers around my neck, our faces only inches apart. Every part of our bodies connects as she melts into me, swaying to the slow, sultry rhythm. Lights are flashing, swarms of people grinding all around us. We get bumped from behind and I grasp her hips, my erection pressing into her. She raises her eyes to meet mine, piercing me with a stare that nearly has me carrying her to a back room and fucking her.

She leans in, her breath hot against my ear, shouting, "I like your ink!" And my skin tingles as she runs her nail along the lines of the tattoo on my neck. When she backs away and her eyes find mine again, they are dotted with heat. "It's beautiful," she says, staring at my mouth. The rum on her breath urges me closer and I want to taste it from her lips. I want to explore her mouth, flick my tongue against her warmth, drag it down her body until she's writhing beneath me.

Her head comes to rest against my chin, my fingers inching up her flesh, massaging her in slow circles. She shivers, prompting me to splay my other hand across her lower back, pressing her tight against me. I know she feels my arousal, it's practically bursting from my zipper.

We stay like this, song after song. The music continues to pound around us, the crowd falling away. Her scent is intoxicating, sweat and something fruity radiating from her skin, taunting me, until I can't take it anymore.

I bring my lips to her ear, whispering, "I want you to come home with me tonight."

She raises her head, awareness shading her eyes. "Why would I do that?"

"Because I think you want me as much as I want you." I lean down, brushing my lips against hers. She's so God damn soft. "Don't you?"

She hesitates, and for a second I wonder if I'm wrong. "Yes," she finally breathes out, before pulling my lips back down to hers, taking what she wants. And I fucking want to give it.

Her lips part and I slip inside her warm mouth, our tongues sliding against one another, the sweet taste of rum flowing between us. She tastes even better than I imagined and I can't resist deepening the kiss, her fingers responding by cinching the fabric of my shirt as she rubs her firm tits across my chest. Desire rips through me, and she moans when I grip her ass, grinding against her. I break the kiss with a loud pop, both of us breathing hot and heavy.

"You ready?"

She nods, and I take her hand to lead her off the dance floor. "Wait." She stops abruptly. "What about Olivia and Hunter? I need to let her know I'm leaving."

"I'll take care of it." I yank my cell phone out and shoot Hunter a quick text. "All set. Now let's go."

We weave our way outside and wait by the curb to grab a taxi. When I glance over at Vanessa, she's flipping her hair around her finger, lip caught between her teeth.

"You anxious, Blondie?" I whisper in her ear, grazing the shell with my tongue. She takes a hard swallow and nods her head.

"Good. I want you anxious."

# CHAPTER SIX

## ANXIOUS MUCH

### *Vanessa*

His breath in my ear makes me hot all over and he smells heavenly, like sandalwood and man. All man. God, he has absolutely no idea how anxious I am. I'm ready to rip his clothes off right here. That's how badly I want him. He's so ridiculously sexy. That dark brown hair. Those bourbon-colored eyes. Lips that felt perfect moving against mine. And his muscled body that I want to run my tongue over. I'm trying to shut my mind off, but it's impossible. Even when he was pissing me off at the bar, there was no denying my attraction for him.

I don't know why I told him anything about my mother, though. I'm usually very close-lipped about my personal life and my family history. Olivia has been witness to that over the past eight years. Although, she's always been the only one who could pry it out of me. The fact that I was so transparent to him made me feel off-balance. But when I saw understanding in his eyes, it was the first time I felt like somebody really got me.

I'm pressing my legs together as we wait for the taxi. My panties are already wet and if his tongue comes anywhere near me again, they just might combust. Luckily, the taxi pulls up and we climb inside.

After giving the driver his address, he slides next to me, hooking an arm over my shoulder. His other hand finds its way to my leg, and I shiver when his finger lightly sketches patterns on my bare knee. I can't think straight. My brain is short-circuiting, lost in a haze of lust, so turned on I'd be willing to have him take me right here. Yes, right in the back seat of this filthy taxi. The thought actually turns me on more.

I subtly open my legs, hoping he might take the hint and move his hand where I really need it. Instead, he continues to drive me crazy with his calloused finger circling just above my knee.

His warm breath fans my neck, and I bite back the noise that wants to escape when his tongue makes contact with that sensitive spot behind my ear. "You taste so good," he murmurs, "and I bet you're already wet for me."

"Beyond wet," I whisper back, not wanting the taxi driver to hear and think that I'm a sex-crazed freak, even though I feel like one.

Rex inhales a jagged breath, his hand finally wandering higher up my thigh. "I can't wait until my tongue can find out just how much," he says quietly. And when I glance up at him, his eyes denote a hunger that lights a flame inside of me. One that's been buried for quite some time.

I press my lips together, staring out the window in an attempt to distract myself. My skin tingles with anticipation as I try to rein in my breathing that is currently out of control. But I don't have to wait too long. Within minutes, the taxi pulls up in front of his building.

Rex pays the driver and practically jerks me from the seat, latching onto my hand as we fly into the building like two sex-starved lunatics. He hesitates the moment we enter the glass door, glancing up at the flight of stairs then back to me. With a devious grin, he scoops me up under my knees and I let out a yelp of surprise.

"Ahh! What on earth are you doing, Rex?" I laugh, my head dropping back.

He continues striding up the stairs with purpose. "What does it look like I'm doing?"

"Why are you carrying me? I can walk, you know."

"Blondie, shut up and kiss me," he demands. "I need motivation for climbing."

My mouth lands on his, taking small nibbles before sliding my tongue across his bottom lip. He opens for me so I can lick at his tongue, his teeth. I tangle my hands in his hair, drawing him closer, wanting him deeper, until he abruptly breaks away.

"Whoa. That's good. Any more of that and I'll be taking you on the fucking stairway." A sly smile forces one side of my lip to curl, thinking about how hot that would be.

He shakes his head, beginning his climb again. "Don't even think about it. Not this time anyway." And something flutters inside my belly at his insinuation that there might be a next time.

"Holy crap," I utter as he continues up, flight after flight. "How many flights?"

"Twelve," he replies, and he's not even out of breath, nor is he breaking a sweat. The guy is in shape.

We finally make it up to his floor and he sets me down, looking over at me. "You ready?"

"I'm ready, but are you sure you have any stamina left?" I flirt, before he grins wickedly as he jams his key in the lock, nearly breaking the door down when it clicks into place.

He slams the door shut, throwing his keys onto a nearby table. When he misses and they hit the floor with a clank, he doesn't give them a second glance. All of his attention is on me.

My purse falls to the carpet as he stalks toward me, backing me up until I'm flush against the wall. He places his arms on either side of my head.

"Do you have any idea how much I want you right now?" he groans, his breath blowing strong against my cheek, his masculine scent and proximity making me dizzy. He removes my hand from the wall and guides me down to his crotch, a hard bulge beneath his jeans. "*That's* how much." I bite my lip when my palm rubs over the thick outline of his cock. His eyes flick to my chest and he licks his lips, voice lowering. "I want to see your tits."

I grab the hem of my knit dress and slide it over my head, tossing it to the ground. All that's left is a black satin bra covering my D-sized breasts, and matching panties. His pupils darken as I reach around, making quick work of the clasp until the straps fall away. My nipples are stiff peaks, my arousal glaringly obvious. He fixates on them approvingly, inhaling a sharp intake of air.

I've never been shy when it comes to my body. I may not have a perfect figure—my hips are a bit wider than I'd like and I'm somewhat top heavy—but I've always been comfortable in my own skin. I guess showing Jason Standish my budding breasts behind his backyard shed when we were in eighth grade and having him grin like he'd just entered the gates of heaven went a long way toward building confidence. But this is a far cry from eighth grade and Rex is a world away from lanky Jason Standish. And I certainly don't mind being looked at with hooded eyes, just the way Rex is ogling me right now. Like he wants to eat me alive.

"Oh, fuck." He drags in a heavy breath. "They're just as perfect as I imagined they'd be."

A satisfied smile simmers on my lips. "You thought about my tits?"

"Hell yeah. Ever since you walked into the shop."

His words spur me on and I tip my head back against the wall, lips slightly parted. Hungry eyes move lower as I cup my breasts, letting my fingers roam to my taut nipples, massaging them in circles. My skin is hot all over.

"Fuck, I think I might come right now," he says through gritted teeth, his fists clenching and unclenching at his sides.

One of my hands drifts lower, floating down my belly until I reach the waistband of my panties. Slowly, I dip two fingers in, soaking them with my wetness. I watch him, watching me, and it looks like he's barely holding on. Reaching down, he removes my hand and brings my fingers up, plunging them into his mouth. I moan when he sucks and licks them, his warm tongue increasing the ache between my legs.

He glides them out, then in, then out again, making me delirious with desire for him. "Your pussy tastes so good. I want more," he says in a husky voice, and then he kisses me. It's forceful, possessive, hungry. His tongue pushes deeper into my mouth, colliding with mine, his passion lighting a fire inside of me. My hands slide up his bare arms and dive into his hair as I grind against him, the feel of his erection intensifying the throb in my core. His lips break from mine and I whimper at the loss as he trails his tongue down my jawline, the hollow of my neck, my collarbone.

"Rex," I pant, my body blazing, wanting his hot mouth all over me.

"Yes?" he answers, forging a trail of warmth down my flesh.

"Suck on my nipples." My voice is pleading, but I don't care.

He coasts lower, my breasts now heavy and aching for his mouth, and I cry out as he finally takes me between his lips, a shiver of pleasure rushing through my body. With a skilled mouth, he rotates between licking, sucking, and biting, sending another moan from my lips into the charged atmosphere. His head lifts and I glance at him from under my lashes.

"Do you know how much you turn me on? Your lips, your nipples, the way you taste? How hard my dick is, knowing I'm the one who made you this wet?"

"God, Rex," I purr, lips unable to form any more words, my body doing all the talking for me. The spark in his eyes is undeniable, and I feel heady, knowing how much he wants me.

"Come on." He grasps my hand. "I want you on my bed, so I can spread you open."

I'm already about to come apart, and he's barely touched me.

When we enter his bedroom, I take note of how small it is, yet it's relatively clean compared to the rest of his apartment. I'm surprised by the amount of framed photographs lining the room, various sketches of tattoos covering the walls. The room is scarce of furniture, just the bed, two side tables, and a small, three-drawer dresser.

"Get comfortable on the bed and slide your panties off," he says, and I do exactly as he asks, flinging them to the side before crawling onto the mattress. My feet claw at the sheets as I lie back on one of the pillows, anxiously awaiting the weight of his body on top of mine.

He grabs his t-shirt, lifting it over his head to reveal ropes of solid muscle, tattoos, and smooth skin. The only exception a tiny patch of hair leading to the part of his body my mouth is watering just thinking about. As if reading my mind, he shrugs out of his jeans and boxers in one fell swoop, and I moisten my lips with my tongue at the sight of his well-endowed cock.

He climbs on the bed, all the while my eyes are trained on his thick cock and the perfectly cut abs leading down to it. He's actually beautiful, statuesque-like in many ways, and I breathe out a sigh.

"I'm going to ravage your body. First," he rasps as he inches up my frame, his heated gaze searing my skin. "I'm going to start with the arch of your neck, then I'm going to move to those gorgeous, full tits, and finally, I'm going to take the most time licking your wet pussy, before I spend the rest of the night fucking you."

I want to raise my hand and tell him I'm ready now.

A man of his word and holding true to his promise, he begins with my neck, a torturously slow descent, flitting down the curve, to the indent of my collarbone, the sensitive flesh between my breasts. My body responds instantly, nipples growing impossibly hard, sex clenching with need. Or maybe it's want. I'm so delirious I don't know the difference.

He takes first one nipple then the other into his mouth, stopping only to stare at the hardened crests. "God, your tits, they're fucking amazing." His nose circles me before he resumes his onslaught of heat down my skin.

My hands fist in his hair, guiding him lower, wanting him between my legs. "Rex, I—" The words are stunted when his tongue reaches my belly button and I tilt my hips up, pools of desire soaking my pussy. I spread my thighs apart, unable to wait much longer.

"Spread wider," he says, and I shudder at the first drag of his tongue between my slit, the flood gates opening, my arousal spilling out.

"Oh God," I shout, before I feel it again, and again, and again. His tongue exploring, tasting, lapping up my juices. "Deeper, Rex, God, your tongue—"

"I could eat your pussy all night," he murmurs, and I can barely hold on now, the coil in my belly ready to snap when he pushes two fingers inside of me, stroking my walls as he's licking my clit.

"I'm—gonna come," I moan, my hips bucking off the bed, heart pounding as he sends me over the edge, screaming his name.

I'm shattered, my body floating as his tongue continues to pleasure me, letting me ride out the wave of my intense orgasm. He shifts back up my body as my breathing slows, heart attempting to find a steady beat again.

He skims his lips against mine before pushing a sweaty strand of hair away from my face. "Did I tell you how much I love your pussy?" He grins, and I can't help but smile.

"I think you just showed me." A flush creeps across my cheeks. "I really enjoyed that."

"Hmmm, yeah. I kind of got that sense." He looks down between us at his throbbing cock. "I think I have something else you might enjoy." He stretches across me, pulling the drawer of his bedside table open. For a split second I wonder how many women have lain here before but quickly put the thought out of my head as he rolls the condom on, positioning himself above me. My hands drift down his chest, wanting to touch him, to feel every solid ridge and plane of his muscles under my fingertips.

He grabs hold of his cock, easing inside my folds, pulling back then pushing in again. The teasing of his arousal is exquisite torture and I tremble as he stretches me. His eyes close and he groans. "Oh fuck. Your pussy is so tight." Slowly, he rocks into me, holding his weight with his hands, eyes penetrating mine.

Streams of whimpers leave my mouth as he thrusts in and out of my pussy, his hips gyrating in a rhythmic motion. The smell of sex surrounds us, arousing me beyond belief. Defined lines of an eagle tattoo on his chest ripple with his movement as the moonlight slants through the window, his face in and out of shadows. I raise my hips to meet his as I climb higher, watching his muscles grow taut, face strained with pleasure.

"I can feel your pussy squeezing my cock. Fuck, you feel good," he mutters, his voice deep, breathing choppy.

"Rub my clit," I moan, my nails digging into his shoulders hard enough to puncture the skin. He reaches between us and the moment his finger touches me, I explode into a million pieces. "Oh God, Rex."

He pounds into me a few more times, dots of sweat building on his forehead, his cock thickening inside of me. "Jesus, I'm gonna come," he growls between heavy breaths. The pulse of his shudder vibrates through me and I grab his ass, pulling him in deep so he can give me everything he has. Exhaling roughly, he drops his head and licks the sweat from my neck, placing a few open-mouth kisses there before he rolls off. "Holy fuck, Blondie." His breathing is still erratic as he turns his head to me.

"You're not so bad yourself," I tease, and his mouth curves up into a grin. He's got a great smile. There's something so sexy about it, yet it's also charming. "So...." I pause, leaning up on my elbow, not wanting to get too personal, which is bizarre because we just had off-the-charts sex. "I was wondering about your tattoos, what they symbolize?"

After disposing of the condom, he lies down next to me, and I still can't get over how beautiful his body is. I trace my finger over the eagle tattoo that starts on his rib, the wings flowing into the middle of his chest. It's done in black and white, a subtle hint of red in the feathers.

"Like this one, it's beautiful," I say, admiring the way it cuts across his muscle. "What does it mean?"

He stares up at the white chipped paint on the ceiling, almost as if he's contemplating whether he wants to answer. There's no trace of his eyes when he finally does. "It reminds me of my dad. He loved eagles when I was a kid, so it's kind of in memoriam."

"Oh, I'm sorry."

"That's okay. Shit happens, you know?" But his words are not as empty as he's trying to make them appear.

"What about the one on the back of your neck? The angel wings with the dagger?" I ask, very curious what this one means.

"Hmph, well, it's my way of saying there's no such thing as angels, I suppose."

"Oh." I'm not sure what to say after that, so that's when my meaningful questions stop and I opt for something a bit lighter. "So, how did you get into tattooing anyway?"

"Boy, you sure ask a lot of questions." His eyes rake over my body. "I can think of better things to do." He leans forward to take my nipple between his teeth, and I moan as he gently bites and sucks, worshipping it into a hard peak.

"You're distracting me and I'm looking for information," I choke out, but my feet are beginning to move anxiously on the bed. He's really good at this—too good.

"So, how did you become a tattoo artist?" I ask again, his mouth continuing to travel south, my mind slowly following its lead.

He raises his head, feigning irritation. "You're continuing to talk when I have other plans for you? Plans that I think you'll enjoy a lot more than hearing about my boring background." I shoot him an insistent glare and he relents with a loud sigh. "Okay, I'll answer this one question, and then I'm having my way with you."

"Deal."

"So...." He kisses the underside of my breast. "I went to school for illustration...." His tongue drifts lower, lunging into my belly button, and I can't help the whimper that escapes. He smiles, knowing he's getting to me. "It was impossible to get a job as an illustrator, and at the time, a friend of mine in Boston worked at a tattoo shop. God, you smell so good," he mumbles, my body squirming beneath him as his nose circles the outside of my sex.

"Rex—"

"That's it. I went in to watch him work, then started working at the shop part-time, doing odd jobs there, watching the artists work. One day I stayed late, hanging around doing a sketch, and the owner was impressed, so he offered me an apprenticeship and the rest is history." His fingers spread me open, tongue finding my clit, and I clutch a handful of sheet.

Not more than a second later, I'm missing his mouth when he stops abruptly. "Are we done talking now?" His velvety tongue resumes its torture of my clit, back and forth through my wet seam.

"Hmmm...."

"How does my tongue feel on your pussy?" He groans, my legs falling open the only response to his question. "Hell, yes. Spread nice and wide... Fuck, you're ready for me again."

"Hmmm," I moan once more as his tongue flutters back and forth over my clit, and I grip the headboard behind me. "It feels so good, Rex."

As his tongue penetrates my entrance, he pushes a finger inside, fucking and licking me as my hips arch against his hand, his mouth. The pleasure begins to build and my limbs tingle. I need more.

"More, Rex, faster," I say hoarsely, and he doesn't hesitate, another finger joining his tongue, and within seconds, I come apart, screaming his name.

I lie here, trying to get my breathing under control, expecting him to stop. Instead, he continues to lap at me as I slowly come down from the high, almost as if he can't get enough.

"You're very skilled at that," I tease when he finally settles beside me.

"Well, it helps when you have a good subject. If it were up to me, like I told you, I'd eat your pussy all night long."

My cheeks flame red for no other reason except—I don't even know why.

"You're kind of cute when you blush." He reaches for a bottle of water on the side table. "Want some?"

"No thanks." Glancing at the table next to me, I find a framed photograph of three boys, all wearing baseball shirts. The two in the back are obviously Rex and Hunter, a little boy kneeling in front of them. "You and Hunter haven't changed a bit." I lift the picture to examine it more closely.

"Yeah." He polishes off the water, throwing the bottle in a nearby trash can.

"Who's this little boy? He's adorable."

He spins around with ice in his eyes, expelling a loud breath, the playfulness from earlier, gone. "What's with the fifty questions? Listen, I'm going to take a shower."

With another audible breath, he stalks off to the bathroom, slamming the door behind him, and I suddenly feel as if I've been slapped in the face. I guess it's not okay to ask questions, even though we just fucked and he went down on me. Twice.

Whatever.

I wait until I hear the shower running then slide off the bed, fishing around the house for the remainder of my clothing. I'm not sticking around. There's really no need to.

As soon as I'm dressed, I snatch my purse from the floor, fuming, wanting to scream though I have no idea why. I shake my head as if to clear it and am about to walk out the door when Rex's arm stops me. I pivot to find him dripping water all over the carpet, a towel wrapped around his waist.

"Listen," he blows out a breath, "I'm sorry I acted like a dick. And you don't have to go."

"Yes, I do." I snatch my arm away. "I need to get up early tomorrow." It's not true, but he doesn't need to know that.

He curls his fingers into a fist, his jaw ticking, seemingly fighting for control. "I-I can't talk about it, okay?" Tilting his head to the side, his gaze slides to mine and I know exactly what he's looking for—understanding. Since he gave it to me earlier, I feel like I owe him that much.

"Sure." I break away from his eyes, digging inside my purse to distract from the sudden awkwardness claiming me.

"Hey." He slips his index finger under my chin, forcing my eyes back to his. "I had a good time tonight."

"I did, too." My response is soft, a ghost of a smile creeping across my cheeks.

"So, can I have your cell? Maybe we can get together again? Well," he chuckles, "as long as I promise not to act like a dick."

"I guess you kind of owed me one for acting like a bitch," I pipe back, and he laughs, surprising me by pulling me in for a kiss.

"So, we're even now," he says against my lips, his erection pressing against me through the towel, making me want to rip it off. I dig in the purse that's now crushed between us, finding a pen and a scrap piece of paper. He backs up long enough for me to write my number down.

"Here." I hand it to him, and he stares down at it before looking back to me.

"This *is* your number, right?"

"Yeah, why?" My smile falters and I frown.

"Just double-checking, I want to make sure I didn't destroy my chances to see you again," he replies, folding the paper into a square. "All right, I'll walk you out."

"Rex," I grin, "we're standing right in front of the door, and you've got a towel on anyway."

"True." His eyes lower to his towel. "But who wouldn't want an eyeful of my junk?"

"Oh my God. I'm going now." I giggle as I walk out the door, the echo of his chuckle staying with me long after I've left the building.

# CHAPTER SEVEN

## POLAR OPPOSITES

"I'm impressed," Stevie says, looking beyond me at the butterflies and cherry blossom tattoo I just finished on India's lower back. I have to admit myself, it looks fucking awesome. "I love the way the butterflies appear to be flying through the tree." He clasps my shoulder. "Nice work, Rex."

"Thanks."

Once I give India aftercare instructions, she hops off the chair, sliding her shirt back down over the bandage. She's definitely got a nice rack, but for some reason when I stare at it, all I see are Vanessa's tits.

That's fucked up.

I still lick my lips at the thought and begin cleaning up my station when a familiar voice sounds from behind me.

"Hey, bro."

I spin around to find my brother, perfectly dressed as always in a dark grey suit, crisp, white dress shirt, and polished black shoes. Then there's me in my ripped jeans and t-shirt. Talk about opposite ends of the spectrum.

"What's up, man?" I give him a nod of my chin. "They allowed you out of the boardroom for an afternoon break to consort with the riff-raff?" I chuckle and he glares at me.

"No one *allows* me, I own the company, Rex," he retorts, twiddling with the watch on his wrist.

"Man, I love fucking with you, Hunter. Your feathers ruffle so easily." I turn back to my station, scrubbing it down with a cloth.

"And since when do you know what the word consort means anyway? You purchased a dictionary?"

I nod my head but don't look back at him. "Yeah. It arrived yesterday."

He laughs. "So you want to go grab some lunch?" he asks, and I'm already suspicious. He rarely ever takes a lunch, never mind paying me a visit in the middle of the afternoon. I have to wonder if this has something to do with Vanessa... or tomorrow.

Pausing with the cloth in my hand, I toss him a questionable stare over my shoulder. "What gives?"

"Do you want to get some lunch or not?" he asks again, checking the time on his watch.

"Okay, give me a sec to finish cleaning up. I'll meet you out front."

A few minutes later, Hunter and I head out, and I definitely know something's up. The tension is thick between us and he's being particularly quiet, which is so unlike him.

"Okay, now are you going to tell me what the hell's going on?" I wait for an answer as we make our way toward the pizzeria a block down from the shop.

"So what happened last night after you texted me? You totally disappeared."

I stuff my hands in my pockets, kicking up rocks on the sidewalk. This can't honestly be what he wants to talk about, but I'll play along anyway. "Yeah, well we went back to my place, and let me tell you, Vanessa's got a puss—"

He holds a hand up to his side, blocking my view. "I'm good, thanks. I really don't want to hear about your sexual escapades, Rex, especially when it concerns Olivia's best friend," he says, and I chuckle.

"She asks a lot of questions though, man." I hold the door open to the restaurant, letting a couple of guys pass before we walk inside.

"Rex." His tone is somewhat scolding. "That's what women do. They're all about the details. Oh wait," he taunts, "you wouldn't know that, would you?"

"Fuck off." I smirk, before we make our way toward the seating in the back.

Hunter snaps his fingers as he slides into the booth, his eyes darting upward. "I almost forgot to tell you. You'll never believe who I ran into the other day?"

"Who?"

"Old Mrs. Clawson." He chuckles, removing the silverware from his napkin.

"No shit? She's gotta be what, like in her eighties or something?" I ask, twirling the salt shaker on the table.

"Yeah, she is. She remembered me though. Which means she probably remembers the time she caught us climbing the oak tree in her backyard and you nearly broke your leg trying to get down so fast."

I smile at the memory as another more fascinating one takes shape in my mind. "And let's not forget that not too long after that she caught me smoking pot in that same tree. You saved my ass, if I remember correctly."

"Well," he says, "if you can call you having to rake leaves from her yard for an entire week saving you, then I guess I did."

The waitress drops our menus on the table and we order drinks before she takes off. I lean back against the worn leather seat, crossing my arms over my chest. "So... you're stalling and I want you to tell me what the hell's up."

"Well," he says, clearing his throat, and I'm waiting for the bomb to drop. "I'm going to ask Olivia to marry me."

"Oh, man, is that it?" I breathe out a sigh of relief. "Jesus, you scared the shit out of me. No wonder you were acting so strange. Well, good for you. She's a hot chick, you scored big with her."

"Would you mind not calling her a chick? She's so much more than that." He flips me a sharp stare while idly folding his napkin.

"Whoa, getting bitten by the love bug has also made you super sensitive. Lighten up, bro. I think it's… great. She's good for you."

"Yeah, she is." He grins, and something about his expression is childlike, reminding me of when we were kids. I'll admit it's good to see him this happy. But that's about as sappy as I'm going to get.

"Jesus, this is a whole new you. I feel like fucking fairies are gonna start dancing around your head any minute."

He busts out a laugh, throwing his napkin at me. "I can't wait to see fairies flying around your head."

"Yeeeeaaah. It'll be a cold day in hell before that happens," I respond, just as the waitress brings over our drinks.

"Speaking of which," he adds, taking a swig of his soda, "remember that Vanessa is Olivia's best friend."

"Yeah, and is that some secret code for something?" I ask, eyeing the pizza choices.

"It just means, don't hurt her."

I glance up from the menu. "Bro, a few fun facts for you. One, I'm not hurting anyone. Two, we just met. Three, we're not in a relationship. And four, we're consenting adults who want to fuck." I drop the menu down on the table and push it to the side.

"Well, I hope sometime in the near future you decide to grow up," he grumbles, knocking back the rest of his soda.

"News flash. I'm all grown up. What you see is what you get. Courtesy of our mother, Diane Grayson," I bite back, her name on my tongue leaving a very bad taste in my mouth.

Hunter tilts his head sideways, scrutinizing me. "You can't blame her forever, Rex. At some point you have to take responsibility for your own life."

"Oh yeah? Let's see. The list is endless." I lift my fingers, flicking them against my palm one at a time. "First, she killed our brother by not being present, when she should have known the babysitter was doing horrible things to him. Second, her family took a back seat to alcohol and her desire to screw, and third, she couldn't give a rat's ass about us—so yes, I *can* blame her forever."

He rubs a finger over his lower lip, carefully choosing his next words. "Well, I care about you, Rex, and that's a lot of baggage for one person to carry."

"All right, what's say we change topic? What kind of pizza do you want to get? I vote sausage."

"I vote pepperoni," he says with a smirk.

"We're never gonna agree on fucking anything, are we?" I taunt, lacing my hands on top of my head.

"Looks that way," he remarks, fighting back a grin.

# CHAPTER EIGHT

## ISN'T IT IRONIC?

*Vanessa*

Trent greets me the moment I walk inside Heavenly Lattes, tipping his baseball cap in my direction. "Hey, Vanessa, I'll get busy on your latte. Oh, we've got double fudge doughnuts today, interested?"

"That's an affirmative, Trent." I sashay over to a table in the corner. I'm in a particularly good mood and I also know why. My body is still buzzing from last night with Rex. In fact, I've been so distracted, it's ridiculous. And this is so unlike me. Typically, I live off of my checklists and calendar, but not today. First, I show up in the conference room an hour early for a presentation. Then I forget to ask Tillie to order drinks for the meeting. I smile to myself. Just this once, going thirsty wouldn't hurt anyone.

My phone chimes and I scoop it out of my purse, sliding the screen open. My lips curve into a grin when I see it's a text from Rex.

**I can still taste you on my tongue.**

Holy shit. I press my lips together, and my thighs, looking over my shoulder as if someone can actually see what he just typed. Then my fingers get busy with my own special reply.

*Do you want another taste?*

Anticipation floods my belly as I wait for his response.

*Hell, yes. Right now.*

Jesus.

*Can't right now. Meeting Olivia. Tonight?*

*If I have to wait that long, I will. Although, I'll be thinking about your pussy all day. And your tits, I'm definitely thinking about your tits.*

I peer over my shoulder again, biting my lip, desire churning in my belly.

*Me too... I'll be thinking about you, not me. Actually, I'll be thinking about wrapping my lips around your—*

That should give him a little more to think about. I toss my cell in my bag, a satisfied smile atop my lips. Olivia happens to stroll in at that moment, waving as she makes her way over.

"Hey." There's a slight tilt of her head as she surveys me. "Wow. What's with the flushed cheeks, V?"

"Why, whatever are you talking about?" I drop back against the booth, patting the seat next to me. "Sit."

She throws her purse down, sliding onto the ripped leather, an excited gleam in her eyes. "Okay, so let's have it," she rubs her hands together, "tell me about last night. We were all supposed to hang out, but then I saw you all of about five minutes before you disappeared."

"Last night, hmph." I tap a finger against my mouth, attempting to keep a straight face. "I can't recall. Must not have been that memorable."

"Not memorable my ass. You were with Rex. I've *seen* Rex, remember? Of course, I've seen Hunter too," she giggles, "so I *know* it had to be memorable."

A huge grin finally splits my face in two. "Okay. Yeah, I guess you could say it was memorable. He's hot. It's kind of ironic," I shake my head and laugh, "that he was the guy from the tattoo shop *and* Hunter's brother."

"It's funny, even though Hunter and I have been together over a year, I feel like I don't know Rex all that well. He's kind of closed off," she remarks as Trent pops over, setting our drinks and doughnuts on the table.

"Thanks, Trent," we say in unison, and he laughs, his floppy hair blocking his deep-set eyes.

"I love being bombarded by two beautiful women at once," he flirts, before spinning around and heading back behind the counter.

Olivia watches him walk away, then turns back to me. "I really want to find someone to set him up with. He's so adorable and sweet. It's hard to believe he's not taken."

"That could be just the problem. He's too sweet." I take a bite of the doughnut, the crumbs falling onto my lap.

"Yes, we all know how you like them twisted, so you're definitely not a candidate. Anyway." She takes a sip of her latte, smiling when the taste hits her mouth. "Where were we? Oh right, Rex. Yeah, he closes himself off as I said, so it's hard to get to know him."

"Well," I say, recalling how he reacted when I asked him about that picture, "I got a little taste of that last night."

"What do you mean?"

"I saw this picture next to his bed. He and Hunter were in it, but they were a lot younger, and there was this cute little boy in it, too, but when I asked him about it, he shut down, and got very defensive." I swirl the straw around my drink before taking a sip.

"Oh." Realization dawns, sadness etched on her face, and I suspect she must know who it is.

"Who is it Liv?" I ask, and she lets out a sigh before meeting my eyes.

"It's just that it feels odd talking about it. It's Hunter's story to tell, not mine."

"Liv...."

"Okay." She heaves out a sigh, louder this time. "It was his brother."

"Was?"

"Yes, he died when he was fourteen." More words come, but it's almost as if she has to push them out. "He committed suicide."

My hand flies to my mouth and I gasp. Now it all makes sense, and I'm overcome with nausea at my reaction, although I had no way of knowing. "Oh God, I feel horrible."

Her shoulders rise and fall on a deep breath and it seems like she wants to say something else, but she doesn't.

I immediately drop my head in my hands, shaking it from side to side, unable to fathom the trail of devastation that left behind for their family. It's no wonder Rex closes himself off. The pain must be too great to bear.

Letting out a deep breath, I remove my hands to face Liv again, a tear creeping down her cheek.

"Every time I think about it, it makes me so sad for Hunter, for both of them," she says, and that's one of the many things I love about Liv. She's such a compassionate person, always caring so deeply for others.

Reaching to the center of the table, I grab a napkin and hand it to her. "Thanks for telling me, and it's certainly not something I would ever repeat. But it definitely helps me to understand him better, that's for sure."

"Yeah." She wipes her nose, then tosses the napkin in her purse.

Quiet settles over us for a short while as we finish our lattes and pick at our doughnuts. I'm not the least bit hungry now. The thought of what happened to Rex's brother weighs heavily on my mind. I'm even more anxious to see him tonight.

"Stella, you can't wear that costume to school, sweetie." I hear a woman speaking from behind me and turn to find a little girl with curly blonde hair, rosy cheeks dotted with freckles, and a big smile. She's wearing a Cinderella dress and twirling around the shop.

"What is it?" Olivia asks, tapping me on the shoulder, my head lost in another place and time.

I shift back in my seat, biting the tip of my nail. "I was just remembering all those times that Stella took me out for Halloween because my parents were working. I was the only one on my street whose babysitter took them out trick or treating." A bitter sound makes its way from my mouth. "My mother and father would always tell Stella to be sure to take pictures of me, but they never even looked at them. Anyway," I shoo the memory away with my hand, "whatever."

Olivia doesn't try to comfort me with words, but instead, places a gentle hand on my arm, diffusing the anger swirling inside of me.

"So... do you want to hang out tonight? Hunter has a late meeting so I probably won't see him."

"I can't tonight." A smile finally breaks through the melancholy. "I'm hanging out with Rex."

"Is that so?" she inquires, and now her lips are tipping up into a smile as well. "You know, I invited you last night because I figured it would get you out and you'd have some fun, but nothing more."

"Hmph, that's kind of like dangling a mocha latte in front of my face and daring me not to drink it." I click my tongue between my teeth. "So as I said, I'm hanging out with Rex tonight."

"And what, pray tell, will you be doing with Rex Grayson?"

"Absolutely anything he wants." Laughter bubbles up from my throat and before long, we're both howling so loud we're getting rude stares from other customers. "It's her." I glance around, pointing a finger at Liv. "It's all her."

# CHAPTER NINE

## I KNEW YOU WERE TROUBLE

While I'm waiting for Vanessa to show, I actually decide to pick up the apartment. It's starting to look like a shithole—well, starting might be a slight understatement. Gathering up all the dirty clothes, I throw them in the laundry bin, then move on to the mountain of dishes in the sink, all from my take-out extravaganza. I'm not sure what my objection is to doing dishes right after I eat. I'd rather let them stockpile, creating a tower that could smash into a million irreparable pieces—sickly reminiscent of my life in some way.

And now I'll stop because I sound like Dr. Billings, the therapist I saw for several years after my brother died, when my whole world fell apart. I've seen her a few times since I moved back to New York, and I know she would frown upon me thinking about myself this way.

Vanessa asking me questions about the picture brought it all back, though. I don't know why after all these years I still have such a hard time talking about it. Maybe it's because I still shoulder that blame. But as much as I condemn myself, deep down, somewhere in the recesses of my distorted mind on a good day, I know it wasn't my fault. The burden rests solely on one person—my self-centered, drunken mother.

That woman has marked me, gouged my skin so deep. Her and that fucking babysitter. There's only one moral to my story. Women are cruel and dishonest, and they can't be trusted. They are, however, good for one thing.

I huff out an aggravated breath and finish cleaning up. By the time I'm done, sweat and funk stick to my body leaving behind a repulsive odor. I hop in the shower quickly and find myself scrubbing harder than normal. Maybe I'm trying to wash off more than just dirt.

It's nearly six when I'm finished and I expect Vanessa in the next half hour. I've been thinking about her all day. There's something about how direct she is. A woman who knows what she wants sexually and is not afraid to ask for it, is such a fucking turn on. Plus, she's okay with taking the reins. Most of the women I've been with are not that vocal, and they like to be led.

Even thinking about her now, I'm already hard. I can't wait to have my hands and mouth all over her. That scent of hers stayed with me today like a shadow. Every time I moved, it followed, impossible to escape.

After pulling on a pair of jeans and a clean t-shirt, I make my way out to the small living room to wait, when there's a knock at the door. Everything south of my brain goes numb the moment I open it. Vanessa has her arm resting against the doorframe, those shapely legs crossed at the ankles in a sexy stance, and she's wearing a short skirt, cut just above the knee. *God,* I love skirts. A barely there tank top shows every single curve of her breasts, my tongue jutting out at the thought of her nipple in my mouth again.

"Are you going to invite me in?" she asks, the sound of her voice extracting me from my lustful haze.

"Hey, uh yeah, come on in." I usher her inside and close the door, taking a moment to check out that ass of perfection. As she tosses her purse onto the sofa, I come up behind her, wrapping an arm around her waist. My nose skims her neck and I inhale deeply, getting the first hit of what I've been craving. "Your scent has been on my mind all day," I whisper against her ear, "your pussy, your skin," and she sucks in a gulp of air. "You smell like fresh rain and something... sweet."

She shivers as my lips follow a path along the line of her jaw, her head lolling to the side as I feather kisses across her cheek, her ear, her throat. A tiny noise travels from her mouth into the space between us, my dick instantly hard at the sound.

Draping her hair over her shoulder, I place one more kiss on her nape before dropping to my knees. My hands anxiously dip down to touch her, the pad of my thumb trailing the length of her leg, surprised when I reach her bare ass. My hand freezes, my cock twitching gratefully in my jeans. "Christ, Blondie, you're going commando?"

"Hmm-mmm," she mumbles as I reach around to cup her sex. She's already wet and I'm at risk for coming in my pants—again. What is it about her that has me wound so tight I could snap at any moment? It's as if my body goes into overdrive and I'm at her mercy.

My finger takes a slow slide between her pink lips, another sexy moan slips out and I groan. "Your pussy is so hot, so slick, you turn me on so fucking much," I murmur and she whimpers.

"Rex," she whimpers again, "I need your tongue." And the way she says it, hoarse and full of want, has my dick straining against my jeans.

I jump to my feet, gently grasping her shoulders and turning her to face me. Her hands come up to frame the day old growth on my jaw, eyes focus on my lips before wandering back up to mine.

I bring a hand up between us, dragging her plump lip down with my finger then sucking it into my mouth. She tastes so God damn sweet. When her tongue darts out to touch my upper lip, a spark of heat sends me into a frenzy and I attack her mouth, plunging my tongue in as we hold onto each others' faces, angling to get deeper.

Seconds later, we break away, her cheeks pink, our breathing accelerated.

"I'm starving for you," I rasp, and I don't even care how it sounds. It's so fucking true. I'm not deprived sexually by any means, but for some reason, I want her so badly I can't see straight.

"Well, I'm yours for the taking." Her tongue pokes out to tempt me, an alluring smile curling her lips.

Mark my words. She's going to be my downfall. Straight into oblivion.

Without warning, I grab her under her knees, flipping her over my shoulder, and she squeals when I smack her bare ass. "And I intend to take you, in every way possible." I stride the short distance to my room, letting her down, and her hands immediately go for her skirt. "Leave it on," I demand. "Just remove your top."

She pitches me a curious smile, but does exactly as I ask. My eyes remain on her the entire time as she teases me, ever-so-slowly sliding the tank top over her head until it falls behind her, leaving her in a sheer lace bra, the stiff peaks of her nipples pinching the fabric.

"Take your bra off, too," I order, my breath catching in my throat as she submits, the satin tumbling away, her pink crests taunting my anxious lips. I lift my t-shirt off then lower my head to run my tongue over her breast, my hand latching onto the other, squeezing and kneading her skin. She shudders as her nipple tightens, fingers clutching my hair, positioning me exactly where she wants.

"Ahhh," she cries out, my teeth nipping at her flesh. "Rex, please," she practically begs. I know what she wants and I have every fucking intention of giving it to her.

When I stand back up, I take a strand of her hair between my fingers, twirling it around, gazing at the desire looming in her eyes. "Do you know what I want?" I ask, my tone low, and she shakes her head, biting down on her bottom lip. I tug it free, then find her eyes. "I fantasized about you the other day... you were riding me." My arms slip around her back, yanking her against me, needing her to feel what she does to me, my dick rock hard for her.

She rubs against my cock, a shiver ripping through me as her nipples brush my chest. I edge closer, my hard breath blowing in her ear.

"I want your pussy all over me. I want you to fuck my mouth."

She gasps and it does a free fall into the air between us. "Rex. If you keep talking like that I'm going to come right now."

"Well, then we better get to it," I wink, "because the only place I want you coming, is all over my face."

She flashes me a killer smile and that's when I notice she has this cute little dimple on her left cheek. It strikes me as odd that I'm even noticing that shit, but I shake it off. Right now I have more important things to think about.

Taking her hand, I lead her over to the bed, motioning for her to sit. I shuck off my jeans and boxers as quickly as possible, Vanessa's eyes widening when my cock springs free. I'm so erect, thick veins straining against my skin, and it nearly does me in when her pink tongue peeks out and skips across her lips.

Fucking aroused beyond belief, I take a pillow, propping it against the headboard before lying on my back. Her gaze moves over my body, eyes alight with appreciation and heat.

"Straddle my face." My voice is husky, my control wavering. She shoots me a sexy grin before hiking up her skirt and bunching it around her waist, then caging me in on both sides with her legs.

I've just officially entered the fucking promised land.

"Hold on to the headboard." My voice is hoarse as I bring her close and slip my hand between her thighs, spreading her lips apart. She smells so fucking good, so intoxicating. "Your pussy, Christ, you smell good."

"Taste me," she purrs, my tongue instantly responding to her request, licking through her wet folds, circling her clit. She shivers and I glance up at her, breasts bouncing with the sway of her hips, hot little noises falling from her parted lips. She looks like a fucking goddess.

A groan climbs from my chest as I continue to devour her, sliding my tongue back and forth over her sex, consuming her like I can't fucking get enough, and I can't. I've tasted a lot of pussy in my time, and none of it compares to hers.

"Rex," she whimpers, fingers tugging at her nipples, squeezing them as she rocks into me. I grip her hips firmly, holding her tight as I delve deeper into her pussy. She moans when I flick my tongue through her center, lapping up her juices.

"Jesus, I could do this all day. You taste so fucking good."

"Don't stop," she cries out, continuing to rock against my face, a steady stream of whimpers tumbling from her lips, her body aching for release. "Oh God," she shouts, and I speed up, working her faster, licking up and down her slit until she bucks against my mouth, limbs trembling, orgasm tearing through her.

She mewls quietly as I slowly bring her down, brushing back and forth over her wetness, wanting every last drop of her in my mouth. "Holy shit." She laughs, before finally shifting off of me and plopping back against the pillow. "Wow."

I twist on my side so I'm facing her, a mischievous grin settling on my lips. "I've got mad skills."

With a subtle turn of her head, her eyes meet mine. "Yeah, that, and a raging ego." She giggles and I laugh right along with her. Raising up on her elbow, she extends her hand to draw circles on my chest, mapping the planes of muscle. I didn't think my dick could get any harder.

I was wrong.

"So, do you like fill in the blank questions?" she breathes out, leaving me in the dark because I'm unable to process any thoughts at the moment, so fucking turned on by her it's ridiculous.

"Sorry?"

"My text?" She gets up on her knees, backing herself down the bed. My dick does a happy dance because he knows where she's headed. "I think I said, hmph," she taps a finger against her mouth, "I want to wrap my lips around your—"

Her tongue finishes her sentence, licking from the base of my shaft all the way to the head, and I groan, afraid I might lose my shit right now. She's warm and wet against my skin and I've fucking died and gone to heaven. A burst of air leaves my mouth when her tongue rounds the swollen head, circling the sensitive area underneath, and now I want inside her mouth.

"Jesus, that feels good."

"Hmmm," she hums against my dick, "you're so hard," she moans again, and my hands dive into her hair, hips rolling toward her. Knowing what I want, she opens and surrounds me with those sultry lips, sliding my cock in and out of her mouth, gripping me hard. Her hand does this twisting and pulling thing as she sucks me off that's driving me insane.

"Take me deep," I pant, and she brings her hands under to cup my ass, pulling me in deeper, my cock hitting the back of her throat.

"Christ," I growl, before reaching down and grabbing my dick, guiding myself in and out of her mouth as she takes me hard and fast. "Shit, I'm gonna come," I grit out, my body jerking from the sheer force of my climax. She doesn't budge, though, finishing me off, swallowing every last drop from my cock. When she finally lifts her head, she's got a wicked grin on her face.

"You see," she rubs a finger over her swollen lips, "I've got mad skills, too."

I shake my head, pulling her back up to me and kissing her, my taste all over her lips. "Yeah, you do."

There's an awkward silence that fills the air as we lie next to one another, and I'm not quite sure what to make of it. It doesn't last long, though, because Vanessa sits up and scoots off the bed, plucking her bra from the carpet.

"So," she hesitates, "I should probably get going."

I sit up and scratch my head, tossing the sheets off. "You can... stay if you want. We can... hang out... watch a movie or something? Although, I don't know if I have any movies you'll like. I'm not into chick flicks."

"Chick flicks," she repeats, strapping her bra on and taking a seat back on the bed. "What makes you think I like chick flicks? I'll have you know, I was a tomboy growing up."

"Oh really?" My eyes roam her body. "That's hard to believe. There's nothing boyish about you."

She playfully smacks my arm. "I used to climb trees and play with those little, green army men. Oh, and I had a thing for G.I. Joe."

"All right," I challenge, slinging myself over the bed, collecting my boxers and shrugging them on. "Game on. Let's go check out my movie collection and you can tell me if anything looks good. I'll be honest, though, there's a lot of death and destruction out there."

"That's cool." She tosses her hair over her shoulder as she walks away. "I'm into death and destruction."

"Seriously?" I shake my head and laugh as I follow after her into the living room. She makes a beeline right for my movie collection.

"No way!" She kneels on the floor, thumbing through the stacks of DVDs in the cabinet. "You have my favorite movie."

"Oh yeah, what's that?" I grab two bottled waters from the fridge, then walk back out to the living room. I twist the caps off and set them on the table before sinking down into the couch.

"*Die Hard*." She holds the DVD up in her hand with a big smile.

You've got to be shitting me.

"Bullshit." I smirk, because there's no fucking way that could possibly be her favorite movie.

"No, seriously," she gestures with her hands in the air, "I'm a huge Bruce Willis fan and Bruce Willis barefoot, well...."

"So you want to watch *Die Hard*?" My voice raises in pitch, shock making it difficult to digest this newly discovered fact about her.

"Yeah. But I need popcorn. Do you have any?" She pushes to her feet, sauntering into the kitchen in just her bra, that hot little skirt, and of course, no panties.

I'm still thinking about what's underneath her skirt when she calls from the kitchen, "Do you have anything here? Where's all your food?"

"I've got food," I yell back, making my way into my kitchen that's more like a rabbit hole. When I walk in, she's on her tiptoes, reaching up to a cabinet. I come up behind her, rubbing my cock, which is already hard again, against her ass. "What do you want?" I whisper just above her ear. "What are you hungry for?" I place a wet kiss against her neck, trailing a finger up the length of her thigh.

She leans her head back, her breath warm against my jaw. "What I really want," she says seductively, "is hot, melted... buttery popcorn."

I squeeze her ass and she grinds against me. "Don't start something you can't finish," I warn, nipping her lobe. She squeals just as she spots the glass jar of popcorn.

Reaching above her, I grab the pot on top of the cabinet. "You see, I have the essentials."

She spins around, glancing down at my hard-on. "You certainly do have the essentials," she flirts. "But what the heck is that in your hand? You don't have a popcorn maker?"

"No. I make it the old-fashioned way," I tell her as I place the pot on the stove. "Can you get the butter out of the fridge? And the oil is right behind you on the counter."

"Geez, I haven't seen popcorn made like this since I was a kid." She moves next to me, her eyes suddenly very far away, like she's lost in a memory. "My dad made it once for my babysitter and me."

"Oh yeah?" My shoulders stiffen, that word making me cringe as I try to focus on pouring the oil then dumping the popcorn in the pot. "You and your dad close?"

"No," she admits, a crinkle of sadness between her brows, "not at all." She clears her throat, as if she's trying to bury the feeling. "What about you? Were you and your dad close?"

My hand stills on the pot, an exhale of breath leaving me. "Well, we were, but I was only twelve when he died, so...."

Empathy fills her voice. "Oh God, I'm so sorry."

"Hey, that's life." I say it like I'm trying to be hard, as though it doesn't matter, but it still hurts like hell even now. I didn't have a whole lot of years with my dad, yet it doesn't make me miss him any less.

"No." Her words are steadfast as she touches my jaw, forcing me to look at her. "That's the part of life that's hard. It sucks, and I'm so very sorry." She holds me captive with her eyes, but it's too much and I snap my chin away, continuing to shake the pot, trying to forget all the shitty things about my life.

"I'll just wait for you in the other room." There's hurt in her voice, and I've done it again. I close my eyes and pinch the bridge of my nose. I'm a fucking expert at pushing people away.

Shit.

Regretfully, I scrub a hand over my face then walk back out. "Okay." I carry the bowl of popcorn out to the living room, trying to pretend like nothing happened. "One bowl of incredibly buttered popcorn made to order." She gives me a slight smile, and I take a seat beside her, holding the bowl out. "Do you want to taste it to see if it meets up to your standards?"

Her smile grows wider and for some reason I feel a bit better. "That's pretty good, but it needs more salt."

"I knew you were gonna say that," I reply, producing the salt shaker I was hiding. "Here you go. Have at it."

I grab the remote and flip the movie on, both of us relaxed, feet kicked up on the coffee table. I'm thankful she's quiet. I can't stand talking during a movie, unless it's me doing the talking. "Enjoying the movie?" I stretch out, hooking an arm over her shoulder. She leans into me and I take a quiet breath, the smell of raspberries radiating from her skin.

"Yup." She finishes off the last of the popcorn, then places the bowl on the table. I barely had any, but I don't care. She resumes her position against my shoulder and we settle back to watch the rest of the movie.

"I love that movie," she says as the credits roll. "I think I've seen it like ten times."

I gulp down the remainder of my water. "That's a pretty surprising discovery I've made about you. What's next? You gonna tell me you like cowboys and Clint Eastwood movies, too?"

"Well, speaking of cowboys...." She flexes her toes, grinning at me.

"Oh no. You don't, do you?" I ask, throwing the empty bottle onto the table.

"I was just going to say that the highlight of my day was getting accosted by the naked cowboy in Times Square."

"Who?" I'm not sure I like the sound of anyone naked accosting her except me.

"Oh, right." She nods her head in understanding. "I forgot you haven't been back in the city that long. He's this guy who hangs out in Times Square wearing only cowboy boots, a hat, and briefs. He has a guitar placed over his crotch so it appears that he's naked." She points a finger my way, pressing her lips together to squelch a laugh. "Oh my God, you should see the look on your face, it's priceless.

"I can't believe, especially being from around here, that you don't know who he is. Anyway, we had a bit of a chat. But it was funny because it reminded me of when I first moved here," she recalls, a reminiscent smile on her lips. "I had just met Olivia and we came across him and she thought I was insane when I started dancing with him in the middle of the sidewalk."

"I guess she had you pegged from the beginning," I quip, and she sticks her very mature tongue out at me.

My dick twitches at the gesture, eyes lingering on her mouth. "If you want to come a little closer, I have something you can do with that tongue."

"Oh, I can think of a million things I can do with my tongue." She drags it across her bottom lip and my cock rejoices. "Later."

"My cock doesn't like the word later," I tease, and she flicks my shoulder.

"Seriously, though, I'm going to take you to Times Square sometime and introduce you to the cowboy." She snatches her water from the table, taking a brief sip. "He's a hoot."

"Actually, it's kind of coming back to me now." I try to keep a devilish smirk at bay. "While I've never met him, I have a vague recollection of who he is."

Her cute little nose crinkles. "Wait, you acted like you didn't?"

"I just like hearing you say the word naked."

"Oh God, you're a jerk." She tosses a pillow at me and I hurl it back in her direction.

"Anyway," I fling her a salty smile, "cowboys really aren't my thing."

"What is your thing?" She takes a drink but keeps her gaze on me.

"Strip clubs." My lips hitch up into a grin and she smirks.

"Why doesn't that surprise me?"

"Actually, I'm kidding. I do like to ask Hunter to go, though, just to razz him." I grab onto her feet and lay them on my lap. "I remember, a few years back, when I took him for the first time. I've never seen anything funnier in my life." I chuckle. "You should've seen the mortified look on his face. Like he'd stepped into hell. He refused a lap dance and couldn't get out of there fast enough."

A relaxed sigh falls from her mouth as I massage her legs. "You guys seem close? Are you?"

I hesitate for a second, pondering her question. I'm not sure there's an easy answer to that, at least not one I'm willing to share. "We are, I suppose. We're very different and don't tend to agree a lot. But, Hunter has always had my back. He's always been there for me."

"What about you? Brothers or sisters?" My hands work their way down to her feet and she giggles. "Ticklish?"

"Little bit." She pinches her fingers together, her mouth curling into a smile that quickly falls away. "No. No brothers or sisters, and my parents are only children, too. It was pretty lonely. Geez this conversation took a depressing turn," she says, trying to make light of something that doesn't seem all that funny.

A brightness crosses her face though, replacing the sadness. "I did have my babysitter, Stella," she reveals, a sudden onset of tension bearing down on my shoulders, and I roll them, anxious to move away from this conversation. "She kept me company a lot since my parents were always working, took me lots of places, even spent holidays with me. I remember this one time," she reaches down and touches her knee, "I was running on the sidewalk and I fell really hard. I didn't want her touching it because it hurt so badly, but she promised she would be gentle. And she was." She smiles, lifting her hand. "She had this first aid kit and she pretended to be Doctor Stella. She made me laugh and then it didn't hurt so much anymore."

"So what happened to her? Do you keep in touch?"

"No," she says, no longer wearing the smile from a moment ago. "My mother sent her away."

"Why?" My hand pauses on her leg as she releases a weighted sigh.

"Probably because I was getting too attached to her. My mother had a thing about emotional attachments," she confesses, her tone bitter.

"Oh." Words escape me because there's really no way to follow that up. It speaks volumes all on its own.

"We didn't have any naked cowboys in Boston," I say, attempting to change direction and maybe cheer her up.

"Bummer." Her lips quirk up into a grin. "It's still a great city, though. Do you miss it?"

"I don't miss the city so much but I miss the guys I worked with at the shop. We had a great team there. Amazing artists. But," I admit, "I love Manhattan and feel like I belong here."

"Yeah, me too. Seattle is a great city, also, but I'm really happy here." She giggles when I find another ticklish spot. Okay, I'm kind of crazy about her laugh. "So do you want to watch another movie? You can pick this time."

"Okay. But be prepared. I'm putting on *Goodfellas*." I tickle her foot as I get up and she laughs. The DVD is already out on the table and I open the case, then pop it into the player. "Do you want more popcorn?"

"No, I'm good," she replies, making room for me next to her.

The movie starts, both of us glued to the television. We're both so engrossed in the drama that before we know it, the show is half over and I think I caught Vanessa yawning once or twice.

"Now about that tongue." I nudge her with my arm but she doesn't respond. Tilting my head to the side, I see her lashes lying against her cheeks, a sleepy smile on her lips. She's probably the most beautiful thing I've ever seen, not that I would ever tell her that.

I brush a golden strand of hair from her cheek, leaning forward to press a kiss to her forehead, but my lips stop short. Instead, I click the remote off then lift her into my arms, carrying her to my room. She makes a little noise of protest, but doesn't wake.

I lay her down gently, sliding her skirt off and covering her up with the blanket so she can be more comfortable. Then I shift on my side, staring out at the moon. I'm restless. I've never had anyone in my bed unless we were fucking. But she fell asleep and it's no big deal. It's just one night. I can handle it.

Twisting around, I rest my head on my hand, staring at her. Her blonde hair is cascading over the pillow, face at peace, troubles temporarily at bay. I raise up on my elbow and edge closer, placing a kiss just above her brow. "Goodnight, Blondie," I whisper.

It's just one kiss. I can handle it.

# CHAPTER TEN

## HOT AND SERIOUSLY TWISTED

*Vanessa*

"I don't know how on earth you got me to the gym at six thirty a.m., V. This has got to be the definition of crazy," Olivia says, huffing and puffing as she walks on the treadmill beside me.

"Liv," my breathing is steady when I respond, "I do this almost every single day. Once you get used to it, it's a piece of cake. It gets you energized for the day."

"Well...." She lets out a wide yawn. "I prefer to be sleeping in the comfort of my bed when the sun comes up. Which reminds me, what happened last night? I texted you a couple of times and you didn't respond."

"Oh," I answer with a grin, trying to keep my balance while thoughts of Rex tap dance through my head.

"And you're grinning because....?"

"I was at Rex's. We... you know, and then we hung out and watched a movie, actually two, but I fell asleep." I smile, vaguely remembering Rex carrying me to his bed.

"You watched a movie? With Rex?" Her eyes pop open in surprise when she glances over at me.

"Yeah, why?" I look over at her, awfully curious what she means.

"Well, he doesn't typically," she bends her fingers in an air quote, "'hang out' with women. He only, you know, has sex with them. At least that's what Hunter told me."

My cheeks pull in at her insinuation. "Well, I don't know what to tell you. He hung out with me, so maybe he's changing his policy. Plus, I don't know if you remember, but *you're* the one that got this little ball rolling when you invited me out to the club."

"Hey, I'm sorry, V." She wipes the sweat from her forehead. "I don't mean to imply anything. It's just that Rex isn't the relationship type, you know, and I don't want to see you get hurt."

"Liv," I take a quick sip of bottled water, "who said anything about a relationship. We're fucking and watching movies. Lighten up," I urge, and she bursts out laughing. "You already know my take on relationships. They suck, remember?"

"Yes, I know. But I'm only bringing it up because I know Rex fits your profile," she says, breathing heavy, pushing the button to slow the treadmill down.

"Profile, what profile is that?" I use the towel to wipe beads of sweat off the back of my neck.

She clicks her tongue against her teeth, staring at me like I should have the answer to her riddle. "You know, hot and seriously twisted."

I laugh so hard I nearly fall off the treadmill. "Well, yeah, he's definitely that."

"So," she steps off the treadmill, "do you want to hang out tonight?"

"I can't tonight. I need to head over to Ryder's bar. One of my clients is having a small informal gathering there next week and we need to go over the details. Maybe I'd be up for something tomorrow night, though." The treadmill slows and I hop off, walking with Olivia toward the locker room. "So, what's on your agenda for today?"

She lightly flicks her towel against my arm. "You know the usual, writing hot sex scenes and then re-enacting them with Hunter during his lunch hour... hopefully on his desk."

I shake my head and snort. "Ah, just another day in the life of an erotic romance author."

"Precisely." She grins, waggling her eyebrows at me.

I walk into Ryder's place distracted, digging through my briefcase to find notes for the event, when I notice the hint of a familiar tattoo staring me in the face, and smile. Rex is sitting at the bar, his back to me. With a few short strides, I make it over and snag the stool next to him. His head swings to the side when the stool squeaks beneath me.

"Hi y-ya B-blondie," he slurs, before turning away, his eyes cast down, hand flicking ice around in the empty glass. His words, bloodshot, glazed-over eyes, and red cheeks tell me everything I need to know. With fierce determination, he taps three times on the counter to catch Ryder's attention and order another drink.

"Rex, what's wrong? You okay?" I ask, placing a hand on his arm.

His eyes stroll over to where my hand is then up to me. "H-here we go with the twenty questions again, huh? Maybe I'm just not in the f-fucking mood to answer your questions, did you ever think of that?" He glares at me, his head bobbing from side to side. "What do you want to know for anyway? So you can use my answers against me? Because that's how women are, you know… they can't be trusted." He stands up, gripping the edge of the bar when he nearly falls over. "But fucking, yeah… now we're talking. Women are great for that." He latches onto my arm. "Do you want to go fuck? Because I'd be up for that."

Suddenly, all my concern for him goes right out the freaking window. I rip my arm from his clutches, grasping the handle of my briefcase so tight that my knuckles turn white. "You know what, Rex," I bite back, staring straight ahead. "Whatever. Sorry I asked, or even cared for that matter."

"Yeah, you cared… right. It's all bull-sh-shit," he mumbles into his drink.

Ryder comes over but when he sees Rex's current state, doesn't refill his glass. "Hey, darlin'," sweetness oozes from his voice, "you didn't get my message?"

"No, what message?" I ask, trying to shrug off this sudden coat of anger, and the fact that Rex gets to me this way.

"I don't have the time to meet tonight. It's too busy, so I was hoping we could meet late afternoon tomorrow?" He stocks the bottle of liquor back on the shelf behind him.

"Oh, no I didn't get it, but that's fine—"

"Darlin?" Rex interrupts, glaring at Ryder. "What's up with that?" Then he spits his venom back on me, spewing angry words in my direction. "Something I should know? You screwing him, t-too?"

"Rex," Ryder warns, "you're out of line, man."

My mouth is still hanging open but I manage to compose myself, holding a finger up in front of Ryder. "I got this."

I wait until Rex turns to face me, my muscles burning, seeing red everywhere I look. "You know what, Rex, I don't know what your problem is *now*, but I don't really give a shit. And for your information," I bark, "I'm not screwing Ryder, but if I was, it's none of your God damn business. And you know what else?" I seethe, raising my voice, drawing the attention of patrons nearby. "I don't even know why I'm wasting my breath talking to you right now." I stand up from the stool. "Because you're not worth it. I'll talk to you tomorrow, Ryder," I say, starting for the exit.

"You're right. I'm n-not," Rex grumbles as I walk out the door.

My breathing is noisy, legs crackling with disgust as they power me toward my destination. I happen to glance up at the sky, a deep, dark gray that reflects my state of mind. I don't know what the hell that was about and I don't even care, or at least I'm trying hard not to. Olivia was right. I sure do know how to pick men. To think I actually believed there might be a decent human being inside of Rex, but it turns out he's an asshole just like the rest of them.

I push the glass door to my apartment open, nearly hitting a woman with bright red hair and freckles in the face with it before offering a quick apology and darting to the elevator. "Hurry up," I say out loud, my foot doing an impatient tap. But no one's listening and it takes forever to get to my floor. All I want is to close the door to my apartment and completely shut out the world.

Finally, when the car stops, I stomp out of the elevator and down the hall, jamming my key in the lock. When I get it open, I throw my briefcase on the black leather couch and cross the living room to the kitchen, honing in on the fridge. I need something to take the edge off. There's a bottle of white Zinfandel on the bottom shelf. And while it's not hard liquor, it will certainly do.

After retrieving a glass from the cabinet, I pour the wine, the glugging sound serving to calm me. With heavy feet, I carry myself and my temporary solace back out to the sofa. I plunk down, toeing off my heels and crossing my legs before propping them up on the table. Within two seconds, I've polished off the glass and am making my way to the kitchen for a refill.

My mind is whirring with anger and a couple of other emotions I can't seem to put a name to. I don't know why I'm letting Rex get under my skin. He's just a guy—one of the many that have disappointed me in my life, beginning with my father.

I laugh to myself. It's amazing how the people that bring you into the world set the tone for your entire life. We try to flick them away—their habits, their mannerisms, their stupid actions—but somehow they manage to crawl their way in, when all you want to do is scrape them off.

There's not an ounce of my being that wants to be like my mother or my father, because quite frankly, I'm not seeing many redeeming qualities there. And that little fact, in and of itself, makes me wipe away the dampness now sitting on top of my cheeks.

Since I've been sulking, I have no concept of how much time has passed when there's a knock on the door, tearing me from my depressing train of thought. I wasn't expecting anyone so I consider not answering, until the pounding grows louder.

I squint when I reach the door, peering through the peephole to find red eyes amidst a ruddy complexion—Rex. How did he even know my address and what is he doing here? For a second, I think about ignoring him. But the problem is, even after the way he treated me, some sick part of me still wants to see him. I'm basically an asshole magnet, a plague I can't seem to escape. With a deep breath, I turn the knob, steeling myself for whatever else he has in store for me tonight.

Rex jerks his head back as the door opens, seemingly as surprised as I am that I answered it. His hands are shoved deep in his pockets, feet shuffling on the floor. A softening settles in his dazed eyes, and yet again, I'm curious what that's all about.

My grip on the door jamb is strong when I decide to speak to him. "How did you find me, Rex? I never gave you my address, and more importantly, what do you want? I don't know what you're doing here, but you're drunk. Just go home."

"I texted Hunter for your address, and... I can't go home. I don't want to be alone," he admits, his voice gravelly from drink.

My tongue pushes against my cheek, attempting to control the anger threatening to spill out at his audacity, thinking I'm actually going to sleep with him after the way he treated me. "Are you kidding me? If you honestly think I'm going to do anything with you after your comments at the bar, you're sadly mistaken."

"I'm not here for that," he says, and I'm unsure whether to trust him. "I just want to talk, that's all. Can you just give me a few minutes?"

I wave him in, closing the door, but not budging from my spot. "So talk, Rex, you've got fifteen minutes."

He stumbles over to the couch and collapses onto it, scrubbing a hand clumsily over his face. "I'm fucking drunk."

"Yeah, I know," I retort, arms folded over my chest, feet planted firmly on the carpet.

"I never get drunk."

I let out an exasperated sigh, tapping my foot on the rug. "Why are you here, Rex? What do you want?"

He raises his head to look at me, eyes drooping, shoulders almost sagging as if in defeat. I know something's tearing at his insides, but I refuse to ask questions. I'm not interested in getting beat up again. If he has something to say, he'll just have to own up to it.

"Today is my brother's birthday," he murmurs, taking a brief pause, his eyes darting around the room before they fasten themselves to mine. "He's fucking dead though, so he won't be celebrating."

The puzzle pieces fit together, and my hard shell cracks because I know what it's like to put up a shield to block out the pain. And when I look at him now, that's all I see—years of pain filling his eyes, creasing his skin, seeping into his soul. Empathy softens my resolve and I walk over, dropping down beside him. I want to reach out, but fear of rejection keeps me at a distance.

"What fourteen-year-old commits suicide?" he says bitterly, and while he asked a question, I know he's not looking for an answer. "I'll tell you. A fourteen-year-old boy who'd been molested for almost two years... who couldn't handle the memories anymore... whose mother had no fucking clue about it because she was too busy drinking and fucking anything with a dick," he spits out, swiping a hand across his mouth. "She was so fucking useless. If he hadn't finally confided in Hunter, we would never have known."

His shoulders curl further over his chest as he stares at the floor. "I found him," he says, voice hoarse with so much anguish that my breathing halts. "He was on the floor of his bedroom. So cold and pale, so lifeless. I'll never get that image out of my head as long as I live."

"I'm so sorry, Rex." Compassion outweighs my fear and I move closer to him until our arms are touching, though I know it's not enough to make that horror go away.

Nothing could ever be enough.

He edges forward, placing his head in his hands and I rest my own hand on his back. "It just fucking sucks, you know." Craning his head to the side, he meets my eyes and holds them. "I owe you an apology. I'm sorry for the way I treated you and all those awful things I said to you in the bar, and also for what I said about you and...," he pauses a beat, swallowing hard before he says his name, "Ryder."

"Apology accepted," I say warily. "Just don't do it again. But... I'm still not sleeping with you because you acted like an asshole."

A hint of a smile curves his lips. "That's okay, Blondie, I'm too fucking drunk anyway. I don't think I could get it up."

"Oh my God!" I giggle, relieved when he laughs, too. "Hey," I place a hand on his knee, my voice growing serious, smile fading, "I'm really sorry about your brother. I bet he was a great kid."

"Yeah, he was." He fists a hand against his mouth, clearing his throat a couple of times as if he's trying to hold back the emotion. "You got anything to drink?"

"I sure do."

I spring up from the couch and head into the kitchen. There's a six pack of Poland Spring water in the fridge, so I open it up and snag one, grabbing a clean glass from the dish drainer and filling it. Not more than a minute later, I come back out to the living room to find Rex slumped against the couch, fast asleep. I set the glass on the table and sit down next to him. My fingers brush away a stray wisp of hair from his forehead. He looks so incredibly peaceful and even though I don't believe in wishes, I find myself wishing that for him—peace. I wonder how much more pain lies beneath the surface, what he's endured, the burdens he carries.

I remember my words to Olivia, and shake off those wayward thoughts. My main problem now is what to do with him because he's too heavy for me to carry to my room, yet I don't want him to be alone. He's way too drunk.

Plodding over to the linen closet, I retrieve a comforter and pillow for him. When I return to the sofa, he's snoring lightly and it makes me smile. Without waking him, I lay him down gently on the pillow, swinging his legs around so he's laid out, then remove his shoes. He mumbles something in his sleep that sounds a lot like Blondie. I'm sure it's a mistake though, because that would be ridiculous.

After covering him up with a blanket, I traipse to my room, changing into a tank top and sleep shorts. I snatch my pillow and favorite purple blanket, a housewarming gift from Olivia when I moved in seven years ago.

I arrange my pillow and blanket on the sofa directly across from him and snuggle in. I'm not all that tired and don't have to go into the office until noon tomorrow, but still need to get some rest. My eyes have a mind of their own though, and refuse to close. Instead, they peek over the blanket, catching a glimpse of Rex. Drunk Rex. I shake my head, but then get up and shuffle to the other couch, standing over him. For just a minute, I stare at his face bathed in sleep before pressing a kiss to his cheek. "Goodnight, Rex," I whisper, and he stirs.

"Goodnight, Blondie," he mumbles before turning on his side.

I lie back down, my eyes close, and I fall fast asleep.

# CHAPTER ELEVEN

## THE SWEETEST THING

Fuck. My head is pounding as if someone took a sledgehammer to it. I blink my eyes and see light streaming through pale yellow curtains. Where the hell am I? When they open completely, it all comes rushing back. Last night, getting cocked, opening up to Vanessa. I smile, letting out a wide yawn, when I notice her on the other couch. She slept here with me? Well, that was... sweet. Then I notice a bottle of Tylenol and a large glass of water on the table. Hmph. More sweetness.

I pop two pills on my tongue, washing them down with a huge swig of water, the liquid doing nothing to remove the rancid taste in my mouth. The need to pee and brush my teeth is strong, so I wander around her apartment until I find the bathroom located down the hall and to the right. I relieve myself, then after washing my hands, squeeze some toothpaste on my finger and roll it around my mouth.

When I come back out, my eyes have finally adjusted to being awake. As I scan the room, I notice Vanessa has a lot of really nice shit in here: leather couches, flat screen television, a kitchen with those fancy stainless steel appliances. And as I look to my right, a great view of the city. This place must cost serious bucks.

The clock on the wall says it's six in the morning, which means I have several hours before I need to be at work. I glance over at

Vanessa. She moves, causing her tank top to ride up, baring the smooth skin of her stomach. My dick responds instantly and I will it to calm down. There's a pretty good chance she wants nothing to do with me after last night. And who could blame her. I acted like an asshole.

I guess there's only one way to find out.

I'm quiet as I make my way over and kneel down on the floor, taking a minute to just watch her. There's a strand of hair stuck to her lip, and I gently push it behind her ear. I bend down, lips touching the flesh of her belly, scattering kisses all over her skin. She makes a tiny noise in her throat, her eyelids fluttering open.

"Morning." My voice is low, lips wanting to attach themselves to her again.

"Morning," she rubs her eyes, "what time is it?"

"It's early. Only six." My nose circles her belly button and she whimpers, but I stop abruptly to meet her gaze. "Is this okay?" I ask, wanting to make sure I'm not overstepping.

"Yes, you're forgiven. Now keep going." She smirks, and I smile against her, my tongue continuing to wander along her delicate curves. When I glance at her, she's biting her lip and I move up her body, suddenly wanting to capture it between my teeth. I hover over her, that sweet mouth taunting me, drawing me in.

"Blondie?" I whisper against her.

"Hmmm?"

"Did I tell you how much I love your lips?" I eagerly brush her mouth with my own.

"No, you told me how much you love my tits and my pussy." She grins.

"Well, I love your lips, too." My tongue darts out to swipe across her bottom lip.

"Rex?" she breathes out.

"Yeah?"

"Shut up and kiss me."

"I like it when—"

She ends my sentence, her hands sinking into my hair, urging me forward. My lips land on hers, my eager tongue reaching into her warm, wet mouth. She pulls me in, sucking, playing, exploring, as we twine around one another. I honestly can't get enough of her. I could drown in her taste, the smell of her skin, the feel of her pussy.

I shift so my weight is on top of her, feeling her heat through the thin fabric of her shorts, my cock pushing against the zipper of my jeans. She moans into my mouth as she rubs against my dick, sending a vibration of want through me. And I'm so God damn hungry for her. I've never wanted anyone like this before and I'm not sure I really understand it, but the last fucking thing I'm doing right now is analyzing it.

Reluctantly, I break from her lips, staring at eyes that are half-lidded, lips parted and swollen. "Jesus, you drive me crazy, you know that?" My breathing is hurried, completely out of control. "I want to fuck you so badly right now."

She only has one response, and it's the best fucking one I could hope for. Her hands drop to the band of her tank, lifting it up and over her head, a sexy smirk lining her mouth. I lick my lips at the sight of her puckered nipples before cupping her breast, tugging on her with my teeth.

"Hmmm," she moans, and I swear to fuck I could come just by hearing that sound alone.

With one last flick of her nipple, I release it with a pop, my eyes darting around the room until I find what I'm looking for. "How attached are you to that table over there?"

She looks at me quizzically, trying to figure out what the hell I'm talking about. "Huh?"

"Because I want to fuck you on it." I smirk, biting the edge of my lip.

"No attachment whatsoever," she comes back with immediately, no hesitation, nothing but mischief alight in her pale blue eyes.

Like I said—such a fucking turn on.

Bounding to my feet, I reach under and she squeaks when I grasp her ass, her head falling back on a laugh. I go for her neck, sucking on the skin there, wanting to leave my mark.

When we reach the table, I set her down. She pushes everything off—books, papers, candles, and any other girly shit that was on there—then leans back against it. Topless, with just those sexy shorts, she eyes me as I reach down and slide my shirt off, strolling over my tattoo. I tilt my head to the side, crossing my arms over my chest and shaking my head.

"What?" Her lips quirk up at the corners.

"It's just that you're so unexpected."

"Is that good?" she questions as I close the gap between us, pushing her silky waves away from those stunning eyes.

"Yeah, it's real good." Our eyes meet and hold for what seems like an overpowering minute before I lower my thumb to her nipple, rolling over the hardened peak. She reaches out a slender finger and traces the lines of my eagle tattoo, skimming my chest with her nails.

"Hmm," she murmurs, as I continue playing with her nipple. "I like how rough your finger feels." She looks down at it, then back up to me. Her eyes are clouded with lust but I see something else there, something I didn't see when we first met.

A spark.

I see hope.

An unfamiliar tingling sweeps over me and I quickly brush it off. I can see whatever I like, but when it comes down to it, there's no hope for me.

"Hey." The sound of her voice brings me back to reality, where I need to stay. "You okay?"

"I will be once you're spread open on the table."

Her tongue does a slow waltz across that full bottom lip before she hooks her thumbs into her shorts and slides them down, taking her panties with them. Hands behind her on the table, she hops up and reclines back, her body like a fucking temple and I intend to cherish every inch of it.

Without taking my eyes from hers, I remove my jeans and boxers, my cock firmly pointed in her direction. Her tongue darts out to moisten her lips as she drops back on the table, spreading her legs for me and crooking a finger, urging me closer.

My only thought right now—life is fucking great.

I snag a condom from the wallet in my jeans, then stalk toward her. Each footstep feels like an eternity because I want inside her so badly. When her hand flies over her stomach, moving toward her pussy, I have to stop her.

"No. I won't last if you do that, and I want to be inside you too much right now. Let's save that for another time," I say smugly, and I'm rewarded with a cat-like grin as she opens her legs even more for me.

Jesus.

After rolling on the condom, I climb over her body, holding myself up on my elbows. My hand disappears between us, and I run my finger lightly over her slit, coated with her arousal. I hiss a breath through my teeth at how drenched she is, something primal going off inside of me that makes me want to bang on my chest. *I* did this to her.

"Rex," she purrs, making my cock harden even more. "Fuck me, I want you to fuck me hard."

"You want it rough?" The heated spark in her gaze is the only response I need. "Then hold on for the ride, baby," I say, and something flashes in her eyes as she smiles back at me. It makes me hesitate for just a beat, before I put it out of my head. "Fuck, you're wet. My mouth is watering. I can't decide if I want to lick you, or fuck you."

"Rex," she breathes out on a pant as I massage her clit over and over. "Stop talking, your words and your finger are going to make me come. Hmmm," she moans again, pushing herself into my hand, wanting more.

I position myself at her drenched entrance before sliding the tip in slowly. Apparently, it's too slow for her because she grabs my ass and pulls me in, my cock so deep inside her pussy, filling her, while she stares at me with an intensity I'm not used to. There's absolutely nothing modest about her and she has no idea how much that turns me on. This is a girl who knows exactly what she wants and isn't afraid to go after it.

"Fuck me harder, Rex," she screams out, and I rock into her, in and out, harder, rougher. I groan when she squeezes my ass again. "Rub my clit," she begs, and I lower my finger to the pink folds of her pussy, circling her, moans of pleasure dropping from her mouth.

"You feel so good," I groan, watching heavy breaths fall from her parted lips, lust coloring her cheeks.

"I'm gonna, come," she calls out, and there's no way I'm going to last either. She feels too fucking good.

"Come for me," I groan, my neck corded tight, cock ready to burst inside of her.

"Ahhh," she whimpers as she spasms around me, her pussy throbbing, sending me over the edge as I continue to pump into her.

"Fuck," I growl, as I come ferociously inside of her before crashing my lips to hers, the salt from our sweat mixed with the sweetness of her lips.

I break from her mouth, panting, my head falling against her breast. It's not until she starts laughing that I raise my head. "What's so funny?" I try to catch my breath. "I'm not sure there was anything funny about *that*."

"I've never fucked on a table before," she giggles, "and that was amazing."

I shake my head and laugh, too. "Yeah, it was. And... I've never fucked on a table before, either," I admit, suddenly unsure as to why I feel the need to spout off when I'm around her. It's like she's some kind of fucking truth serum.

"Really?" she asks, seemingly happy with my response.

"Yeah, really."

"Hmph," she says with a wide smile. "Well, I'm actually thinking this table should be reserved for fucking. I don't want to eat on it anymore after that, anyway."

"You're insane," I reply, rolling off of her and lying on my back.

"So where's the most unusual place you've ever had sex?" She shifts on her side, propping her cheek on her fist.

"I don't know if they're that unusual, but I had sex once in a parking garage, and another time in a press box at a baseball game. What about you, oh adventurous one?"

"Hmph." Her eyes flick upward in thought. "Probably in the fitting room at a department store. There was a curtain of course."

She's silent for a minute, almost contemplative, before reaching out a finger to follow the lines of the guitar strings running alongside my neck. No words are spoken, but I know they're coming. Questions. More fucking questions. And so I wait, hoping she'll remain quiet.

But they come anyway.

"I love this tattoo... does it have any special meaning...." She hesitates, knowing how much I enjoy answering questions.

My wall instantly begins to slide up between us, but when I turn my head sideways to look at her, something in her eyes makes me wonder whether she really is like all the others. She almost looks like she cares. But the war I constantly fight within myself won't allow me to take my wall down. Instead, I reach over it, handing her this small piece of information.

"It's to remind me of my brother. He loved strumming the guitar as a kid. He couldn't play for shit, really, and sounded pretty awful, but," I shrug, "it was his favorite thing to do."

She continues sketching the strings with her finger as my mind roams to my freckle-faced brother. "What was his name?" she asks softly.

I huff out a deep breath, not wanting to reveal anything else, still warring with a brain that thinks she has some ulterior motive. Most women do. But for some unknown reason, I continue. "Tyler," I respond, emotion clogging my throat. "His name was Tyler."

"Tyler," she repeats, and then she does something completely unexpected. So unexpected, I don't know what to make of it. She leans forward, placing a kiss to my tattoo before lying back down on the table. Her lips no longer on my skin.

But I still feel them.

# CHAPTER TWELVE

## DEATH AND DESTRUCTION

# *Vanessa*

I'm not sure why I just did that. There's a part of me that feels it was too intimate. But I saw the devastation in his eyes last night when he talked about his brother, and I want him to know that I empathize with his pain—that he's not alone. He's lying stock still, though, not saying a word, and I need to do something to lighten the moment.

"So," I sit up and ease myself off of the table, "I'm going to hop in the shower. I don't have to work until noon and I'm going to try to meet Olivia beforehand. Do you want to join me in the shower?" I ask as he gets up, his muscles rippling with his movement. He's ridiculously sexy and I can't help myself.

"Can I take a rain check?" He snatches his jeans and t-shirt from the floor. "The idea of being near you when you're wet and slippery is very appealing, but I need to get home. I have a couple of errands to run before work, so I'll just shower there."

"Sure." I paint on a smile in response even though disappointment looms over me. There's something comfortable about having Rex around and I'm not all that anxious for him to go.

"Maybe we can get together later, though," he grins, buttoning up his jeans and toeing on his sneakers, "for more death and destruction? I'd say let's go to a club, but it's not really my scene."

My smile is genuine this time when I answer. "Sure. That sounds good." I slide my tank over my head. "I'll walk you out."

He gets to the door, pausing with a hand on the knob, turning back around to face me. "So...." He clears his throat as his eyes cast downward, one hand shoved in his pocket. "I'm not great with words, but... well, thanks, for last night... for not turning me away."

"Hey." I lower my head to the side looking for his eyes, and don't speak until they meet mine. "You're welcome. I'm glad I was here."

Our gazes fall away and he opens the door. "I'll see you around, Blondie."

"Yeah, see ya, Rex."

Five minutes later, I'm still standing in the same spot, unmoving. I quickly shake off my untamed thoughts and come back down to earth. The fact that he called me baby while we were having sex means nothing, and the fact that I'm even thinking about it now is utterly ridiculous. I hope he didn't notice my reaction when he said it, though. I'm sure it was a slip and it doesn't mean anything.

So why am I thinking about it?

I laugh at myself and head over to my purse, digging around for my phone. When I finally find it, I dial Olivia's cell. She answers on the first ring as if she was expecting my call.

"Hey," she says with a pop in her voice, "are we still meeting up this morning?"

"Hey to you, too, and yes, we are. I just need to hop in the shower."

"You haven't showered yet?" she asks, and there's a loud rustling in the background.

"No, I haven't," I reply with a grin that she can't see.

"You sound awfully happy. My bitch detector isn't going off. What's going on?" She laughs, and the sound of her crunching on something vibrates in my ears.

"Well, if you must know, Rex just left." I pull a file from my bag, smoothing down one of my nails as the other end of the line goes quiet. "Hello? Liv, you there?"

"Yes, sorry. I'm standing outside of Adele's Coffee House and it's very busy."

"All right, well, let me shower and I'll meet you there in about an hour." I toss the file back in my bag and make my way toward the bathroom.

"Actually, meet me at Victoria's Secret, instead," she suggests.

"Victoria's Secret?" I laugh. "Again?"

"Again." She giggles, before we hang up.

The door jingles as I walk inside the palace of lingerie. It's been a while since I've been in here, but it's a place that Olivia frequents very often since she started dating Hunter.

I sneak up behind her as she lifts various bra and panty sets in the air, scrutinizing them. "Are you old enough to be in here?" I ask in a deep voice, and she spins around, startled.

"Very funny." She laughs. "Wow, you look great!" She eyes me up and down. "Fresh-faced. *Someone* had a good morning."

"Yeah, I did. But we can talk about that later. So how long should I expect to be in here? Weren't you just here last week?"

She lets a pair of underwear drop back into the bin. "Yes, but one can never have too many sets. You never know when they might come in handy. Especially when I visit Hunter's office tomorrow during lunch."

"You're shameless now," I tell her, as we get in line for the register. "This is such a different side of you. I really like it, and I really like seeing you this happy."

She curls her arm around mine. "Thanks, V. Me, too. Now we need to work on you. Find you a good man that can live up to your expectations."

I look away, chewing on my fingernail, a pang of something jabbing at my stomach. Whatever it is, it can't be good.

"Oh no," she tugs on my arm, "please don't tell me you're falling for Rex. Listen, I'm not saying he's not a good guy, but I think he's got a lot of issues."

"Yeah, Liv," I glare at her, my face pulling tight, "like I don't."

"You know what? You're right. I need to keep my mouth shut. I just don't want to see you hurt. I want to see you happy." She smiles and my bitterness fades away.

"I know you do."

After the sales girl rings up another six pairs of panties to add to Liv's collection, we stroll out the door, heading into the sunshine.

"I'm really in the mood for a BLT. Let's go to the deli around the corner." I tilt my head back, letting the sun warm my face. "God, I can't wait until the hot summer kicks in."

"Yes, I know how you like it hot, V."

From the side I see her smirking. "Yes, hot and *hard*."

We burst out laughing and by the time we traipse into the deli, we still haven't stopped. Olivia isn't watching where she's going and ends up slamming into a wall of muscle, only to look up and see that it's Hunter.

"Hey! Fancy meeting you here." She reaches up on her tiptoes and kisses him.

"Hi, sweetheart. Hi, Vanessa. I'm actually just on my way to a meeting uptown. Stopped to grab a sandwich." His eyes drift to the shopping bag and he grins. "Another shopping spree?"

"Uh huh." She dangles the bag, giggling like an excited schoolgirl.

"Hmmm... well, on that enticing note, I hate to leave. I'll call you later." He presses his lips to her cheek. "I love you, sweetheart."

"Love you, too," she replies, and he pinches her ass and flips her a wink before he struts out the door.

I look over in the corner and spot one table for two that's still available. "I'm going to snag that table, Liv. Just order me the BLT, a side of fries, and an iced coffee."

"Fries, too?" She perches a hand on her hip.

"Yes, I'm feeling depleted. Starving, actually," I mumble as I walk toward the table. She says something else under her breath that I'm not close enough to hear. I'm sure it has something to do with Rex.

My phone chimes as I gaze out the window, looking at all the people that make this city I love so unique. I pull it out of my purse and smile when I see it's a text from Rex.

*We're on for death and destruction tonight, right? My place, seven?*

He'd probably run in the other direction if he saw my grin.

*Yup. Bring it on.*

*I might even stop and get more popcorn. I can't have you complaining if we run out during the movie. I need to focus on the destruction.*

*Oh really, that's too bad because I'll be going commando.*

*Jesus, I'm hard now.*

*Hmmm...*

I close my phone, attempting to wipe the smug smile from my face just as Olivia heads in my direction.

"Do I want to know?" She places our food on the table, taking the seat beside me.

"No, you don't. But," I wave a finger in the air, "there's something I want to know."

"Oh yeah?" She steals one of my French fries, popping it into her mouth. "What's that?"

I narrow my eyes at her and playfully smack her hand. "Paws off my fries. Get your own," I say, before she grabs one more. "So have you talked to your parents? Or, more importantly, have they recovered from finding out that you're an erotic romance author and not the VP of a cosmetics firm?"

She expels a sigh which means it can't be good. "Oh, that."

Leaning back in the chair, my fingers idly wipe the condensation from the side of my cup. "Yeah, now spill."

"Well, when I spoke with them the other night, my mother asked if I had been attending church on Sundays, and confession of course to atone for my sins, while my father wanted to know if I was living an honest life now." A tiny laugh slips from her mouth and she presses her lips together. "I told them that maybe if they read one of my books they wouldn't be so uptight. Neither of them thought it was funny. In fact, I think I heard my father spit his coffee out."

"Oh my God! I love it. However...." I clear my throat, sitting up straighter in my chair. "If you'd like me to attend church with you, I'd be more than happy to, although I can't think of anything I need to confess." My lips turn up as I shove a handful of French fries into my mouth.

She takes a bite of her sandwich, angling her head to the side thoughtfully. "I'm sure we could come up with something you need to confess."

"Nope." I'm adamant and she laughs, nearly spitting her coffee on the table. "And now you're starting to spit, just like your father."

# CHAPTER THIRTEEN

## THE TIN MAN

"Hey, Rex, I'm talking to you. Where the hell did you go?"

Jaden's gruff voice pulls me out of my thoughts, dragging me away from staring at Vanessa's message and back to the next customer at the front desk.

"Sorry, man, just a lot on my mind." I stuff the phone in my back pocket, walking with him toward the counter, when he slaps me on the back.

"A lot of *who* on your mind?" He chuckles, before trudging out the door of the shop.

I shake off the runaway train going through my mind and try to focus. Chloe, a girl who came in two weeks ago to consult with me on a tattoo, is here. She said she'd be back when she finally worked up the emotional courage. Four months ago, her boyfriend died tragically in a motorcycle accident, and she wants to pay tribute to him. I'm going to help her do just that.

"Hey, Chloe," I greet her, a somber smile on her thin lips.

"Hi, Rex. Well," she shrugs, her shoulders dropping on a sigh, "I'm back, and I'm ready."

I shoot her a comforting smile, hoping to ease her nerves, to let her know it's going to be okay. "Come on."

She follows me back to my station, taking a seat on the chair. Another sigh leaves her, and it weighs heavily in the air. "So, I've decided where I want the tattoo." She points her index finger to the area on her arm, just beneath her shoulder. "I'd like it to cover this whole spot," she says, circling the skin.

"Great," I tell her, as I prepare the needle and the various inks.

Chloe is quiet for a bit as I get everything ready, but I know the silence won't last for long. It never does. But I don't ever invade a client's emotional space. I know when they're ready, they'll talk. And they always do. Getting a tattoo is like therapy.

"I don't want to ever forget him," she says quietly, as the first prick of the needle hits her skin. She flinches, another minute going by before she speaks again. "I'm not one of those people who takes a lot of pictures, and now I'm wishing that I had. I'm afraid," she pauses, wetness pooling in the corners of her eyes, "that one day I'll wake up and I won't remember his eyes, how blue they were, how full of life they were... and the next day I'll wake up and I won't remember his smile. Then the day will come when I'll wonder if he was ever real. Sooner or later, he'll just fade away. I don't ever want him to fade away, you know?" she says, a tear crawling down her cheek.

I lift the needle off of her skin, placing a comforting hand on her shoulder. "Now he won't ever be far from your mind, or your sight," I soothe, and she raises her weepy eyes to meet mine.

"Yes," she responds on a soft sob as I reach for a tissue and pass it to her.

My chest grows heavy, a weight of guilt sitting on top of it. I suddenly can't remember how many freckles my brother had on his cheek, or the sound of his voice. I breathe out a pained sigh before I go back to helping Chloe heal. That is what's important right now. Not my bullshit.

There's very little conversation after that. Chloe is lost in her thoughts and I'm concentrating on making this the best damn picture she'll ever have. After a little over two hours, I'm finally finished. She's had her head turned the entire time, but the moment the buzzing ceases, she shifts my way.

"All done?"

"Yup." I wipe her skin, a prideful smile covering my face. This is a damn good tattoo.

When her eyes find the tattoo in the mirror, her mouth hangs open, nothing but awe dropping out of it. "It's... it's beautiful and perfect. It looks just like him." Her eyes climb to mine. "Thank you, Rex. It's not enough, but thank you." She flings her arms around me without warning and I hug her small frame in return. "You just gave me my memory back," she whispers, "until I see him again someday." She backs away and I begin wrapping up her tattoo. "You have a good heart. To be doing this kind of work, you have to have a good heart."

"Nah, I don't have a heart. I'm a bit like the Tin Man." I chuckle, even though it's a God damn depressing statement.

Reaching out her petite hand, she taps on my chest which takes me aback. "You do. You just haven't found the right person to make it beat hard enough for you to feel it." She kisses my cheek, then walks to the register without looking back.

The rest of the day goes by in a blur, burdened by thoughts of my baby brother and Chloe's words. There's a mild nagging in my chest. I feel like I need to see Vanessa and have no idea why. It's fucking with me because I don't need anyone... because relying on anyone other than myself only leads to disappointment and a false sense of hope.

Everyone has gone home, so I finish cleaning up my station before locking up the shop and heading to my apartment. On the way, my phone beeps and I yank it out of my pocket to discover a text from Vanessa. I slide the screen open and smile.

*I arrived a bit early for death and destruction, but you're not here.* :(

Did she seriously just give me a sad face? I type back a quick reply.

*On my way, don't get your panties in a twist. Oh, that's right, thank fuck you aren't wearing any.*

I wait for her response which comes quickly.

*Hmmm... and I'm already wet, too.*

*Jesus. I'm running, be there in ten.*

Shoving the phone back in my pocket, I literally start sprinting toward my apartment, knocking over anyone in the way.

By the time I make it there, I'm slightly out of breath, but nothing that seeing Vanessa won't cure. There's something about her that breathes a little bit of life into me, even though I'd never admit that openly. I actually like being around her, and not just for a quick fuck.

The elevator doors open and the first thing I see when I step off are mile long, smooth legs peeking out from under a skirt so short it should be illegal. Not to mention the snug t-shirt covering her perfect tits. Vanessa has her head angled, leaning against the wall, and she looks sexy as fuck.

"Hey, Blondie." I bound toward her, completely invading her personal space. My lips are inches from hers, her breasts flush against my chest.

"I'm glad to see you," she murmurs as my hand slides down her spine, past her lower back, reaching under her skirt to cup her ass. The softness of her skin forces my eyes closed as I gently massage it, and then her mouth is on mine, the warmth of it sending a jolt of electricity straight to my core. She moans as her greedy tongue slips between my lips, flirting, until she gently eases out, her sweet breath brushing against me.

"I like that welcome." My finger slips past the seam of her ass, grazing her clit, feeling the wetness between her thighs. "I guess you do, too," I say with a smug grin, and she narrows her thumb and forefinger together.

"Just a smidgeon."

I nod my head toward the door. "Come on. Let's go choose our path to death and destruction."

She flings her heels off the moment we walk inside and jumps on the worn leather sofa. I rub my eyes with my palms, then scrape a hand through my hair.

"Hey, you all right? You looked wiped out." She leans forward, curling her legs underneath her.

"Yeah. Fine. Just a long day. You want a beer?" I ask, already making my way to the fridge.

"No, I'm good. Thanks," she answers, but I still feel her eyes on me when I come back out and cross the room.

"Are you sure you're—" She starts to say, but stops herself. "Never mind."

I know she's holding back and I'm not surprised. She's so accustomed to me snapping at her all the time. But I'm not used to anyone being that interested in what I have to say. Doubt shows up, taking the form of a muted quiver inside my chest.

Collapsing beside her, I flick the cap off the beer. "So you had a good day?" I ask, even though my desire to talk right now is nonexistent.

"Yeah. Work was really busy." She sprawls out, resting the edges of her cute little feet against the table. "I met Olivia earlier today and we ran into your brother at the deli, too."

My fingernails begin to pick at the label on the bottle as my mind wanders from our conversation. Tension sits on top of my shoulders, as if a hand is gripping me hard, or maybe it's the fucking vice squeezing my chest, holding me hostage. An explosion is brewing, each second I hold my feelings in moving me toward utter devastation. But then again, that's my life. Dealing with the ruins, things collapsing around me and trying to figure out how the hell to get through it all.

Alone.

"Rex? Did you hear me?"

Instead of answering her, the words finally push past the knot in my throat. As painful as they are, they have to come out before I annihilate everyone around me.

"I had a client today," I mumble, continuing to tear at the label, "a girl, probably in her twenties, but wise beyond her years. She'd lost her boyfriend in a motorcycle accident and wanted his picture tattooed on her arm so she'd never forget what he looked like." I take a sip of beer to wash down the emotion threatening to spill out. "I realized that I struggle now to remember certain things about my baby brother and I don't have any pictures except that one you saw. I could probably ask Hunter, but... I don't know, I guess I feel like... I don't deserve to have them."

Vanessa doesn't bombard me with words or questions. Instead, she moves closer, laying her head on my shoulder, her hand on my arm. I breathe out a sigh. I'm so damn tired of shouldering all my shit... alone.

Each second that goes by, I let a little more of it go as she draws patterns on my arm, nuzzling into my neck. She seems to understand me, even when I don't understand myself. A voice in my head whispers something that I'll never say aloud.

I'm drawn to her.

I rest my head on top of hers, breathing in the scent of her shampoo. "You smell like raspberry candy," I whisper, and she smiles against my neck. "If I remember correctly, you taste like candy, too, although I might need a refresher."

"I thought we were doing death and destruction," she pouts. But it's not annoying, it's cute. "And I want my popcorn."

"Okay," I chuckle, "death and destruction *first*. And I'll make your popcorn now."

Even though I'm not anxious to move, I push up from the couch and shuffle into the kitchen. As I grab the pot and pull the popcorn down from the shelf, I'm thinking that if this is going to become a habit, I might need to purchase an actual popcorn maker. The thought freezes me in my tracks, my pulse thrashing against my wrists. I don't know what the hell I'm saying. This is *not* going to become a habit. No fucking popcorn maker required.

"Okay," I announce, trotting back out and handing her the bowl, "popcorn with extra butter and salt made to order. Now, we need to decide on a movie." I open the drawer underneath the television cabinet that contains hundreds of movies, holding one up at a time as if they're on display. "First option... *Scarface*."

She tilts her head, a smile tipping her lips. "Hmph, I love Al Pacino but that may be a bit too much death."

"Okay." I drop the movie back in and pluck out another one. "*The Godfather*? Some mafia action?" I question, and she just shakes her head, continuing to stuff handfuls of popcorn into her mouth.

"I've got it!" I call out with confidence. "*Die Hard 2*?"

"Yup." She smiles while crunching on some kernels. "That's the one. More Bruce Willis."

I shake my head and laugh before I pop in the movie, grab the remote, and sink down next to her.

"Hey, by the way. I'm curious about something," she says, and when I turn to her, she holds up her hands, adding, "I know, big surprise." She's smiling as she says it, so it puts me at ease.

"What now? Bleeding me for more information?" I tease, and she pinches my thigh.

"Well, when we met it was at a club, so I was wondering about when you said you don't frequent clubs." She digs her hand into the bowl and grabs some popcorn, tossing it in her mouth.

"Mostly because I don't like to drink a lot. I drink beer, but I'm not one for the heavy stuff because I've seen what it can do. My... mother has a drinking problem. So," I shrug, staring at the wall, "I don't like to put myself in situations where people are getting loaded. They tend to do and say stupid things." My eyes wander back to hers. "The way I acted last night was a perfect example of that."

"Yeah. I get it. I don't really drink much either." She lets out a bubble of laughter. "Stella used to give me these little lectures about drugs and alcohol. I don't recall how old I was, but she would tell me how drinking was so bad for your liver and drugs were bad for your brain. I remember wondering why she was even talking to me about it because I was young, you know? But now I appreciate that she did. Besides," she adds, her lips quirking into a grin, "I'd much rather go to a movie or a museum."

"Museums are cool," I tell her, and her eyes widen in surprise.

"Seriously? You really think that?"

"Hey, don't look so surprised." I give her shoulder a little shove. "Think about it. Art is how I make my living. It's something I'm interested in, that I'm passionate about, so yes, I like museums. I'll have you know, I've been to the Metropolitan Museum of Art *twice* since I've been back."

Her eyes narrow, regarding me with a speculative gleam. "Hmph. Interesting *and* impressive."

"I can see you sizing me up in that little brain of yours," I joke, and she throws a handful of popcorn at me.

"I'll have you know there's nothing little about my brain," she protests, as I take some of the popcorn from my lap and munch on the kernels.

"So, is the interrogation over now? Can we watch the movie?" I quirk a brow and her lips flip at the edges.

"Yeah, I'm done... for now. Popcorn?" She waves the bowl in front of my face. "Before it's all gone."

"No, thanks. I'm good."

"Okay then," she smirks, "more for me."

"You're a piece of work, you know that? Now," I put a finger to my lips, "shhh, no talking during the movie," I instruct, and she giggles as she inhales more popcorn.

I love that she doesn't talk during the movie. I've had to endure women who can't stop yapping when I'm trying to focus. It's irritating, but she's definitely not. I turn my head in her direction when I notice she's clutching her stomach, her face a milky white.

"Blondie, what's wrong?"

"I don't feel so good all of a sudden," she groans. "My stomach, I think I'm gonna be sick."

Before I have a chance to respond, she springs up off the couch, running toward the bathroom. I follow behind her quickly and get there just as she's kneeling in front of the toilet. "It hurts, Rex," she whimpers, still holding her stomach, and I gather her hair up, lifting it away just as whatever food she ate spills out.

"It's okay, I'm here," I whisper, rubbing calming circles on her back. My skin tingles with insecurity. I don't know how to do this. The only person I ever tried to look after was Tyler and we know how I fucked that up.

Seconds later, after her stomach is completely emptied, she collapses back onto the floor. She's freezing cold, her skin pale, and I'm really worried. I don't know what to do for her.

"I'm freezing," she mumbles, and I immediately lift her off the cold tile floor and into my arms, carrying her to the bedroom. I draw back the covers with my free hand and lay her down, removing her skirt before settling her underneath them. Jogging back out to the hall, I quickly grab a heavy blanket from the closet and return to her, pulling it up to her neck to keep in the warmth.

When I reach my hand out to touch her cheek, she's still so cold and I'm thinking maybe I should take her to the hospital. "I want to take you to the doctor," I say, hoping she can hear me.

"No," she mutters, "I can't move... just stay with me." Her lashes are fluttering and I don't like how little color is in her cheeks. My teeth grab onto my lip hard, the metallic taste of blood rising to the surface. There has to be something else I can do.

"I'm just gonna get a warm washcloth. I'll be right back." I kiss her cheek, which is like ice, and frantically run to the bathroom, grabbing a hand towel from the rack and soaking it in warm water. My head starts to pound and I grip the counter for support. Worry knocks hard against my chest, but I refuse to answer. Instead, I blow out a hard breath before wringing out the washcloth then hurrying back to her.

The mattress shifts under my weight, and I scoot in next to her beneath the covers. She groans when I press the cloth to her head.

"Rex," she whimpers, her eyes now closed, head moving from left to right.

"Shhh... I'm not going anywhere." I wrap my arms around her and bring her to my chest, hoping to help warm her with my body heat. Soft cries pierce my ears so I squeeze her as tight as I can without hurting her, stroking her hair over and over, trying to calm her and maybe myself, too.

Eventually, the sound of her quiet breathing assures me she's asleep, easing the ache in my chest. But I still don't close my eyes. The minutes tick by and I lie awake, listening for any noise, any change in her breathing. Her body is warmer and I expel a sigh of relief.

I can't imagine anything happening to her.

My mind is hindered by jumbled thoughts. After my dad died, everything changed for me. I felt like I had no one. Hunter tried as best he could to be there, but he was still young himself. Besides, it wasn't his fucking responsibility. The person I needed was my mom, but she was never present. Because of that, even at my age, I'm incapable of knowing how to care for someone. It's pathetic and sad.

Bile churns my stomach as I glance out the window, lost in my past, in memories of my mother; my drunk, alcoholic mother with her nose in a bottle or with one of her lovers, instead of where it needed to be—with her family. With her son who was left in the hands of a disgusting human being who did horrible things to him. My teeth grind together, anger swells within me. But it's forgotten the moment I hear Vanessa's hushed words.

"I need you, Rex," she mumbles in her sleep, and something erupts inside my chest.

She needs me.

"I'm here, baby. I'm right here." I press a gentle kiss to her forehead.

And maybe, just maybe—I need *her*, too.

# CHAPTER FOURTEEN

## UNRAVELING

*Vanessa*

Light pricks my eyes and I awake disoriented. I squint and wriggle my body, trying to recall where I am. Of course, the rock hard chest beneath my cheek makes things all too clear.

Rex.

I smile against his smooth skin even though I've got nothing to smile about at the moment. My stomach is burning, a million needles seem to be poking at it from all angles, my throat dry, mouth consumed by a rotten taste—all remnants of a night that is now slowly coming back to me. This is what it must be like to get run over by a truck. Every one of my muscles ache, my head heavy.

"She wakes." The low rumble of his voice vibrates against my cheek.

I lift my head, immediately slapping a hand over my mouth. "Morning," I mumble, not wanting him to be repulsed by the horrible stench of my breath. "How long have you been awake?"

He takes my hand, moving it away from my mouth. "All night. How are you feeling?"

"Like a train wreck," I respond miserably. "And why were you up? You couldn't sleep?"

He pauses as I stare at him expectantly. "I just wanted to make sure you were okay, is all. No big deal."

"Oh." A little piece of my heart softens at his words. He took care of me last night. That much I do remember. I put a hand up between us again. "I need to brush my teeth. My mouth tastes like ass."

He chuckles, pushing a matted strand of hair behind my ear. "Ass, huh? Don't move," he orders, sliding out from underneath me. And even in my tattered state I can still appreciate his amazing form as he strides away.

When he comes back, he has a cup of water and a toothbrush in his hand, a small line of toothpaste covering the bristles. He places them on the table next to the bed before taking a pillow and propping it against the headboard.

"Do you think you can sit up?" he asks, and I nod my head as he helps me lean back against the pillow. Sitting down cross-legged in front of me, he takes the toothbrush from the table and holds it out. "Open," he commands, and I do so willingly, staring into his rich amber eyes as he gently glides the brush over my top and bottom teeth. "Stick out your tongue," he instructs again, smiling, and when I do, he brushes that as well. "There. No more ass."

"Thank you," I respond sheepishly as he hands me the cup of water, touched by his kind gesture.

Who would've known he could be so sweet?

He lifts the back of his hand to my forehead. "You're nice and warm. That's good." Then he drops his hand to his lap. "You scared the shit out of me last night."

"I honestly don't remember ever feeling so horrible," I admit, "but I think I know what it was."

"What?" He tosses the toothbrush on the table.

"I went out to dinner with a friend for sushi, and obviously it was bad. Food poisoning at its finest." My stomach grumbles, a loud reminder that it's completely empty.

"Jesus, you need to get something in your stomach. He looks toward the kitchen, then back to me. "I don't have a whole lot, but I'll make you some toast. Sound good?"

I rub my belly, my mouth pulling down into a frown. "I'm not really hungry, Rex."

"Well, you need to eat something. Everything exited your stomach last night, remember?" He gets up off the bed and walks away, unwilling to take no for an answer.

My lips tug at the corners, a small piece of me admittedly happy that he's worried about me, even though I'm more than capable of standing on my own two feet. I've looked after myself for so long that it's hard to let someone in. But right now, my achy limbs coupled with the nausea rolling around in my stomach won't let me argue. With each twist of my belly, I'm being warned never to eat sushi again.

"Almost ready," Rex calls out from the kitchen just as I glance over at the clock. It's already 8:30 and there's no way I'm going to make it into work today. My eyes travel the room, spotting my purse on the carpet, and I reach down, fishing for my cell phone. I slide it open and dial the office. Matilda Draper, the receptionist, picks up after the second ring. She's always so enthusiastic.

"Platinum Events, this is Matilda, how can I help you?" Her peppy voice and the way she's chomping on her gum has me giggling. With her excitement, that subtle Georgia accent creeps into her last few words.

"Hey, Tillie, it's Vanessa."

"Hey, Vanessa. What's shaking?" She blows a bubble, popping it in my ear.

"Tillie. Does Jonathan know you're sucking down gum at the front desk while you're greeting people?"

"Of course not," she laughs, "I stuff it in my cheeks when he walks by."

I shake my head even though she can't see me. "Well, I'd keep it that way if I were you. Anyway, I wanted to let you know I'm not going to be in today. I'm not feeling well."

"Oh no," she replies with upset in her voice, "what's wrong?"

"I got food poisoning after my sushi dinner last night." I cringe, recalling the night in my head.

"That's awful. Do you want me to bring you some soup or something during my lunch break?" Her concern for me carries a smile to my face.

"No thanks, I'm good," I answer just as Rex walks in with my toast. "I've got everything I need." My words are a bit quieter but she bubbles up when she hears them.

"Okay, good. Well, I'll let Jonathan know. Feel better!"

"I will, Tillie. Thanks." I toss the phone back in my purse as Rex perches on the edge of the bed.

"Everything okay?" He hands me the plate and a napkin.

"Yes. I just called into work. I'm not in any shape to go in today."

His eyebrows pull in and he bites on his thumbnail. "Well, I have appointments starting at noon today so I have to go in to the shop, but you're more than welcome to hang out here if you want."

I nibble on the toast, wincing as the rough texture hits my throat. "Thanks, but I'm going to head home and just lounge in bed all day. With any luck, I'll sleep the rest of this off."

He reclines against the headboard next to me, crossing his legs at the ankles. "Are you sure you're going to be okay? I mean, maybe you should follow up with a doctor or something?"

"Rex," I lay my hand on his arm, "I'm fine. Seriously."

"I don't do well with shit like this." He tilts his head back against the wood. "I haven't since... well, since... Tyler." He shrugs, cracking his knuckles in his lap.

"I can understand that." I know it's hard for him to share so I remain quiet, not wanting to press him further.

"I don't like feeling helpless...." He pauses, blowing out a breath, and just when I think he's going to open up more he changes direction. "Anyway, did Olivia talk to you about dinner next Wednesday night? I can't believe my brother is finally going to pro—"

"*What*?" My eyes widen in shock. "He's popping the question?"

"Oh shit." He bunches a pillow under his neck. "Hmph... I don't think I was supposed to say anything and now you're sworn to secrecy. Hunter will have my nuts in a sling if this isn't a surprise."

"Rex." I shoot him a hostile glare. "Do you seriously think I would tell Olivia? Why would I do that? I want her to be completely surprised." I clap my hands together. "I'm so excited for her! She deserves this and she loves your brother like crazy."

"Even though love sucks, right?" he teases, the edges of his lips lifting into a grin.

"Yup, it does," I smirk, "just not for her."

"Yeah, this is huge for Hunter. I've never seen him so happy. He honestly doesn't care about anything else, even work."

"Well," I half-joke, "I guess that's what sucky love does for you."

He tilts his head to the side, meeting my stare. "Yeah, I suppose it does."

Our eyes hold for a bit too long and it makes me uncomfortable, so I break away from his gaze, changing the subject.

"So, I've been meaning to ask you?" Hesitancy makes my voice crack and I see his jaw grow tight. "Don't get nervous," I reassure him. "It's nothing crazy. I noticed the tattoos on your bicep and was interested in knowing what the symbols mean."

"Oh." He blows out what I conceive to be a relieved breath. Pointing a finger to his upper arm, starting with the thick, black Asian symbol on the left, he explains, "Well, this one means ears, and this one," he moves to the upper right, "means eyes. And this one here," he traces the one in the middle on the right, "means undivided attention. And the bottom right one," he taps against it, "means heart."

"So what does it mean, to *you*?" I run the pad of my finger over the design and his eyes follow the path, staring at the ink on his skin.

"Well, that I watch and listen, and give people my attention as they open their hearts and share their stories. It reminds me that what I do every day is important."

"I love that, and your passion for your work," I say, and if I'm not mistaken a small hint of red colors his cheeks. It's the first time I've seen him blush and he looks adorable. But I think I'll keep that to myself.

"I feel pretty disgusting. Can I take a shower?" I cast him what is hopefully a seductive smile, meeting his gaze. "You have to shower, too, don't you?"

"Why indeed, I do." A mischievous grin forms around his mouth, lighting his eyes. He holds out his hand to me. "Let's go."

I slip my palm into his, a tingle coursing through me at the smooth, yet slightly rough feel of it.

"You okay?" he asks.

"Yes, fine," I say back quickly. I can't let on how much he affects me.

When we get into the bathroom, he opens the stall door and turns the handle for the shower, standing just outside of it. "We need to give it just a second, it takes a minute to warm up. Need help getting undressed?" He grins, and I put a hand on my hip.

"I'm mostly recovered, I think I can handle it," I profess as he continues smirking. He takes his boxers down, my eyes involuntarily following the direction of his hands, landing on his erection.

A sexy grin is sent my way before he steps inside, holding his hand out to me yet again. I quickly slide my shirt over my head and remove my bra, immediately aware of how hard my nipples are and the ache building between my legs.

I'm definitely feeling better.

I climb in, my back to his front, the length of his arousal pressing firmly against my ass. The stream of water flows over my face, my breasts, my arms, warming me, but nothing like the warmth I feel when Rex snakes his arm around my belly, nuzzling his face in my neck. I rub my cheek against the rough stubble on his chin, instantly on fire, wanting that same sensation on the apex of my thighs.

"Your skin is so smooth," he says, but then throws me off with his next words. "Is this okay? Am I hurting your stomach?"

"I'm fine. Your hands feel good," I murmur, but feel deprived once he removes them. A minute later, they're on me again, only this time in my hair, massaging shampoo into my scalp, goose bumps popping up all over my arms. "No one's ever taken care of me like this before," I say quietly, and his hands still.

"No one?"

"No one." I don't say anything else, I can't. The spots flooding my vision make the memories hard to recall.

Or at least, that's what I tell myself.

Rex cups my shoulders, spinning me around to face him. A mixture of dark and light dilutes the brown of his eyes as droplets of water drip down his face, his chin, over the defined muscles of his chest.

"Let me... try?"

The tenderness in his words melts some of the hurt away and my breath quivers, his desire to care for me tugging on battered yet vulnerable strings.

"Tip your head back," he urges, his fingers gently combing through my hair, rinsing the suds away.

His gesture makes me feel like a child, but that child is long gone, only the shell of her remains. In her place stands a fiercely independent woman who tries her best not to need anyone. Although the face staring back at me when I raise my head causes doubt to skate across my mind.

Rex takes the bar of soap and lathers up the washcloth. Beginning with the bend of my neck, he smoothes it over my skin, down the length of my arms, then back up again. He glides the cloth past the base of my throat, over the swell of my breast, sneaking his thumb underneath to caress my nipple. The tip beads up and I moan, the need for his mouth on me overwhelming. My bottom lip falls open, breathing accelerates, as he trails leisurely down my belly, skimming my waist, lowering to his knees to massage my legs. A noise escapes my throat when his lips replace the cloth, his tongue doing a painstakingly slow sail up my calf, along my knee, and when he reaches my thigh, I whimper his name.

"Rex."

He peers up at me, his eyes the color of night. "Please, I need to taste you again."

The way he's looking at me, the sweetness in his words, bring unshed emotion to the surface, making it impossible to do anything but nod my head in response.

He smiles against me, the roughness of his cheek has me incredibly aroused, hot, wet. His nose rubs back and forth over the softness of my inner thigh, fingers sliding up my wet skin, teasing me, and my whole body hums with anticipation.

I brace my palms flat against the tile wall before he hooks my leg over his shoulder, spreading me open. He dips a finger into my folds, drenched with want for him, and I moan loudly when his tongue finally lashes out, running through my wetness.

"You like that?" He looks up at me, my arousal soaking his lips, taking away what I want most right now.

"*God*, yes," I pant, before his tongue lightly brushes my clit and I arch into him, wanting him deeper. Ripples of pleasure shoot through me, every movement, every flick of his tongue, making me delirious. I no longer feel the stream of water rushing over me, only the warmth of his breath, the softness of his tongue, the ferocity of his mouth, devouring me.

My hands drag through his hair, clutching tightly, holding him against my sex as he delves further, exploring, sucking, teasing. He drives me crazy with desire, consumed with a need I'm not sure I've ever felt before. I only know it goes beyond sexual, and at that last thought, my mind dizzies when his finger joins his tongue, teasing my clit, and I'm lost.

"Ahh…." My legs begin to quake as he increases the pressure of his tongue and I pulsate around him, sending me into the oblivion of the most amazing orgasm I've ever had. I think I actually see stars.

As I float back down to the here and now, I'm vaguely aware of Rex's mouth still on me. He doesn't stop until I finally urge him back up, my hands gripping his shoulders.

"I can't get enough of you," he murmurs, sliding his tongue across the seam of his lips. He leans forward, rubbing his wet, firm chest against my hardened nipples, reaching the tip of his tongue out to mine. I respond instantly, wrapping my arms around his neck, curling my fingers into his dark hair.

Our tongues twine, breaths mingling in the most sensuous dance. I don't want to pull away. And so I don't. Instead, I hold on to him tighter, licking into his mouth, loving the way I taste on his tongue. He grinds his cock into me, now impossibly hard, and I want him inside of me.

I can't seem to get enough of him, either.

"Jesus," he rasps after he backs away from my lips, "I need to be inside you." His voice cracks with a desperation I haven't heard before, almost as if he needs this like he needs air to breathe.

"I want that, too," I murmur, and he gives me a quick kiss on the lips before he opens the shower door and heads straight for a drawer underneath the sink. I'm personally praying for a tower of condoms.

When he pivots back around, all hotness, tattoos, and divine male, I watch him roll the condom on, inch by glorious inch, before stalking back to me.

"How do you want me?" His eyes are piercing, and I feel as if that's a very loaded question.

"Every which way." And there may be some hidden meaning in my statement that fortunately he doesn't pick up on.

"I think that can be arranged." He lifts my leg under the knee, looping it around his back. Nudging my swollen entrance with the head of his cock, he eases in slowly. I lean back against the wall, moaning when he slides in all the way.

"Fuck, you feel good, baby," he growls, and there it is again. I know it doesn't mean anything to him, but my stomach does a tiny flip when the word reaches my ears.

I'm not sure what's happened but something has definitely shifted. He continues to thrust into me with a punishing rhythm, all control seemingly gone, as though he needs to desperately wash away whatever is eating at him. He plunges deeper, lips seeking out my neck, my ear, sucking on the skin, and I whimper when he takes my lobe between his teeth.

"Come inside me, Rex," I moan, and he hisses a loud breath, my nails digging into his shoulder blades as he pounds into me one final time. Tremors rack his body as his orgasm rips him apart, taking everything he has and giving it over to me. Whatever has him this rattled, I want to be able to carry it away, ease his pain, even if only for a little while.

"Oh God," he groans, burying his face in my neck, his heavy breaths blowing against my skin. His heart is racing in time with mine, each beat laced with emotion and pain, sorrow and regret.

Invisible scars form a cloak around his body and when he lifts his head, lines of pain are etched across his skin. His gaze burrows into my thoughts, making me transparent, yet I see him so clearly it almost scares me—because I see myself.

I frame his face with my hands, my thumbs doing a slow caress of his jaw. "I understand, and it's okay."

Flecks of gold shine a light on the pain in his eyes as the air shifts between us, our stare intense, breathing erratic. His eyes close briefly and he drops his forehead to mine. "He kept telling me about her, but I didn't listen," he says, his voice a strained whimper, and I'm stunned into silence by his confession.

I'm just about to say something when he pulls out of me abruptly, leaving me with a hollow feeling in my chest. Opening the glass door, he yanks a towel off the rack and wraps it around his waist. He walks out of the bathroom and I'm left standing here, unsure of what to do or say next. Fear sends my muscles into a temporary paralysis while my heart aches for him. Instinct tells me to reach out, to provide comfort, but the thought of being kept at arm's length holds me back... again.

My next movements are calculated as I figure out what to do. Slowly turning the knob, shutting the water off, stepping out of the shower, locating a towel. I peek out of the bathroom and see Rex sitting on the bed, his elbows resting on his knees, head in his hands. Heaving out a deep breath, I walk over and sit beside him, but say nothing.

"I'm sorry. I shouldn't have told you that," he says, unable to look at me.

"What? *Why*?" I fist my hands in my lap, fighting the urge to move closer and touch him.

"I-I just... shouldn't have."

My heart scrunches tight in my chest at the struggle in his voice and the battles he's facing within. I can't stay quiet. "Rex, I—"

"Please," he pleads, getting up, pacing the small space in front of the bed, "no fucking questions, I can't talk about it. I won't." He grips the dresser with his back to me, chin down, blowing out a hard breath. "No one else knows. I've never told anyone. Not even Hunter."

Before I know what's happening, he's on me, pinning me to the bed. Both my hands are in his firm grasp, held above my head, his gaze burning into mine. "You're unraveling me," he admits, closing his eyes and shaking his head. A minute later, his eyelids flutter open and in an even quieter voice he says, "You're fucking unraveling me."

He shakes his head again, his face set in a pained frown. Warm brown eyes scroll over my face and land on my lips, lingering there. He reaches out, the backs of his fingers brushing my cheek before he touches his mouth to mine. His tongue skips across my lips slowly, and I open for him as we join together in a brief dance, my heart stammering and doing a dance of its own—making me realize one glaring fact.

I'm caught up in the web that is Rex Grayson.

Our kiss becomes the slightest whisper against my lips and he backs away, clearing his throat. "I need to get to work."

He springs up and starts slamming drawers, pulling out his clothes. The air around us is so thick again I can practically feel it between my fingers. My body wants to stay rooted where it is, but my brain is telling me to go and let him have his space.

I stand up and secure my towel before plodding to the bathroom. By the time I come back out, Rex is dressed and has his keys in hand. He gives me the once over before opening one of his drawers and tossing me a t-shirt.

"Here, wear this if you want."

"Thanks." I don't say anything else. I'm completely at a loss for words. I hold my head up high, attempting to be the strong person I know that I am, but inside I'm crumbling. Outside, it's even worse, I see little pieces of myself being scattered about the room. I wish I knew what he was thinking. What he was feeling. He just told me that I unravel him. Is that a good thing? I feel like it is, but his actions tell me otherwise.

"So," he stares down at the carpet, "I'll talk to you later?"

"Of course, yes." I try to catch hold of his eyes but he's averting my gaze.

"If you could just lock up when you leave, that would be great." He walks toward the living room, jingling his keys around his fingers.

"Sure."

He's almost to the door when I realize I can't let him go just yet. I tear out of the bedroom, calling to him, my towel nearly falling to the ground in my haste.

"Rex, wait!"

He pauses with his hand on the knob, eyes fixed on the door. "Yeah?"

"Thank you... for...," I'm tripping over my words which is a first for me, "for last night, for... taking care of me."

Turning back, he finally meets my eyes. "It was nothing, really." He shrugs, expelling a deep sigh. "You make it pretty easy."

And then he's gone. Leaving me to wonder if I'm the one who's unraveling.

# CHAPTER FIFTEEN

## WHAT LIES BENEATH

I'm sitting on a bench in Washington Square Park, arms folded across my chest, head tipped back, the sun beating down on my face. I don't remember the last time I sat on a bench in a fucking park, but I had to leave my apartment. The desire to run was overpowering and I had to get away from her—from Vanessa.

For whatever reason, she's fucking with my head. Women have fucked with my head my entire life. But this is different. I can't seem to stay away from her or stop thinking about her. Let's be honest. The sex is fucking amazing, there's no question. But it's more than that. I may be an asshole, but I'm not a liar. Somehow, she's reached into the core of who I am, pulling me up from the bowels of my shitty little life.

I don't know why I let that slip out in the shower. But there's a relief flooding my chest that I've told someone—that I've told *her*. I've carried that burden for far too long; it has eaten away at my insides like a poison. Driven by guilt. Shame. Hatred. First, toward my mother and then toward myself. All the regret, the "if onlys" that whiz through my mind, burying me in a quicksand I can't escape. Sinking deeper with no hope for ever getting out.

I have secrets. Everybody does. But I know better than anyone how secrets can destroy everything and everyone around you. Hunter already blamed himself for too many years over Tyler's death. As the oldest, he felt responsible, as if he could have prevented it or stopped it. When in reality, there is only one person who could have done that. Even the thought of my mother makes me want to spit the sour taste out of my mouth.

My cell phone rings and I'm thankful for the interruption. I slide the screen and Hunter's name appears. "Hey, bro, what's up?"

"Hey, you at work?" he inquires, and there's the sound of rustling papers in the background.

"No, I'm at the park."

"At the park? Since when do you go to the park?" he asks, now banging on the keys of his computer.

"Listen, are you talking to me or are you typing?" I bite out.

"You know how busy I am, Rex," he says in a condescending tone.

"Yes, we *all* know how busy you are. So, why are you calling me, then?"

"Can you meet me at Tiffany's on Wednesday morning?" And I can actually hear the smile in his voice.

"Hunter, it's Friday. That's five days away, and why the hell would I want to do that anyway?" I tease.

"Because Olivia's ring will be ready then and I want you to see it before I propose. And I'm reminding you now because it's on my mind. In fact, it's the only thing on my mind."

"If I must," I retort, smirking.

"I can just see the wiseass grin on your face right now, little brother." He muffles the phone, saying something to his secretary about a contract.

I chuckle. "Yes, and you would be correct."

"All right, I have to run into a meeting. So I'll see you Wednesday around ten thirty?"

"Sure, see you then."

With my phone still in hand, I scroll through the list until I see Vanessa's name. Still angry with myself for the way I left, an idea flashes in my head and I send her a text.

*Hope you're feeling better. I'm sorry I left so fast. Maybe I can make it up to you tomorrow afternoon?*

When she doesn't reply almost instantly, my stomach lurches with disappointment, and that's exactly the same time I realize I need to snap the fuck out of this—whatever *this* is.

I'm navigating my way through street vendors and hurried pedestrians when the smell of coffee hits my nose and lures me into a small café near the shop. As I'm waiting in line, my cell phone dings and I can't help the fact that my lips twitch thinking it could be Vanessa. When I slide the screen open, the twitch turns into a full-blown smile.

So much for snapping out of anything.

*Hey, was on the subway, and yes, I'm feeling better, thanks. What did you have in mind?*

I'm suddenly thankful I have the whole day off tomorrow. I type out a quick reply.

*I'll let you know. I'll text you the address.*

*Oh. Sounds mysterious. Okay, I'll talk to you later then. x*

I blink a couple of times at the letter *X* before I respond. What the hell does *that* mean?

*Okay, later*, I type back. *Without* an *X*.

# CHAPTER SIXTEEN

## ART ART ART

*Vanessa*

I'm standing next to the huge stone pillars, just atop the long length of steps leading up to the Metropolitan Museum of Art. My cheeks feel like they're going to burst from grinning so big. I might as well hold up a sign that says, *I have this stupid smile on my face because I'm waiting for Rex Grayson*. It's that obvious.

I don't know exactly what happened yesterday, and maybe I don't need to right now. But the one thing I do know is, I haven't felt excitement like this in a long time. I'm bouncing from heel to toe and even though no one can hear me, I'm singing on the inside.

It doesn't take long before I spot Rex walking down the street. Even from this distance, it's impossible not to notice that cocky strut of his, and I certainly can't ignore the women that are turning their heads. But I definitely don't blame them.

He pauses when he sees me, a smile tugging on his lips as he climbs the steps two at a time. When he finally reaches me, he takes his aviators off and hooks them over the top of his t-shirt. "Hey." Leaning in, he presses a kiss to my cheek, the growth on his chin making my skin prickle.

"Hey." As he backs up, I tap my watch three times, attempting to withhold the grin that wants to fly from my lips. "You're late."

His fingers encircle my wrist and he lifts my hand, staring at the time. "No. I believe *you* were just early." He smirks, gently releasing me from his grasp. "So, are you ready to do this, or what?"

"Yeah." I nod my head toward the building. "So, The Met, huh?"

"Yeah, well, I figure in case you have any doubts about my ability to be cultured, today they will all be wiped from your brain."

"Yeah, we'll see," I mumble as he lets me go before him, placing his hand on the small of my back. Goose bumps swarm up my legs, his touch triggering a response that I'm unable to control and find impossible to hide.

"Everything okay?" He retrieves his wallet from his back pocket as we enter the museum and head toward the admission desk.

"Yes, I'm fine." I turn my head and bite my lip, uncertainty spreading through me in a rush. I'm overcome with a sudden shyness, which is so foreign to me.

"Listen." He latches onto my arm, pulling me out of the way of three teenagers anxious to move past us. "Are we cool? I mean, are you upset about yesterday?" His eyes bore into mine, searching, for what I don't know.

"No, not at all. We're good." Although, I don't know what the heck that means. So I change the subject. "I think you're stalling though."

"Stalling?" He stuffs the wallet back in his jeans, continuing to hold my gaze.

"You know, delaying having to go inside and show your true colors."

"That sounds like a challenge, Blondie. And I'm more than happy to meet and exceed your challenge." He dips down, his warm breath pouring in my ear. "In more ways than one." The roughness of his skin scratches my cheek and I close my eyes before they flicker open to a knowing grin. "So shall we go in?"

"Yes, let's." I smile, picking up a map from the counter. He holds out his elbow and we link arms, strolling into the main lobby of the museum. Grandiose statues of a medieval mounted knight and an Egyptian pharaoh greet us.

Rex stops just in front of the pharaoh, looking up at the sculpture towering over us. "Now, that was the life. The absolute power of the pharaoh. Ruler of everything, God—"

I throw my head back on a laugh. "The life? You better wake up from that demented dream of yours. This is the twenty-first century, Rex. Let's go." He chuckles and I tug on his arm, still surprised by the fact that we're here... and that he knows anything about pharaohs.

"So, where do you want to start?" He plucks the map from my fingers and opens it, pointing to one of the exhibits. A smug smile forms around his mouth. "We can start with nude statues of the middle ages, if you like."

"Give me that." I snatch the map back, scrolling over our options. "Actually, let's start with impressionist paintings. I love that period."

"Oh yeah? Do you have a favorite?"

"Yes," I respond with a smile as we weave our way around a tour group. "But I'm not telling you."

"What? Why not?" His brown eyes narrow in curiosity and I smile. He's really cute.

"I'd rather show you," I tell him, and he pinches my side before pulling me close.

"Yes, I'd prefer that, too," he teases, and my skin flushes, tiny hairs raising on my arms.

We work our way through crowds of people, making me realize that Saturday was not the best day to come to the museum. The last time I was here, it was with Olivia, probably about six months ago. It was a weekday and much easier to navigate our way around.

When we finally arrive on the fifth floor, I glance over at Rex to find him grinning. "What?"

"I happen to like this era, too. Maybe after you show me your favorite painting," he winks, "I'll show you mine."

"You've got yourself a deal." I grab onto his hand because it feels like the natural thing to do, but then that nagging uncertainty creeps back in and I let go.

We leisurely stroll past several works, studying them, until we find ourselves at the end of the narrow room. My whole face lights up when the painting comes into focus. Rex follows me until we're finally standing in front of it. "This is it."

The picture is made up of dots of color—matted greens, oranges, blues, blacks, and yellows—blending into people in their Sunday dress, all out enjoying an afternoon in the park by the Seine in Paris.

"Georges Seurat's, Study for *A Sunday Afternoon on the Island of La Grande Jatte*," he utters confidently, "good choice."

My eyes blink a few times and I must look at him as if he has three heads.

"Don't look so surprised. I told you. I know my art." He stares at the painting for a long minute before turning to me. "So, why is this your favorite? What draws you to it?"

I let out a nostalgic sigh, continuing to stare at the picture, "Stella loved art and when we'd go to the bookstore, she would show me a lot of the works she liked. I remember seeing this on a page in one of her books and loving it right from the start. Something about the colors and the way the dots of paint come together to form each image, and the way he uses shadows and light. Plus the depth of field. I can actually picture myself there," I wave a finger toward the water, "in one of those boats, enjoying that lazy Sunday afternoon." The thought makes me smile.

"Well, shit. Now I'm the one who's impressed," he says, and I flick his shoulder before he laces our fingers together, leading the way out of the room and down the stairs. "My painting is on the fourth floor."

We make it down one flight, stepping into the room, and I'm in awe of the masterpieces lining the walls. The ability to create beauty like this is nothing short of magnificent. Rex leads me to the far corner, stopping at a painting of a river landscape. The plate on the wall shows that it's a Monet.

"*Vetheuil in Summer*," I read the words on the plaque. "It's really pretty. So why do you like this one?"

Rex extends an arm over his chest, elbow resting on his hand, finger pressed to his mouth in contemplation. "It reminds me of when my dad used to take us fishing. And the time he tried to teach me how to bait a line but I sucked at it. He thought it was pretty funny though, but he was very patient and didn't give up until I finally got it."

"I like it. I love the way Monet used color and light so the sun looks like it's reflecting off the water. It's so interesting to me, too, that it's all done in simple brushstrokes, yet there's such a contrast between the riverbank and the sky. The sky has a dull texture, while the water looks like it's glistening."

I turn to Rex and his gaze is fixed on my face, eyes a bold brown. His attention shifts to a spot over his shoulder then returns to me, nothing but mischief in his stare. Before I know what hits me, he curls his arm around my waist and ducks behind a stone pillar, pressing me up against it. His lips come down softly on mine, teasing and playful, before he pulls away.

"What's that for?"

His thumb skates over my bottom lip. "I guess hearing you talk about art turns me on. I can't get over how enormous your brain is."

"Art. Art. Art. Art," I joke and he grips my waist, planting another kiss on my mouth.

Grinning, he asks, "Do you want to blow this joint?"

"No. We still have a lot more to see." I brush my hands down my tank and skirt to make myself presentable again before lightly tapping his chest. "Later."

"You say that word way too much for my liking." He chuckles, and we open our map again to figure out where to go next.

After visiting the Arms and Armor, European, Medieval, and Contemporary Art exhibits, we decide we've had enough art for one day. Side by side, we follow the crowd toward the front exit. My stomach clamors on the way out, protesting my long bout without food, and it garners Rex's attention.

Wide brown eyes survey me. "I think we need to feed you. That was some growl." He stops just short of the double doors. "They have a restaurant here. Do you want to just eat here?"

"Actually, I have a craving for a hot dog from one of the street vendors out front." There's another rumble in my belly at the mention of food.

"All right. Let's go get you a hot dog then."

The line at the cart is fairly short considering it's nearly five. Rex orders me a hot dog and gets two waters but nothing else. We take a seat on one of the steps in front of the museum.

"You're not eating?" I plow into the hot dog, suddenly realizing just how hungry I really am.

"No. I have to help Zeek move some furniture into his girlfriend's apartment tonight, so we're going to grab something later." He motions toward my food with a smile. "But you enjoy that." He reaches out with his thumb and wipes the side of my mouth. "Stray ketchup. So," he pauses, "this was... fun." He's smiling as he says the words but it's almost as if he's having a hard time admitting it.

"Yeah, it was. Oh, and tomorrow if you're not busy, I thought I could bring you to see the naked cowboy." I finish half my hot dog and decide to take a break.

He gives me a firm shake of his head. "Uh, hell no."

"Oh come on, where's your sense of adventure?" I bump his shoulder with my own. "It'll be fun."

"Listen, there's only one person I want to see naked tomorrow, and it sure as hell ain't that cowboy."

# CHAPTER SEVENTEEN

## FORCED SENTIMENT

I glance at my watch and notice it's eleven. As I'm wondering where the hell my brother is, my mind drifts back to the last few days. Mostly to the time I've spent with Vanessa. I chuckle, thinking about her unsuccessful attempts to lure me to Times Square. Although, she did manage to nearly whip my ass in pool. Maybe I should've chosen the cowboy.

I'm still trying to decide which would've been more humiliating, when I catch sight of Hunter weaving through the crowd, his cell phone pressed to his ear. He ends the call just as he reaches me.

"You're late," I snarl, pushing off the side of the building.

"Yeah, I know." He shakes his head, staring at his watch. "I got caught in a meeting that wouldn't end."

"Well," I kid as he holds the door open for me, "my time is valuable, too."

"Let's go wiseass." He sidles up next to me and as we walk in, I'm greeted by condescending stares from all the women, their noses in the air. Apparently, they've never seen a guy with tattoos before. Hunter, on the other hand, is being looked at like a piece of meat they want to gnaw on until they pierce the bone.

We head to the glass cases at the far end of the store and I rub my hands together eagerly. "All right… let's see this bubble gum ring you're buying for Olivia."

The blonde, smartly dressed woman behind the counter clad in diamonds and a very expensive Rolex watch dismisses me and my sarcastic remark, honing in on Hunter.

"Can I help you?" She addresses him in a sugary sweet voice that I imagine helps her sell a lot of this shit.

"Yes," Hunter replies in that smooth tone that brings women to their knees. "I had an engagement ring put aside for me. The name is Hunter Grayson."

"Of course, let me get that for you." She walks to the back and a few moments later returns with a small blue box, handing it to Hunter. "Would you like to do the honors? And might I add, the ring is exquisite."

With a prideful smile, Hunter takes the box from her hand. "Thank you." He flips it open, plucking the ring from the velvet setting while my mouth hangs open.

"Holy fuck, bro, it's huge," I comment, and the sales clerk coughs like my profanity got stuck in her throat.

"Rex," Hunter eyeballs me, "have a little class, will you?"

I look over my left shoulder and then my right. "You remember who you're talking to, right?"

"Point taken. So…." He holds the ring up to the light, the freaking thing is sparkly as hell. And expensive. It must be so God damn expensive. "What do you think?" he asks with a smile of utter contentment.

"I think it's sparkly as hell." My voice rises, and a tall brunette walking by laughs and tosses me a wink.

"It better be. I'm paying thirty thousand dollars for all those sparkles," Hunter says matter-of-factly. Of course to him, that money is just a drop in an oversized bucket.

Realizing we're in Tiffany's, I try to keep my mouth from gaping too wide. "Well, I always knew you were slightly touched in the head, but this confirms it."

He punches the side of my arm playfully. "I can't wait to see the look on her face when I give it to her tonight. I love her, man," he admits quietly, staring at the ring.

"I know, bro." I slap him on the back. "I know."

While he's waiting for them to package the ring, I wander around the store when a woman with a blonde ponytail leaning over a jewelry case catches my eye. For a second, I think it could be Vanessa, until she turns her head. The dark green eyes giving me the once over are definitely not the pale blue ones that turn my world upside down. Hunter's voice barges into my thoughts.

"You ready?" he asks, and I nod as we make our way out of the store. Needless to say, it's not a place I'm anxious to return to anytime soon. "So, do you have time to grab lunch?"

"Hunter, Rex?" I hear the voice that grates on my nerves like nails on a chalkboard. My reaction is immediate—I want to sprint in the other direction.

"Mother," Hunter addresses her, and she leans in, offering her cheek for a stiff kiss.

"Diane." I make no move when she repeats the gesture with me. I'm not playing her bullshit games.

Her eyes immediately scroll over the tattoo on the side of my neck before she speaks. "Rex, I'm your mother, and as such, should be greeted accordingly." She smoothes a hand down her perfectly styled, chin-length, black bob. The designer suit and matching shoes she's wearing do her a disservice. They don't hide the disheveled woman inside.

"Well, *Diane*, you have to earn that title and I don't believe you've accomplished that." My words are bitter and Hunter elbows me as though that will change anything. It fucking won't.

She raises her chin and makes an uncomfortable noise in her throat. And she damn well should be uncomfortable. Her two sons can't stand the sight of her, and only one of us can fake it.

I stare at the woman in front of me, my only resemblance to her the deep brown of our eyes. My mouth curves into an involuntary sneer as I watch her—cold, affectionless—and a chill runs down my spine. For a split second, I wonder if I *am* like her, and that thought scares the shit out of me. It makes me want to scrub my skin raw to get rid of any trace of her.

She eyes the Tiffany's bag, peering over the edges to get a closer look. "What's in the bag, darling?" she asks Hunter, who, while he might never admit it, is as anxious to get away from her as I am.

He heaves out a frustrated breath before glancing at his watch. "I left you three messages last week, Mother, to tell you about it, and I didn't hear back from you."

"I'm so sorry." But there's nothing genuine in her words, and I'm waiting for the excuses to come pouring out. "I was at a book signing in Napa last week."

Fucking excuses.

"I guess they don't have cell phone service there," I mumble under my breath, and that earns me a trademark snarl from her thin, painted lips.

"I'm planning on getting engaged tonight if all goes well." Hunter draws her focus back to him, a nervous twinge in his voice.

Her mouth twists in disgust as though she can't bear to say her next words. "To that erotic romance author?"

"To *Olivia*," Hunter emphasizes, the conviction in his tone making her take a step back.

"That's wonderful, darling," she forces out. And that's all it is—forced sentiment—because she doesn't care about anyone but herself. That hasn't changed and it never will. My nails dig into my palms. This little charade has gone on long enough and I'm done.

"I have to get to the shop." I turn to Hunter. "I'll see you tonight."

"Sounds good. Thanks for meeting me, Rex," he says, and I smack him on the back before stalking off.

As I'm leaving though, her shrill voice stops me in my tracks. "You're not even going to say goodbye?"

I attempt to blow out a calming breath before I spin around. "Goodbye, Diane," I mutter with disdain. And then I walk away from the one person who has always walked away from me.

The journey to work is one giant daze, my head filled with shit I don't want to waste my energy thinking about. But I do know one thing. Hunter is right. I have to let this go, this seething hatred that consumes me, eats away at me piece by piece, effectively paralyzing me. I can't spend any more of my time thinking about a woman who never thought about me a day in her life. She's just not worth it.

I've yet to find a woman who is.

# CHAPTER EIGHTEEN

## A BRIGHT IDEA

# *Vanessa*

"I think that's it for the liquor order," I tell Ryder, scanning the paperwork for the Hamilton Juices event next Friday with one hand, while holding the phone to my ear with the other. "I believe you've got it."

"Awesome, darlin'. So let's try to meet up sometime next week. I've got two people lined up to bartend for the party, too."

"Great. Thanks again, Ryder. I'll talk to you later." I hang up just as a knock sounds on my door. "Come in," I call out, and Matilda peeks her head in.

"You got a second?" she asks, and even from this distance, I can see the mischievous sparkle in her deep green eyes.

"Absolutely, Tillie. Come on in."

She bounces through the door, smacking on her gum. Red curls dance over her shoulders, smile as happy as ever. Taking a seat on the leather chair across from me, she sinks back, tapping a pencil against her bright red lips.

"Okay, what's going on?" I drop the paperwork on my desk and lean back in my chair. "You look even happier than you normally do, if that's at all possible."

"Well...." She waves the pencil in the air like a wand, a smile tickling her lips. "Guess who's going to be helping you out at the Hamilton launch?"

"Hmph...." I rap my fingers against the side of my chair, my eyes floating upward. "Claire?"

"No! Me!" Tillie squeals, jumping up from her chair. She braces her arms on the desk. "I just finished talking with Jonathan. He's finally considering promoting me!"

"It's about damn time!" Matilda's been with the firm for four years as our receptionist but she's so incredibly capable and I've been pulling for her. "I'm so glad he's finally seeing the light."

"Yes, me too. I can't wait to come out from behind that desk." She blows a bubble and pops it with her finger.

"Now, you *do* realize you'll have to forgo the gum chewing, right?" I tease, and she giggles.

"Yes, I don't think our clients would appreciate that. I can manage it for one day." She plops back down in the chair with a contented sigh. "So, you want to maybe catch a movie later tonight? That movie *Demolition* is playing and I know how much you love death and destruction."

"I'd love to, but I can't tonight. I have plans." I grin, my mind straying to Rex and our private little death and destruction showings. Even though tonight is huge for Olivia and I'm excited for her, a part of me wants to just hang out with Rex alone.

"Yoo hoo." She waves a hand in front of me. "Earth to Vanessa?" she says, and my eyes snap back to her. "Where did you go? You seemed like you were in another galaxy."

"Nowhere in particular," I respond, fighting back a smile.

"Yeah, well, wherever it was, promise you'll take me next time," she jokes, and I laugh. I can feel the red creeping over my cheeks, settling in nicely with the ridiculous grin I'm sure I now have covering my face. She smacks her gum, pursing her lips at me. "Care to tell me about it?"

"Not really," I lie. "Well... there is this guy." I try for nonchalant even though there's no way she's buying it.

"Some guy, huh?" She twirls a ringlet of hair around her finger. "And does this guy have a name?"

"He might," is all I offer, swiveling in my chair, but other than that I remain tight-lipped.

"And his name *is*?" she presses, edging closer to the desk as if waiting for a big secret.

I roll my chair forward, meeting her halfway, and whisper, "Rex."

"Rex," she repeats, testing it out on her tongue. "I like it."

"I'm glad you approve, Tillie."

She pulls a pack of gum from the pocket of her slacks. "Gum?"

"No, thanks." I smile, watching her stuff more in her mouth. "Maybe you should practice going cold turkey on the gum to prepare for the Hamilton party."

She hesitates and you'd think I just asked her to jump off a cliff. Although in her mind, it's probably the equivalent. "Nah," she says, and we both break out into laughter.

When our laughter subsides, I notice her eyeing one of the pictures on my desk. She lifts it up, examining it.

"I love this picture of you and Olivia," she comments, admiring the photo of us in Central Park two years ago on Liv's birthday. It was a beautiful summer afternoon and we rode the boats that day, enjoying a picnic afterward. I'll never forget it. I bought Olivia a dozen colored balloons and we let them go one at a time, watching as they floated away in the sky.

"I love photographs," she continues, "I always take a ton of them because I like to remember everything. I have so many now, I should probably start scrapbooking or something."

That's when an idea pops into my head and I spring up from the chair. "Listen, Tillie. I'm going to take an early lunch. There's something I need to do." I grab my purse from the bottom drawer of my desk and stride toward the door. "I'll see you later."

"Oh. Okay," she replies, a bit confused about my behavior.

She's not alone.

Excited, I hop on the elevator, my hands fidgeting at my sides. I'm willing the floor numbers to pass by more quickly, but if anything they seem to slow the longer I stare at them.

When I finally make it to the lobby, I charge out of the building like a woman on a mission, hunting for my cell phone the moment I push through the glass doors. I send Hunter a quick text to see if he has a couple of minutes to spare for me. His response: *I always have time for you, Vanessa, come on by*. His words draw a smile from my lips. Olivia has found herself a great guy and I'm thrilled for her.

The wait for a cab is longer than I'd like, but I finally manage to hail one and scoot inside. My palms are sweaty, head already overthinking what I'm about to do. But somehow, even though my brain is hesitant and my thumbnail worse for the wear, my feet still propel me through the bronze doors of the building.

Everything about this structure screams wealth and elegance, from the marble floors and gold accents, to the famous paintings on the wall. I start for the elevator when a tall, burly, and very balding security guard motions me toward the desk. After a quick phone call upstairs alerting Hunter of my presence and getting clearance, I'm sent on my way.

Once inside the elevator, I tap my foot anxiously as the car ascends to the fifty-seventh floor. This is actually the first time I've been to Hunter's office. I know Olivia makes frequent trips here and the thought makes me giggle. Torrid and sordid are not words I would have used to describe her before, but ever since she met Hunter, I can't think of two words that suit her more perfectly.

The car dings and I step off, immediately taken aback by the enormity of the space and the floor-to-ceiling windows offering a breathtaking view of the city from every angle. White leather furniture occupies the wide open area accented by glass tables and exotic plants. It's sparse, yet it doesn't look barren.

This is a side of Hunter I rarely see, but a glaring reminder of the wealth and power he possesses, yet never flaunts.

A tall woman with a black pants suit and straw-colored hair drawn up in a slick ponytail comes over to greet me. "Good afternoon, Miss Hilliard?"

"Yes." I'm suddenly feeling completely out of my element, like a little fish in a large ocean.

"Mr. Grayson is just finishing up a conference call and he'll be with you shortly." She pats the top of her head as if to make sure there's not a hair out of place. "Can I get you some coffee or a danish?"

"No, thank you," I reply, taking a seat on one of the leather couches. I pick up a magazine without glancing at the title, but quickly discover it's all about software and place it neatly back down on the table with the others.

Minutes pass, and I spend them crossing and uncrossing my legs, checking my phone for new texts, and digging for a piece of gum in my purse. I suddenly realize I should've taken Tillie up on her offer.

Uncertainty forces my teeth to dig into my lip, feet to shuffle restlessly along the floor. I'm rethinking my decision about being here and am just about to leave, when the double doors to Hunter's office open. He struts out in his dark grey suit accompanied by a crisp, white shirt, looking every bit the high-powered executive.

His arms reach out, embracing me in a warm hug. "Good to see you, Vanessa. Come in, come in."

Upon entering his office, the first thing I notice is that the size of it rivals my entire apartment. The space is massive, but again, with not a lot of clutter, making it appear that much larger. An oversized mahogany desk sits alone on one side of the room, while two chocolate brown couches and a table occupy the other. A full bar lines the far wall, next to it a door to what looks like a private bathroom. The backdrop to this glorious arena is the Manhattan skyline.

"I honestly don't know how you get any work done in here, Hunter, the view is spectacular. I'd just stare out the window all day."

His deep chuckle echoes throughout the space as I walk over to the window overlooking his unique view of the world. "I know you didn't come here just to admire the view," he remarks, and when I turn around he's strolling over to his desk. "Come, sit."

I exhale a breath, letting my nervous energy float out into the expansive room. "As much as I love the view, you're right, I didn't." Dropping my purse to the floor, I collapse onto the chair across from him. "I wanted to ask you something."

"Sure, anything." He rolls his chair forward, steepling his fingers on the polished wood.

"Well, first, Rex told me about your little brother and I'm very sorry."

He blinks a couple of times, almost as though he didn't hear me correctly. "He told you?"

"Yes. But only very briefly. He was hurting and I think he just needed to get it out." My lips feel dry and I lick them a couple of times, then continue, "I was wondering...," I twiddle my hands in my lap, "if you had any pictures of Rex and Tyler that I might be able to borrow to make a copy? Rex mentioned not having many and I thought maybe I'd... you know," I shrug, "get one framed for him as a surprise."

Hunter relaxes back in his chair, the edges of his lips teetering into a smile. "Is this for his birthday?"

"His birthday?"

"Yes, it's tomorrow. Although...." He hesitates as if maybe he said too much. "He doesn't typically like to celebrate it, to be honest, so I'm not all that surprised if he didn't mention it."

Curiosity flares in my brain but not enough to ask any more questions. I almost feel like I'm prying and it's none of my business. Although, I care for Rex. Maybe a little more than I should.

"You care for my brother," he states, reading my thoughts, and that's *definitely* not a question.

"Yes," I admit sheepishly. Even the mention of him starts the fluttering in my stomach. I wish it was from hunger because somewhere deep down all I hear are Olivia's words of warning. But the heart is an involuntary organ and doesn't heed warnings. "He's interesting."

Hunter tips his head back, letting out a meaty laugh. "Yes, that would be an understatement, Vanessa," he says, and I can't control the grin that breaks free. But the airy smile on his face soon disintegrates as he reaches a hand out to slide open the top drawer of his desk. He sets a small wooden box down and opens the latch, releasing a sigh before he touches what I'm assuming are pictures inside. He lifts up the pile and flips through them, nostalgia and sadness streaking his eyes. Clearing his throat, he passes them over to me. "Take a look."

I carefully open my palm as the memories slip into my hand, grasping them as the treasures that they are. Pictures of a young Rex: free, innocent, unburdened. One after the other, I look through them, finally landing on a close-up shot of he and Tyler wearing backward baseball caps, shades of happy covering their eyes, their mouths, their cheeks. I raise it up, showing it to Hunter. "This one. Can I take this one?"

"Absolutely." He smiles when he sees my choice. "That's a great shot."

"Thanks, Hunter."

"Sure." He gives me a manila envelope. "You can put it in this."

"Great." I carefully place the envelope in my purse, ensuring it doesn't get crushed amidst all my crap.

"So, I'm assuming you never got the voicemail I left on your cell?" he asks, and I stare at him with a blank expression.

"No, what voicemail?" I sling my purse over the arm of the chair. "I had a bunch, but there wasn't one from you."

"I must've dialed the wrong number, then. It was about tonight." His fingers toy with the collar of his shirt. He's sweating already and it makes me giggle. "What's so funny?"

"Nervous about pop—" I press my lips together making a loud sound "—ping the question?"

"Rex told you that, too?" He seems stunned, as though his brother broke some kind of code by telling me.

"Yes. It was an accident, though. It slipped out. But, I couldn't be happier for you, Hunter. Olivia is madly in love with you." Tiny beads of sweat break out across his forehead. "You don't need to worry," I whisper, "she's going to say yes."

"You think so?" He wipes the moisture from his temple, worry abundant in his voice.

"Oh, I know so."

His cheeks puff up before exhaling a large dose of air in my direction. He puts the box of pictures in the drawer, then stands up and walks over to where his jacket is hanging up. Digging into one of the pockets, he lets out another hearty breath as he pulls out a blue velvet box. He ambles back over and leans against the desk, legs crossed at the ankles, presenting it in his palm. "The ring."

"Boy, you really are nervous. I kind of gathered that's what was in the box," I say, and he chuckles. "Let me see that sucker." I hold out my hand as the soft velvet tickles my skin. With a gentle flick of my finger, it pops open, my eyes following suit. Inside sits the biggest and most beautiful engagement ring I've ever seen. "Holy shit, Hunter! It's gorgeous!"

He laughs and his next words are so surprising to me, and very sweet. "Do you think she'll like it?"

"Hunter," there's a calm reassurance in my voice, "it could be a ring from a thrift store and she'd love it. Because it's from you. And honestly, I'm ecstatic. She deserves this so much, and so do you." My cell phone chimes, reminding me that I have a two-thirty meeting to attend. "Oh shoot. I have to go. I've got to get back to the office for a meeting. Is there anything you need me to do to help with tonight?"

"Just make sure she shows up," he kids, but I don't think he's actually joking. He plucks the ring box from my hand. "Come on, I'll walk you out."

I'm not sure what possesses me, but when we get to the bank of elevators, I throw my arms around him and he stumbles back, surprised. "Thank you for the picture," I say with appreciation, "and good luck tonight."

As the doors close, I expel a gratifying sigh. I reach into my bag and find the envelope, pinching it between my thumb and forefinger, then tuck it away safely. I can't wait to see the look on Rex's face when I give it to him. There are a lot of things he seems to want to forget. I'm glad I'll be giving him something wonderful to remember.

"Evening, Henry," I greet the doorman to Olivia's building. He welcomes me, tipping his hat in my direction.

"Good evening, Miss Vanessa. And might I say you're looking particularly lovely tonight," he compliments, holding the door open for me.

"Yes, you might." I wink, flipping my hair over my shoulder before stepping onto the elevator.

This may be Olivia's night, but it's impossible to deny the obsessive clockwatching I've been doing all day, or the way my mind wouldn't allow me to focus on anything else. Tillie practically left bruises on my leg during the meeting from the amount of times she had to kick me under the conference table to bring me back on topic. Even now, I can't seem to remember.

My phone chimes and it's a message from Rex, almost as if he knew I was thinking about him. I slide the screen to unlock it and smile.

*Hey.*

*Hey back.*

*Ready for tonight?*

*Yup.*

There's a long pause and I wonder if he'll respond.

*I really want to see you.*

My pulse leaps underneath my skin as my shaky fingers type out a reply.

**Me too.**

And just like that, you couldn't drag me off of the cloud I'm floating on. That's the most peculiar thing about all this—I'm not *that* girl. The one who gets giddy over a guy or walks around in a dreamy state. I'm the one with the barricade, the wall around her heart that refuses to let anyone in. But Rex has found a way in, a loophole in my façade, probably without even realizing it.

I'm just about to knock on Olivia's door when it opens and we both stare, wide-eyed. She's wearing a teal, knee-length satin dress that makes her eyes appear an even deeper blue. Her hair settles in rich, dark waves over her shoulders, a subtle sweep of makeup showcasing her natural beauty.

"Liv… I don't even know what to say. You look beautiful."

"Funny," she reclines an arm against the doorframe, "I was just going to say the same thing about you. Is that a new dress?"

"Maybe." I strut through the door, tossing my purse on a nearby sofa. "So what are we doing?" I'm trying to play along with the charade, attempting to keep her guessing.

She applies some lip gloss in front of the hall mirror, puckering her pout. "I have no idea. Hunter was very mysterious. He just said his car would be picking us up at seven. But that's all I know. So…," she slinks over to the sofa, dropping down beside me, "what's going on with you and Rex? Everything okay?"

I grin and point a finger at my face. "Does it *look* like things are okay?"

Her eyes thin and she glares at me. "Don't play games, V. You know I'm concerned about you."

"Liv, chill out. Everything is fine. More than fine, actually. So don't get your panties ruffled. Well," I grin, "that's if you even have any on. Should I assume you made yet another trip to Victoria's Secret today?"

I continue to stare at her as I plow through my purse, feeling around for some lipstick.

"Even though I know you're changing the subject, the answer is yes, I did."

I shake my head and smirk. "Hunter must be a happy man."

"He will be later." She elbows me then checks her watch.

"You seem nervous. You okay?" I ask, still trying to make sure I don't give anything away.

"I'm okay. It's just—Hunter was acting kind of strange today." Her teeth pierce her lip. "I hope nothing's wrong."

"Oh," I flap my hand in the air, "you know how men are. I'm sure he's fine."

The cell phone chimes, making her jump, and she gets up to retrieve it from her bag. After looking at the screen, her eyes make their way back up to me. "The car's waiting outside."

It's time. And I'm not sure who's more excited. Her or me.

# CHAPTER NINETEEN

## ASSHOLE OF THE YEAR

"You ready for this, bro?" I ask Hunter as he paces the private dining room doing last minute checks to make sure everything is perfect.

He ignores my question, and instead, examines the perimeter, ensuring all the candles are lit, flowers arranged accordingly, soft music playing at the right volume in the background. I almost want to laugh at him. But in this situation and given how nervous he is, that would be cruel. It's just that I've never seen him this caught up in someone before and it's unsettling to me.

I know what's really bugging me though. I've been on edge since that annoying encounter with my mother. I already feel like shit because I blew off a whole lot of steam at Zeek. Fortunately, he knows me so he let it slide, aware that I was fighting my demons. Unfortunately, it's a war I wage all too often and I'm sick and fucking tired of it.

The sound of laughter startles me from the hell that is my mind. I stand back, remaining in the shadows, taking a moment to just admire Vanessa from afar. My breath stills as I steal a quiet glance, noticing every little detail; the way her hand sweeps her hair over her shoulder then comes back around to softly tuck it behind her ear, the angle of her cheek, the bare skin of her neck, the dip of her collarbone. All the cold from the day leaves my body in a rush, replaced by warmth flowing through my veins. A shiver begins its journey up the crook of my spine, rooting my feet to the ground with a realization.

Somehow, she makes it better.

I watch as her chin subtly travels to the side, tentative eyes scanning the room, searching. So I step out of the darkness into the light of her blinding smile when those eyes land on me, our gazes locked, our connection undeniable. She sashays across the room, giving me a chance to take in the black dress that clings to her every curve, leaving little to the imagination. Her golden tresses cascade over her shoulders kissing her breasts, skin dusted with a pink glow. She's like a fucking masterpiece. I make a lame attempt at swallowing, but my dry throat makes the action futile.

"Hi," she says when she's finally standing in front of me.

"Wow. You're a stunner as always, Blondie. You look... beautiful." I lift a finger, running the back of my knuckle down the side of her cheek and her eyelids flutter. "Beautiful," I whisper, and it's as if I've had an out-of-body experience when the words I've spoken actually reach my ears.

"You clean up pretty well yourself." Her eyes roam the white dress shirt and black pants that I typically wouldn't be caught dead in, but I knew Hunter wouldn't appreciate ripped jeans. "You even brushed your hair," she teases. "I might need to mess it up later."

"I'm counting on it." I step as close to her as possible, digesting the small space between us. "Hi there," I say, her breath so close I can practically taste her on my lips.

"Hi again." She brushes her mouth softly against mine. "So are you going to kiss me, or keep talking and make me wait, because you know, you have a habit of doing that."

"See, that's the thing. I can't wait another minute." I put my hands on either side of her face, my thumb drawing her bottom lip down, so soft and smooth. "You were on my mind today," I breathe out, my tongue doing an upward sweep of her lip. She opens on a sigh that I freely catch before our mouths join together.

It's as if she's sampling me, every corner of my mouth being explored with her warm tongue, and I'm completely at her mercy. I think I finally understand the phrase 'bringing a man to his knees' because that's exactly what she does to me.

Forgetting where we are, one of my hands moves lower, taking a fistful of fabric and tugging her up against me. The touch of our bodies so close together incites a riot within my chest. A spell that is broken when a cough sounds from behind us.

"Did you forget you're not alone?" Hunter reprimands, and we quickly back away grinning, me with a hard-on and Vanessa with red, swollen lips.

"Sorry, Hunter," Vanessa apologizes, fixing her dress, but I set her straight immediately.

"You don't have anything to apologize for, *does* she Hunter?" I glare at him until he gets my message loud and clear.

"No, you don't." Hunter knows that intimidation shit doesn't work with me. I'm not one of his employees. He punches me in the arm to make amends and takes Olivia to the center of the room for a dance. I nod toward the table.

"You wanna sit?"

Her eyes wander to where they're huddled together then back to me. "Sure." I pull a chair out for her and she takes a seat.

"Such a gentleman," she taunts, and I lean over her chair, my lips resting above her ear, the smell of her raspberry shampoo causing a momentary lapse in memory.

"You wouldn't say that if you knew what I was thinking right now."

She sucks in a breath and I grin before planting myself next to her.

"So how was your day?" she asks, her voice cracking, skin turning a soft shade of pink.

"Honestly, it sucked," I admit, staring off into the distance, my mind forcing away thoughts of my mother trying to break through the blockade I've constructed for myself.

"Rex? Hey," she taps my shoulder and I turn back to her, "you're so far away. Where'd you go?"

I take a long pull of the beer, desperately needing help with my response. "I ran into my mother today," I say through gritted teeth. "She never changes, you know?"

"Maybe someday—" she starts to say, but I instantly cut her off.

"No. There is no maybe someday for us. Too much shit has happened and my life isn't a fucking fairy tale. I'm under no illusions when it comes to my mother. I've learned not to expect anything from her because that way I won't be disappointed."

"Have the two of you ever tried therapy?" she interjects, and I fucking snap.

"Been there, done that. It's impossible to be in therapy trying to fix something when someone doesn't show up because they don't give a shit about fixing it." My hand goes to my head, rubbing at my temples. "I can't fucking talk about it, anymore, *okay*?" I raise my voice much louder than I'd intended.

"*Okay!*" she barks. "I'm going to use the bathroom." She pushes back her chair, the legs scraping harshly against the wood floor, the grating noise a slap across my face. I'm being an asshole... again.

"Fuck!"

Hunter and Olivia stop dancing and Olivia walks over to me. "What's wrong? Is Vanessa okay?" She looks toward the door then back to me. "I'm going to go check on her."

"No." I grab her arm, halting her. "I'll go." I dart toward the door, my eyes seeking out the sign for the ladies' room, releasing a breath when I find it. With an apprehensive fist, I knock three times on the door. "Blondie, it's me, open up."

"No."

I bang my head against the door, practically able to feel her leaning against it on the other side. "I'm sorry. I know I acted like an asshole. I just... it's really hard for me to talk about her."

She doesn't say anything but won't relent and open the door. Now I'm at a complete loss. I typically don't have a problem getting women to talk to me, but then again, Vanessa isn't like most women.

"Okay," I begin, trying a different tactic. "So, did you know I'm pretty much the biggest contender for the asshole of the year award. You might have even voted for me...."

The lock clicks on the door and she opens it, crossing her arms tightly over her chest, a smirk that she's trying to hide overpowering her mouth. "Asshole of the year?" She bites her lip, staring me down. "I think I voted for you *twice*."

The door closes and I back her up against it. "Twice, huh?" A loose wisp of hair falls against her face and I push it behind her ear. "I'm sorry. Jesus. I say that a lot, don't I?" I grab the back of my head, dropping a heavy breath onto the ground before meeting her eyes. "But I am."

"Okay." She skirts around me but stops. "I think we should get back. This is Olivia's big night, after all."

"Right," I agree, following her to the room, catching Olivia and Hunter in a heated embrace. Similar to one I could be enjoying if I hadn't acted like such an asshole. I cough loudly, interrupting their floor show, Olivia's face turning a bright red.

"So, who's hungry?" Hunter asks, pinching Olivia's ass then rubbing his hands together.

I can't get over the change in my brother and I don't know what to make of it. I'm not even sure why I'm trying to analyze it. He's happy. It's really that simple.

For him.

But then again, he doesn't carry around the same shitty baggage that I do.

Two waiters clad in tuxedos walk in carrying silver trays. They make their way over to the round table and set them down beside it. Vanessa and I look at each other quizzically when we see the burgers and fries, while Olivia starts laughing.

"I thought we were having prime rib? What the fuck is up with the burgers?"

Hunter and Vanessa join in, and it appears I'm the only one who doesn't think this is funny. I can get a freaking burger any day of the week.

"They're Olivia's favorite," Hunter elaborates, scooting her chair closer to his side. "I hope you like apple pie, too."

"All right, there's obviously some little private joke I'm missing out on and that's fine. I'll admit these burgers look amazing. Come on, Blondie. Let's dig in." I hold her chair out for her and she sits, but I still feel a cold wind blowing from her direction. Moving closer, I put my hand on her arm until I get her attention, those pale blue eyes cutting right through me. "I meant what I said. I really am sorry."

"I know." She gives me a half-smile and I take it as an opening to place a kiss to the corner of her mouth.

"You know it's impossible to stay mad at me." I point a finger toward my cheek. "This face, it's irresistible, isn't it?" She shakes her head but she's smiling now. I just might be forgiven.

There's a lot of talking during dinner, but me, I'm doing most of the listening. Hunter has decided to tell stories of when we were kids. Most, I'd like to forget. Although, there are some good ones, like the fishing one he's telling now.

"We were out in this little fishing boat that our dad had. It was nothing to write home about, but it was lived in, you know? I remember seeing Dad sitting out on the dock, just watching us. He was smoking these cigars that he only ever smoked when he sat out on the dock. Remember that, Rex?" he says, and I nod in acknowledgement, a pang hitting my stomach thinking about him and those darn cigars.

"Anyway, nothing was happening, the water seemed pretty quiet, until all of a sudden something grabbed hold of Rex's line, and instead of Rex reeling it in, it was more like the fish was reeling Rex. He was such a lightweight and the fish was so heavy, I had to hold him down so he didn't go overboard. But we did get the fish, and boy was he a beauty."

"Aww," Olivia and Vanessa say together. Vanessa tilts her head sideways, her lower lip jutting out in a pout. I want those lips. She has the sexiest fucking mouth I've ever seen.

"Yeah, but who's the lightweight now, tough guy?" I lean back in the chair and lace my hands together above my head, the muscles in my biceps flexing.

"You got me there, little brother. Unfortunately, I don't do that much working out in the boardroom. But I have much better ways now." He throws Olivia a devilish grin, practically eating her up with his eyes alone.

"Okay, then." I spin around to Vanessa. "You want to dance with me, Blondie?"

"Sure."

I take her hand in mine, helping her up. Her skin is soft and pliable, molding perfectly to my own. We reach the middle of the room and the song changes, her demeanor shifting right along with it. "What is it?" I ask, my thumb doing a continuous stroke over her knuckles as the words to Gavin DeGraw's "Chariot" play softly in the background.

Her eyes glaze over, a wistful haze clouding them. "I used to sit in my room and listen to music just like this over and over when my parents were arguing. It took me to another place. A happier place. I felt hopeless a lot of times when I was growing up, but music," she shrugs, "always gave me hope. I know that probably sounds weird."

"Come here." I gather her up and press our bodies together, my arms wrapped around her waist, hers settling around my neck. "I don't think it sounds weird at all." I catch her eyes, now seeing a small piece of that lost girl from the first day in the shop. "Hope comes in all different forms. Sometimes," I tilt my head to the side, my voice growing quieter, "when I look at *you*... I see hope."

Her gaze fogs, eyes widening then narrowing, mouth slowly tipping up into a smile. "Rex Grayson. That has to be the sweetest thing anyone has ever said to me."

"Yeah, well," I counter, "don't get too used to it. That's about as far as I go in the sappy department."

"A bit of a stretch, huh?" she jokes, playing with the hair at the base of my neck, tingles working their way through every part of me.

"Speaking of stretching, how 'bout you stretch those lips a bit closer and kiss me?"

She smiles as if she likes the idea, moistening her lips with her tongue, my eyes dropping to her mouth as she does. Her long, golden lashes fall against her cheeks just before her breath skips across my skin. I fall prey to her, drugged by her presence, her lips on mine, fingers tickling my flesh, the scent of raspberry everywhere around us. Our tongues scrape against one another, fiery and hot, seeking and giving.

I ease out of her mouth, practically panting because of my desire for her. "I want you so much," I murmur, resting my forehead on hers, my breathing rapid. The rise of her chest against mine telling me she feels the same. "Can we get out of here?"

"Are you insane?" She laughs, the sound light all around me. "He hasn't even—...," she backs away, spying on Hunter and Olivia, saying in a hush, "proposed yet."

"Well I wish he would hurry the hell up. I've got needs."

Vanessa snorts, making me chuckle and drawing the attention of Olivia on the other side of the room.

"What's so funny, V?" she calls out from across the table.

"Rex has jokes, that's what's so funny." She slaps me on the shoulder and I'm wondering why I'm getting turned on from hearing her sound like a pig. Is there *anything* about her that doesn't turn me on?

"You guys ready for dessert?" Hunter yells over to us and my response is immediate.

"Hell yes." But there's only one person I'm looking at when I say the words, and it earns me another slap from the object of my desire.

"Let's go." Vanessa tugs on my hand, pulling me back over to the table.

"I think that chair is too small for you. Why don't you sit on my lap?" I offer, wiggling my brows, grabbing my dick through my pants.

"*You* are relentless," she comes back with, and she may be shooing me away with her hand, but the glimmer in her eye tells me something entirely different.

The waiters return again, filling everyone's glasses with

champagne and bringing out a dessert tray. I have to wonder what Hunter is doing. Dinner is nearly over and he hasn't made a move yet. But I'm starting to see a thin layer of sweat on his forehead so it must be almost showtime.

"You okay, bro?" I ask, and Olivia looks over at him as well.

She raises a hand to his temple. "You're sweating, babe. You feeling all right?"

"Yeah, I'm fine, sweetheart. It's just a bit warm in here." He fingers his collar, attempting to distract Olivia and probably trying to catch his breath. I honestly never thought I'd see the day my brother would be getting engaged. This is one for the books.

Puzzled, Olivia looks over at Hunter once the desserts are set down on our plates. "Parfaits? No apple pie?"

"They were all out. So this was the next best thing. It looks delicious, doesn't it?" His voice is beginning to crack, and that's when I finally figure out what's going on.

"Yes, it does." She smiles at him before picking up her spoon and diving in to the parfait. Not more than two seconds later, her spoon falls against her plate with a clatter. "There's something in my strawberry...." she mumbles as she shakes her head back and forth in disbelief, cheeks red, eyes filling with tears.

Her jaw drops to the floor and hangs there, hands shaking as she tries to steady them enough to pluck the ring from the strawberry. Meanwhile, Hunter is already on his knees beside her and I think I even hear Vanessa sniffling.

I'm not cut out for this shit.

"Sweetheart," he whispers, and she's already gone, tears rolling down her cheeks, staring at the ring in her hand. "Sweetheart, look at me." He tilts her chin, smiling up at her. I sigh and roll my eyes, wondering what we're doing here. This is a pretty private moment.

"I don't think I've ever been so grateful for a train ride in all my life. And I don't know if it was the moment I first spotted you in the station, or the moment I spotted you in the café after looking for you for so long, not knowing whether I'd ever see you again. My heart spoke to me in a voice that was so loud it was impossible to ignore. My lungs filled with air for the first time because you breathed life into me, Olivia. You made me want things, and up until the time I met you, I didn't want very much. But now I want everything... and I want it with you. Every part of me—my mind, my heart, my body, my soul—belongs to you. You keep them safe. You look after them, and I want to do the same for you. I promise you that I will treasure every part of you with everything that I have, everything that I am. I love you, Olivia Redmond, and I want you to marry me, to be my wife forever and always."

I glance over at Vanessa, a single tear escaping down her skin, and she quickly pats it away. She breaks from her trance, a bittersweet smile trapped between her lips, but something seems off. The expression on her face is not a happy one. It tugs at me, and I guess I'm getting sucked into the moment too, because I place my hand on top of hers, threading our fingers together.

This is the last time I'm attending one of these things. It's fucking with my head.

We're both silent as Olivia's tears continue to fall, and now even Hunter looks weepy, waiting on her expectantly, as if his entire life hangs in the balance. I suppose for him, it does. That's how much he loves her. For a second, I wonder what that's like. And for an even longer time, I let my eyes drift to the girl sitting beside me, but quickly snap them away when she catches me staring.

"Yes, Hunter. There's nothing I want more than to marry you," Olivia manages to say through a neverending stream of tears. Hunter wastes no time, grabbing her, swinging her around before they kiss to seal the promises they just made to one another.

"Good." I sit forward in my chair. "Now that that's over, can we go?" And Vanessa glares at me before I get pelted one more time for that comment. I give her the stink eye right back. "Hey, you're three for three. Watch it."

She jumps up from her chair, rounding the table to hug Olivia once Hunter finally lets go of her. "I'm so happy for you, Liv.

You deserve this and I love you so much."

Olivia pulls away with a twinkle in her eyes, holding Vanessa at arm's length, assessing her. "You knew about this all along, didn't you?" Then she points a finger at me. "And you too."

"Maybe," Vanessa and I say in unison before we start laughing.

Hunter comes around to me and I stand up, gripping him in a hug. "Congrats, bro. I'm really happy for you."

"Thanks, Rex. And just so you know, I'm giving you advanced warning. I want you to be my best man."

I pat him on the back a few more times as I let his words sink in, my stomach sinking right along with them. "But, Hunter, you know I'm—"

"There are no buts." He breaks our embrace, determination in his gaze. "You're my brother and I love you. It's that simple. And I know we disagree on a lot of things, but this isn't something I'm going to take no for an answer on. So don't fight me on it, *okay*?"

"Okay," I reply, resigned, knowing he's right.

The walls begin closing in on me, the lump in my throat growing, making it difficult to breathe. I need air desperately. "I'm gonna get some air. I'll be back." I don't wait for a response. Instead, I head in the direction of whichever door will get me outside the fastest.

I push through the crowd waiting to get in, finally making it outside and releasing a huge breath I didn't realize I'd been holding. Bending over, hands on my knees, I let out a couple more slow breaths. That's when I feel a hand on my shoulder.

"You okay, Rex?" Vanessa's sweet voice fills my ears, her warmth instantly surrounding me.

I get to my feet, my hands fisted at my hips. "Yeah." I shrug, looking down at the ground, kicking a piece of loose concrete. "This shit is hard for me. I just don't do well with it, you know?"

"Yeah, I do know," she says, and when my eyes climb to hers, I can see that she does. Somehow, she understands. She gets me. Even as fucked up as I am.

Pinching the fabric of her dress, I draw her closer. "Come home with me," I say against her lips. "Will you?" I ask the question, my stomach cinched with nerves as I wait for her answer.

"Yeah. I'd like that," she replies in a soft breath, and for some reason my heart knocks against my chest knowing she wants to be with me. Even if it's only temporary.

"I want to go in and say goodbye first, though. Come on." She reaches between us and threads her fingers through mine, leading me back inside.

I might just follow her anywhere.

"Congratulations, again." She gives Hunter a hug before moving on to Olivia. "Call me tomorrow, okay, Liv. And enjoy the rest of your night celebrating," she says, as they exchange a mischievous wink.

"So, I guess you're gonna be stuck with my brother for life," I tease, embracing Olivia.

"Yup," she grins, "and I wouldn't want it any other way." She looks lovingly at Hunter and he returns her expression tenfold.

"All right, man, I'll catch up with you tomorrow."

"You got it," he says, before we head out, and I glance back one more time at the two of them with a slight smile, guilt fueling my brain because all I want to do is run from all this fucking happiness.

"That was nice of Hunter to have the car take us back." Vanessa stares out the window, the lights and colors of the city whizzing by us in a blur. A quiet settles over her, but not a comfortable one, the air suddenly heavy with unshed thoughts.

"You all right, Blondie?"

"Hmph?" She swings her head around. "Yeah. Fine."

I pat the seat next to me. "Come closer. You're too far away," I tell her, and she readily moves over, laying her head on my shoulder—and I find myself liking it, a rope of confusion pulling tighter in my gut. "What are you thinking about?" Leaning my chin atop her hair, my fingers sketch shapes on her arm, goose bumps marching along her skin.

With a heavy sigh, she says, "Olivia. I'm just thinking about how happy I am for her."

"Is that all? Because you seem... I don't know, sad or something." My hand pauses on her arm as I wait for her reply.

"I just hope they'll be happy together, that's all. I didn't have good role models for marriage. But they love each other and that will be enough, right?"

"You know what? And I may be out of my mind for saying this, but I actually think they'll be very happy. They really do love each other and I think with that, they'll be able to get through anything."

She lifts her head, shifting to meet my eyes, the glow from passing cars casting shadows on her face. "You going soft on me, Rex Grayson?"

"Never. I can't afford to tarnish my badass reputation."

Her eyes hold me until she edges closer, touching her lips to mine in a whisper of a kiss that leaves me wanting more.

"That's all I get?"

"For now," she adds, going back to my shoulder.

"You seem really tired." I close the door to my apartment, dropping my keys and wallet on the coffee table.

She doesn't acknowledge my comment, just continues walking toward the bedroom, shedding her heels as she goes. I follow behind, half-expecting her to collapse into bed. But that's not what she does. Instead, she perches at the edge of it, her eyes, a sultry gray-blue, seeking out mine. "I-I need you to touch me, Rex."

The words come out like a plea, which strikes me as odd because the last thing she has to do is beg me to put my hands on her. That's all I want to do whenever she's around.

I join her on the bed, tugging on the hem of her dress. "Lift up, baby," I instruct, and as she raises her ass, I peel the dress over her head, whistling a breath through my teeth at the sight of her lacy red bra and thong.

Moving closer, my nose trails up the length of her neck, her head falling back as she lets out a needy moan. "Do you know what I was thinking about all night?" I murmur, my voice deep, and she shakes her head from side to side. "Every time you touched your silky hair, crossed and uncrossed your legs, or brought the glass of champagne to your mouth and I watched you swallow," I whisper, my teeth nipping her lobe, "I was thinking about my lips on every inch of your skin, starting right here." I lick the sweet spot behind her ear and she whimpers. "Then working my way down here," I groan, as my fingers squeeze her tight buds through her bra. "To your pretty pink nipples. Then—"

"Rex—"

"Shhh, baby, I'm not done. Then I envisioned moving lower to your stomach, my tongue tasting your flesh, strolling past the curve of your hip—"

"Ahh," she cries out, her nipple hardening as I flick it back and forth through the fabric.

"—until finally I'm sliding my tongue between your thighs. And when you're so wet, only when you're dripping for me," I rasp, and she purrs as I rub a finger across her panties, damp with want, "then I'd bury my cock deep inside your pussy, fucking you slowly, wanting to hear my name on your lips as you're coming apart—"

"Rex, please," she pleads, spreading her legs for me, her body buzzing with need.

"Lie back," I direct, and with her feet flat on the bed she scoots toward the pillows. Her eyes never leave mine as I jump off, ridding myself of my pants and boxers, and discarding my shirt.

Her searing gaze continues to burn into me as she unclasps her bra, dropping it to the carpet. The next to go are her panties, as she slips them down her legs, kicking them to the side. There's a hunger in her eyes as she stares at me, but there's something else there, too. I don't know what it is, but it's gnawing away at me.

I crawl over her, unable to help noticing the fire in her gaze has dimmed. An uneasiness settles over me. "Blondie—"

"Shhh." She puts a finger to my lips. "Don't talk," she says, before cupping my neck, pulling my mouth down to hers for a kiss.

I attempt to shake off the discomfort, focusing instead on the goddess beneath me. Our tongues collide as she holds me where she wants me. Licking, devouring, searching. The smell of her—her skin, her pussy—is all around me. And my cock is rigid and erect, so damn hard for her.

Breaking the kiss abruptly, my anxious lips trail down her body, following her scent. I spend extra time caressing her nipples with my tongue and fingers, pulling and twisting, sucking until they're stiff and sensitive. A strangled sob of pleasure leaves her as she holds her tits, pushing them into my mouth. Her legs begin moving wildly on the bed as she grinds against me, and I'm so turned on, I'll probably come if she keeps that up.

"Rex," she lets out a jagged whimper, "I want your mouth between my legs." And that's all I need to hear before I lower myself, spreading her thighs apart, my eyes closing on a deep inhale. I separate her pink folds, and she bucks against my face at the first tease of my tongue to her sensitive clit.

"I love how wet you get," I mumble, before my tongue gets lost inside of her as I lick her pussy, sliding a finger in and out, fucking her with my finger and my mouth, my cock wanting to be next.

I'm bathing in her slickness, her hot liquid coating my throat, my tongue, as she writhes and moans, her hands diving into my hair to pull me in deep.

"God, that feels good. You're going to make me come, Rex."

"Come, baby," I groan, before my tongue sweeps over her clit one final time and she explodes around me, climax completely overtaking her as her sex pulses against my mouth. I drag out her orgasm, kissing and sucking her clit, licking her until all those sexy little mewls have subsided.

As I inch back up her body, I'm struck by the glossy look in her eyes. "What's wrong? Did I hurt you?" I ask softly, and she shakes her head instead of answering me. I immediately climb off, propping myself on my elbow beside her. Even though my dick is hard and I want her desperately, that's not what is important right now. "What is it?" I push a sweaty lock of hair behind her ear. "You look like you're about to cry."

"No, I'm not," she states matter of factly. "I'm not a crier."

"Bullshit. And you've been upset since we left the restaurant. What is it?" I ask again.

She stares straight ahead, and that's when I see the tiniest of tears creeping down her cheek. I know she's trying to hide it from me, but it's too late. "I don't know. I just feel... empty."

"Come here, baby," I say, curling her into my chest, tucking her close.

Everything about her disarms me: her smile, her touch, her spirit. Little by little, she's diffusing the bomb that constantly ticks, the one threatening to rip me apart—and I don't even think she gets it.

My mouth opens to speak, but my fucking tongue gets caught in my throat when I need it the most. I'm unable to form the words to tell her how far from empty she is, that I've never met anyone quite like her before. But the only thing that slips out is a frustrated sigh.

I guess I'll just save it for another day.

# CHAPTER TWENTY

## BROKEN PROMISES

*Vanessa*

A sliver of light reaches through the curtains, tapping me on the shoulder, awakening me. And I wake up to the most beautiful sight—a sleeping Rex Grayson. I watch, his dark lashes splashing across his cheeks, the angle of his strong jaw, the peaceful smile on his lips. I listen to the continuous beat, the steady sound of his quiet breathing.

Last night's conversation comes back to me and I exhale a shaky breath, knowing why I was so upset. I just couldn't admit it fully to Rex. After watching Olivia and Hunter, I finally realized I want that kind of love. There's a huge part of me that craves it desperately. The only problem is, I don't know how to get it. I'm not sure I know how to give it either.

I wish the people that brought me into this world had been better teachers—that I had been one of those children whose parents knew how to show their love with kisses and hugs rather than dismissive glances, with long, heartfelt talks instead of the 'ignorance is bliss' theme that ran through my house. Buying me off was much easier than paying attention to me. My mind tumbles down a road that is paved with sadness.

*Daddy poked his head in to say goodnight. I didn't see him at dinner because he was working so I guess he just got home.*

*"Goodnight, Vanessa," he said.*

*"Daddy," I called out, just as he was closing the door.*

*"Yes?"*

*"Can you read me a bedtime story tonight? You said you would last night." I held my breath and played with my fingers while I waited for his answer, hoping he would say yes.*

*But then I heard that clinking noise. The same one I always heard when I asked for a story. He dropped a lot of coins in my piggy bank, then looked over at me.*

*"There. Now tomorrow Stella can take you to the bookstore and you can buy a brand new book. I promise we can read it tomorrow night."*

*"Okay, Daddy," I said, knowing that promises meant nothing and tomorrow would never come.*

I force a deep breath from my lungs, trying to expel the memory and focus on the present. And the biggest question of all, looming over my head like a dark cloud. Why is all this surfacing now?

The answer is right next to me.

Fear prompts my lungs to constrict as that thought settles into my brain. But when I look over at Rex, I feel like I could jump and it might just be okay. Maybe he's the one who would catch me if I fall.

When his eyes blink open, I realize it might be too late. I may have already fallen.

"Morning," he says with a sleepy smile, stretching his arms above his head, the eagle soaring across his chest. He swivels on his side, brown eyes studying me. "How are you this morning? Better?"

"Yes. I think so. Just had an off night." I do my best to distract from my true feelings, feelings he probably doesn't even return.

"An off night, huh?" He strums up and down my arm with his fingertip and my skin prickles.

"Yeah."

"Well, you're entitled. Hey, can I ask you something?" His tone is hesitant.

"Sure. I think you're entitled to ask me a lot of somethings, a bit of payback perhaps?" I giggle, but he doesn't laugh. His face grows serious, his gaze straying beyond my shoulder before returning to mine.

"I've been wondering something. What did you mean when you said no one had taken care of you like that before?"

"Oh." Tension pulls my cheeks in, my lips forming a straight line. Now I'm the one who's not looking at him, but instead, focusing on the space between us. "My parents were... busy people. Both attorneys, not around a lot. Stella was always looking after me but it wasn't the same. I always wanted it to be my mom, but well... it never was. I was very stubborn and didn't want Stella doing things for me. Things like washing my hair. So I would try to do it myself but never did a very good job."

I swallow a breath as the teasing I endured fills my head. "Sometimes I would go to school with greasy hair and my mother would get very upset, but still she wouldn't take the time to wash it. She didn't want anything to do with me, I guess." I finally gain the courage to meet his eyes. "I mean, don't get me wrong. I know there were kids who had it a lot worse than me. I at least had a roof over my head and food, but still, I thought it was pretty fucked up. They basically pushed me off on someone else because they didn't want to make time for me. I guess when it comes down to it," I shrug, "I wasn't important enough."

"You know, there's always someone who has it worse, but that doesn't make what you've experienced any less fucking real to you. And well, I—" Looking past me to the side table, he glances at the clock. "Shit, I have to get to work. I have a nine o'clock appointment."

"Okay," I reply back, curious now as to what he was going to say. "I need to get going, too. I want to see if Olivia can meet for breakfast before I go to work."

"I wish I didn't have to go, though." He presses his erection into my thigh. "I'd much rather stay here with you."

"I can see that," I tease with a smirk. My fingers lift the sheet and I peek underneath. "Yes, I can definitely see that."

He rolls over on top of me, nestling between my legs. "Do you want to grab a bite to eat tonight? I get off of work about seven." His lips sail along the edge of my jaw, skimming my neck. The rough stubble on his chin is heavenly.

"Sure, that sounds good." I angle my head as he peppers wet kisses along my skin, eliciting a shiver that travels to my toes. "Your lips feel so good on my skin," I whimper, and he smiles against me.

"I'm particularly fond of them on your skin, too." He grins, giving me a chaste kiss on the mouth before pushing off of me and heading for the bathroom. "I better shower now." He mumbles something under his breath, then disappears behind the door.

After the shower goes on, I jump off the bed, dress quickly, and tiptoe into the kitchen. I'm going to see what, if anything, I need for the surprise I have planned tonight for his birthday.

Each cabinet I open reveals that he has very little to work with, so I'll need to pick up a ton of ingredients and also grab some pots from home as well. I shake my head at the lack of food he has here. But then again, since we've been hanging out, I have yet to see him cook. The bag of popcorn I glimpse in the corner has a huge smile forming on my lips. It looks new and makes me take a pause when Rex's voice catches me off guard.

"Blondie?"

"In here," I reply, thinking fast and turning on the faucet.

"What are you doing?" His jeans are hanging low on his hips, fingers combing through his wet hair. I need water just to douse the flames of heat whizzing through my body.

"Just getting a drink of water."

"With no glass?" he observes, and I laugh it off, hopefully distracting from my strange behavior.

"Oh yeah, right." I open a cabinet, pull out a glass and fill it with water. "You want some?" I offer, draining half of the glass for show.

"No, thanks. I've gotta run, but I'll see you tonight, right?"

"Yes, I'll meet you here around seven. Let me just grab my purse. I'll walk out with you."

I come back out of the bedroom to find Rex deep in thought, staring out the window, a faraway look in his eyes. "All set." More than a minute goes by and he doesn't respond. "Rex?"

"Huh?" he startles, pivoting his head toward me.

"Ready?"

"Yeah." He snatches his keys from the coffee table, and it's almost as if he's not here with me anymore. A part of me wants to see if he's okay, but my instinct tells me he needs space so I let him be.

Once we get outside, we're swept away into a whirlwind of people passing by us. There's loud conversation in every direction, overpowered only by the honking of taxis.

"So I'll see you later, Rex. Have a good day." I try to sound peppy but worry betrays my voice.

"Yeah, a good day," he responds with a bitter laugh. "You too." He kisses my cheek and struts off in the opposite direction. I tap a finger against my arm as I watch him walk away, wondering what that was all about.

When he finally disappears from view, I hunt for the cell phone in my purse to call Olivia. I dial her number, the phone ringing several times with no answer. I'm just about to hit end when she picks up, laughing loudly in my ear.

"Hey, V!"

"How's the morning after?" I joke, hearing Hunter's deep chuckle in the background. "Sounds like it's pretty good."

"It's fantastic," she sings, and I don't think I've ever heard her sound so happy. The joy in her tone thankfully drowns out the longing in my belly.

"So do you think you can sneak away for breakfast? I have to check out a new meeting venue at eleven thirty right off of Broadway, so I thought we could meet up before then," I suggest, walking toward the subway.

"Sure, that sounds good." She muffles the phone, whispering something to Hunter, and I giggle.

"All right." I peer at my watch, noticing it's eight thirty. "Do you want to meet at... say ten? I was thinking we could go to Community Food & Juice, they're between one hundred twelve and one hundred thirteenth street. They have fabulous pancakes."

"That's perfect. I'll see you then." She laughs again, and the line goes dead.

I shake my head and silently give myself a pep talk. I've got too many things to think about today and I need to stop brooding.

Olivia isn't there when I arrive at the restaurant, so I snag a table outside and order two coffees and some pancakes. I love this place. It's more upscale than a typical diner, but the food has that down-home taste as if you're sitting and eating at your grandmother's house for Sunday breakfast. Not that I'd know anything about that.

My cell phone rings and I wince when I see the number at the other end. My mother. I consider hitting ignore and letting it go to voicemail. But it's been about a month since we've spoken and if I don't get it this time, she'll probably keep harassing me. I let out what I hope will be a serenity inducing breath before I answer it.

"Hello, Mother," I say with the lack of enthusiasm she instills in me, taking a sip of my latte as I listen for the sharp-edged tone that awaits.

"Vanessa. I'm glad you picked up. I need to discuss something with you," she responds, as cheerful as ever.

"Well, Mother, let's just dispense with the pleasantries and get down to it," I reply, and she clears her throat, completely disregarding my comment.

"I wanted to inform you that I'm getting remarried and I realize it's soon but it's happening, and there's nothing you can do to change it." The lack of emotion she displays is astounding. She might as well be in a courtroom prosecuting a case.

"Wow, Mother," acid spews from my tongue, "being a bitch is a great way to lessen the sting. I really appreciate that."

"*Vanessa Summer Hilliard.*" Her attempt to sound forceful is negated by her lack of power over me or my responses, evidenced by my bitter laugh that silences her.

"*Really*, Mother? That didn't work when I was a child and it certainly won't work now. Have you told Dad?"

"I'm seeing your father this evening and I plan on telling him then." Her voice oozes so little sincerity I feel sick to my stomach. Did she ever care about him?

"Okay, then. Is that all? I'm rather busy." I pick at my fingernail repeatedly, cursing her in my head.

"Yes, that's all. I just thought you should know."

"Gee, thanks. And an extra thank you for the pick-me-up. Goodbye, Mother." And I hang up without even waiting for her to say goodbye, dropping my head in my hands, wondering how I could've been so blessed.

"V. You okay?" The sound of Olivia's voice and the feel of her sincere hand on my arm pulls me up from my bootstraps.

"I guess. I just talked to my mother. She's getting remarried."

"Already?" she asks, surprise lacing her tone.

"Exactly. It kind of makes you wonder, doesn't it? Maybe she was seeing this guy while they were married. Who knows? Honestly, Liv, I'm so thankful they live in Seattle. I don't think I could handle it if they were close. Anyway," I wave my hand in the air dismissively, "I don't want to ruin my morning any further by talking about them. Tell me about you."

She flops her hand down right in front of me, and I come face to face again with the sparkling boulder on her finger.

"Liv." I grab her hand. "That ring is beautiful, and enormous. You may need a forklift to pry it off."

"I'm never taking it off," she says, staring at it with a dreamy smile.

"So... spill it. Tell me about your night." I lean back, sipping my coffee and dusting off any lingering remnants of my mother.

She sighs, tucking her fist under her chin. "It was amazing, V. So romantic. I mean, I know I've always said I'm not the flowers kind of girl, but he had rose petals and candles everywhere when we got back to his place. It seems surreal to me. I kind of feel like I'm living someone else's life, you know?"

"It's a life you deserve so hard, Liv. I can't think of anyone who deserves it more." I finish off my coffee as the waitress brings our pancakes, placing them on the table.

"I can definitely think of someone who deserves it just as much, though," she implies, her eyes boring holes through my skull. "Speaking of which, you and Rex looked pretty cozy together last night. And even I'll admit, he seemed pretty relaxed. How are things going?"

My cheeks warm and I already know I'm blushing. "Good. We have a good time together, and... I like him."

"Yes, well, the flush on your face is a dead giveaway, not to mention the way you were staring at him last night."

"Was it that obvious?" I ask, hoping it wasn't that apparent to Rex.

"Just to me, I'm sure, because I know you. Just—"

"I know," I interrupt her, well aware of what she's going to say, and getting tired of hearing it. "Be careful, and I will."

Olivia's big, blue eyes narrow. "Don't get bitchy with me. I care about you."

Her word choice hits a nerve, striking a chord of insecurity deep within me. I huff out a breath. "I know you do, Liv. But I'm a big girl and I can take care of myself. I've done it my whole life." I stare down at the plate in front of me, picking at the pancake with my fork. "Hey, I want to ask you something."

She nods as the waitress refills her coffee. "Sure, anything."

Self-doubt creeps into my head and I can't help the next words that fly from my mouth. "Do you think I'm like my mother?"

"No," she emphasizes, dropping her fork with a rattle, and I look up at her. "I don't think you're anything like your mother. She doesn't have a caring bone in her body. You're the total opposite."

"Thanks for saying that." I exhale a relieved breath, needing reassurance after that harrowing phone call.

She covers my hand with her own. "I'm not just saying it, V. I mean it."

"Okay."

"So what are you doing tonight? Hanging out with Rex again?" She smirks, twirling a piece of pancake with her fork.

"As a matter of fact, I am. But, it's his birthday and he doesn't know that I know it's his birthday, so I'm making him a surprise dinner." I motion to the waitress to get the check.

She leans forward with wide eyes. "You're cooking... for a guy?"

"Don't look so surprised. You know I can cook. I just never had a desire to do it before," I say, just as the waitress comes by with our bill. "Thank you."

After she walks away, Olivia sets her sights on me again. "Yes, I know, *that's* why I'm surprised."

"And on that note," I push my chair back, "I have to run. I need to go see this venue and then run some errands before I head to the office." I throw some money on the table. "Breakfast is on me, Mrs. Grayson."

Her lips turn up into a beaming smile as she stands to see me out. "I like the sound of that. It has a nice ring to it."

"I hope so." I laugh, and we march arm in arm out into the sunshine before parting ways.

"Have fun tonight," she yells, and I whirl around, lifting a hand in the air.

"You know I will."

The space for the event is perfect and the walk-through doesn't take as long as I thought. After I've said my goodbyes to the management staff and leave the building, I notice that I'm only a few blocks away from Intricate Ink. Without even realizing it, my feet are pulling me in that direction. It appears they know what I'm thinking better than I do. I want to see Rex.

Of course, when I'm finally standing in front of the shop, my legs seem to be singing a different tune. They won't move, frozen as if they're having second thoughts. I know I am. And now I'm overanalyzing my behavior, which I never do. I'm just about to hightail it out of here, when the door jingles and Rex's deep voice calls out to me.

"Blondie? What are you doing here?"

"Oh, hey. I was in the neighborhood so I thought I'd drop by and say a quick hello," I reply, my tone even, trying to appear casual when inside I'm anything but.

"Come on in. I have about fifteen minutes before my next tattoo." He holds the door open and I follow him inside. "Do you mind sitting with me while I sketch?"

"Not at all." I'm excited to see his work, get a glimpse at this other side of him.

We go to a room in the back, a black curtain the only thing separating it from the rest of the space. The room is small. A simple table is set up with inks and needles, and across from it, a small drafting desk. There's an old, weathered reclining chair in the center.

"Have a seat," Rex suggests, but just as I'm about to, he catches me off guard, crowding me and pinning me against the wall.

"Hi." He brushes his lips over mine, the smell of mint on his breath mixed with his own scent has me quickly aroused.

"Hi," I breathe against his lips.

"I like this." His voice is throaty as he hooks a finger into the low-cut V of my blouse, grazing the curve of my breast. "I like this a lot."

"You might like this even better," I whisper, popping the first two buttons to reveal a red and black satin bra.

His eyes darken, and he takes my hand, placing it over the large bulge in his jeans. He's already hard. "Do you see what you do to me?"

He teases me with his lips and his words while my tongue sneaks out to taste him and he groans.

"Your tongue is delicious, just like the rest of you. I wish I could take you right here, open those legs and taste your pussy," he says quietly, grinding his cock against my sex, the satin of my panties already wet.

The curtain opens and we pull apart abruptly.

"Oh, sorry, man."

"That's okay." Rex adjusts himself before skating around the very tall, muscular guy completely covered in tattoos from his neck down the length of his arms. "Zeek," Rex nods, "this is Blon—Vanessa. Vanessa, Zeek. He manages the shop."

"Nice to meet you," I greet him, an embarrassed flush warming me when he glances down at my open blouse. I bring my arms up to cover my chest and he smirks. Rex doesn't notice as he's already sitting down at the desk sketching.

"Sorry to interrupt," he apologizes and I let out a nervous laugh. "I just need to get some ink and I'll be out of your way."

"Oh no, it's fine," I come back with, trying to ease the awkwardness of the moment. I nab a chair and slide it next to Rex. "Well, that was an interesting meet and greet," I joke once Zeek leaves the room.

"Nah, Zeek's cool." He continues drawing as I button my blouse, peeking over his shoulder at his art. I'm fascinated by how his large hand glides over the paper effortlessly, back and forth, creating fluid lines, vines, and flowers. It's mesmerizing.

"Wow. That's amazing, Rex."

"Thanks. I'm finishing up a back tattoo of a flowering tree that I started last month. I'm stoked because it's actually one of the more detailed tattoos I've had the opportunity to work on."

He pauses with the pencil in his hand, looking over at me. "So how are you? Good day?"

"Hmph. Well, that depends... if a good day includes having your bitch of a mother call you to tell you she's getting remarried."

"I'm sorry. That sucks." He drops the pad and pencil on the desk, swiveling his chair to face me, taking both my hands in his. "You okay?"

"Yeah. I guess. It's just that she's so—insensitive." My mouth pinches tight, finding it difficult to speak about the woman who doesn't deserve to call herself my mother. "It's hard for me to describe." I sigh, and he nods his head in acknowledgement. Of course he understands. His situation is even worse.

"I'm sorry, Rex. I know you get it."

He lifts his hand to cup my chin. "No need to apologize. We all have our crosses to bear." Tugging me forward, he touches his lips to mine, then reclines back and resumes his drawing. All the stress from before leaves me, as if his kiss cleansed my body of all its impurities. That is, until there's a knock on the wall.

A woman walks in and she is absolutely stunning. Jet black hair, green eyes, and one of those hourglass figures that can easily be seen through her tight tank top and jeans. A halo of jealousy swirls around my head as I stare at her waiting for some sort of introduction.

"Oh, hey, Sienna," Rex says casually, looking up from his sketch. "Have a seat, I'm almost ready."

Of course *this* has to be the recipient of the tattoo. Visions of her shirtless with his hands all over her back make my stomach harden. All I want to do is wring her neck and my intense reaction surprises me.

"Oh, sorry. Sienna, this is Vanessa. Vanessa this is Sienna."

I plaster a smile on my face and reach out to shake her hand. "Nice meeting you," I say, narrowing my eyes when she stares at Rex instead of me.

"I'm really excited about this, Rex," she chirps, a sneer beginning to root itself at the corners of my mouth. Even her voice is sexy.

"Hey, Rex, I've got to get back to work."

"Okay, baby," he says, and I'm not sure if I'm imagining the trace of disappointment in his voice. But I'm sure as hell not imagining the way it lights me up inside at the way he called me baby, in front of her. "All right, well, let me walk you out." He turns to address Sienna. "I'll be right back and then we'll get started."

With his hand at my lower back, he guides me to the front door, and surprisingly walks me outside. "I'm glad you came by." He leans against the window of the shop, arms crossed over his chest, a cocky smile sitting on his lips. He waggles his finger at me to come closer and then grabs me possessively, crashing his lips to mine.

By the time I pull away, I'm breathing way too heavy to be standing on a public street. But I'm glad I'm not the only one.

"So we're on for seven, right?" I touch a finger to my lips, my composure choppy at best.

"Yup." He digs his hands in his pockets, looking far too sexy for me to leave alone with that green-eyed monster. "Oh, you know what? Here." He pulls out his keys and loosens one from the ring, handing it to me. "Just in case I'm running late, you can let yourself in."

"Okay." I take the key, shuffling my feet along the sidewalk. "Have fun tattooing that green-eyed temptress in there." My nostrils flare as I toss my hair over my shoulder, unable to hide the thick layer of jealousy covering me.

"Hey, smartass," he calls out, and I whirl around, walking backward.

"Yeah?"

"I'll be tattooing her, but she's not the one I'll be thinking about." He winks, then disappears inside, and I'm left standing here with a pounding heart and the ground moving beneath my feet.

I'm checking my list as I leave my office for the day. Lists are basically my lifeline in the event planning business. If one thing goes amiss, it can literally ruin an entire function. I can't afford to forget anything because there's absolutely no room for error. The upside, or downside in some cases, is that it carries over to my life. Of course I say all this realizing that I've had my share of mental lapses as of late. The cause of my forgetfulness brings a smile to my face.

I scroll through my to-do's for tonight to get everything ready for Rex's surprise, noticing I only have one thing left—wrap up the framed picture of him and Tyler. I reach into my briefcase and pull it out. My heart warms, while my belly does a strange flutter at the thought of giving it to him. I really hope he likes it.

"Heading out for the night?" Tillie asks as I stroll past her desk.

"Yes." I return the picture to my bag. "And you should go home, too," I add, pushing the sleeve of my blouse back to check my watch. "What are you doing here so late anyway?"

"What else?" She points to Jonathan's office. "He has an early morning meeting tomorrow and he needed packets made up for everyone attending. I'm almost done though. I'll be out of here soon."

"Okay, good. Well, I have to run. I have *plans*," I say with a hint of mystery as I make my way to the elevator.

She leans way over the desk, poking her head out. "Have fun."

"Oh, I fully intend to," I reply, nervous energy pulsing through my body at the thought of seeing Rex. He doesn't seem like he's had a whole lot of happy in his life, and somewhere deep down, in a place where it's difficult for me to admit, I'm secretly hoping I can be the one to give him that.

# CHAPTER TWENTY-ONE

## WHAT A DAY

I'm surprised at how well I managed to get through the day, considering everything it represents. The fact that my mind and hands were occupied with back to back tattoos served me well. Dr. Billings would be proud. Even Zeek, who knows it's my birthday, hasn't said shit to me about it.

With Sienna's tattoo finished, I begin cleaning up the back room. Pride takes up residence in my chest—this is the one thing in my life that makes me feel good about myself, like I have some sort of worth. A small piece of relevance in this world.

"Yo, Rex," Zeek pokes his head around the corner, "I wanted to let you know I got some shots of Sienna's tattoo for your portfolio. It came out fucking spectacular, man."

"Thanks." I smile, knowing he's right. "I guess she really liked it. She offered herself up to me when we were done."

"Are you fucking kidding me?" He walks in further, taking a seat on the leather chair. "And I know you're taking her up on it, right?"

I pause with my hand on the cloth, surprising myself by grinning when I answer. "No, I'm not."

"Are you fucking crazy?" he asks. "Did you see the bod on her? And she's willing?"

"Yeah, she's definitely hot, but—"

"Wait a second," he chimes in. "Does this have anything to do with that blonde chick that was here earlier?"

"Maybe."

"Maybe, my ass." Zeek chuckles. "Man, it must be nice to be you." He gets up, snatching a couple of rags from the drawer. "I'm gonna finish out there and then I'm taking off. Did you want to grab a beer?"

"Thanks, Zeek, but I've got plans with the blonde chick," I joke, and he mumbles to himself, brushing past me then disappearing.

I fish the ringing cell phone out of my pocket, my lips forming a snarl when I see it's my mother. The ignore button gets pushed immediately and I shove the phone back in my jeans. It's obvious what she wants, and she should know better than to try to acknowledge me, today of all days.

Determined not to focus on her tonight, I push those thoughts away and instead think about Vanessa. I chuckle at myself, probably looking like a crazy person to anyone on the outside. But they don't know me. Whenever she's around, it's like my lips runneth over. I can't believe some of the shit that comes out of my mouth. I guess she brings it out in me.

Adrenaline runs rampant through my system as I round the corner to my building, practically sprinting now.

When I step off the elevator, she's not here. But then I remember I gave her a key, so she might be inside. If not, I can hurry and take a quick shower before she arrives. I jam the key in the lock and push the door open. My keys fall to the ground as my vision blurs, eyes darting around the room. Black and white balloons, a white tablecloth with flowers and candles on my table that barely seats two. The smell of something I can't make out drifting through the air.

What the fuck?

The reality of who I am and where I come from smacks me hard in the face, the chest, the knees, nearly knocking me off my feet. The oxygen slowly being drained from my lungs allows very few words to slip out.

"What is this?"

Vanessa turns around at the sound of my voice, her bright smile transforming into a line of confusion across her brow when she sees my face.

"What the fuck is this?" I ask again, and her response tells me she must think I'm joking.

I'm not.

"What do you think this is?" She balances a plate in one hand and the other one on her hip. "I wanted to do something special for your birthday."

I dig my hands into my hips as my feet begin pacing the floor in circles, my breathing uncontrolled. "You had no right to do this. I didn't say you could do this. I didn't give you a key so you could come in here," I flail my arms in the air, "and do this."

And then I snap, and it's as if someone flipped a switch inside of me. "How the fuck did you know it was my birthday?" I spit. "Were you snooping around? Asking more fucking questions? I don't celebrate my birthday *ever*!" I shout, my neck corded tight with anger. "You don't fucking know me. You don't know what this day means to me. I don't fucking celebrate it!" I yell again. "So you need to take your fucking flowers and your fucking balloons and get the fuck out!"

She stares at me blankly as if she's looking into the face of a stranger. "*What* did you just say?" she asks, an eerie calm in her tone. But I see the storm coming, as I watch every single ounce of happiness drain from her body on a heavy exhale of breath. "You think I was fishing around for information about you? That I was going behind your back?" She takes a few steps forward, still gripping the plate with her fingers, dealing me a menacing glare that has no effect because I can't see past my rage. "What kind of person do you think I am? Because I've got a news flash for you. I wasn't sneaking around, plotting and scheming when you weren't looking. Your *brother* told me about your birthday.

"What *is* all this?" She gestures toward the room with her free hand, her voice rising to a shriek. "The *fucking* flowers and the *fucking* balloons. I wanted to do something for you. I know how little happiness you've had and I thought I could change that for you, give you a little piece of something good. But you know what?" She lets out a foul laugh. "I'm the idiot. I've never done anything like this before and now I know why. Because assholes like you don't appreciate it. Because you're not capable of appreciating it."

I don't know why she's still standing here talking to me after everything I've said. But I need her gone. So I do what I do best, what I've become a master at—I push away. Because the reality is, I'm not good enough for her. I'm not even good enough for myself.

The filter for my mouth completely dissolves until suddenly I have no control over my thoughts or my words, self-hatred spewing out of me and I'm helpless to stop it.

"What do you think we're doing?" I gesture between us, then scrape a rough hand through my hair, staring at the carpet so my eyes don't reveal the truth. "We have a good time. We fuck and it's amazing. I love fucking you. But that's all this is. Don't make this something it's not."

And when I finally dare to look up, that's when it happens. My life passes right before my eyes, moving in slow motion as if I'm watching a scene in a movie unfold.

Shock forces her eyes to widen, mouth to hang open as the plate she's holding clatters to the ground, shattering, sauce splattering on the wall, the floor, her dress, but she doesn't flinch. Instead, she shoots daggers at the asshole standing in front of her.

Good. I want her to hate me. She couldn't possibly hate me more than I hate myself.

Even from this distance, I can tell her eyes are glistening, her lower lip quivering, and I know that I've hurt her. But it's for her own good. As soon as the next words leave her mouth, though, my heart squeezes so tight I find it difficult to breathe.

"Thank you, Rex, for making me feel like a whore for the first time in my life."

Refusing to look at me, she walks over the broken plate, the pieces crushing under her heels. Eyes glued to the door, she's looking for a way out of the hellhole I've just created for her. When she reaches it, she pauses, her head turning slightly to the right, but still she doesn't meet my eyes.

"You were right about one thing. I definitely don't know you. Because I mistook you for someone who was worth it." She laughs bitterly. "And you're *so* not worth it." Her hand reaches for the knob before everything crashes down around me. "Goodbye, Rex."

The lock clicks, the door slamming so loudly behind her, frame rattling on its hinges. The noise confirmation to my ears of what I've always known.

She's right. I'm not fucking worth it.

The silence that follows her departure leads to a different kind of insanity. One that I'm not familiar with... loneliness. But it doesn't last long before rage wraps itself around me, keeping me in a tight hold. I haul back and punch the nearest wall, needing an escape, but the only thing I get is what I deserve—a balled-up fist covered in blood—and even then it's not enough. So I hit it again, pain my only friend now, a way to numb the absolute agony I'm suffering. And it's my own fucking fault.

I pace the room, breathing heavy. Blood drips onto the floor, but I make no attempt to soothe myself. The only soothing balm I've ever known just slipped through my fingers. And who's the fucking asshole? I am. Because I let her go. I didn't just let her go. I kicked her out the door.

Devastation seeps through every pore of my apartment: food covering the walls, smeared blood mixing with faded white paint making for one hell of a fucked-up piece of art. I stomp to the kitchen to escape the view, sagging back against the counter when I see the birthday cake. Jesus. She even made me a fucking cake. My gut twists and I can't bear it any longer so I flee the kitchen and collapse onto the couch, burying my head in my hands as life deals me yet another blow. I'm not sure how much more I can handle.

After a few minutes, I finally manage to lift my head, my eyes blinking slowly as I take in the scene around me. Something shiny on top of the television cabinet draws my eye in and I move closer to it, hesitating in my tracks when I see it's a birthday gift. My feet continue to move slowly toward it, almost as if it can bite, before I'm finally standing in front of it. I let out a hesitant breath, then snatch it down, tearing open the card. The picture on the outside is a rose tattoo, and when I open it, it reads:

*So you never forget. xo*
*Vanessa (aka Blondie)*

I rub my forehead in confusion before I anxiously rip open the package, staring at the picture in disbelief. My legs buckle and I drop to my knees, clutching it to my chest. When I feel like I can bear to look at it again, I hold it out in front of me. It's a close up shot of Tyler and me at the baseball field, hats backwards, goofy smiles on our faces, Tyler making a peace sign behind my head. I run my thumb over his cheek, over the freckles that I couldn't remember.

One lone tear sneaks out from my eye, pain burning a path down my skin. "Blondie," I whisper, the horrid realization of what I've just done drowning me like a fucking tidal wave.

My eyes survey the room, staring at the wreckage of efforts born out of kindness. She thinks I'm worth it. Or at least she did. I pick up the card from the carpet, rubbing over the letters of her handwriting, desperate to feel her aura around me. But I feel nothing. Because she's gone.

A different type of pain that I've never experienced before lances through me, and now the only thing I want is to take back the last fifteen minutes of my life—roll back the tape so I can try again—so I can have another chance.

I spring to my feet, placing the picture frame on top of the cabinet before grabbing my keys from the floor and hightailing it out the door. Determination to find her and explain fuels me, my heart racing as I punch her number into my cell phone and it repeatedly goes to voicemail. But I won't let that deter me. I head in the direction of her apartment, figuring I can catch the subway, when I spot her through the window of Ryder's bar.

Vanessa is standing next to Ryder, and the moment she sees me walk through the door, her lips lock with his, my blood boiling in response.

He has no right to kiss her; she's mine.

"What the fuck?"

She breaks away from Ryder's lips, wiping her mouth, shoving a chunk of hair over her shoulder.

"What are you doing?" I ask, all the while knowing I have no right to the answer. She doesn't owe me a God damn thing now.

She stares back at me, deadpan. "Just living up to my reputation. Once a whore, always a whore, right?"

I wince, feeling the color drain from my face, limbs going completely numb. "I'm sorry, I shouldn't have said all those horrible things, Blondie. I just need a chance to explain." I sound lame, even to my own ears, but I don't know what else to say to make this better.

"Don't call me Blondie," she huffs, folding her arms protectively over her chest. "My *name* is Vanessa, and anyway, you were right. All you were was a good fuck, so there's nothing to explain. I'm pretty sure we're done here," she says, devoid of emotion, scanning the bar as if I'm wasting her time. "Is there anything else?"

The sting of hearing those same words I dealt her is like a knife twisting in my chest. "No," I respond in defeat.

"Good, then we're done. Goodbye, Rex." She turns her back on me, her voice flat, empty, and inside I'm completely gutted, because deep down I know what I just lost.

The best thing that ever happened to me.

# CHAPTER TWENTY-TWO

## A DISTANT MEMORY

*Vanessa*

The minute Rex walks out the door, my legs give out on me and I collapse behind the bar. I'd like to think I'm strong and tough, but as I try to fight the tears from falling, the only thing I realize is that I'm a big ball of hurt. His words made me crumple inside, and now all I want to do is suck into myself and disappear.

I've never felt so low in my life. I finally allowed myself to begin to care for someone only to have it thrown back in my face. No one has ever made me feel like this before. And no one ever will again.

Ryder crouches down on the floor beside me. "Hey," he wipes a single tear away with his finger, "you okay?"

"I'm great," I reply, still trying to maintain my tough exterior.

"No, you're not."

"No, I'm not." I glance up at him, begging him with my eyes. "Take me home with you. Please, Ryder, I don't want to be alone tonight."

The way he closes his eyes and sucks in a breath tells me maybe he's not as over me as I thought. But selfishly, I need him tonight. I can't be alone. I don't want time to think about Rex, where he can creep into my mind, crawl back into my heart.

"*Please*," I plead again.

He finally opens his eyes with a new resolve, laying a gentle hand on mine. "You know I can't say no, Vanessa. When it comes to you, that word isn't in my vocabulary."

"Thank you," I reply, squeezing his hand.

"Okay, let me get Vince to take over and we'll get out of here." He reaches for something under the counter and comes back with a box of tissue, handing me one. "Here."

"Thanks, Ryder."

About five minutes later, he returns, and I still haven't moved. My ass is stuck to the sticky, dirty floor and I couldn't care less.

"Come on," he lifts me from the ground, "let's go." His strong hand grips my elbow, tucking it underneath his arm as we make our way outside.

Silence floats back and forth between us, but I can tell he wants to say something. "So, are you going to tell me what happened? I mean, that kiss was rocking and all, and I played along with your game, but now you owe me an explanation." He doesn't look at me, but from the side I can see his lips twitching at the corner.

"Rocking, huh? Well, you always were a good kisser, Ryder." I elbow him, even though he can see right through me and my tactics.

"It won't work with me. I know you too well, so stop redirecting."

"I need a drink first. Actually," I laugh, even though all I want to do is cry, "I may need a lot of drinks."

"Okay." He nods toward his street as we reach the corner. "I've got that."

By the time we reach Ryder's apartment, I'm feeling even worse than I did at the bar. My stomach is tight with longing. There's only one place I want to be, and it's not here. But after the way Rex treated me, how he disregarded me as if I meant absolutely nothing to him, I can't go back. I won't.

"All right," he says, once he unlocks the door, "make yourself comfortable. I'll get the shot glasses." He stops midway to the kitchen, swerving around. "This must be bad because you don't really drink that much."

I fall back on to the couch, kicking off my heels, reclining my head against the soft cushions. "Yeah, well, I may just make up for that tonight."

"Okay." He raises up the bottle when he comes back out. "I've got Yankees shot glasses and a bottle of Patron."

"Perfect," I reply, eager to take the edge off my emotions. "I'd forgotten how nice your place was, Ryder. It's really homey in here," I add, looking around the room but not really seeing anything except my own anguish.

He sets the alcohol on the table before copping a seat next to me. "Are we going to continue to talk about my decorating abilities or are you going to tell me what the hell is going on?"

"Are you going to pour me some comfort or what?"

"Tiger," he mumbles under his breath as he pours us each a shot. Raising his glass, he clinks it against mine. "To the truth."

"Yeah, what's that saying?" I knock back the entire shot, followed by one more, before waving it in the air. "The truth shall set you free. In my case it should be, the truth will make you feel like absolute shit." I hold out the tumbler. "Another, please."

"You'll get another *after* you start talking." He holds the bottle tight against his chest. "Well...."

"Fine," I huff. "I don't even know where to start." Warmth fills my belly, sending me on my way to the numbness I crave. "I made dinner for Rex because it's his birthday today and he freaked out on me and said some pretty awful things, the worst one being that we're just fuck buddies and that's it." I put a hand to my head, attempting to rub the memory from my brain. "It hurt. A lot."

"Because...." Ryder sets the bottle on the table. "Because you care about him."

"Cared. Past tense," I insist, although the words don't sound very convincing.

He cocks his head to the side, shadows of disbelief covering his face. "You need to talk to him. Because I can tell you this. The look on his face when he walked into the bar was not the look of a guy who was desperate to talk to his," he makes air quotes with his fingers, "fuck buddy."

I wave the shot glass in front of him. "I talked, so pay up," I say, determined to make Rex Grayson a distant memory.

The third and fourth ones go down smooth and I like the way I'm starting to feel. Edging closer to Ryder, I lean my head on his shoulder and close my eyes. He tips his head against mine.

"Tomorrow you'll feel better. I think you'll see things a lot more clearly in the morning."

"I don't want to see things more clearly. I want to keep drinking." I pout, collapsing onto my back.

"Well, I'm not going to let you do that." He takes my hands and pulls me up from the couch. "I'm putting you to bed."

I shuffle my feet, stumbling beside him on the way to his room. "I like the sound of that." I giggle, and he chuckles.

"You see, you've already had too much to drink. You've lost control of your faculties."

"That was my goal but you wouldn't play along," I slur, nearly falling over.

"Sit," he commands, sliding off my shoes then pushing me back on the mattress. "Sleep." There's a blanket at the foot of the bed and he covers me from head to toe. "I'll be on the couch if you need me."

"Hey, Ryder," I mumble, my head already making a dent in the pillow. "Thank you."

"Don't mention it. Now get some rest."

The room goes dark, yet my eyes won't close. Particles of light streaming in from the partially open curtains form shapes of nothingness—a little too familiar for my liking. My mind is racing along with my heart, body tossing and turning, not allowing sleep to rescue me. The image of Rex's face when he walked into the apartment haunts me, then again when he entered the bar. I wonder now what he was going to say. What made him act so crazy?

How could I have been so wrong in thinking there was something a bit more between us? I felt it. I feel it even now. Even after everything he said to me, I still want him. But I'm not that type of a girl—the forgiving kind. When I hurt, I hurt deeply within my core and I have a hard time letting go.

In eighth grade, when my best friend, Sherri Zuckerman, told me my boyfriend, Corey Thompson, was a dirtbag and he would only hurt me, I believed her. That is, until I found her sucking face with him in the janitor's closet. She was my closest friend and I trusted her. After that, we were done. I never spoke to her again.

I change sides, fluffing up the pillow under my head as if that will make a difference. A muffled sound perks my ears up and I realize it's my phone but can't see a thing in the blackness. The cool sheets get pushed aside as I sit up on the bed, feeling around for the lamp switch before flipping it on and spotting my purse on the chair. I plod clumsily over to it and pluck my cell from the bag, jumping back on the bed and scrolling through my messages.

There are four voicemails from Rex, which I refuse to listen to, and I can't even count the number of texts.

*I'm sorry*; *Please forgive me*; *I need to talk to you, I really am sorry*; *You can't ignore me forever*; *Call me, you have to talk to me.*

No, I don't.

The phone chimes in my hand and I startle, seeing yet another text from Rex.

*I'm so sorry. Please call me, I need to hear your voice, to know that you're okay.*

That one goes straight through me to a place that's raw, an open wound around my heart. He went from saying we were fucking to needing to hear my voice? I'm sorry, I'm just not buying it. Tonight certainly proved my theory, though.

Love definitely sucks.

I shut my phone off, tossing it onto the carpet, then bury my head under the pillow and pray for relief from a sleep that never comes.

# CHAPTER TWENTY-THREE

## TONGUE-TIED

Hunter opens the door, rubbing the aggravation at the late hour mixed with sleep from his eyes. "Hey, Rex," he groans, his voice gravelly, "Happy Birthday."

"Yes. Happy fucking birthday to me." I stumble through the door, plopping down on the nearest sofa.

"You reek of alcohol and you don't drink hard liquor." He scratches his head, closing the door behind him.

"You're very observant, bro," I chastise, my voice growing louder. "You're right on both counts. But I'm making an exception tonight." Actually I made an exception last week too, but I won't tell him about that.

"Hey, keep it down please. Olivia is in the other room sleeping and she's exhausted."

"Oh. Sorry," I speak in a hushed tone, "wouldn't want to wake sleeping beauty."

"Listen. I know it's your birthday, and I'm completely understanding of that, but is this why you came here? To throw your bitter attitude in my direction?" He glares at me, rubbing the back of his neck. "Because if that's the case, you can go. It's three in the fucking morning, Rex."

"Okay, okay." Anxiety filters through my system over having this conversation, and I run my hands down the front of my jeans, wiping the sweat from my palms. "Why did you go and fucking tell Vanessa about my birthday?"

Hunter blows out a breath, taking a seat in the chair across from me. "Oh shit. It was an accident. It just slipped out, Rex. Tell me what happened."

"I came home to find her in my apartment, preparing a celebration." I scrub a hand over my face. "I didn't even know how she knew it was my fucking birthday. But you know how I feel about it."

He raises his head, an apology in his eyes. "I really am sorry. I didn't intend to tell her. But I'm sure whatever happened can be fixed."

I slap an arm over my head, gritting my teeth. "I'm not so sure."

He sits up, crossing an ankle over his knee. "Why? What did you do?"

I glance toward the kitchen, my lips suddenly dry. "Do you have anything to drink first?"

"Not for you. Keep talking, little brother," he says with a heavy stare.

"I freaked out, pushed her away, said some pretty rotten things, told her all we were doing was fucking, nothing more." I expel the words fast, anxious to be rid of them. The sooner I can forget about this night, the better.

"Jesus, Rex." He exhales an exasperated sigh. "Maybe I spoke too soon. It's going to take an act of God to fix it. Olivia says she doesn't forgive that easily. But you better get off your ass and figure something out, though."

"I know." I cover my face with my arm, trying to shut out the world. "She won't answer any of my calls or my texts."

"Of course she won't. My advice," he offers, "start taking responsibility for what comes out of your mouth. Go find her and tell her the truth." He starts to walk away, but turns back. "I'm sorry about what happened. Listen, stay the night. Take one of the guest rooms. You'll feel better after you get some sleep."

There's only one thing that will make me feel better. And that one thing wants nothing to do with me.

Three hours later, I'm still awake, staring at the ceiling, wondering how I got here. It's not much of a mystery. My thoughts taunt me as the consistent pattern of my life emerges. The shit I've muddled in for so long has become familiar to me, so much so that I don't even recognize I'm wallowing in it. I've become too comfortable in my own misery.

Until now.

Last night was a wake-up call. The one person that finally comes along, giving me a glimmer of hope, the possibility of climbing out of this pit of despair I've become entrenched in—I cast aside like she was nothing.

I rub my eyes, gritty from lack of sleep, attempting to rid myself of the image of Vanessa in my apartment. Hurt rippling from her eyes and cheeks, the slant of her mouth. I squeeze my lids shut, regret hardening my stomach.

The sound of Olivia and Hunter's laughter catapults me back into reality. The clock reads 6:15 and that means Hunter is getting ready to take off for work. I decide to wait until they're gone before I get up. I'm assuming by now that Hunter told Olivia what happened last night and I don't feel like hearing her shit, too.

I reach around to the end table, sliding my cell phone over. Immediately unlocking it, I search through texts and voicemails, holding in a breath as I check for any sign from Vanessa. Of course there isn't one.

The moment the door closes, I climb off the bed and head straight for the bathroom. After taking a piss, I find myself in front of the mirror. I grasp the ledge of the counter, taking a closer look at the face staring back at me. Dark circles drag my eyes down, remorse lining the outer corners. My reflection teases me, another reminder of who I'm not, more so than who I am.

With a heavy hand, I twist the faucet to cold, splashing some water over my face. I'm actually shocked that I don't have a hangover. I'd readily welcome that kind of suffering though. The kind I can control as opposed to the jagged blade that's slicing me open, pain spilling out from every crevice of my body.

I dry my face with a towel, blowing out a breath, mulling over what to do. I already know what I want to do—I want to go see Vanessa. She typically doesn't go into work until later in the morning, so I can probably catch her if I hurry.

Fuck it.

The knowledge that she wants nothing to do with me doesn't deter me. My footsteps bear down on the pavement, moving quickly toward their destination. When I reach the subway, I traipse down the stairs and push through the crowd at the turnstile, unaffected by the dirty looks thrown my way. Little do they know I could give two shits. I've dealt with a lot worse.

There's a man delivering boxes when I arrive at Vanessa's apartment building, delaying my entrance, allowing more time for the sweat to find its way down my skin. By the time I can get through the glass door and step on the elevator, I'm bouncing from foot to foot, attempting to form a script in my head. I want to make sure I say the right thing. At this point, I'm not even sure what that is—I guess like Hunter said, the truth would be nice.

The car finally stops on her floor, and I steel myself with a meaty breath before walking out. I'm just about to knock on the door when it opens suddenly. Vanessa falters, stumbling back in surprise, her purse dropping to the ground.

"What are you doing here, Rex?" she asks flatly as I bend down to help her pick up her belongings. "I've got it," she snarls, waving me away, unwilling to meet my eyes.

The chill in the air sends a shiver up my neck and I can't stand that I've done this to her. Even with that, it takes me a second to respond, so fucking happy just to be in her presence that I'm tongue-tied.

I push back up to my feet. "You didn't leave me any choice. You wouldn't respond to my calls or my texts and we need to talk."

She slings her bag over her shoulder, intent on pushing her way past me. "There's nothing left to say, Rex. I'm pretty sure we covered everything last night."

My body blocks her, but I make sure to keep my hands to myself. "Can you just give me five minutes?"

There's a release of breath as she raises her eyes to the ceiling before finally allowing them to find mine. "Fine. Five minutes, Rex. I have to get to work." She stands aside, letting me walk in. Relief floods my chest at having made it this far.

"Can I sit?" I ask, motioning toward the couch. She looks at me with a bored expression, as if she has better things to do. Little does she know, I can see right through the tough-girl act she's trying to dish out.

"Be my guest." She sets her bag and briefcase down but continues to stand, glancing at her watch.

"I'm sorry, Blon—I'm sorry for the way I acted yesterday. I was out of line in so many ways and I honestly regret it. I reacted to something that had nothing to do with you." I pause, gesturing toward the sofa with my hand. "Will you please sit your ass down? You're making me nervous and I'm already fucking nervous as it is."

Her lips begin a slow curl toward a smile, but then shift direction, as if they've changed their mind. "Well, I wouldn't want you to be *uncomfortable*, Rex," she says, and I certainly don't miss the sarcasm dripping from her words.

She takes a seat at the other end of the couch, as far away from me as possible, fiddling with her fingers in her lap. An excruciating breath forces its way from my lungs as I try to push the words out before they get caught in my throat.

"The man that raised me. The man that I loved who I thought was my father... was not my father."

"I don't understand."

I scrape a hand through my hair before continuing. "My father is a drug dealing, lowlife piece of shit who's rotting away in prison right now. One of the many men my mother decided to screw along the way."

"I'm sorry." Those beautiful eyes of hers fill with sympathy, or pity, I'm not sure which one. But I know I can't continue to look at them.

I stare at a spot on the wall, hoping that will make this easier. "I didn't find out until I was nineteen but ever since then, I can't tolerate acknowledging my birthday. I feel like my whole childhood was a lie. Hunter is my half-brother, as was Tyler, and my mother is a liar."

I know I'm rambling but I can't stop myself. "Every year when my birthday rolls around, my way of coping is to ignore it. So yesterday just reminded me of everything bad in my life... the absolute shit that I come from, and when I walked in, it hit me, and I freaked out and acted like an asshole. I know I hurt you and I'm sorry. I'd do anything to take it back," I plead, my eyes trailing back to her face. "Anything."

"Okay."

"*Okay*?"

"Yes, I accept your apology," she says, and I breathe out a sigh of relief, moving closer to her. But she backs away.

"This doesn't change anything for me, though." She kneads her hands together, her shoulders rising and falling on an exhale of breath. "You hurt me and... I don't know if I can get past it right now. I understand that you've had a shitty past, Rex, and I'm truly sorry for everything you've been through. But you know what? We all have stuff we have to come to terms with, and you can't go around using it as a warrant to hurt people. It's time to grow up. Get therapy or do whatever you have to do so it doesn't happen again."

Ouch. But I definitely deserve that.

"What does that mean for us?" I ask, unsure as to whether I really want the answer to my question.

She stands up, snagging her purse from the carpet. "There is no us, Rex. Not now."

Her words punch me in the gut, but I should know better than anyone how one mistake can cause irreparable damage.

"Not now, or not ever?" The question leaves my mouth and I'm completely aware of my teeth clenching as I wait for her reply.

There's a long stretch of silence before she responds, instilling a seed of hope in my subconscious. "I don't know."

"Well, we're still friends, right?" That's the last thing I want, but at this point I'll take whatever scraps I can get.

"Friends, Rex?" She tugs on the strap of her bag as though it's her lifeline. "We're a bit beyond that, don't you think?"

"So what now, then?"

"Rex," she huffs, taking yet another glimpse of her watch. "I can't do this with you right now. I have to get to work."

I get up off the sofa, following her out the door. "Then when?"

"Rex."

"Yes, Blondie?" I try to coax a smile out of her, but right now it's like getting blood from a stone. She won't even give an inch. She's so damn stubborn and so fucking beautiful at the same time. It's driving me insane that I can't reach out and touch her.

"I have to go." She closes the door behind us and I follow her to the elevator, neither one of us saying anything.

The entire ride down to the lobby, I'm staring at her and she's focusing on the numbers as we descend, still clutching onto that strap like she needs protection from me. Maybe after last night, she does.

Her eyes drift from the panel to the dried blood on my knuckles. "What happened to your hand?" she asks, eyes softening with concern, giving me hope that she still cares about me.

I cover up my fist with my other hand. "I had an accident with the wall."

The doors open then and she bolts. A dull ache slices through my chest, knowing she wants to run from me. But I catch up to her and grab her arm. "Wait," I plead, and her eyes move to my hand so I wrench it away. "Listen." I dig my hands in my back pockets so I don't touch her again, but leave our eyes connected. "I never got a chance to thank you... for that picture of Tyler and me. It's... it's the best gift I've ever gotten. I just want you to know," I trail off, discomfort forcing my gaze away because I don't want her to see right through me. "It means a lot."

"You're welcome." With a nod of her head she turns and breezes past several people before my voice stops her in her tracks, again.

"Blondie!" I yell out, and she whips around just before reaching the glass door. "I can remember now," I shrug, "he had five freckles." A half-smile softens her lips and then she disappears into the crowd.

That smile—something else I never want to forget.

# CHAPTER TWENTY-FOUR

## THE FAN CLUB

*Vanessa*

Hurried, I turn the corner of my apartment and slump against the nearest building, letting go of my purse and briefcase. I clutch my stomach, trying like hell to breathe and even harder to suppress the tears that threaten to fall. I didn't realize how difficult it would be to push Rex away. The vulnerable part of me wanted to fall into his arms, while the tough side of me had to keep him at bay.

I can't erase the look on his face when he talked about the picture. It made me want to wrap my arms around him and never let him go—to be the one who takes away his demons. But I can't be his savior and I certainly won't be his punching bag.

For a second, I wonder if I was too hard on him—until the memory of last night kicks me in the gut and I realize I probably wasn't hard enough. Trust is a fragile thing and once it's shattered, the pieces are difficult to put back together.

The problem is, I'm drawn to him, like a moth is to a flame. I know myself, though, and sooner or later I'll get burned. As hard as it is, I have to distance myself. Even though it's the last thing I want to do. Trying to temper my thoughts, I gather my bags and focus on getting to work. That will be my salvation now.

I'm barely inside the glass doors before Tillie bombards me.

"Morning, sunshine! I have three phone messages for you here and you had four messages about the Hamilton launch already. I left them on your desk with the guest list. Oh, and Jonathan had to go to California for a last minute meeting with a potential client so he needs you to sit in on the Chelsea meeting, and—"

"Take a breath, Tillie." I pick up the message slips from my inbox on her desk. None of them look too urgent until I get to the last one, that says Rex. Just seeing his name on a sheet of damn paper has my heart skipping a beat. This will bode really well for me staying away from him. "Tillie, what's this?" I flip the paper around so she can see it. "It just says *Rex*."

"Oh yeah," she smirks, making a noise with her throat, "I'm supposed to deliver the following message." She snaps her gum inside her cheek. "Rex called and he wants you to know he's thinking about you. Oh," she leans closer, whispering, "and he sounds hot."

My lips quiver at the corners and I can't help the shake of my head that ensues. "Gah!" I grumble, before retreating to my office and closing the door. What is he trying to do? I just left him not more than thirty minutes ago. I guess telling him I needed space meant absolutely nothing.

Stacks of paperwork on my desk lift my spirits, telling me I'll be so busy next week that I won't have time to think about Rex. I plop down in my chair, stowing away my purse in a side drawer then logging on to my computer. The amount of e-mails I have to reply to is staggering, but I figure I'll dig into those first.

After going through nearly a hundred of them, I settle in with all of the details to prepare for the Hamilton event. Next Friday will come quickly and I need to make sure I have everything in order.

While I'm reviewing the orders for food and drink, my eyes can't help but wander over to that silly pink slip with Rex's name on it. I mentally scold myself for acting this way, as if my brain isn't already on Rex overload. Picking up the slip, I crumple it into a ball and throw it in the wastebasket. There. Done and score.

If only it were that easy.

My phone rings and my ears go on high alert, while my mouth lets out an aggravated, "What now?" A small breath of relief departs my lips when I see it's Ryder.

"Hey, Ryder, what's up?"

"Hey. I'm just checking on you. You left before I woke up this morning and I wanted to see how you're doing?" His voice is filled with concern, reminding me of how sweet he is. Of course, that doesn't do it for me. I prefer them sick and twisted.

"I'm fine, why?"

"Are you the same girl who was in my apartment last night?" he teases and I giggle.

"Oh. I'm doing okay."

"Did you speak to Rex?" he asks, and there's loud chattering in the background.

"Well, he came to see me today...," I swallow, "to apologize."

"And... hold on," he muffles the phone, "I'll be right there. Okay?" He comes back on the line. "Sorry. So what happened? Did you kiss and make up?"

"No," I reply, although his idea sounds much better than my reality. "I told him I can't be with him right now and to get some therapy."

"You did not!" he yells into the phone.

"Oh yes, I did." I kick off my heels, flexing my toes under the desk.

"Vanessa," he reprimands, "you know that's not what you want."

"Actually, it is. I can't shake off the feeling I had last night and I'm not sure it won't happen again."

He's quiet for a minute but then says, "People make mistakes, darlin'."

"Ryder." I exhale an abrasive sigh. "If anyone knows that, it's me. But...."

"But you're scared." He finishes my sentence for me as if he can read my mind.

"Okay, yes. Happy?" I bite back, immediately regretting my outburst.

"Hey, take it easy there, tiger."

"Sorry." I close my eyes, tipping my head back against the cool leather of the chair.

"I forgive you. You see, everyone makes mistakes." And I can picture him smiling as if he were right in front of me.

"Okay. I have to get back to work now, Doc. I'll drop off the check for our session later."

He chuckles into the phone. "You do that. Later."

"Bye, Ryder."

No sooner do I start sorting through the orders when the intercom sounds.

"Vanessa, Olivia is here. Can I send her in?"

"Sure, thanks, Tillie."

A minute later, there's a subtle tap on the door and Liv pokes her head in, a curtain of chestnut strands swaying around her face. "Hey, V. Is this a bad time?"

"No, it's fine. The boss is in Cali. Come on in." I pile the papers and set them on the corner of my desk while Olivia takes a seat, elbow bent on the armrest of the chair, studying me.

"You okay?"

Oh God, not her too.

"Yes, I'm fine," I state in a firm tone, and I'm not sure who I'm trying to convince more.

"Really? After everything that happened last night, you're fine. And why didn't you call me?" She purses her lips, narrowing her deep blue eyes.

I settle back in my chair, figuring this is going to be a lengthy conversation. "How do you know what happened last night?"

"Well, I stayed at Hunter's and apparently Rex came by at some ridiculous hour. He was really upset."

"He was?" I ask, fishing for reassurance, something I can hold on to, believe in.

"Yes. He—"

My hand halts her words. "Before you say anything else. You were right. I got hurt."

"Oh, V," she says softly, coming forward and resting her elbows on the desk. "I didn't want to be right. And honestly, after talking with Hunter this morning, I'm not so sure I am."

"What do you mean?" I jump in, desperately needing confirmation of Rex's words.

"I don't know. Hunter said he'd never seen him like that before. I get the feeling he cares about you."

Hope blooms in my chest, but is stunted by my own insecurity. Or maybe it's a lack of faith.

"Well, he could've fooled me. Oh wait." I let out a harsh laugh. "He did."

"I can't believe I'm actually saying this." She gives me a tight smile. "But maybe you should give him another chance."

Stunned, I do a double-take. "You're kidding, right, Liv? After all the warnings to stay away from him? Now you're joining the Rex fan club," I proclaim, my hand going to my temple to ease the mounting tension.

"What does that mean?" she questions, and I shake my head, brushing it off.

"Never mind."

Her cell phone dings and she retrieves it from her purse, a wide smile curving her lips as she views the screen.

"Let me guess. Hunter?"

"Yup." She practically bounces as she gets up from the chair. "I have to run. We have a lunch date."

"On his desk?" I tease, coming from behind mine to walk her out to the elevators.

The car opens and she steps on, flashing me a flirty grin and a glimpse of her lacy pink bra. "Maybe."

"Hussy," I mouth, just as the doors close.

I casually stroll past Tillie's desk, watching as she stares intently at her computer, her long, manicured nails tapping feverishly on the keyboard. "Any messages?" My words come out casual, but I can't help biting on my lip.

"Nope, nothing new." She continues to focus on her work.

"Okay, thanks." My stomach dips with disappointment but then I remember I asked for this. This is what I want.

Maybe if I keep telling myself that, I'll start to believe it.

# CHAPTER TWENTY-FIVE

## CRAZY TALK

"Rex. It's good to see you," Dr. Billings greets me as I step further into her office.

A large part of me feels like this is a mistake. But something prompted me to make the appointment, and since I'm here, I might as well see if she has anything valuable to offer.

She takes a seat across from me in her swivel chair, white-lined pad placed on her lap, black hair pushed up into a high bun. Her matching designer glasses rest against her face, blue suit perfectly pressed. She looks more like an attorney than a therapist, until she opens her mouth.

"So, Rex," she begins, folding her hands across the length of the pad. "I was both surprised and pleased to get your call. It's been a few months and it sounds like we need to catch up."

I don't respond right away. Instead, I glance around her small office, books neatly organized on the shelf, framed academic degrees lining the walls. I'm aware of the stiff leather couch I'm sitting on, where hundreds of other patients have sat before me spilling all their fucked-up issues, and many will after me as well.

"Rex." The even keel of her voice gets my attention.

"Yeah?"

"So, tell me what's happening. Tell me how things are going."

"They've been better." My knee is bouncing with nerves, wanting to be anywhere but here. I hate this fucking place. It always makes me feel like I'm crazy.

"Expound, please." She taps her pencil against her pad in time with the second hand ticking on the clock, driving me toward temporary insanity.

"I met a girl. A girl who's making me say and do crazy shit." I bite down on my thumbnail, watching Dr. Billings fight back a smile.

"What do you mean?" She starts jotting down notes with her pencil, making me wonder what the hell she's writing. I've barely said anything.

"Just crap I normally wouldn't say. I find it coming out, even *wanting* to say it sometimes."

"Are we talking about feelings, Rex?" She pauses with her pencil in mid-air, appraising me in a way that only a therapist can.

"Yeah. And I don't know how to handle them. Well," my other leg joins in on the bounce, "I may not get a chance to now anyway."

"I'm not following."

"It was my birthday yesterday, and you know I hate that fucking day. Well, I came home to find her, Vanessa that is, making me dinner and I lost it. Said some hateful things to her and I'm not sure she'll forgive me. She's actually one of the reasons I'm here." I exhale a smug laugh. "She calls me on my shit. She basically told me to stop using the past as an excuse to be an asshole."

Dr. Billings raises her chin, head tilted slightly to the side. "I like this girl already."

"It just reminded me of how fucked up I am, where I come from." I brace an arm firmly against the couch as if it can give me the support I need. "Everything feels so fucked up sometimes."

"What does, Rex?"

"I'm the product of a selfish, alcoholic mother and a low-life asshole for a father. The only positive thing I can think of is Hunter." I swallow hard. "And Tyler, of course. Hunter never treated me as anything less, even when I told him the truth."

"And why would he? He loves you. Blood doesn't change that. Look, Rex," she places her pad on the side table, "I see people all the time who come from dysfunctional families, who end up closer to friends or other people's families than they are to their own. Tell me, who brought you up, Rex? Who raised you?"

"Daniel did," I mutter, recalling the memories I have of him as a child.

"Daniel was your father in the ways that mattered, Rex. He loved you; he raised you until he passed away. That's the only father you've ever known." She rolls her chair closer. "You know, Rex, you have to stop looking at yourself in such a negative light all the time. You're a good person."

"Am I?" I stare at the yellow paint on the wall, thinking about Vanessa. "She gave me a picture of Tyler and me as a gift, so I would remember him."

"That's a lovely thing for her to do. She must care about you." She says it with a reassuring smile on her face, yet I don't feel sure about anything.

"I think she did." Regret rolls off of me in waves, my stomach dizzy with it.

"And I'm sure she still does. Whatever you said," she laughs, "I'm sure it was a whopper, but nothing that can't be fixed. You just might have to work a bit harder than you're used to. But...." Her fingers toy with the pearls around her neck. "It sounds to me like she might be worth it."

My lips turn up of their own volition. "Yeah, I think she just might be. And... I-I've been thinking about Tyler a lot, too. Trying to remember what you said about not blaming myself. But it's so fucking hard sometimes. He told me over and over again how he didn't like that babysitter." I thrust a hand roughly through my hair, guilt shrouding my words. "He was trying to tell me, in his own way, give me clues, but I didn't listen. I thought he was being a pain in the ass because he was younger and wasn't able to tag along with Hunter and me. If only I had listened, maybe, just maybe—"

"Rex." She sits forward on an exhale of breath. "I don't want you to do this to yourself. There is no maybe. You were a child. Period. You were not responsible for your brother in that way. There is only one person who was, and since your father was no longer living, we both know who that was. Now, tell me." She leans back in her chair. "Have you had any interaction with your mother?"

"I've run into her, but that's about it. She hasn't changed and she's not going to. There's really no hope for any kind of a relationship there."

"Okay. And while we've discussed it before, I seem to hear more acceptance in your voice now. So this is what I'd like you to think about. Why don't you start using your energy on the people that matter in your life, as opposed to the ones that take away from it. I don't want to see you continuing to let the past define you because that will lead you down a dark road, Rex... and you've traveled that path before. It's time to chart a new course." She gets up and walks behind her desk. "Since I squeezed you in today and we didn't have a lot of time, why don't we schedule another session?" she suggests, flipping pages in her appointment book.

"Do I have to?" I joke, pushing off the couch and heading for the door. "I'll be in touch."

"Okay, Rex. You know where I am. Feel free to reach out via phone if you need to. Take care of yourself."

"Thanks, Doc."

The protective coating I have whenever I'm sitting in her office slides away the moment I step outside. Everything changes when I walk off—the bright sky turns dark, the sun hiding behind my clouded past. Uncertainty swells within me as my feet hit the cement, but there's one thing that keeps me going now. One person who has shined a light on a side of me I never knew existed, who makes me want to get to know the person she sees when she looks at me.

And I sure as hell won't give her up. Not without a fight.

I pull my cell phone from the pocket of my jeans, finding Vanessa's number and sending her a text.

***Hope you got my message. And just in case you're wondering, I'm still thinking about you. And I'm so sorry... for everything.***

I'm not expecting a response, which is a good thing since I don't get one. I shove the phone back in my pocket, checking my watch and discovering I've only got ten minutes until I need to be at work. My day consists of back-to-back tattoos so there won't be much time to breathe or think—which works for me.

The shop is crazy busy when I arrive and the energy here brings me the best kind of high. The humming of the tattoo machine is music to my ears, the smell of cleaning products and sterile air making me feel right at home. And this is my home now. Dr. Billings was right about that. Zeek and the other artists I work with have become like my family. We share stories and bond over our art, something a lot of people don't understand.

"Hey, man," Zeek yells when I walk in. "How ya doing?" he asks, while Stevie and Jaden look up and give me a quick chin nod before focusing back on their clients.

"Good. Ready to get to work." I head to my station, my mind still back in Dr. Billings' office.

He comes over holding one of our portfolios. "Check it out. These are the photos I took of the tattoo you did on Sienna. It's fucking brilliant, man."

"Wow." And I'm actually impressed with my own prowess. "You're right, I am fucking brilliant," I brag, closing the book and handing it back to him.

"And fucking full of yourself," Jaden calls out, earning a chuckle from Stevie.

Zeek shakes his head and cackles. "Well, she obviously thought so, too. You just missed her. She came by to express her *gratitude,* I guess, and damn if I didn't wish I was the one she was grateful to."

I point a finger toward the floor. "She was here?" I ask, and he nods. "Well, I'm glad I wasn't then."

"That's right." He gives me a shove. "You have more important things to think about."

"Yeah, I do, asshole, like getting my station ready for my next tattoo," I jab, starting for the back of the shop.

I'm not used to this—this tightening in my chest, these feelings I don't know how to handle—being consumed by thoughts of a woman. I've never had female friends, never needed them or wanted them, and to be honest, why would I? My opinion of women stems from my mother, and we all know what a fine example she set for me.

But Vanessa's changed all that.

She walked in with her brutal honesty and her confident as hell sway, and made me look at myself. Made me want to trust. Made me want to say and do shit you couldn't have paid me to do before.

Fuck.

I delve into my pocket for my phone and slide the screen, checking for any sign of her. But there is none. My eyes dart around as I contemplate what to do. I've never chased after a woman before, but then again, I've never met one quite like Vanessa. I let out a jagged breath and type her a text.

### *Is there any way I can see you tonight?*

My foot taps against the grainy floor as I wait for any acknowledgement from her, smiling when the chime sounds, but frowning when I read her words.

### *No.*

### *Why not?*

*I have plans.*

*Bullshit.*

*I do have plans.*

*Okay, then tomorrow night?*

*I can't. I have work to do.*

*So when can I see you then?*

*I don't know, Rex.*

*Fine.*

What the hell else am I supposed to say?

Frustration surges through me with the uncontrollable force of a gale wind and I toss my phone onto the table, only to end up picking it up off the floor. When I push to my feet, Zeek is right behind me.

"You okay, man? You seem a bit edgy." He sizes me up with his deep green eyes.

"Yeah, I'm good, thanks. Just ready to get to work."

He clasps my shoulder, forcing my eyes his way. "Listen, I know how frustrating they can be. I've got more than I can handle with Tabitha. Sometimes she has me so twisted up, I don't know if I'm coming or going. And, I prefer to be coming," he jokes, squeezing my shoulder again.

"Yeah, I hear you on that one. Thanks, Zeek."

"Don't mention it." He walks toward the front of the shop, then swings his head around. "Hey. You want to hang out with Tabitha and me tonight? I want to watch a ball game and she hates baseball. It would be nice to have some more testosterone in the room. If you don't have any plans."

"Sure. I'll come by." Because I definitely don't have any other plans.

Not more than a minute later, the sound of my brother's voice alerts me to his presence and I glance toward the door where he's chatting with Zeek. He heads toward my station, his face set in determination. Of what, I have no idea.

"Hey, bro. To what do I owe this honor? Two visits in less than a month to the other side of the tracks. You feeling okay?" I chuckle, and he shoots me his signature older brother smirk.

"I actually just came by to check on you. The last time I saw you, you weren't in the greatest shape." He leans back against the counter, one hand in his pants' pocket, legs crossed at the ankles.

"I'm all right," I volunteer, which is a load of shit and he already knows it. "I went to see Dr Billings."

"Oh yeah, how was that?"

"It went well in that Dr. Billings sort of way. It always does when I'm in there, but the moment I step out into the real world my shit clings to me again."

"More importantly though, did you talk to Vanessa?" And just the mention of her name has me shifting on my feet.

"Yeah."

"And, how did it go?"

"Hmph... not well." Regret rolls off my tongue. "She doesn't want to have anything to do with me right now."

"I'm sorry, man. But you can't blame her, can you? You were pretty harsh." His voice is sympathetic, but his words cut me deep because I know he's right.

"Yeah, I know. Do you think Olivia might put in a good word for me?" I ask, my jaw clenched so tight my teeth are beginning to hurt.

A frown settles around his mouth. "I think she already did."

"Well, from the look on your face, I'd say it didn't go well." And without realizing it, I'm digging my fingers into the back of the chair so hard it could leave a mark.

"Olivia said she's got a mind of her own." He picks up my sketches from the table, admiring them. "She's not easily swayed."

That's my girl. Or at least she *was* mine. The thought makes my stomach harden.

I snag the seat in front of Hunter, dropping down with an annoyed breath. "Yeah. She's pretty much ignoring my texts. Maybe I should just give her the space she needs."

"Or maybe you need to step up your efforts." He drums a foot against the floor, grinning smugly. "Since when do you ever take things lying down, Rex? You've never had a problem going after what you wanted before, so what's different now?"

Hunter's words stay with me the rest of the day, long after all the customers have gone and I'm closing up the shop alone. With nothing but time and eerie silence swirling around me, I realize he had a point. I don't sit back and wait for things to happen. But in this case, for whatever reason, I'm worried about being rejected. Then again, what have I got to lose?

I slide the screen on my cell and type Vanessa out yet another text.

**Go out with me.**

Her response is immediate. I'll take that as a good sign even though her words are not encouraging.

**No.**

I try to be playful.

**That doesn't sound very convincing. Is that a maybe?**

*No.*

Well, that didn't go well. I guess there's always tomorrow.

# CHAPTER TWENTY-SIX

## COMPLETELY INCORRIGIBLE

*Vanessa*

It's been six days since I've seen Rex, not that I'm counting. Nights are the hardest. When I close my eyes, I can see that lopsided grin, feel his lips against mine, the pressure of his rough hands trailing my body. I've been spending a ridiculous amount of time with Olivia and Ryder, and they've been terrific. The sting is still there, but somehow it helps me forget, if only for a short time.

Every day Rex sends me messages and I continue to come up with excuses as to why I can't see him. I know that if I give in, I'll crumble and fall into his arms.

So much for being strong.

I have no idea what we had. But I know it was more than sex and it was starting to mean something—to me. That's where I fault myself. I should've known better because he's too messed up in his head. There were so many signs along the way, but I chose to ignore them.

I'm one to talk really. My past isn't sparkly and glittery, laced with fairy tales and kisses goodnight. There were no blankets of unconditional love wrapped around me, keeping me warm and safe. For me it was the chill of the unspoken word, a house weighted down by silence. Strangers pretending to be a family.

My chest seizes up at the memory.

*I pressed my hand to the glass, watching Patty play ball with her dad, and my belly started to hurt. She looked like she was giggling and having so much fun and I wanted so badly to be her. My lips dropped into a pout but I tried to smile big when she looked up at the window and waved to me.*

*The screen door slammed and her mom came outside with a happy smile, and I wanted that, too. Even though I couldn't hear Patty from there, I knew what she was saying because it was Sunday and on Sunday her mom always made brownies. I let out a big breath, staring at the hard ground, wondering if I jumped, if my parents would notice, if they would even care.*

I can practically still smell the melted chocolate from the brownies her mom made every Sunday. Such a simple thing, but to me, it was everything, because I never experienced it yet longed for it so desperately.

Now I'm older, but the feeling is the same—a physical ache in your gut from wanting something so badly, and in this case, even when you know it's probably not good for you. And that's the fucked up part about all of this. I actually think Rex could be good for me. He brings out qualities in me I didn't know I possessed, makes me feel things I didn't know I was capable of, makes me want things that absolutely terrify me.

I grab onto the edge of my desk, inhaling a deep breath through my nose and exhaling through my mouth. That's what this is all about. This is my fear talking. After what happened, I'm afraid to fall because somewhere deep down, I know he could be the one to truly hurt me. The other night is glaring proof of that.

"You all right, Vanessa?"

Tillie's voice ships me back to the now and I release the death grip I have on my desk. "Yes, I'm good." I flap a hand in her direction. "Come in. So," I continue, slapping a smile on my face. "You ready for the Hamilton launch tomorrow night? This is the big time."

"Yes," she says, her enthusiasm bursting through her grin. "I can't wait. I have my dress and shoes all picked out, and I'm getting my hair done right after work. If I know you, you've got everything done right down to the last letter. This event is going off without a hitch."

"Yes, which reminds me." I glide my chair up to the computer, clicking my to-do list on the desktop. "I need you to finish putting the name tags together. That's the last thing on my list. Can you have that done by tomorrow at noon?"

"Absolutely!" She springs up from the chair, continuing to chomp on her gum. "I'll get to that right now."

"Great, thanks. Oh, and Tillie," I remind her, and she spins around just as she reaches the door, her red ponytail flapping in the air, "don't forget, no gum tomorrow night."

She clicks her heels together, a hand to her forehead in salute. "No worries. It shall be done."

A nostalgic smile crosses my lips at her eagerness, remembering when I first started out at the company seven years ago. Even then all I could think about was rising to the top, working my way up and getting my own office with an actual window. Maybe even a decent view of Manhattan. And I made it happen. I'd love for Tillie to have the same success.

I finish printing out the list of attendees for the party when my cell phone alerts me of an incoming text. Without looking, I already know who it is. And of course, I'm right.

**Go out with me.**

I shake my head at his persistence and even smile because there's no one here to bear witness to it. Then I type back a reply. The same one I've sent all week.

**No.**

Not more than a second later, he responds.

*You know you want to.*

I bust out laughing so loud, anyone listening might think I was crazy. He's completely incorrigible. My fingers get busy on the keypad.

*No I don't.*

*Come on, go out with me.*

*No.*

My fingers parade along the edge of my desk as I wait for his reply.

*Okay.*

Time stops when I see his response. I think my heart does, too. Panic swells inside of me, causing my limbs to feel shaky, and I'm sitting down.

I type back with hesitant fingers.

*Okay?*

*Yeah.*

What the hell does that mean? Is he giving up? And what's wrong with me? I'm the idiot that's been saying no and pushing him away. I can't expect him to follow me around like a puppy dog with his tail between his legs.

I'm about to bite my newly manicured fingernail when I think better of it. Instead, I bury my cell phone in the depths of my purse and get back to work, attempting to push Rex Grayson out of my mind.

Since I can't get him out of my heart.

"Thanks for meeting me," I tell Olivia, as we sit on the cushy leather sofa in the lobby of the Clark building where the event is being held tomorrow. "Here." I hand her the latte I picked up from Starbucks. "Mocha Frappuccino, extra chocolate."

"Thanks, V." She winks before taking a sip. "Just what I needed. Geez," she settles back, adding, "I feel like I've seen you more this past week than I have the rest of the month combined. Hunter's feeling a bit neglected." She laughs as she crosses her legs, her foot bouncing in circles. "But he'll deal."

"Yeah," is all I say, staring at my coffee like it has the answer to all of life's problems.

"Hey." Her voice is soft. "You okay?"

"I miss Rex." The words come out so quiet I can barely hear them, but they resonate loudly within my core.

"I know you do, sweetie." She sets her coffee down on the table, turning to face me. "I don't understand why you won't agree to see him. You're being stubborn. And if I recall correctly, you've said the same thing to me a time or two before."

My throat is thick with feeling. "I'm scared."

"Because...." She waits, and the uncertainty is clear in my tone when I answer.

"I don't know."

"I think you do know. Because you were falling for him. And I get it." She giggles, pinching me playfully in the arm. "I'm in love with a Grayson, too, remember? Those Grayson boys are pretty hard to resist."

An uneasiness washes over me, knowing that Rex had a different father, but I blink it away. "I didn't *say* I was in love with him. We haven't even known each other that long," I protest.

"No. You didn't. But you were definitely beginning to fall for him."

She stretches her head to the side, trying to catch my eyes. "Right?"

"Yes. But I'm having a hard time letting go of what he said to me. It hurt, you know? I guess I'm afraid to let myself get in deeper because I'm afraid he'll hurt me again."

"I don't know what to say, V. I'm not going to blow smoke up your ass and tell you that he won't. I have no way of knowing that. I also know that your view on relationships was tainted from the start, and that it's hard for you to let go and forgive. But in this case, it might just be worth it. I can't decide that for you, though." She taps a finger against her lips. "But I do know this. You haven't been yourself in a week. So I think that says something." She giggles. "I just don't know exactly what it says."

My eyes rove to the quiet cell phone sitting on the table. It's been several hours since Rex's last text. I'm wondering if he's given up on me. It's not like he doesn't have a million other prospects. The idea of him with anyone else gives me heartburn in the worst way.

"You willing it to ring?" Liv asks, picking it up and placing it in my hand. "You can always be the one to call." She huffs a loud sigh. "But I know you won't." She glances up at the large clock on the wall. "I have to run. I have a meeting with my editor. Think about what I said, okay?"

"I will, Liv. Thanks." I stand and walk with her past the bronze doors out into the sunshine.

"I'll talk to you later. Oh!" she calls out with a blast of energy. "I made an appointment for us at Josie's at eleven on Sunday morning to look at wedding dresses." She twirls her hand whimsically in the air. "So add it to your list. And by the way, this place is gorgeous, V. Good luck with the event tomorrow night."

"Thanks," I reply, and she gives me a quick kiss on the cheek, taking off down the street, her brown locks dancing behind her back.

My cell phone chimes an incoming text and I jump, hoping maybe it's Rex, but my spirits take a dive when I see that it's Ryder.

**Pick up your cell in two.**

As soon as it rings, I answer it, interested to see what his cryptic message is all about. "Hey, Ryder."

"Don't sound so thrilled to talk to me. Should I take this to mean you haven't gotten back together with Rex?"

"Ha! Were we ever together? I think we were just screwing, weren't we?" I bark, earning me a dirty look from an elderly woman walking by.

"You know...." He pauses as if contemplating his next words. "I'm not into guys or anything, but Rex is good looking, and if you don't want him, I'm sure there are a ton of other women who do."

"Is this your idea of reverse psychology? Something that's supposed to motivate me?"

"Did it work?" he asks, and I laugh.

"Not really. So anyway, are we set for tomorrow night?"

"Yeah. I'll be there around five. Hang on," he says, and I duck into a small pastry shop to grab a croissant. "Okay, so yeah, what time will you be there?"

"I'll be there at four. Hold on a sec, Ryder." I step up to the counter, taking a quick look at the sandwich menu. "Can I have tuna salad on a croissant please, to go?" I hold the phone back up to my ear. "Okay, so I'll be there and Matilda will be there to help me around the same time."

"The cute little redhead is coming to the event? Since when does she attend these things?" Ryder asks, but there's more than just curiosity in his voice.

"Since my boss is considering her for a promotion," I reply, paying for my food and striding out the door.

"Oh, okay."

"Hmph. And by the way. The cute redhead is single," I hint, waiting to see how he'll respond.

"Good to know. Thanks, darlin'. All right. I'll see you tomorrow."

"Yup. See you then." I end the call but proceed to scroll through my text messages, just to make sure I didn't miss any new ones from Rex.

I didn't.

His voice is in my head, though. I hear him calling me Blondie, feel his smile tickling my skin, the deep rumble of his chuckle. If I were an artist, I could paint it on a canvas. Beautiful, bright yellows and oranges with streaks of red. He makes me feel alive.

Maybe I should take an art class. Or maybe I should just pick up the damn phone.

# CHAPTER TWENTY-SEVEN

## A CRIPPLING FEAR

### *Vanessa*

A million things need to be done before we leave for the event, and what am I doing? Glancing over at my phone for the hundredth time today. I haven't heard from Rex since his text yesterday and I don't know why I'm surprised. For an entire week he apologized, asked me out, then apologized again. Still, I turned him down. All because of fear.

Fear is a powerful thing. It can motivate you to achieve greatness, yet it can also cripple your existence, threatening to hold you back from the very things that could actually enrich your life.

I want to take that step forward, really I do. Yet each time I lift my foot it feels unsure, shaky, worried about taking too big of a leap. Mostly, though, I don't want to trip and fall, get a gash that's too deep to ever heal. I'm already working through the ones I was privileged enough to receive earlier on in my life. I don't need any more.

"Okay. The boxes are all set to go," Tillie announces, walking into my office with a confident strut. Her hair is a waterfall of red with a dress and shoes to match.

"Wow, Tillie, you look great! That's a lot of red."

"Too much?" She looks down at herself, running her hands along the seam of her dress.

"Absolutely not. It suits you. You look stunning," I compliment, watching her cheeks add more red to the ensemble as I gather up the last of my paperwork and deposit it in my briefcase.

"All right." I scan the paper quickly. "Let me just go through this list one more time before we head out, just to be sure we have everything." I check off the last of the items with black pen. "Okay, looks good. Let's go."

"I'm so excited I can hardly contain myself!" Tillie exclaims in the company car on the way over. "I still can't believe that I'm going to get the opportunity to move up from answering the phones."

"Why not, Tillie?" I take out the small mirror from my bag to check my lipstick. "You work hard, and you don't just answer phones, either. You basically organize the department." I close the compact and stow it in my purse, then turn to her. "You deserve this."

"Thanks, Vanessa. That means a lot," she replies, a grateful smile turning up her lips.

"Okay, so when we get there, I'm going to need you to set up the welcome table with the name cards and organize the promotion packs in the larger hall. And if you could go around and be sure we have enough chairs at all the tables that would be fantastic."

"Absolutely."

The car pulls up to the Clark building and we gather our things, sliding off the leather upholstery and into the late day sun. George, who heads up logistics for all the events, greets us at the door.

"Hey, Vanessa." He rolls a cart onto the sidewalk. "A good portion of your boxes arrived this afternoon. Is this everything else?"

"Yes, it sure is. How's the room looking?" I ask, as we accompany him through the double glass doors to the lobby.

"It looks good. It's everything you requested, and the tables and chairs have been set up accordingly." He motions with a hand toward the boxes on the cart. "Where do you want all this?"

"In the main ballroom would be great, thanks."

"Okay. I'll get to that and check in with you later. Let me know if you need anything else," he says with a nod, taking off for the main hall.

Someone pinches me from behind and I turn around to find Ryder, complete with an enthusiastic grin. "Hey, you."

"Hey, yourself. You ready for this?" His gaze drifts over to Tillie as he blatantly checks her out. She plays right into it, fanning her hair over her shoulder, shooting him a flirty smile.

"I am. You remember Matilda, don't you, Ryder?" I smirk, waving my hand as if she's on display.

"Please, call me Tillie." She extends her hand to him and I almost keel over laughing when he brings it to his lips for a kiss. Her cheeks continue to darken, so obviously enthralled by Ryder's charm.

"Okay!" I clap my hands together. "I'm going to make sure everything is ready." My eyes dart from Tillie to Ryder. "Care to join me?" I ask, and feel a pang in my belly when I catch the familiar scent of sandalwood from someone passing by, instantly reminding me of Rex. That prompts me to hunt for my cell phone and check for any new texts or voicemails, exhaling a winded sigh when I discover there are none. It's been a whole day now and I've heard nothing from him.

Desperately needing a distraction, I push through the doors to the main ballroom, a smile giving way when I notice it looks perfect. Round tables with white linen tablecloths and simple arrangements of exotic flowers are scattered about the room, buffet tables along the perimeter, the bar taking up the length of the far wall. There are two violinists seated toward the back that will play classical pieces during the event, something Jonathan felt adamant about and I didn't argue.

Ryder goes to chat with the bartenders, while Tillie takes care of getting the welcome table ready for the arrival of our guests. I glance at my watch, noticing it's only five fifteen and we're forty-five minutes ahead of schedule.

I grab the numbered place cards from one of the boxes and begin setting them out on the tables, when someone clearing their throat garners my attention. I swivel around to find Ryder nodding his head toward the entryway, smiling.

A strange awareness prickles my skin, and as my head turns to find out the source of his amusement, I nearly lose my footing.

Reclined against the doorframe in a black leather jacket, white t-shirt hanging loosely over a pair of blue jeans, and a mess of dark hair, is Rex.

It feels like it's been raining for days, but the moment I see him, the gray morphs into a panorama of color. I want to clutch at my chest, the sheer sight of him filling the hollow space inside of me.

I will my shaky legs to move without giving out but keep my poker face on, not wanting him to know he's getting to me. As I inch closer, I notice his hair, slightly longer in the front, making me want to reach out and smooth it to the side. It suddenly feels like an eternity since I last saw him. The smile he's wearing soothes the ache that's been growing since we've been apart.

"Hiya, Blondie," he says in that cocky as hell way of his, eyes dancing, my heart doing a pitter-patter of its own.

"Rex. What are you doing here?" I try to keep my voice quiet, not wanting to draw any attention. "I'm working."

"I kind of got that," he says, "but you weren't really responding to my messages so you left me no choice."

"Come on." I gesture with my head toward the hall and he follows. His scent alone makes my knees wobbly and I find myself closing my eyes briefly and inhaling him.

I walk up to the welcome table that Tillie conveniently disappears from and open the guest book. I'm fiddling with the pages when I feel Rex pressing up against me from behind, his lips in my hair. His hands remain at his sides, yet I feel him everywhere as if they were touching me, his nearness a cocoon around my body. My cheeks warm, goose bumps flare up all over my skin.

"I couldn't let another day go by without seeing you. I miss you," he whispers and I suck in a breath. "Tell me you don't miss me and I'll walk away. I swear I'll leave you alone. You won't ever have to see me again."

Every ounce of my being wants to scream that I don't, but my hearts wins out, the truth flowing endlessly like a river. "I can't."

"Go out with me," he whispers again, his breath making me hot, his voice caressing the deepest part of me. The cold, dark place only he's been able to reach.

I blow out a breath, my walls tumbling down around me, shield cracking under his persistence. Turning around, I let my eyes wander over his face; the endless brown in his eyes, the smooth edge of his brow, those full, sculptured lips, that strong jaw coated with a dusting of stubble. The face that keeps me awake at night, haunting me, daring me to live, to take a chance.

And I want to so desperately.

"What do you want, Rex?" I exhale, slumping against the table, my strength disintegrating before his eyes.

"It's simple. I want *you*."

"You're still relentless," I breathe out with what little breath he hasn't stolen from me.

"Is that a yes?" He edges closer, his voice deep, our knees practically touching now.

"Okay." I choke out the word, squeezing it past the ball of nerves in my throat.

"*Okay*?" he repeats, his eyes telling me he doesn't believe what he heard.

"Yes," I confirm, and the answering grin I'm gifted with is blinding.

"Great." He runs a hand through his hair, staring at the ground before returning his deep brown gaze back to me. "Okay, so... I'll be in touch."

"You'll be in touch?" I laugh, and his face grows serious, eyes piercing mine.

"I missed that sound." He closes the gap between us, and my eyelashes flutter when his lips, warm and soft, find my cheek. "I'll be in touch."

And then he walks away, leaving me mesmerized by his ability to do what no other could before him—somehow chisel his way into my heart, carving out a spot all his own.

Once he's gone, I sag back against the table, attempting to catch my breath, but finding it impossible to hide the runaway smile on my face or the relentless pounding inside my chest.

The rest of the event goes off without a hitch—a whirlwind of conversation, captivating speakers, laughter, and drink. I couldn't care less though. I'm sitting on a cloud in a crystal blue sky, floating. The only thing I can think about.

I've got a date with Rex Grayson.

My feet are on fire by the time I stumble to the elevator of my apartment building at midnight. The event was a huge success and every part of my body is feeling it. A relaxing breath leaves my mouth as I slide off my shoes, looking forward to soaking my tired muscles in a warm bath.

With heavy eyelids and a smile that hasn't left my face since Rex paid me a visit, I slink onto my floor, hauling my briefcase that suddenly feels like it weighs a ton over my shoulder. A glint of silver in front of the door catches my eye, and moving closer, I discover a giant tin. There's a note on top, so I drop my bags to the ground and unfold it, grinning when I see Rex's handwriting inside.

*Meet me tomorrow night at 7:00 at Loews Theater on 39th Street for some death and destruction. I trust this will be enough popcorn for you.*

*Until tomorrow.*

*Rex*

I press my lips together to suppress the squeak that wants to escape at his thoughtfulness. I've never looked forward to death and destruction so much in my entire life.

# CHAPTER TWENTY-EIGHT

## ARE YOU PAYING ATTENTION?

Why the hell do I have to work on Saturdays? I should've taken the day off today. I've done four tattoos and if you asked me what the hell they were, I couldn't even tell you. There's only one thing on my mind and that's seeing Vanessa tonight.

I hope she liked my present. I'm not really a flowers type of a guy, but maybe the popcorn let her know I was thinking of her. If she knew how much, it would probably scare her off. I know it terrifies me. But I'm trying to push past the fear and focus on what Dr. Billings implied in our session. *Pay attention to the people that add value to your life.* And Vanessa definitely adds value to mine.

The image of her from yesterday is stamped on my brain. Those sky blue eyes with a sparkle that draws me in like no one else before her, lips that when they smile make me forget my own name. And her heart. She's got so much heart. I don't even think she realizes it.

"All right, Zeek, I'm heading out," I call out, my feet so anxious I can barely keep up with them.

"Early tonight, huh? You got a hot date?" He chuckles, rubbing hand sanitizer between his fingers.

"Something like that." I keep walking, trying to stifle the grin threatening to expose me.

"I figured as much." He props his elbows on the counter. "You didn't act like a dick today."

"I try my best, asshole," I joke, and he straightens, stretching his arms above his head.

"See ya, man."

"Later." I wave my hand in the air as I plod out the door.

The air is crisp, serving as a wake-up call to the strange shit happening in my life. I'm fucking excited about seeing a girl. It's certainly not something that I ever expected but I'm finally acknowledging it, accepting that I want to see where this goes. For the first time in, well, since I can remember, I feel hopeful. Emotions are unfamiliar territory for me so I know I need to tread lightly. Otherwise, fear will pull me under and I'll end up drowning. I've already let that happen once. I refuse to let it happen again.

The theater is packed when I arrive and there's no sign of Vanessa. Doubt festers in my head and I run a jerky hand through my hair, worrying that maybe she changed her mind. I quickly shrug off the thought and zigzag through the crowd to the concession stand. I want to get her that buttery popcorn she's so fond of.

A high school student with blue hair and a nose ring helps me out, and I make sure to have him put extra butter and salt on it. I don't know how she can eat this shit, but I love seeing the smile on her face when she does.

I find an empty corner and wait, trying to avoid checking my watch every few minutes. I'm sure she'll be here. She's probably just running late.

Not more than ten minutes later, she walks through the doors. I stand back and watch her as she scans the lobby for me. Her big, blue eyes are wide, blonde waves bouncing over her shoulders as she peers over heads and around bodies until she finally spots me. And that's when I see it.

The smile that makes me forget to breathe.

We walk toward one another until we meet in the middle, both of us talking at once.

"Hi."

And then we laugh.

"You showed," I say, and her brows dip low in confusion.

"Of course. I never pass up an opportunity for death and destruction." She plucks a kernel from the tub of popcorn and pops it in her mouth, crunching down on it. "Oh, and popcorn."

"And to think," I shrug, "I thought maybe it was my sparkling personality that brought you out."

"You're an added perk," she teases, elbowing me as we search for theater four. "By the way, was this the biggest popcorn they had?" she asks as I hold the door open for her. "Because I like the extra large."

"Somehow I already knew that." I grin and she elbows me again, harder this time. "So where do you want to sit?"

"I'm flexible. I just can't sit too close to the screen."

"Okay, how about here?" I point to a row in the middle of the room. "Good?"

"Yup," she replies, and I follow behind her until we take our seats. "Hey." She flicks her gaze to mine. "Thank you for that tin of popcorn. That was really thoughtful." Her lips meet my cheek in an appreciative kiss that makes me grin.

I did something right.

"So what are we seeing anyway?" She continues to munch loudly on the popcorn and I can't control my laughter from spilling out. "What's so funny?" Her blue eyes narrow as she arms her hands with bunches of popcorn, ready to strike.

"It's just that you're too darn cute. That's all."

Her eyes soften and the popcorn lands in her mouth instead of on me. "Okay. In that case, you've been spared."

"Shhh... quiet. The movie's starting," I warn, and she shakes her head, giggling.

I honestly couldn't give two shits about the movie. The fact I'm so close to her again that I can hear her laugh, smell her raspberry shampoo, feel her knee brushing against mine. That's the only thing I'm focusing on—everything else is static.

In the back of my mind, I know she probably still doesn't trust me. But I'm going to prove to her that she can, that she matters to me. I know I'll probably fuck up. If I'm lucky, though, maybe she'll be there to catch me.

The beginning credits roll and she gasps from beside me. "Oh my God," she says in a hushed voice. "It's *A Good Day to Die Hard*. You remembered."

Of course I did. There's not a single thing I don't remember about her since we met. And as soon as I heard they were having a Bruce Willis marathon, I was all over it.

I'm not even paying attention to the damn movie. Instead, I'm stealing glances at her, watching the way her cheeks puff up every time she takes a handful of popcorn, her eyes focused on the screen. It's still crazy to me that she loves these movies. Although, if I had to sit through a chick flick with her, I would. I just wouldn't tell her that.

Halfway through the movie, I lean over, my breath barely a whisper above her ear. "I'm so glad you're here," I say, and she shivers when my lips graze her skin.

She turns her head and smiles, and I know she feels it too. I reach out, threading our fingers together, and she looks down at our hands before returning her attention to the screen. Her lips curl at the corners, my heart racing in response.

It's a good thing I've seen this movie, because I couldn't have recalled one single detail. The only thing I do have memorized is the girl sitting beside me, who stands up and stretches now that the show is over.

"That was awesome!" She tosses her empty box of popcorn into the trash on the way out. "Didn't you think?"

"Yeah, it was great."

We follow the hoards of people back through the lobby and out into the night. The sky is filled with stars and the New York City streets are buzzing with energy. As much as I miss Boston sometimes, there's something about this city that makes me feel alive.

"So, what do you want to do now?" I casually slide my hand over, twining our fingers together again. I'm not usually one for holding hands, but I can't not touch her.

"I don't know. Let's just walk. It's a beautiful night. So," she pauses, "did you ever make out in a movie theater when you were younger?"

"Hell, yes."

"Geez, don't hold back." She giggles, her lips edged with sarcasm.

"Hey, you asked. It was ninth grade with Emily Sanchez. Kind of hard to forget. It was the first time a girl's hand had wandered down to the promised land."

Her head falls back as she laughs. "The promised land?"

"Fuck, yes. What about you?"

"No. I never did, but always wanted to," she says, sounding regretful.

"Well, you're about thirty minutes too late. All you had to do was say something and I would have obliged. I could've been your first."

The twinkle in her eye when she turns to the side tells me she wants to say something else, but instead I'm on the receiving end of a comfortable silence as we continue strolling the streets of Manhattan.

We walk a few more blocks until a small shop comes into view, the display window filled with cakes and a variety of pastries. Vanessa stops to admire the sweets, and I think I see her mouth frothing at the corners.

"You want to go in?"

"What gave it away? My longing looks at the chocolate croissant," she teases, and I grab her, tugging her up against my body, swallowing any distance between us.

"You. Are. Feisty," I breathe out, my eyes lowering to her lips, tongue anxious to taste her again. But I hold back. After the fucked up comments at my apartment, I want her to know that she means more to me than just my physical attraction to her. "Come on, feisty. Let's go in so you can get your fix."

After ordering some dessert, we take a seat at a table for two by the window. I watch in amusement as she eats her croissant slowly, picking it apart as if it were a frog in biology class back in high school.

"I went to see my therapist," I blurt out, taken aback by my blunt admission.

She pushes her plate to the center of the table, giving me her undivided attention. "Oh? How did that go?"

"Good. She confirmed what I've always known. That I'm crazier than a shithouse owl."

"*What*?" She laughs. "What does that mean?"

"I don't have a fucking clue. It's something I heard my father say once when I was a kid and it kind of stuck with me." I pick at the cake with my fork, thinking about my dad.

"Hey." The soft tone of her voice draws my eyes up. "I'm sorry... about what you told me about who your real father was. That had to turn your life upside down when you found out."

"Yeah." All that shit comes back to me, remembering just how fucked up I was, and how I made sure everyone around me felt it. "I was a mess. Lashed out at everyone. It was Hunter who finally put me in check. Made me own up to my shit. Kind of like you," I tease, tapping her leg with mine under the table. Although I'm not sure she realizes how serious I am. "Whatever though, you know. It's not easy for me, but I'm trying to work through the fucked-upness of my past."

"The fucked-upness?" She giggles, twisting her leg around mine, and I like feeling this connected to her. "I guess I have a bit of that too."

"Have you talked to your parents?"

Her posture stiffens the moment I bring them up. She stares down at her coffee, picking at the edge of the cup with her fingernail.

"No. Not since my mother's call about her getting remarried. I haven't heard from my dad in a few months."

"That stinks." I reach for her free hand, hoping I can give her some sense of comfort. I don't think I'm very good at this kind of stuff, but I'm trying.

"It is what it is. Honestly, I'm really grateful for the people that are in my life now. Those are the ones that matter."

"Does that include me?" I ask, finding myself holding in a breath.

"Yeah, Rex, it does." She glances up from her drink at long last, giving me an amazing view of her eyes, complete and utter sincerity filling their blue depths.

"Good. Hey," I scrub my free hand across my chin, "I—I know I'm not all that great with this communication stuff, but I want you to know I'm working on it. Just fair warning, though, I might fuck up sometimes."

She stands up and rounds the table, taking a seat in my lap. Her fingers weave through my hair as she rests her forehead against mine. "You can be so sweet, Rex," she breathes out, giving me a brief kiss. Her lips are soft and supple, and I relish the way she feels against me. All too soon though, she pulls away, and I want her back.

I want her everywhere.

"Let's go."

Since she's already on my lap, I decide to carry her out the door, wanting to keep my arms around her for as long as possible.

"What are you doing?" she squeals, one of my hands on her ass and the other around her back.

"What does it look like? I'm trying to cop a feel," I joke, and she shakes her head, laughing, her silky hair flapping against my face.

"Are you intent on carrying me the entire way to my apartment?" Her cheeks rise with her smile and she's so damn adorable.

"You know I've got the stamina." I wink, squeezing her ass. It's kind of hard not to when it's right under my hand.

"Yes, that you do," she says with a knowing grin, just as I set her down gently on the ground.

"That's it?" She puts her hands on her hips, feigning frustration.

"Well, truth be told, you're kind of heavy."

"Ahh! You sure know a way to a girl's heart," she huffs, stomping off playfully, and I catch up to her, wrapping an arm around her waist and pulling her to my side.

By the time we make it back to her building, she's yawning like crazy. It's only eleven but yesterday was probably exhausting for her. As much as I don't want the night to end, I know it has to.

"So, you know you're not getting any tonight, right?" she deadpans, standing in front of the door to her apartment.

I let out a low chuckle, pivoting to face her, rolling the ends of her hair between my fingers. "I already got what I came for."

"Oh really, and what's that?"

"I got to see you smile again," I whisper, and she jerks her chin up, mouth falling open. Edging closer, I let my thumb graze her bottom lip, and she shivers as I drop a kiss on the corner of her mouth. "Goodnight," I murmur, strutting off toward the elevator. But then I remember something and turn back. "Hey, Blondie?" I call out, just as she's putting her key in the lock.

"Yeah?"

"I just realized I didn't tell you how beautiful you looked tonight."

And then I make my grand exit, walking off with a lightness in my chest and the memory of the beaming smile I just left on her face.

# CHAPTER TWENTY-NINE

## I'M LATE, I'M LATE

### *Vanessa*

The sun's rays pour through the curtains, swaying with a gentle breeze that tickles my face—and I smile. I guess that's what one night with Rex Grayson will do to a girl. And he's definitely doing something to me. Butterflies somersault in my belly when I think about our date, all the sweet things he said, how hard he's trying. Just that fact alone is good enough for me. He wants to make an effort, which means he wants to see where this can lead.

I stretch my rested arms out to the side. Sleep came easy to me last night. Even though I had other things on my mind. As much as I wanted to drag Rex into my apartment and maul him, I'm glad I maintained some semblance of self-control.

A reminder tone sounds on my phone and for the life of me, I can't recall what I need to be reminded of this morning. That is, until I slide my phone off the nightstand and see the words *Here comes the bride,* quickly reinforcing where I'm supposed to be—at Josie's Bridal, meeting Olivia.

"Shit!" I yell out loud, before scrambling out of bed to get ready at lightning speed, throwing on whatever clothes I can find, and drawing my hair up in a ponytail. I won't even have time to get a coffee. That's how late I am.

When I show up at the shop, Olivia is just beyond the entrance tapping her foot, arms huddled close to her chest. I probably screwed up her appointment and now she'll have to reschedule.

"Hey, Liv!" I shout, enthusiastically, trying to distract from my tardiness. She knows I don't make a habit of being late, quite the opposite actually, so I'm not sure why she's so upset.

"You know you were supposed to be here forty-five minutes ago, right?" she bites back, and I'm also not used to seeing her so edgy. That's usually my role in our friendship.

"Wait, aren't I usually the bitchy one in this relationship?" I make a lame attempt at a joke but her lips don't budge. "What's wrong with you? You seem stressed."

"And you seem happy," she utters miserably before slumping down in a red velvet chair.

I take a seat next to her, resting a hand on her arm. "What is it? Did you and Hunter have a fight?"

"No." She lowers her chin to her chest, and that's when I see the tears falling freely down her cheeks onto her blouse.

"Hey," I murmur softly. "What's going on? Talk to me, Liv."

"What if Hunter cheats on me?" she sobs, sinking even lower into the chair as if she wants it to swallow her up.

"What are you talking about? Hunter is head over heels in love with you. It's disgusting actually," I joke, and she lets out a tiny laugh through her misery. "Listen, I know years ago your ex-fiancé, who shall remain unnamed, cheated on you with a bimbo, but he was a complete douchebag. Hunter isn't like that. End of story."

"You really think so?" she says in a barely there voice, tear-filled eyes peering up at me.

"Of course I do. You know what this is? This is just nerves, and I know exactly what will cure it."

"What?" she asks, sprinkles of hope for a remedy clear in her eyes.

"A trip to Victoria's Secret, what else?" And I start laughing, thankful when she joins in. I pull some tissue out of my purse and blot her tears away. "Come on." I tug on her hand. "We've got wedding dresses to try on."

Four hours and twenty-five dresses later, she's found the most beautiful gown. So beautiful in fact, that as she's trying it on I feel an unwelcome tear building in the corner of my eye.

Suddenly overwhelmed, my stomach clenches tight, steeped in yearning. After everything I saw my parents go through—a nonexistent love, an affectionless marriage—never in a million years would I have thought I'd want to share my life with someone. But somehow, I feel hopeful, like maybe there's a chance for me after all.

I rise up from the chair and walk over to Olivia, gently touching her shoulders and shifting her away from the full-length mirror to face me. "You look absolutely beautiful, Liv. Wait until Hunter sees you. Honestly, you look like you just walked right out of a fairy tale."

"And you look...." Narrowed blue eyes scrutinize me. "Dare I say... happy?"

"I saw Rex last night," I confess with a sheepish grin.

"I knew it! It's about fucking time!"

The bridal consultant clucks her tongue, distaste clear in her expression, unable to reconcile the foul mouth belonging to the body donning the elegant dress.

"He was so sweet, Liv." I flip my ponytail around my finger. "He seems to want to try—I don't know—to see if this could be anything."

She lays a hand on my cheek. "Well, of course he wants to try. Because it's you, and you're worth it. I'm glad you're letting him in. I know it's not easy for you to do."

"That's the odd thing," I go on, turning her around and helping to unfasten the pearl buttons on the back of the dress. "It seems easy with him for some reason. I don't even recognize who I am when I'm with him."

"Here," the sales clerk interrupts, "let me help you with the rest of those buttons."

I step out of their way when my cell phone pings. My purse is sitting in the corner of the dressing room so I make my way over to retrieve it, grinning like an idiot when I see it's a text from Rex.

*I've been thinking about you all morning.*

*Really?*

*REALLY. I don't know why I didn't kiss you last night.*

*Me either.*

*Do you want to come over tonight and make out?*

"Oh my God!" I laugh, and Olivia spins around.
"Everything okay?"
"Yes, fine," I say through a fit of giggles before I type back eagerly.

*Can I bring my popcorn?*

*Yes.*

*Absolutely then.*

*Now I won't be able to concentrate the rest of the day because I'll be thinking about your lips.*

*Hmmmm.*

*Don't do that. I have to work here.*

*Sorry.*

*Come by at 8.*

*Okay.*

I'm about to throw the phone back in my bag when it chimes again.

***Can't wait to see you, baby.***

How can six typewritten words make my pulse dance under my skin? I type back two, hoping they have the same effect.

*Me too.*

"All set?" Olivia smiles as she walks up to me, glancing back at her dress hanging on the wall.

"Yes." I nudge her shoulder then take her hand in mine. "Let's go admire your dress one more time before we go, shall we?"

"Splendid idea," she replies, and we do a slow stroll up to the gown. "I love it so much." She runs her hands over the silky fabric. "The subtle beading and the way it's off the shoulders and cuts in at the waist, but then flares out at the bottom."

"Me too. It's classy yet very sexy." Then something occurs to me. "Wait, what about the train?" I ask, surprised it doesn't have one. "You didn't want one?"

"Well," she says with a gleam in her eye, "it would be kind of hard to walk on the sand with a long train."

I scrunch my nose up and my eyebrows follow. "Sand, what are you talking about?"

She lets out a happy sigh. "I kind of forgot to tell you that Hunter and I are going to get married on a private beach in Hawaii."

Disappointment pulls my mouth down into a frown, wanting to be there to see my best friend get married. "Oh."

"Why the long face? You're coming too," she adds, and I grab her and hug her so tight, my purse digs into her arm.

I pull back, shaking my head. "That was pure evil."

She giggles. "I know, but I had to do it. And the look on your face was priceless. Do you honestly think I wouldn't have my best friend there on the most important day of my life? After all, I can't very well get married without my *maid of honor*, now can I?"

"Liv...." I start to talk but my words are cut off by a swell of emotion that I force back down so I can continue. "I don't know what to say. But I guess I'm saying yes, even though you're not really asking me." I let out a laugh that turns into a sigh. "Hawaii," I say dreamily. "I've never been."

"Hunter is flying anyone out who I want to be there. He's just amazing." Her voice exudes nothing but love and admiration. "You, my family, Rex of course," she says, grinning wickedly.

The picture in my mind elicits an uncontrollable twitch from my lips: the sun gleaming off the golden sand, snow-capped waves crashing onto the shore, my hair swaying in the salty breeze—and Rex.

Sounds like paradise to me.

# CHAPTER THIRTY

## ADRENALINE RUSH

I asked her if she wanted to make out? I'm acting like a fucking teenager who's never had a hard-on before in his life. We know *that* couldn't be further from the truth.

But the reality is, I don't even recognize myself when I'm with her. It's like some alien being has taken over my brain and I can't be held responsible for what comes out of my mouth. That should probably piss me off in some way. But surprisingly it doesn't.

"Rex, fucking awesome, man," Scottie says, admiring his tattoo, dragging me back down to earth. "That makes four you've done for me since you've been here."

"Should I expect you back next month for number five?" I joke, and he rubs his bald scalp, contemplating my question.

"I'm not sure. I'd like to, but my wife would probably divorce me. She told me the first two were hot, but now she thinks I'm going a bit overboard." He stands up and checks out the skull on his bicep. "She may not like this one, but I fucking love it. Thanks, man."

"Sure. Let me get it wrapped up, then you can get the hell out of here and so can I," I tease, and he chuckles, his round belly shaking with the sound. But I'm not really joking. The rush of adrenaline pumping through my veins tells me there's somewhere important I need to be.

Thankfully, I get back to my building with a half hour to spare. It's a shithole as usual, and I'd like to get it picked up a bit before Vanessa arrives.

After hiding my dirty clothes in a big pile in the closet, quickly scrubbing the dishes, and making sure the bathroom is presentable, it's nearly seven. I take a fast shower to scrub the remnants of my day off before sliding on a pair of jeans and a t-shirt, then running my hands through my hair a couple of times.

The loud knock that sounds is music to my fucking ears, the smile on my face evidence to prove it. And when I open the door, my lungs seem to have a problem functioning. Staring back at me is the most beautiful creature I've ever seen. It's not just the golden mane surrounding her high cheekbones or the way her shirt hugs her tits, or even the curvy waist and hips leading down to those luxurious legs. What really makes me lose my breath is the light in her eyes, the tip of her lips that tells me she's just as happy to see me as I am to see her.

My gaze lands on the tin of popcorn she's holding on to for dear life. "I see you brought your staple," I say, and she laughs, holding it out for me to take.

"Yes, for sustenance."

The tin and her purse drop to the floor with a thud as I yank her inside, wrapping my arms around her waist, needing to feel her against me. One of my hands wanders to the back of her neck, holding her close. Then I kiss her, our lips fitting together so perfectly it's as if she is the only person I was ever meant to kiss. And as she opens for me and my tongue slides against hers, I'm alive. More so than I've ever been—more so than I ever dreamed I could be.

She's awakened me, lifting me from a place of darkness. I'm not fucked up when I'm with her. I don't feel like I'm damaged beyond repair. And while I know she can't be the one to fix me, she makes me feel like I've got a shot at something I never thought was possible, that I rejected for so long.

Happiness.

She moans into my mouth as my thumb strokes back and forth over the sensitive skin behind her ear. When she reaches between us and takes my face in her hands, I feel like she's got me.

*God*, she so fucking has me in every sense of the word.

Our kiss becomes softer but she continues to lick at me, her tongue lashing out to catch my lower lip, and I let her because, well, it feels so fucking good.

"I think that's a pretty good start to our makeout session." She smiles against my mouth, fisting her hands in my hair. "I like your hair longer like this, it gives me something to tug on."

"You know... it's a good thing you finally stopped pushing me away because I would've resorted to drastic measures."

"Oh *really*." She angles her head back to get a better view of my eyes. "And what might those have been?"

"Well." I hook a finger through her belt loop, tugging her closer. "I might have kidnapped you and tied you up until you submitted."

She smiles as if she likes the idea, mischief written all over her face. "Hmmm...," she moans, licking her lips and my cock hardens.

"You into that, Blondie?" I ask, trying to quell the discomfort in my jeans.

She grins. "With you, maybe."

"Well, I don't think I'd want you tied up, I like your hands on me too much."

"Well, maybe I could tie *you* up." She smirks, brushing her lips against mine again.

"Now that's definitely food for thought. Speaking of which, you hungry?" I reluctantly let her go and grab my wallet from the table, tucking it into my back pocket.

Her hand goes to her stomach just as it starts to growl. "Yeah, I guess I am. I haven't eaten since lunch."

"Come on. Let's go feed you." I weave our fingers together before we head down to the elevator, passing a guy on the way who gives Vanessa the once over. My jaw pinches tight as my hand squeezes hers.

I've never really been one for public displays of affection before, but it doesn't bother me with Vanessa. I actually like it. Or maybe I just want everyone to know she's mine.

"What do you feel like eating?" I ask when we get down to the street, looking to my left and right, trying to figure out which direction to go in.

"I've got a craving for Italian. There's that small place I walked by on the way here, around the corner from you." She points just down the block to the right. "What's it called? Gianni's?"

"Yeah. We can go there. The food is actually really good."

The walk to Gianni's takes all of about two minutes. I hold the door open for Vanessa when we get there, only to have some drunken asshole plow into her on his way out. She loses her footing and stumbles back, my arms shooting out to catch her.

Rage grabs a firm hold of me, clouding my vision. "What the fuck, man? Why don't you watch where the hell you're going!"

He curses under his breath, then mumbles a couple of insincere apologies before he shuffles down the street, struggling to maintain his balance.

"You okay, baby?" I clasp her shoulders, looking her over from head to toe.

"Yeah, I'm fine. He just startled me is all," she assures me with a bright smile.

"Gotta love the effects of excessive alcohol," I snarl as we head into the restaurant, the past shoved in my face in an instant.

"Wow, it's really dark in here," Vanessa comments, the only illumination coming from overhead lighting and small red votives on each table. "Do we just seat ourselves?" she asks, and I nod.

We find a booth in a quiet corner. Vanessa goes first and I slide in next to her. "So what's good here?" She picks up the menu and begins flipping through the pages.

"Pretty much everything. I think the veal parm is their specialty, though. I'm actually gonna get the shrimp parm. That's really good, too."

"Okay," she asserts, closing the menu. "I'll get the veal. So," she fastens her hands together in front of her on the table as we wait for the server, "I saw Olivia today. She tried on wedding dresses."

"Oh yeah?" I hook an arm over the back of the booth, settling in close to her. "How did that go?"

"It was great. She found the most beautiful dress and she's so happy. I really see how much your brother loves her. He's really good for her." Vanessa looks up at me with those enormous blue eyes and I tug on my lip, feeling like I should say something, but not knowing what the hell to say.

"Yeah. I'm happy for my brother, too." I lay my hand on top of hers. "It's funny to see him like this, though. He's usually all business with women, or," I chuckle, "the arm candy he was sporting over the years. This is a completely different side of him I'm not used to seeing." I stare down at our fingers, the past creeping up on me, my memories on overload. "We were so different growing up, you know? He was playing little league while I was hanging out with my friends on the railroad tracks trying cigarettes for the first time. He was running track on the school field while only several feet away, I was smoking weed." My laughter at the recollection turns into a bitter scowl. "I didn't understand it until I found out we had different fathers, then it all made sense."

"What was your dad like?" She rests her other hand on my knee, and I appreciate the fact that she's trying to turn this around for me.

Nadine, one of the waitresses here, shows up to take our order. "Hey, doll, how are you?" she asks, placing all of her attention on me.

"I'm good. Nadine, this is Vanessa, my...." I hesitate, not entirely sure what I should say. But I certainly don't want to say the wrong thing. "Girlfriend."

"Nice to meet you," Vanessa says, the smile lifting her lips and the way she squeezes my thigh tells me I made the right choice.

"Damn it, Rex. That means there's no chance for me then, is there?" She raps her pencil against her pad, tossing Vanessa a playful wink.

"No. Sorry," I reply, as Vanessa huddles up closer to my side, marking her territory.

"All right, then what can I get you to eat?"

"We'll have one veal parm and one shrimp parm, and I'll have a beer." I turn to Vanessa. "What do you want to drink, baby?"

"Just a large water with lemon, thanks."

As soon as Nadine walks away, Vanessa taps my chin. I shift to face her, rewarded with a hard kiss on the lips. I'm barely able to resist the temptation to drag her tongue into my mouth.

"What was that for? Not that I'm complaining." I twist a strand of her hair, curling it around my finger.

"Can't your *girlfriend* give you a kiss?" There's a subtle lift of her head and I internally give myself a high five. I'm getting better with this stuff.

"My girlfriend can give me anything she wants," I whisper, my lips resting just above her ear.

"I'll make a mental note." There's a visible change in her breathing, her legs shifting under the table. "Wait, what were we talking about?" She laughs, just as Nadine sets our drinks down then ambles away. "Oh yeah, your dad. I want to know what he was like."

"Hmph," I sigh, "I guess what I remember most is that he was always around. Even though I knew he had a very busy job, he always left his shit at the office, and when he was with us... he was with us. I think he probably overcompensated too at times for my mother, but he always had us on the forefront of his mind." I rub my chin thoughtfully. "He was funny and he made great peanut butter and jelly sandwiches."

After a few more minutes, Nadine brings our food, disrupting my trip down memory lane. "Here you go. If you need anything else, let me know."

"Thanks," we both say before she saunters away.

"You know the one thing that sticks out for me, though?" I recall, taking a swig of my beer. "He took me to his office one day and all of my school drawings were taped on his wall." Even now, my heart warms at the memory. "I remember how happy that made me, that he was proud of me, that he thought my pictures were good."

She lays her fork down on her plate. "Just think what he would say if he could see you now. You're exceptional, and you're spreading your gift to the world, Rex. Your art is on people's skin... forever."

"Yeah." Contentment rolls around inside of me because I know she's right. I love what I do. It's the one thing that has always made me feel as though I have some worth... until now.

There's an easy silence that accompanies us as we continue eating, yet Vanessa seems distracted. When she finally breaks the quiet, I understand why. "My dad never had time for me like that. Work was everything to him. It's what he lived for. That's why he always bought me things. I think maybe he thought that could take the place of his love, but he was so wrong." Sadness pours from her eyes and I want to take it from her, to rid her of the pain. "I didn't care about any of it. I would have given anything if he had just paid attention to me, climbed a tree with me, or came to one of my school plays... anything. By the time he and my mother decided to grace me with their presence at my graduation, I just didn't care anymore. It was too little, too late."

She holds her head up high, letting out a deep breath. "But you know what, I'm all grown up now, and it is what it is, right?" But she doesn't sound all that convincing to me.

"Hey." I caress her with my voice, wrapping my fingers around her wrist, drawing her gaze to mine. "I guess one thing I've realized is that we're never too old to be affected. It still hurts and that's okay, baby."

She lays her head on my shoulder and I press my lips to her hair. "I don't know how to get rid of the anger though, how to let it go. I just don't think I can."

"One day at a time. You might not be able to today, but maybe at some point you will."

"Boy...." She lifts her head with a lopsided grin. "That therapy is really working wonders. I'm impressed," she says, and I knock her shoulder playfully.

I don't realize how long we've been talking until Nadine finally comes back again to clear our plates. "Do you two want dessert or coffee?"

"What do you think, Blondie?"

She holds her hand against her belly, scrunching her nose up. "I'm stuffed. But maybe some to go?"

"Good idea. What does Gianni have for dessert tonight?" I ask, and she points to a chalkboard behind her. "Cheesecake, chocolate fudge cake, carrot cake, cannoli, and homemade vanilla ice cream."

"I'll have a piece of the chocolate fudge cake, please." She continues staring at the board. "Rex, what are you gonna get?"

"I'll have a piece of cheesecake. Thanks, Nadine."

"Oh good!" Vanessa says with excitement. "I was hoping you'd get something different so I could try it."

"Oh, no you don't," I warn, sliding out from the booth. "Hands off. You've got your dessert."

"*What*?" She fists her hands on her hips, eyes pinched with intimidation.

"Sorry, Blondie. That shit won't work with me. I'm not scared. But...." I pull her by the hand out of the booth. "If you're really nice, maybe I'll give you a bite."

"I can play nice." She casts me a flirty smile, just as Nadine comes back with our to-go bag, and I pay the bill.

"Here you go. All set." She hands Vanessa the bag. "Oh, hope you have an umbrella by the way, it's pouring out," she adds as we steer ourselves toward the door, peeking through the window at the torrential downpour.

"Oh shit. It's seriously raining." I glance over at Vanessa to test the waters, see what she wants to do.

She nods, an excited glow in her eyes. "I'm game if you are. We really don't have far to go anyway."

I fucking love her adventurous side. The fact that she's not worried about her hair or any of that shit is such a turn on. And now I can't wait to get her back to my apartment.

"You ready?" I take hold of her hand. "Let's make a break for it."

And we dash out the door, heavy raindrops drenching us instantly, thunder pounding our ears. Vanessa squeals and we run as fast as we can toward my building.

"Ahhh!" she squeals again, the force of the rain nearly drowning out the sound of her voice. We finally get to the front entrance, weighted down by our soggy clothing, but Vanessa is laughing and it's contagious.

Once inside the door she shakes her head from side to side, flicking droplets of water all over the floor. "Oh my God, I'm soaked," she says through a fit of giggles. But her laughter stops the moment I meet her gaze and hold it.

"Even soaking wet, you're the most beautiful thing I've ever seen."

I watch as her face transforms, that dazzling smile I've grown familiar with, come to look forward to, appears, but this time it's mixed with something else—a shyness that I've yet to see from her. A different side of her to appreciate.

I close the unwanted gap between us, her chest rising and falling with heavy breaths as is mine. The heart that I didn't think I had stumbles inside my chest because I realize I almost lost this—lost her. Stepping even closer, I lift my thumb to her cheek. Beads of water fall from her long, thick lashes, and I pad them away, never once leaving her eyes.

"I can't believe I almost let something so precious slip right through my fingers. I'm such an asshole."

"No. You're not." Her head does a subtle shake, a small smile on her lips.

My ears hone in on the sincerity in her voice and it calms me, slowing my heartbeat. The worry of loss still looms over my head like a dark shadow as I wait for it to pounce. I've become way too accustomed to losing the things I love most in this life.

My brain short circuits. Why is that word in my head? It shouldn't be. It can't be. Because I know nothing about it. And bad things happen to the people I care about.

I forget about everything and sweep my tongue across her mouth, the taste of rainwater on her lips, the sweet scent of raspberries swirling around me. She reaches for me, a shiver rocking my body as her gentle hands caress my neck, slanting my head, guiding me to where she wants me. And I've never wanted anyone this fucking much in my entire life. When her tongue enters and finds mine, the thread of control I was barely hanging on to snaps and I cup her ass, a low moan escaping her throat as my aroused cock rubs against her.

I could keep going, ignoring where we are, but she cuts off the kiss. Her breathing is ragged, cheeks flushed red. She peeks up at me with those steely blues, blinking several times while chewing on her lower lip. When she opens her mouth to speak, I suddenly feel sick to my stomach.

"Rex, I... I...."

Panic seizes my chest, my organs burn as I wait for what she has to say. Maybe she's changed her mind about me, somehow realized I'm not good enough for her.

"What is it? Just say it!" My insides are screaming with my words as I force myself to breathe.

"I... I missed you," she confesses, her voice shaky.

A whoosh of relief flows through me and I exhale my assumptions in a big breath. It's pathetic that I always assume the worst.

"I missed you too, baby." I palm her cheek, stroking her skin. And then I realize it's not enough. That's not telling her how I really feel. Dr. Billings reminded me I need to do more of that. So I stuff the fear back down my throat, steel myself for honesty and say the words. "You know... when you walked out on me that night, well, after I forced you out with those awful things I said... I felt you leave me. Your light, it was gone, and it was the absolute worst feeling in the world. All I wanted to do was see you smile and hear you laugh again."

Stunned blue eyes stare back at me, but then a brilliant smile brings her lips up at the corners. "You missed me?" she says softly, almost as if she's trying to reconcile it in her mind, as though it's so hard to believe.

"I missed the fuck out of you." I press my forehead against hers, inhaling a shaky breath. "I want you to stay with me tonight. Will you stay?"

"Yes," she breathes out, without an ounce of hesitation.

"I love that fucking answer." I plant a kiss on her forehead, then throw her and the bag over my shoulder without warning as I take quick strides toward the elevator. She lets out a squeaky little noise of surprise that makes me stab at the button three times before the fucking door finally closes. The wetness dripping from her hair tickles my neck, her rounded ass hovering next to my face. And I can't resist, I move my head an inch and bite down on it through the fabric of her jeans.

"Ow," she whines, and I smooth my hand over it to soothe her. She eases my shirt up, her cold fingers inching up my back, her touch making me tremble. "I've never fucked in an elevator before. I think we should do that sometime."

"If you don't stop talking like that, that sometime might just be now," I say with a frustrated breath, staring at the numbers, willing them to move faster.

"Hmmm...," she teases, and I smack her ass, chuckling at her eagerness to complete her sexual bucket list.

The car finally dings and I continue with her over my shoulder. "Let's go, my sexual temptress." I practically sprint down the hall and push my door open, kicking it closed behind us. When I set her down, my chest is flush with hers. "So what do you want to do now?" I cock a brow, my eyes piercing her fiery ones, and her lips turn up devilishly.

"Everything." Her fingers skate across my stubble, the sight of her tongue swiping across her lip has me adjusting myself in my jeans. "I'm aching for you," she rasps, her voice so sexy I nearly drop to my knees so I can taste her pussy and give her what I know we both want.

"I know the feeling." I lift her hair, and she moans as I trail kisses down her neck.

"Rex."

"Yes?" I continue my descent down her skin, feeling starved for her after being without her for way too long.

"I think we should go get these wet clothes off," she murmurs, but I don't want to take my lips off of her just yet.

"Rex?"

"God, I love the way you say my name, baby. You have no idea how the sound of your voice—makes me hard." My gaze travels lower. "The sight of your nipples, stiff and sensitive—gets me hard." I let my fingers rove over the space between her legs. "The smell of your wet pussy—gets me hard."

"Hmmm... Rex, please. Let's go get naked." Somehow she manages to skirt around me and I chase her to my room, tackling her on the bed. She squirms underneath me when I tickle her ribs, her laughter filling the barren space with happiness. "Stop! Rex, come... on, we're soaked, your... bed."

I finally let up and she climbs off, taking me with her. "Strip, Rex Grayson. *Now*," she demands, as she slides her t-shirt over her head. I do the same, and we're meeting each other item for item until I'm in only my boxers and she's in her bra and panties.

"It seems you're at an unfair advantage. You have two pieces of clothing left to my one," I say, before she falls to her knees in front of me and yanks down my boxers, speckles of mischief in her eyes when she looks up at me. "I like the view from up here," I joke, but my laughter subsides when her tongue darts out to lick my swollen head and a shudder barrels through me.

She seals her lips around my cock, taking me into her warm mouth. And then she sucks. Hard. It feels too good and I know I need to stop her.

"Baby, stop. I want to be inside you when I come." I lift her to her feet then take a seat on the bed. "So, bra and panties *off*."

Her hands disappear behind her back and I hear the welcome flick of the clasp before the straps slide off her shoulders and it falls to the floor. I know I'm staring, but her tits are fucking perfect and I need to get reacquainted with them. That is, until she slips her panties down her legs and I can't decide where I want to go first.

My eyes move slowly over every inch of her skin, drinking her in, my cock twitching against my abdomen. "You are fucking perfect." I crook a finger at her, wanting her near, and she comes willingly.

When she's standing between my legs, I glide my hand up the curve of her spine to her neck and pull her down for a kiss, her breasts nearly brushing my chest, my skin tingling being this close to her again.

I back us up, breaking our connection only for a minute. "I wanted to worship you but I need to be inside you... so badly."

"I want that too," she breathes, and I lace our fingers together while I reach back with my other hand and grab a condom from the drawer. Her gaze doesn't waver from mine, watching me as I roll it on.

Scooting up the bed, I lean back against the headboard. "Hop on my lap," I tell her, and as she lifts her leg, hovering above me, I slide my thumb over her clit and she whimpers. As much as I want to be inside her, I need to feel her. Moisture drenches my finger and I close my eyes, sucking in a sharp breath. She's always so wet for me, so responsive, and my dick grows harder, if that's even possible.

"Your pussy is so wet," I groan, and she rubs herself back and forth against my finger, telling me with her moans that she wants more.

Reaching between us, she takes my cock, replacing my finger, and lingers just below her entrance. She lowers herself down, taking me all the way in until I'm completely filling her.

"Slow, baby." I take both her hands in mine. "You feel so good."

"Oh God, Rex. It's so deep like this. I feel you so deep," she moans, lips parted, head dropping back. But I need to see her. I need to look at her. I *want* to look at her.

"Baby, look at me," I command, and she immediately lifts her head up, an unreadable emotion in her eyes, and I wonder now if she was trying to hide from me so I wouldn't see it. A part of me also considers if mine reflect that same emotion. Because I know something is going on inside of me, shaking my core, unsteadying me. Yet at the same time, nothing has ever felt better.

"This feels so right, you and me." My voice is strained from pleasure as the words slip out of my mouth. Vanessa's eyes shine in response, a pink undertone to her cheeks. She's staring at me like I just gave her the world. And I think maybe I want to.

"Rex... I need to move."

"So move, baby. Ride me like your life depends on it." I grin, and she rotates her hips, rocking her hot as hell body against me. I separate our hands and dig my fingers into her skin, grinding my cock, taking us both higher. My mouth finds her nipple and I suck hard, eliciting a desperate moan from her throat.

"Rex... it feels too good... I'm gonna come." Sweat glistens on her forehead, her lips opening on a shallow breath.

"Come, baby, come all over my cock."

"Ahhhh...," she shouts out, and I feel her pussy clenching and pulsing, squeezing my cock, spurring me toward my own release, which is going to be insane. It's been too long.

"Fuuuck!" My breathing is erratic, and the moment she leans forward and licks my nipple is when I explode, all the pent-up frustration of the previous week releasing inside of her. Unable to manage any words, I frame her face with my hands and lift it from my chest, pressing my lips to her mouth.

"You taste sweet and salty," she says winded, "and it's making me hungry."

"Ready for... dessert?"

I'm breathless, trying to come down from the absolute high she gives me. My body is completely relaxed beneath her, the idea of moving not all that appealing.

"Affirmative." She points a finger at my chest. "You stay here. I'll get it."

"Good. Because that means I get to stare at your ass as you walk away," I tease, and she makes a show of it, wiggling as she saunters off into the living room.

God, I'm fucking crazy about this girl.

Two minutes later she comes back, our to-go bag and plates in one hand, her other hand waving in the air. "Okay, what is the deal with the lack of utensils and dishes in this apartment? I'm buying you some.

Don't you ever eat?"

"You worried about me?" I ask, and she tries to hide a smile as she plops down on the bed next to me. "I eat take out a lot and sometimes if I work late at the shop, I'll just grab something with the guys. I have popcorn though."

She flicks my arm before opening up the bags. "Okay, so cheesecake for you, which I'm trying," she adds under her breath, "and chocolate for me. I'll let you try mine if you let me try yours," she suggests, flashing me a coy smile.

"Nah. That's okay. I don't want any of yours." I grin, taking a bite. "Well, your cake anyway."

"Hmmm... this is soooo good." She closes her eyes, sticking her naked breasts in my direction. "Oh! I almost forgot. Did you know that Hunter is flying everyone out to Hawaii for their wedding?"

"News to me," I reply flatly, continuing to devour my cheesecake, but secretly saving a bite for her.

Frustrated, she sets her plate down on the bed. "That's all you have to say about it. I think it's amazing and so generous."

"He can afford it. He's ridiculously rich. He could probably send his entire company."

"Still, it's really nice of him." She wipes a bit of chocolate from the corner of her mouth. "I'm excited and I've never been to Hawaii. Have you?"

"Nope," I respond without an ounce of regret. "I can count on one hand the places I've been: Boston, New York, California, Ohio. That's it."

She picks up her fork, twirling some of the frosting around with it. "I've traveled a lot in the years I've been doing events, but Hawaii is one place I always wanted to go."

"Here." I hold the fork in front of her face. "You can have the last two bites," I offer, and she opens, closing her eyes and savoring the taste.

"Oh my God. That is really good."

"So," I can't help the nervous twinge in my voice, "I have something for you."

"You do?" She bounces, her tone rising several octaves.

"Indeed I do, Blondie. Indeed I do." I try to sound confident even though inside I'm shitting bricks. I've never done anything like this before and I want her to like it.

Before my nerves immobilize my feet, I zip off the bed, plodding to my closet and taking the gift down from the top shelf. I can feel her eyes on me the entire time, the excitement rolling off of her in waves. A few steps take me back, and I sink down next to her, handing her the package.

It suddenly feels too warm in here and I rub the back of my neck, attempting to lessen the mountain of anxiety my limbs need to overcome. She stares at the wrapping for a long minute, my tension building each second she waits to open it.

"Did you wrap this yourself?" she asks, and I can't manage anything more than a nod in response. A grin tugs at her lips. "It's impressive." She concentrates back on the gift, tearing the paper open in a very unladylike manner.

That's my girl.

"Ahhh." Her lips separate in a gasp as she stares at the drawing. "It's me," she whispers, glancing up at me briefly before returning her focus to the picture. A shaky finger traces the pencil lines of her hair, her eyes, the bowed outline of her lips. "When did you do this?"

"While we were apart," I shrug, "I had a lot of time on my hands. That was the first time you smiled at me. We were at the bar with Hunter and Olivia."

She shakes her head, astonished. "It doesn't even look like me... I mean, it looks like me, but I look—different—happy almost."

"That's the way I see you. It's what I see when I look at you." Her profile changes, and I watch the right side of her mouth curve up, a hint of wetness in the corner of her eye that she quickly swats away.

I move closer and rest my chin on her shoulder, reaching out with my hand. "You see, down here," I point to her mouth, "how when you smile the right side of your mouth lifts a little higher than your left," my finger moves to her cheek, "and here," I run my finger back and forth, "the soft angle of your cheekbone, and over here," my thumb traces her hairline, "the way this one strand always escapes from behind your ear, settling on the side of your face. And up here," I circle my finger just above her brow, "this cute little freckle that doesn't go unnoticed. And last, but not least," I draw a path back down her skin, "the tiny pucker in your cheek that can only be seen when you smile big."

With a voice strained in disbelief, her head turns a fraction, my lips skimming her chin. "It's like you have me memorized."

"I do, baby," I whisper. "I do."

After laying the picture on the bed, she flips her body around to face me, eyes glued to mine. Her hands find my face, fingers gliding over my eyebrow, my cheek, my chin, my lips. "No one has ever done anything like this for me before, and... I don't know how to express to you how much it means to me."

"I think you just did." I tuck that runaway wisp of hair behind her ear. "It's trying to escape again," I tease, and she smiles as I press my lips to hers in a whisper of a kiss. "I'm glad you like it. It's the first portrait I've done that hasn't been inked on someone's skin."

She climbs onto my lap and throws her arms around me, burying her head in the crook of my neck and embracing me in a way that no one ever has before. Her acceptance wraps around me like a cloak in the dead of winter, making my breaths come easier—and I feel like it's okay to be me.

I don't know how long we stay like this, because it feels too damn good and neither of us pulls away until the muffled ring of her cell phone breaks our moment. I reluctantly let go of her so she can shuffle off the bed to answer it.

"Hello?" She squints at the digital clock to see what time it is. The glow in her cheeks morphs into a milky white, lips flattening, face suddenly blank of any emotion. "Yes, I'm here." Her tone turns stale and the air grows very cold around us.

"What? You're coming here? When?" She paces back and forth now across the carpet, gnawing on a fingernail. "Yes, fine. Let me know when you get in." Then she hangs up without saying goodbye and I want to know who the hell that was, and why the hair is standing up on the back of my neck, an urge to protect her overwhelming me.

"Who was that?" I ask, and she doesn't respond. Instead, she's frantic as she scoops up her bra and panties, her clothes that are still damp, and tugs them on. "Wait, what are you doing?"

"I-I need air. I-I can't breathe," she says, clumsy in her efforts to dress, before taking off without another word.

"Wait!" And now I'm scrambling to get my own clothes on, following after her in my bare feet, grabbing my sneakers from beside the door. "Blondie, stop!" I call out, trying to catch up with her as she's running down the stairs, refusing to even take the elevator. I manage to latch onto her wrist halfway down, halting her. She's breathing heavy, nostrils flaring, tension forming a dark cloud around her body. "What's going on? Talk to me, damn it!"

She starts chewing on that damn nail again, and I pull it from her mouth. "It was my father. He'll be in New York tomorrow and he wants to see me. I just—can't—" And then she takes off again and I throw my hands up in the air, chasing after her.

By the time we get down to street level, both of us are huffing and puffing, only for different reasons. She's tired and I'm fucking frustrated.

I bend over with my hands on my knees. "Fuck. What are we doing? It's almost midnight."

"I just need to walk." She stares straight ahead at everything, but I can tell she sees nothing. "I don't want to talk right now, okay?"

"Okay," I agree, but I reach out and latch onto her hand, thankful when she doesn't push me away.

The air around us is laced with an uncomfortable silence, but for the first time, I know it has nothing to do with me. Whatever it is obviously relates to her father, and it must be bad because I haven't seen her like this since we met. I don't like it. This isn't my

Blondie. This is the girl I met at the tattoo shop, pain etched in her eyes.

A feeling of helplessness ties my stomach in knots. I want to help her but I won't force her to talk. Personal experience tells me it will only cause her to shut down.

As we turn the corner, a small neighborhood park comes into view. It's desolate this time of night and she leads me there, taking a seat on an old bench. The wood is worn, beaten down from time and weather. I can't help wondering if that's how she feels—worn down.

Still quiet, she stares at the creaky swings as I wait. Patience is not a strong suit of mine but I know that's what she needs right now, so I swallow hard and grant her space. In the meantime, I gently run my thumb over her knuckles so she knows I'll be here when she's ready.

"Like I told you earlier, I still harbor all this anger," she admits again, voice flat, eyes locked on the playground. "Therapy didn't help me get over it. My mother is a cold bitch and my father is apathetic and removed, affectionless." She clears her throat and I see her fighting back the anger, her shoulders rigid, face like stone. "They never cared about me, never took an interest in me. In fact," she lets out a harsh laugh, "I don't know why they ever had me."

She blows out a hard breath. "I remember this one time," she starts, but has to take a pause before continuing. "I was getting an award for being a person of good character, I think it was in fifth grade. They told me they would be there. And even after everything, I believed them, because it was a big day for me, and because I needed to so desperately. But when I looked out into the auditorium they weren't there. I saw Stella, though. And I saw how big she was trying to smile, because I know she saw the look on my face, how disappointed I was." Her gaze finally finds mine. "I've made a life for myself that doesn't include them. I moved from Seattle so I could be as far away from them as possible. I don't like the stress I feel or who I am when I'm near them, who I become. It's ugly actually and it scares me because it reminds me of my mother."

"You're not your mother, baby," I reassure her, taking her hand and placing it on my thigh.

"No, but I have the potential to be. And that scares me more than anything else." She exhales a pained sigh. "My father will be here tomorrow. He said he wants to talk. I haven't heard from him in months and I haven't seen him in almost two years. And I don't want to now."

I tug on her arm and she nestles into my side. "Call me crazy, but if you have a child, you shouldn't just disregard them like they're nothing. You have a responsibility to them, to care for them, to love them. I guess somehow they missed the parental training class," she bites out.

"If you want, I can, you know, hang out with you when he comes," I offer, unsure as to whether she'd really want me around for that.

A kiss to my cheek bats the insecurity away. "Thank you, Rex. But I need to see him alone. I honestly wouldn't want to subject you to that. It's not pretty." She exhales a sigh, laying her head on my shoulder.

"I think you forget I've seen my own share of ugly. That doesn't bother me. I just want... well, I'm here, that's all, if you change your mind."

"Thank you." She plays with the sleeve of my t-shirt, flipping it between her fingers. "Honestly, just you listening makes me feel better."

"Whoa, did you see that, Blondie?" I point up at the sky and she follows the path of my hand. "It's a shooting star. I think we have to make a wish or some shit like that."

She laughs but it comes out as a snort. "Some shit like that?"

"Yeah, you know what I mean." I pinch her side gently and she flinches.

"I don't believe in wishes," she states in a bland tone. "They never come true."

"Fuck that. We're making wishes. Close your eyes." She huffs out a sigh of protest and I see the remnants of an eye roll before she decides to acquiesce to my demand.

"Okay, I'm done," she calls out. "Hurry up, you're taking too long."

I open my eyes and meet hers. "So what did you wish for?"

"Ahh, I see," she practically tsks, "let me get this straight." She crosses her arms in front of her chest. "First, you demand I make a wish and now you want to know what my wish is. You obviously know nothing about wish etiquette."

"Well, smartass, for someone who doesn't believe in wishes, you certainly know way too much about it," I retort, and she doubles over, howling with laughter. The sound sends a shot of happy straight to my core.

"Now get over here and kiss me. It seals the wish-making."

I won't tell her my wish already came true.

# CHAPTER THIRTY-ONE

## SOMEONE ELSE'S LIFE

### *Vanessa*

"Morning, Tillie," I sing out, feet light as a feather as I make my way toward my office. I'm honestly not sure why I'm so happy. Actually, I know why I feel this way. Last night with Rex was amazing and I refuse to let the weight of my father's visit taint that for me. He's already done enough.

It feels a little bit like I'm living someone else's life lately. Holding hands, kissing under the stars—and that drawing Rex did especially for me. The way he sees me. The way he looks at me. The way he holds me. Even the things he says, knowing how hard it is for him, knowing how hard he's trying... for me. Bombarded by emotion, dizziness overtakes me and my briefcase falls to the floor. I grab onto the wall, these feelings I've never experienced before spinning me on a strange but wonderful axis.

"Vanessa, are you okay?" Tillie runs over, touching my arm, a ridge of concern under her wispy bangs. "Let me get you a chair."

"No." I clasp her elbow, pulling her back. "I'm fine. Just a lot going on, and I didn't eat breakfast this morning so that doesn't help."

She bends down, picking up my briefcase, then escorts me to my office. "Well, I'm going to run down and grab you a bagel with cream cheese. You need something in your stomach. I'll be right back."

"That would be great, Tillie, thanks."

I don't argue with her because I don't think food will hurt. In fact, I'll probably be eating more than my share today to prepare myself for having to deal with my father. Maybe I should have her get me a box of candy bars, too.

Part of me wants to take Rex up on his offer to be by my side when my father shows up. He has the uncanny ability to calm me, but I don't want to use him as a crutch for my fear. I have to face this head on. I'm a twenty-seven-year-old woman and I need to grow up and start acting like one.

Taking a seat behind my desk, I stow my purse in the bottom drawer and boot up my computer. There's a lot I need to accomplish today and I refuse to let negative thoughts drag me down.

My phone chimes and I slide it over, smiling as always when I see who the text is from. I expel a contented sigh before I unlock the screen, reading the words four times before I respond.

**_Morning, baby. I WISHED you hadn't left this morning._**

**_Me too._**

I feel the smile slipping from my lips. What I wish is that I didn't have such a long memory. My stomach swirls with nausea as it comes rushing back.

*When I woke up, the house was quiet, just like it was last year on my birthday. There were no balloons or fun, colored signs. I shuffled into the living room and sighed. All of my presents were wrapped but they weren't home. Same as last year. They were at work, where they always were.*

*Mommy promised when she left that morning that she would be home early. I didn't understand it at all. It was a Saturday so they should have been home anyway. I sighed, sending my bubble gum breath into the air. "This sucks," I said out loud. I'm not even sure if that was a word I was supposed to say or not. But I didn't care, because it did.*

*Stella called me over. "Happy seventh birthday! Don't you want to open your presents?" she asked with a big smile on her face. But it looked fake to me, like she was trying too hard. Maybe because she was here last year on my birthday, too.*

*I lifted my shoulders and looked at all the presents, way too many to count. Other kids would probably be jumping for joy, but not me. I'd have given all the presents away if Mommy and Daddy would have just come home to take me out for ice cream or cupcakes, or something.*

*I plopped down on our perfect green leather chair, swinging my feet underneath me. It felt like someone was pulling down hard on my lips and it was starting to hurt. Then my belly began to get sore, too. It was spreading everywhere because pretty soon my eyes felt like they were wet and I quickly wiped them with the sleeve of my shirt. Because I couldn't cry. Mommy told me over and over that it was bad to cry and that no one wanted to be around a weak, little cry baby. So I held the drops back and instead my belly felt worse. But at least no one would call me a baby.*

*Stella came over and kneeled down in front of me. She took both my hands, and with a smile, said, "Come on, sweetie. Let's go into the kitchen. I have a surprise for you."*

*I didn't move so she helped me down off the chair, still holding my fingers in hers, and we went into the kitchen. There was a single chocolate cupcake on the table with a lighted candle in the shape of a green army man on top. We both plopped down and I sat in front of the cupcake, staring at it.*

*"Make a wish," Stella said excitedly, her face glowing behind the candle.*

*I closed my eyes, but wished for nothing. Because every year I made the same wish and it never came true. I wished I had parents who loved me.*

*So eventually I just stopped making them.*

The smell of coffee yanks me into the present and I blink a few times before I notice Tillie standing in front of my desk.

"Boy, you seemed a million miles away." She blows a bubble that nearly pops all over her face. "All they had left were garlic bagels so I got you one toasted, with cream cheese. But," she winks, "I did get you the grande coffee."

"Thanks, Tillie. I appreciate it." I close my eyes and take a sip of the latte, the warmth serving to help ease the chill of my past. "So sit." I flap my hand toward the chair. "Tell me what's going on."

"Well...," she begins with a twinkle in her eyes, curling her red strands around her finger. "You'll never guess who posted an ad for a receptionist on all the internet job sites?"

My finger thumps steadily against my lip. "Hmph. I give up," I tease.

She points her thumb against her chest. "This girl did. And once we find a replacement, guess who'll be getting an office? Well, it'll be more like a shoebox," she giggles, "but who's complaining."

"That's fantastic, Tillie. I'm so happy for you. And it's about freaking time. By the way," I pick at a small square of white paper, holding it up. "What is this cryptic message from Ryder you left me?"

"What?" She squints to get a better look. "Oh!" She snatches it out of my hand, sticking her gum in the paper and folding it. "That wasn't meant for you. It was meant for *me*."

"Oh?" My voice rises in curiosity and she grins.

"Yeah, he kind of asked me out but I haven't said yes yet." There's a dramatic shift in her expression as she breaks off a piece of croissant. She pops it in her mouth but isn't forthcoming with any other information.

"Because...."

"He's very sweet, don't get me wrong. But...." Tears border her green eyes and she frowns. "Well, my last boyfriend seemed sweet, too, and then he ended up being a jerk, in more ways than one. So, I'm wary."

"Listen, Tillie," I assure her with a warm smile, "I know Ryder really well. And what you see is what get. He is as sweet as they come."

Light makes its way back to her face and her lips soften. "Thanks, Vanessa," she says with a hint of that cute little southern accent she still retains. "Okay, I'm going to get back to work." She stands and straightens her shirt, brushing the remainder of crumbs onto the floor.

After she leaves, I plow through several e-mails and return a few phone calls before my mind strays to the visit with my father. I don't know why I even call it a visit. It will be more like a defensive confrontation.

Without thinking, I pick up the phone, wanting to hear the only voice that will calm me. I dial Rex's number and he answers on the first ring.

"Hey, baby," he says in that rough, sexy rumble that makes me want to give myself over to him in a hundred different ways, yet it also makes me sigh. "You okay?"

I pick at the chipped wood on the corner of my desk. "I'm... nervous about seeing my father. I'm trying not to be, but it's not working."

"I know. But it's gonna be okay. And my offer still stands. If you—" he starts to say, but stops. "Hang on, baby." Then he places the phone down. "Zeek, tell him to hold the fuck up. I'll be there in a few." He comes back on the line. "Okay, I'm here."

"Do you have to go?" I ask, silently hoping the answer is no.

"No. It's fine. So I was saying that if you want me to be there, my offer still stands."

"I know, Rex, and I appreciate it. But I'll be okay. I just might be a raving bitch when you see me later." And even though I'm trying to be funny, it's inevitable.

"Baby, I won't turn you away, so just come as you are," he says, and I can almost see his lips forming a smile. The realization of what he means, that he accepts me no matter what, sends a sudden flash of awareness through me. My nerve endings respond with a tingle of happiness. Something I never saw coming. That I didn't think was obtainable.

"You still there?"

"Yeah, I'm here. Okay, so I guess I'll see you later." I heave out a disgruntled sigh, not really wanting to hang up just yet.

"You will, indeed." And I hear Zeek call to him again so I know I need to let him go.

"I-I can't wait," I manage to squeak out before he hangs up, as if that was the hardest thing in the world for me to admit. If he only knew everything my heart was holding back, he'd probably run in the other direction. And that's the last thing I want.

"Me too. Bye, baby."

"Bye." I try to keep my voice upbeat even though I'm drowning inside. Because there's so much more I want to say. I'm just afraid he won't want to hear it.

Once we hang up, I begin typing a text to Liv when something occurs to me—I called Rex first. Olivia is always the one I run to... but not this time. After the surprise of that soaks in, I finish the message, letting her know I'm seeing my father. Of course, not more than a minute later, my phone rings.

"Hey, Liv. That was fast."

"What's going on? You okay? Why is your dad coming?" She's already overloading me with questions that I can barely handle.

"I have no idea why he's coming. I'm sure it can't be good. You know I haven't heard from him in months, and seen him in even more time. Ugh. You know how I get, Liv. I already feel myself shutting down. I hate that."

"I know you do." There's nothing but empathy in her voice. "What can I do?"

"Nothing." I let out another of a long string of sighs. "Thanks though. I just want to get this over with." And then I can wash my hands of him for another two years.

"How's Rex?" she asks in the same moment I look out the window, seeing the sun burst from a gray cloud. It makes me smile.

"He's great. Fantastic, if I'm honest. Swoonworthy, amazing... shall I go on?"

"Nah. I think I get the picture. I have one of those myself." She giggles, and I hear voices in the background.

"Someone over for lunch?" I'm wondering if it's Hunter.

"No, I ordered Chinese food. I've got a ton of writing to do to make my deadline so I don't have time to go out. Plus, I didn't like my choices here." The bag crinkles in my ear, cueing me that it's time to hang up.

"All right, I'll let you go eat," I tell her. "I'll talk to you later."

"Okay. Good luck with your dad. I'll be thinking about you. Let me know how it goes."

"I will."

Except I already know it's going to go like shit.

I've checked my watch six times in the last five minutes and pretty much worn down the fairly new carpet in my apartment. He said he'd be here at six and it's six twenty. I wonder if he changed his mind about seeing his only daughter. It wouldn't surprise me.

I trudge to the kitchen to get a glass of water, gulping it down fast before filling it up again. I feel completely dehydrated. My throat is dry and it's almost as though I've been stranded in the desert, deprived of water for months. Meanwhile, my body is wound so tight, I could snap any minute.

My shoulders are burdened, my stomach churning. I do so much better when I don't hear from either him or my mother. Why did he have to contact me? Why can't they just let me live my life? They certainly had no issue with it when I was younger.

A firm knock tells me that my time is up. Inhaling a deep breath, I walk over to the door, finally letting it out when my fingers reach the handle. I turn the knob slowly attempting to prolong the impending agony.

When I open it, I come face to face with a man I don't recognize. Time has not been kind to my father. Skin bunches around his eyes and mouth, dark circles line the area underneath his lashes. Wrinkles are engraved on his cheeks and his hair is thinner and more gray than I remember. It's obvious that work is still his life.

"Vanessa. It's so good to see you." He comes forward to try to hug me and I stagger back as if I could get burned. My father and affection don't even belong in the same sentence. I can count on maybe one hand the number of times we've hugged in my twenty-seven years and it's always been awkward. Plus, I'm not going to pretend we are something we're not. And I'm certainly not going to make it easy for him.

"Come in," I say when he continues to stand in the doorway. The air is thick with tension and already my persona is changing. A discomfort settles in my bones, a clear signal that this person is not good for me—even if he is my father.

"Thank you for agreeing to see me." He says it as though he's a business associate I've made time for. And he might as well be, because for all intents and purposes, we're strangers. "I needed to see you. There are some things I need to say and I'm hoping you'll be open to hearing them." He gestures to the couch. "May I sit down?" he asks, and I nod, but take a seat across from him on the other sofa, wanting to keep my distance.

He sits forward on the couch, his elbows on his thighs, fingers steepled against his lips. "Your mother is getting remarried. I'm sure you must know that by now."

"Yes. She called and told me." But I'm unwilling to offer up anything else. I don't have much to say on the subject of my mother.

"Your mother, Vanessa. I'm not going to lie to you," he begins, staring at a spot on the coffee table. "Your mother...," he lets out a wry laugh, "I don't think she ever loved me."

His words don't surprise me, yet still they punch me in the stomach when I already had a gaping wound. I don't know what to say to that. So I say nothing.

"It's not your fault though," he admits, finally looking up at me. "I need you to know that. I'm not sure she was ever capable of loving anyone other than herself. You know?" He stands up, walking over to the floor-to-ceiling window, staring out over the city. "When I initially met your mother, that very first time I saw her in the courtroom, she was larger than life. She had so much passion and drive. A fire in her eyes." He turns his head briefly in my direction. "Like you," he says before looking away again, and I want to tell him not to compare me to her because I'm nothing like her.

"I was so drawn to her. I knew I had to get to know her. I wanted to make her mine from that very first moment I laid eyes on her. And I did." He circles the room as he continues. "Things were good for a while, for several years, but then I noticed everything changing. We both became very focused on our careers, especially your mother. She began to eat, sleep, and breathe law. It became her life and I came second. Then one day," he stops and clears his throat, pain lining his features, "I came home and found her in bed with someone else."

My hand goes to my head to ease the ache building in my temples. I'm not sure I want to hear this. But I have no choice because he doesn't stop there.

"She said it was a one-time thing and I believed her, probably because I needed to at the time. Because I couldn't picture my life without her, even though I felt the distance between us growing. So I thought, maybe," his darkened, blue eyes shift to mine, "if we had a baby then it would keep us together. It would bring us closer. But she really didn't want to have children and I made a decision that I didn't care what she wanted. Because I wanted her more." He scrapes a weathered hand through his thinning hair. "I don't want to go into all the sordid details but obviously she ended up pregnant with you and we stayed together. But we never should have. Because we were a mistake."

He swallows hard, then comes over and sits on the coffee table in front of me. I'm trapped, not only by him, but by his words, afraid of what he's going to say next. The desire to run out the door is overwhelming, but I'm frozen—waiting to bleed some more.

"But you, Vanessa. You were never a mistake," he insists, his voice hoarse, and I don't know where this is coming from. I certainly don't believe him. "I loved you. I'm sorry that I just didn't know how to show it and I was too wrapped up in what I wanted. But you're my daughter and I... I still love you," he confesses, reaching out a hand to me and I flinch, sitting as far back on the couch as possible, hands hidden beneath my legs.

"I don't believe you," I retort, because he must want something from me. Distrust merges with long buried anger and I can't let this farce go on any longer. "Suddenly I'm your *daughter*," I spit. "I've been your daughter for twenty-seven years. Where the hell have *you* been?"

"I know—"

"No." I cut him off with my words and my hand in the air. Rage makes my eyes burn and I want him to see this, the monster of a daughter he created. That little girl inside that was starved for any crumb of affection he would throw my way is gone. So I face him. "You *don't* know. You don't know the first thing about me because you never bothered paying attention long enough to find out. Tossing money and presents in my direction didn't take the place of love and affection. I wanted it back then. I *needed* it back then. But I don't need it now. And I certainly don't want it—not from you."

He takes a seat next to me on the couch and I turn away. I can't look at him anymore. "Vanessa." My name comes out as a sigh. "About a month ago, I had a birthday. I turned sixty, and I looked up and saw no one. Nothing... except for my work. My life is empty and I know I only have myself to blame. Maybe," he laughs acidly, "it's because half my life is over and I realize that nothing has changed. But I don't want to live the second part of my life the way I lived the first. I want to try to be different. That's why I'm here. I want another chance to be a father to you.

"I know it's different now, and that you're older. You don't need me the way you needed me to be there when you were younger, and I wasn't. I know no apologies can make up for that. We can't go back, but we can go forward. I'd like to be a part of your life in some way, if you'll allow me to be. If you can forgive me. I'd like to get to know the woman you are now."

My head is pounding and my hands are starting to hurt from squeezing them so hard. I pivot around, blue eyes that are way too familiar staring at me, expecting answers, when I have none.

"I don't know what you expect me to say. I don't know if I can give you what you want."

"And I understand." He's somewhat resigned as if he knows his request is impossible for me. "All I'm asking is that you think about it."

And the only thing I'm thinking about is seeing Rex. I need to see Rex.

"Okay," I mutter. "I will." I say the words, not even knowing whether I mean them or not. I just need him to go.

"Thank you. I'm staying at the W until tomorrow night. In case you want to reach me." He pushes off the couch and I'm thankful that I don't have to ask him to leave. He's already overstayed his welcome and I think he knows that.

I don't move from where I'm sitting, still trying to absorb what just happened here. When he gets to the door, he pauses, chin down, reaching into his pocket. Something jingles in his hand and he circles back, setting whatever it is down on the table. My heart scrunches tight in my chest when I see it's the silver charm bracelet that Stella bought for me when I turned eight. The only gift that ever meant anything to me.

*"I have a present for you," she said, pushing it toward me on the table.*

*"I don't like presents," I mumbled, but it was hard to look away from the bright yellow wrapping paper and yellow bow. Yellow was my favorite color.*

*"I know," she replied, and her voice sounded sad to me. I didn't want her to be sad because she was my friend. She picked up the small, square box and shook it just a little bit. I heard something rattling around and got excited, bouncing in my seat. Only because it was Stella.*

*I felt my lips doing a funny quiver and she smiled back at me. She* had the whitest teeth I'd ever seen. She must have used special toothpaste.

"Okay." I took the gift from her hand and quickly tore away the paper. When I opened the box, I found the prettiest silver bracelet with puppies and kittens hanging from it. They were my favorite. I think my eyes and my mouth must have smiled at the same time because when I looked up at her, I could see all of her teeth. But then my throat felt funny and I wanted to cry. Instead, I remembered what Mommy said and sniffed in big to hold back my tears. "I love doggies and kitty cats," I said, touching each one.

"I know you do," she said, and then she kissed me on the cheek. "Happy Birthday, Nessa."

And then I gasp as something hits me with so much force I can barely breathe. She *did* know. Because she cared enough to know.

I blink back the tears that are desperate to fall, my chest expanding with euphoria. All those years I thought that I was unlovable, that there was no one who cared about me, when all along there was someone right in front of me who did.

"Where did you get that?" I ask, the words a choppy jumble from my mouth.

He glances down at the fragile, tarnished piece of jewelry, faded from time. "We were cleaning out the house and I came across it. I kept it for you because I knew it was important to you." And then the latch clicks, closing the door on everything that happened here tonight, leaving me wondering if I'll be able to open the one he wants to walk through.

The sky is bathed in darkness, a replica of my pensive mood, as I blindly make my way toward Rex's apartment. My mind is spinning in confusion, unable to make sense of my father's words. The consistent band of insecurity that tightens around my waist still makes me wonder if he has an ulterior motive.

The moment Rex opens the door, it's as if I've walked into the light. I launch myself into his arms, all of the anger and confusion consuming me becomes one big blur and melts away. Large hands grip my waist, holding me, and I feel safe and protected. His strength has become my harbor in this crazy storm that is my life. I've come to rely on him. And while it scares me, it's exhilarating at the same time. Something I never thought could happen—with anyone.

"Whoa." He squeezes me tight, his hand coming up to stroke my hair. "I'm happy to see you too. Hey," he says when I don't respond, "you okay?"

I shake my head against his chest, continuing to nestle myself as close as possible, trying to stifle the emotion that wants to come pouring out. He won't let me hide though, another thing I love—I mean, appreciate about him. Instead, he pulls us apart, taking my face in his hands, his rich, brown eyes searching for the truth in mine.

"No, you're not okay. Come tell me what happened with your dad." He intertwines our fingers, leading us over to the sofa.

We sit down and recline against the back of the couch. Rex pivots to face me, giving me his full attention. The conversation with my father comes rushing back, making me feel lightheaded. I'm unable to reconcile who he used to be with the man who showed up tonight.

"I don't understand what's happened to him," I begin. "He told me he was sorry for everything, that he wanted to make it right, to start over. And...." I clench my fists in my lap. "I wanted to hate him. I thought that I *did* hate him. So my first reaction was to push back, to be angry and resentful, because it doesn't matter now. Where the hell was he when I needed him? But," I let out a pained sigh, "after he left I realized maybe it does matter. Maybe there's a part of me that still wants him in my life."

"Of course. He's your father." Rex strums my palm with his knuckle, soothing me.

"You know." I tug at the ends of my hair. "Growing up, I always felt like there was something wrong with me because I didn't have the perfect family like everyone else I knew, and somehow that made me less than in some way, that made me broken."

"Not broken, baby," he says with a half-smile. "A little bit bent like the rest of us maybe, but never broken."

My eyes move to our hands. "He said he wants to know if we can try to build something, get to know each other now. I just don't know if I have it in me to forgive him."

"Hey." Rex takes his finger, tapping underneath my chin, and I lift my head. "I think you do. I think your capacity to forgive is enormous, because your heart is so big."

The meaning behind his words and the sincerity in his eyes trigger a kaleidoscope of emotions to rocket through my body. A dam bursts as years of sadness, regret, and anger rise to the surface, along with something else more powerful that I've yet to put a name to, and I can no longer hold back. My mother's words finally disintegrate as the tears course down my cheeks.

"I don't cry," I hiccup through a sob, no longer making any attempts to hide from him.

"Yeah, so you've said." A tear lands on his thumb and another follows in its path. "Crying doesn't make you weak, baby. It makes you human."

I press a hand against my face, trying to disappear again. "When I'm like this, I—I just don't want you to see me."

He removes my hand, taking it between both of his. "It's too late, baby. You're the only one I've seen since the moment I laid eyes on you."

My breathing stalls and I can't get it to start up again. Rex tucks a wayward strand of hair behind my ear, his head angled to the side, eyes dancing over my face.

"I haven't been completely honest with you." His voice is hoarse, and my stomach plummets to the ground, anticipating those next words that will send me running out the door with a broken heart— because somewhere, deep down, I knew this was too good to be true.

"When I came home that night on my birthday, I was upset about what the day reminded me of, yes, but there was something else I couldn't tell you. I wanted to push you away, for you to get as far from me as possible, because I was afraid I would end up hurting you." He caresses my cheek with his hand, his gaze burrowing into mine. "But when you left that picture of Tyler and me, you showed me a piece of your heart and then walked away... and I realized in that moment that I wanted you more than I was willing to let you go."

His other hand comes up to my cheek, his eyes continuing to hold me prisoner. "I—I couldn't have dreamed you up if I tried. Because you're too perfect. Too giving, too warm, too beautiful, and probably too good for me. But... the truth is, you make me want to try harder to be better, to be someone who deserves you.

"I don't like to fall, you know? And believe me when I tell you I've fallen a lot in my life. I've been banged up, bruised, fucked up more times and in more ways than I can even count. But I'm not afraid to fall anymore. The only thing I'm fucking terrified of, is that you won't be there to catch me when I do."

"Rex, I—"

He silences me with a finger to my lips. "I'm falling in love with you, Blondie."

"*What?*" I question in a whisper.

Gentle thumbs stroll over my skin, the warmth of his hands and his words making my own fear evaporate. "I said, I'm falling in love with you."

Pure joy, an emotion I've not known before now, encourages more tears to break free, rolling down my face and across his fingers. But this time I smile through them.

"You're doing that no crying thing again," he teases, and I can't do anything but stare into his eyes. The only eyes I ever want to see me this vulnerable. The only eyes I want looking at me the way he is right now.

"I owe you an apology." I reach out and smooth a fringe of hair from his face, a tiny wrinkle of confusion revealing itself. "I accused you of using your past to lash out, all the while I've been doing pretty much the same thing."

"I don't understand." He leans into my hand when it reaches his cheek.

"I may not have been lashing out, but I used my past to keep me from my future, from trusting you, from opening myself up to you and letting you in, for fear that you'd hurt me the way they did. You're not them. I know that now. And I'm sorry."

"You don't owe me any apologies."

"Oh, but I do. Because now I can clearly see what's right in front of me. I can feel without barriers. And I can finally tell you that I'm in love with you, Rex."

"Say it again," he demands, his mouth practically on top of mine now, his breath kissing me in a whisper.

"I'm in love with you." I barely get the words out before his lips are on me, warm and sweet. And I close my eyes and give in, opening myself up to him in every way.

Willingly. Happily. Finally.

# CHAPTER THIRTY-TWO

## WHO KNEW?

She's in love with me. Me. The guy who didn't understand what the fucking word meant, never mind actually having a shot at it.

And I did it. I pushed past the fear of loss and admitted something I've been feeling for a while but was unable to voice. That I'm falling in love with her, too.

I part her lips with mine, kissing her slow and tender, and she tastes even better now if that's possible. But I suppose love does that.

Who knew?

She pushes me down on the couch, draping her entire body over me and I shudder, filled with a bone-crushing desire more fierce than anything I've ever felt before. I've said the words, but now I want to show her how much she means to me.

Our lips and tongues tangle, and I feel how much she wants me, not just with her body, but with her heart. And it's fucking amazing to be wanted this way. Especially by her. Only by her.

And if I'm lucky—always by her.

Taking her lips from mine, she breaks our connection, her blue eyes dotted with so much emotion it nearly takes my breath away. "Rex, I want... well...," she bites her lip, "I know it's going to sound strange, but...."

"Hey," I tell her, setting her lip free, "nothing you say is strange. What is it?"

"I've... I've never made love before," her throat moves on a swallow, "and I want to... with you."

"Well I haven't either, you know? So it's kind of a first for both of us." I roll her over and we end up on the carpet laughing, which was not my intention.

"Is this your idea of foreplay?" she jokes, and I pinch her ass.

"Oh, baby, you ain't seen nothing yet." I manage to tear myself off of her, grabbing onto her arms and pulling her up. "Let's go, hot stuff. I think we should move this to the master suite."

A laugh leaks out, so loud, so happy, and I decide I don't want to ever stop hearing that sound.

"Master suite," she kids when we get to my room, but there's an uneasiness in her tone and I want to take it away. "I'm nervous," she admits, glancing down at her hands, and that's when I notice she's shaking.

Immediately, I gather her hands in mine, steadying her. "Why are you nervous? I've seen you naked before; I can map your body with my eyes closed," I remind her, trying to lighten the anxiety. But there's still no sign of her eyes, and I need to see them. Her truth is always there. "I need you to look at me."

Big, beautiful pools of blue finally stare back at me and I'm gone. I'm so fucking gone.

"I'm nervous because... now you can see my heart."

I trace a pattern down the side of her face, starting with her hairline, moving down past her eyebrow, the curve of her cheek, her chin. "Well, you know what? I'm nervous, too," I tell her, and she shows me that dimpled smile.

"You are?" she asks, surprise lighting her gaze.

"Yes, but it's more than that." I run a finger down her bare arm and she shivers. "I've never wanted anyone more than I want you in this moment. I'm not sure I've ever wanted anything more in my entire life."

"You're getting pretty good with this sappy stuff. So whatever you're doing, keep it up," she urges, her lips doing a soft brush over mine. "And now would be a perfect time to kiss me. Like *really* kiss me."

So I do.

And it's a fucking explosion—of lips and tongue and feeling—of everything we've been holding back. Her arms loop around my neck and mine surround her waist, every body part touching, hearts pounding with such force that I can't determine where hers ends and mine begins.

Warm hands slip under my shirt, making me shiver. The gentle skim of her fingertips, her touch, giving me a high unlike anything else. I rub my cock against her and she mewls softly, propelling me closer.

Breathless, she puts a stop to the kiss, lips swollen, eyes darkened. She lowers her hands, lifting my t-shirt away before gliding her nails over the planes of flexing muscle, tracing the lines of my tattoo. Her fingers work their way down to the clasp of my jeans, flicking it open. That's when I reach down and grip her wrist, halting her from going any further.

"I want to undress you," I say, and the confusion in her features melts away. She immediately drops her hands to her sides, giving me free rein over her body.

Squatting down, I take the ruffled hem of her dress between my fingers and rise to my feet, slowly lifting it up as I go, letting my eyes rove over her form as the dress falls away to the carpet.

"*Jesus*, you're beautiful."

Taking my palm, I smooth it down the curve of her neck, her collarbone, the dip between her breasts. I can feel the hammering of her heart beneath my fingers and my own heart gallops inside my chest, knowing what I mean to her now. For some reason, she chose me.

And I feel like the luckiest fucking guy in the world.

I lift her hand and starting at the bottom, place closed-mouth kisses along the underside of her arm, my lips drifting along its length, goose bumps shimmering on her skin in their wake. I allow it to fall and gently pick up the other one. This time, letting my tongue trail her flesh, the soft moans leaving her mouth urging me on.

Her shoulders are next, and I move behind her, kneading them, her head falling to the side as I do. I kiss my way down to the clasp of her bra, releasing it, and her skin prickles as the straps glide slowly across her arms. "Lean back, baby," I say, and when she does, I reach around to the hardened pink tips of her nipples, squeezing them between my fingers, watching them stiffen further. Seeing how aroused she is, knowing how her body is humming for me, makes me ache to take her right now. But I want to go slow. I've never had this with anyone and I don't want to do anything to fuck it up.

"Rex," she whimpers, and I smile against her hair. I love how well I can read her... in every way.

"I know, baby." One of my hands descends her belly, following the curve of her waist until I reach her panties. I dip a finger inside, exhaling a long, uneven hiss of breath when I find them soaked with her desire. Lowering myself to the carpet, I slip them down her legs, before pushing back up to my feet.

I spin her around to face me, letting her watch as I rid myself of the remainder of my clothing. Her eyes drink me in, gaze landing on my erection, thick and hard, practically pointing against her stomach. Taking both of her hands in mine, I lean forward and kiss her forehead, the tip of her nose, her chin. With one final kiss to her lips, I walk her back to the bed, lying us both down. Blood roars through my veins, the need to please her overwhelming me. Putting myself second was never a part of who I am, until I met Vanessa. Now with her, it's the only thing that matters.

My mouth finds hers and she teases me with her tongue and teeth, nibbling at my bottom lip, sucking it into her mouth. I don't linger there long, wanting desperately to taste her, to watch her eyes glaze over as I make her come over and over again. She stops me though, tugging on my hair to bring me back up to her.

"Show me." Her voice is strained, and my head tips in question.

"Show you what, baby?"

"Show me... love," she whispers, a tear crawling down her cheek, my heart ceasing to beat at the realization that no one has ever done that for her.

I lower my head and shower her face with kisses until all the wetness disappears, then reach next to me on the table. But she grabs my hand, shaking her head.

"No. I've been on the pill, Rex. And I don't want anything between us now. I just want to feel you, with nothing else."

"I've always been safe. I've never—"

She interrupts me with a finger to my lips. "I trust you, Rex."

Three words that send me fucking reeling, as if I've just climbed the tallest mountain.

"Good. Because I would never hurt you."

The intensity of her stare is blazing, cutting right through me. Vulnerability cracks the surface of my tough exterior, making me want to look away. A small part of me even feels the need to run, fear clamping around my chest. But I can't. And I won't. Because those eyes fill me with hope for a second chance—to rewrite my story.

"Rex." She says my name and there's promise in her voice, like that moon Tyler and I used to chase as kids is somehow within my grasp. I hold myself up with one arm, taking my other hand and caressing her face, pressing my lips to the corner of her mouth, down her jaw then back up again.

Her fingers take the lead, encircling my erection, and I nearly come right then, just from her touch alone. She teases her entrance with my hardened cock, rubbing me back and forth over her slit, moisture covering the head. I'm not even inside her yet and feeling her pussy without any barrier is fucking amazing.

I reach down between us, covering her hand with mine as she guides me inside, both of us watching as my cock disappears, a low guttural noise tearing from my throat the moment I enter her. "Oh fuck," I groan as her wet heat surrounds me, squeezing and holding my cock—and it's pure, fucking bliss. I've never not used a condom before, and now that I have, I don't ever want to have to wear one of those fuckers again.

Eager lips open to connect with mine as I thrust in and out at a slow pace, our breathing and bodies intertwined, her hands clinging to my arms for support. She's practically panting into my mouth and I break us apart, my breathing uneven, her skin flushed pink.

"Baby, you feel so good. Jesus. You're so warm and snug. My cock likes it in there," I tease. "He might stay a while." And she lets out a laugh mixed with a whimper, as I continue to sink into her, savoring this—her body, our connection.

I love that I can be with her like this and still joke, still be me. I don't have to say all that lovey dovey shit, because even though I'm crazy about her, that's just not me. And she doesn't expect me to be anyone I'm not. It makes me feel weightless, as if I could take flight. She accepts who I am and there's no better fucking feeling in the world.

"Oh God, Rex, you feel amazing," she murmurs. "I want you so much." Her breathing is ragged, sweat beginning to glisten on her forehead.

"You have me, baby," I groan, locked in her gaze as I push in and out of her pussy, my chest heaving, muscles drawing tight. With a clenched jaw, I rock into her and she arches her hips, both of us giving, taking. It's no longer just our bodies that are entwined now, it's our hearts, too.

"Ahh, I'm close," she moans, and I duck my head, taking her nipple into my mouth, licking and sucking the way I know will make her come apart.

"Come for me," I urge, and she squeezes my biceps, her nails biting into my skin.

"Oh my God, Rex." My name rolls off her tongue as she spasms around me, pulsating, and I know I'm not far behind. "I want to feel you come inside me," she breathes out and I completely lose it, pounding into her a few more times before I come with a ferocity I've not experienced before.

Dropping my head against her chest, I attempt to catch my breath, which is utterly impossible. My hair and body are drenched with sweat, my cock soaked in her juices. In other words, I'm in heaven.

"Do you have any idea how amazing that felt?" I manage to lift my head and meet her eyes, pausing just above her lips, our breaths colliding.

"Hmmm... I think I have some idea." She smiles, and then I take one last look into those soulful blue eyes before my lips find hers, putting everything of my heart into this one kiss so she knows this is real for me.

Our mouths separate, but our eyes remain connected. Nothing else exists right now. Nothing else matters.

"You know I'm crazy about you, right? I mean," I pause, hoping to find the words, "I know I don't always say the right thing," I shrug, "but... well I am."

"I think you do just fine." She raises a hand to let a finger skate over the rough stubble on my chin. "Just be you, Rex. Because that's who I fell in love with."

A strange tingling radiates throughout my chest, hearing her say those words again. Never in a million years could I have imagined this, or her. But now that it's happening, I can't envision anything else. I close my eyes, inhaling what I hope will be a calming breath as the fear of loss creeps back into my psyche, freezing my limbs, rendering me immobile.

She must sense it too, because something changes in her smile. A tiny line marks a path across her forehead. "What's wrong?"

"Nothing." I roll off of her, swinging my legs over the side of the bed. "I'm going to get us a cloth to clean up."

When I come back from the bathroom, she's sitting up on the bed with a scowl, arms crossed over her chest. "Don't do that."

"Don't do what?"

"*You* know what." She glares at me. "Don't shut me out. Not after everything."

I heave out an aggravated sigh, unsure as to whether it's because she knows me so well or because I have to reveal the truth. I sit next to her on the bed, about to slide the washcloth between her legs when she stops me with an expectant stare.

"It's just fear, baby. I lose the people I care about. It's that simple. I lost Tyler, my father...." My gaze slips from hers and I glance out the window. "I don't want to lose you, too."

Her soft hand trails down my arm, bringing my eyes back to hers. "You're not going to lose me, Rex. We just found each other." A wide grin draws the tiny dimple from her cheek. "Well, unless you do something to fuck it up." She giggles and I jump on top of her.

"You got jokes now, huh?"

"Perhaps," she grins, "but I'd probably be a lot funnier if I had some food in my stomach. Please tell me you have food?"

"Hmph... you know I have popcorn." I nip her ear and she laughs.

"Yes, well. I'm starving. Why don't we go shopping and I'll cook for you?"

"I'm thinking we need to stay naked and order take out," I suggest, trying to convince her by attaching my lips to her nipple, flicking my tongue over the crest.

"Sold!" She laughs, and I cease the torture once she agrees. "I could go for some Chinese food. Sound good?"

"What do you want?" I sweep the washcloth between her legs and then clean myself up, too.

"Hmph... chicken with broccoli and vegetable fried rice."

"Okay." I toss the cloth in the laundry and throw on my boxers. "Their number is in the kitchen. I'll be right back."

As I'm walking into the other room, I can't help but think how right this feels, she and I. It feels so normal and I don't know if I've ever had that in my life. I've had crazy, insane, and fucked-up—but never normal. And normal feels pretty damn good.

"Okay," I announce, coming back into the bedroom. "They said they're really busy and it'll be about an hour. I know you're really hungry. Do you want me to go pick it up?"

"No, thanks. I can wait." Her eyes drift from mine, summoned to the window by the light of the moon. "Wow, that is some moon. I don't remember the last time I saw one so bright."

I bounce on the bed beside her, immediately taking hold of her hand, twining our fingers together. "Me neither." And then I chuckle out loud thinking about one of the few memories from my childhood that actually makes me smile.

"What is it? What's so funny?" she asks, and I kind of want to share it with her.

"I was just remembering something. When I was younger, Tyler and I used to try to chase the moon. Sometimes at night, when we were outside on the front porch, we'd see it and just bolt, trying to catch up to it." I smile, thinking about the look on Hunter's face. "Then Hunter would take off running down the street after our asses. He always told us the moon kept moving so we'd never be able to catch it. But that never stopped us from trying."

"So that's where you get your tenacity." She rests her head on my shoulder. "I used to wander off with Stella sometimes," she says, and it's so quiet I almost miss it. "There was this field around the corner from my house and it was filled with wilting wildflowers and overgrown weeds. I remember wondering why no one took care of it, thinking how beautiful it could be if someone just paid attention to it. So," she laughs as if lost in the memory, "I filled my ladybug watering can up and made Stella take me there every day. It didn't hold much water, but I thought maybe if I gave them a little bit, some of them would come back to life. 'They just need someone to care for them,' I kept telling Stella."

Sadness seeps from her words, a piece of me hurting for her. But she has a chance to move forward now and I hope she takes it.

"And did they?" I ask, kissing the top of her head. "Grow?"

"No. But I still kept going back, hoping one day they would."

"What will you do about your father?" I carefully broach the subject even though I know it's weighing heavily on her mind.

"I don't know." The apprehension in her voice thickens the air around us. "But I'm trying to be open. Thinking about maybe giving him another chance. Everyone deserves that I guess, even though it scares me that I'll get hurt all over again."

I swivel my body around so I'm facing her, clutching her face in my hands. "You are amazing. You know that?" And she shakes her head, disbelief swimming in the depth of her eyes. "Well, you are. And you know what else?"

"No," she says, and I'm determined to get this out, to say it as best I can, pushing back the unease constantly forcing its way to the back of my throat.

"You've been showing me little by little that it's okay to be me, and that maybe in some fucked up way, I wouldn't be me if I hadn't gone through the shit, you know? And," I pause, swallowing down this foreign emotion she makes me feel, "I look forward to tomorrow now, more than I ever have in my entire life. And that's because of you."

"You've given me hope, too." And as she presses her lips to mine, I feel it.

I never knew hope could feel so good.

# CHAPTER THIRTY-THREE

## STEPPING INTO A DREAM

*Vanessa*

My nails have seen better days. I think I've bitten every single one on the subway, heading to see my father. I'm sure the people on this train think I'm some kind of lunatic, plotting my next scheme. Nerves rack my belly, and even though Rex was so sweet and wanted to take me to breakfast, I had to say no. The last thing I need is food rolling around in my stomach. The opportunity to lose it is too great.

I sigh Rex's name, and that coupled with the crazy smile taking residence on my face is yet another indicator that I'm psychotic to anyone watching. But I can't help myself. He was so wonderful yesterday. And he's in love with me. *Me.* The girl who never thought she had a chance at love. The girl who got a front row seat to doors slamming and curse words flying down an empty hall, but the walls are always listening—I certainly was.

But I feel like that's behind me now. Or it will be once I talk to my father. I'm getting a second chance at something I've wanted since I was a child, but never thought possible. And while I still don't completely understand my father's motivation, I'm going to try to believe that it's genuine. Because the man who visited me the other night seemed nothing like the distant and unaffected stranger I grew up with.

The subway doors open and I stride through the crowded platform, shaking off the apprehension sticking to me before trudging up the stairs leading to street level. The air is murky and troubled, quite possibly a twin to my respective mood. But I ignore it, steadying my breath, attempting to remember everything I learned in yoga class. Even though that was three years ago.

"V!" I hear my name and recognize the voice calling it, spinning around to find Olivia with a huge smile on her face, hands on her hips. "Uh, hello? You didn't get my messages? Hmph? Perhaps you were indisposed?" She clucks her tongue with a devious smile.

"Yes, I do believe I was," I grin, "and it was very pleasurable, if I remember correctly."

"Oh, I don't doubt it," she jokes. "Remember," and then she mouths a silent *Grayson*, at which point I start laughing, a much-needed distraction to lift my spirits. "So how did it go with your dad? That's why I was trying to reach you." She attempts to hide the Victoria's Secret bag behind her back and I just shake my head.

"Actually, I'm on my way to see my father right now." My tone drops significantly upon the mention of his name.

"Really? What's going on? Is he all right?"

"Well, that depends on how you look at it. He told me that he wants to try to have a relationship." I'm still beyond stunned that this is even happening. The way Olivia stares back at me, eyes wide, mouth open, she seems to agree.

A minute later, she finally picks her gaping mouth up off the cement. "Wow, that's huge. What are you going to do?"

"Even though it scares the shit out of me, I decided that I'm going to give him a chance."

That's when she lunges for me, dropping her lingerie bag and purse to the ground, hugging me harder than she ever has before. "I'm so proud of you," she whispers in my ear, "so, so proud."

I heave out a breath, simply because Olivia is the one person who knows how hard it has been for me over the years. The ways in which my upbringing, or lack thereof, has affected my life have been staggering. Of course, now I realize that I don't have to let it rule me, and at my age, it's high time I learned that.

"Thanks, Liv," I reply, and she lets me go just as someone bumps into us and curses, struggling to get past.

Gripping my shoulders, she stares intently into my eyes. "You're one of the bravest people I know, Vanessa Hilliard. It takes courage and strength to do what you're about to do, and you've got it in spades."

I help her gather her bags from the pavement. "That means a lot to me."

"Make sure to let me know how it goes. Don't ignore my texts this time." She winks, digging in her purse and pulling out some lip gloss. "I've got to run home and then go see my publisher but I'll leave my phone on."

"Okay," I promise, as she finishes putting a shine to her lips. "Oh, and by the way. I almost forgot. Rex told me he's falling in love with me and I'm in love with him, too." I say it off-the-cuff, meanwhile my heart is jumping in my chest. "Just thought you might want to know."

For the second time, her bags along with her lip gloss tumble to the cracked sidewalk, but this time she squeals, "And you were planning on telling me this when?"

"It just happened last night," I confess, wearing my heart in my smile. "Being with him makes me happy. Like *insanely* happy."

"I've always wanted that for you." She moves closer, tugging on the sleeve of my blouse, her lips turning up in a genuine smile. "You deserve it."

"You know what, Liv?" I stare up at the sky, and even though it's a dark gray, it doesn't seem to matter anymore. "I finally feel like maybe I deserve it, too."

My gaze wanders back to her and I see my friend. The person who has been by my side no matter what, who I can always rely on—who loves me. And the cup that I've always looked at as half full, is suddenly overflowing.

"I love you," I blurt out, and now it's me who embraces her, and she giggles. "What's so funny?"

"This love thing is really working for you," she teases, patting my back before releasing me. "I'm glad." She bends down to pick up her things from the sidewalk. "Okay, I've really got to go now. Don't forget to call me. See ya, V." She swings her purse over her shoulder and saunters away.

"Hey, Liv!" I shout out, and she twirls around, her chestnut locks flapping against her face. "Nice bag!" I smirk, her loud burst of laughter and the smile on her face resonating long after she's gone.

My hands are clammy, the past beginning to suffocate me the closer I get to the hotel. Heavy feet want to turn back, to thrust me into a place of comfort—preferably Rex's arms. But I can do this. I *have* to do this. And more importantly, a grown woman should not be afraid to talk to her father. It's just that we've never *talked* this way before.

Insecurity fastens itself to every limb. My steps become slower, more unsteady. I happen to check my watch and realize that I'm early, so I let out a relieved breath as I walk through the revolving doors of the hotel. Since I have a few minutes to compose myself, maybe I'll go splash some water on my face.

I didn't expect to see my father already waiting for me, his dark suit camouflaged against the pleated black leather couch he's sitting on. But I certainly don't miss the moisture he's wiping from his forehead. It's good to know I'm not the only one who's nervous.

One hand poised on his lap, his gaze fixed out the window, he looks as lost as I feel. I notice the consistent tapping of his foot against the marble floor and find myself staring at it. This is such a different side to my father. The confidence and strength he once exuded seems long gone and I wonder if my mother getting remarried was the last straw for him.

I draw in a breath and let it out slowly before walking over, thankful the lobby is fairly empty. The second I see his foot still, I know he's spotted me.

He stands up, tugging on his starched cuffs then rubbing his hands together. "Vanessa," he says, his tone shaky, a confirmation that I'm not the only one who's uncomfortable. "I'm so glad you called. Here," he points to the sofa, "please, sit down."

I perch myself at the edge, and now I'm the one fidgeting with my fingers, picking imaginary lint off my skirt, waiting for what he's going to say next. But I'm surprised by my own voice when I speak first.

"All I ever wanted," I begin, keeping my eyes trained on my hands, "was for you and Mom to pay attention to me. To know that my favorite color was yellow, that I loved puppies and kittens, that my favorite thing in the world was to play with those little green army men. That," I laugh, but the memory makes me sad, "I used to sneak chocolate from the kitchen cabinet. And the ridiculous thing about it is, I don't know why I ever felt the need to sneak it. You and Mom didn't notice, because you didn't care."

"Vanessa, I—"

"No," I interrupt, shaking my head, but still not looking in his direction. "If we're going to do this, you have to let me finish." I pause, trying to gather my thoughts again. "All those important moments in a child's life: birthdays, holidays, awards ceremonies, concerts, graduation. You and mom were nowhere to be found."

My eyes close as I struggle to block out the memories. "I remember watching my friends' faces, and their families', beaming with pride. But I felt alone... like I didn't exist to anyone else. So many times, I wanted to run away, I wished that I had a different family. The only person I had was Stella, and even then, Mom ended up sending her away, probably because she knew that she was the only person who cared about me." Tears build in my eyes as my voice becomes barely a whisper. "I don't understand why she didn't want anyone to care about me."

I steel myself with a big breath and finally pivot my body so I can look at my father, facing my fears, facing my past. "All I wanted was for you to see me. I always felt like I was just something you and Mom had to deal with, an obstacle in your way. There was even a time when I wondered if I had died, whether it would have mattered to you, whether you would have realized that you did love me, but it would've been too late."

"Oh, Vanessa." His eyes crinkle at the corners as his shoulders slump forward, completely crumpling under the weight of my words.

I keep going though, because he needs to hear this. But more importantly, I need to say it so I can finally work toward healing myself. "For a long time, I hated you, or at least I thought I did. I've let this affect so many aspects of my life, and it's held me back. But I don't want it to anymore. I won't *let it* anymore." I pierce him with a frosty glare that I quickly let go of. After all, I'm here to move past this.

A tear slides down his cheek and the anger fizzles from my body, replaced by something I never thought I'd have for my father— compassion. In all these years, I've never once seen him shed a tear over anything or anyone. Rex's words come back to me in a rush—*it makes you human.*

I feel as though I'm someone else when I reach out and touch his forearm, wanting to comfort him, wanting him to know that I can forgive now, that I don't blame him anymore. "Daddy," I say, a word that sounds like it's coming from a little girl, and maybe in some ways it is. A little girl wanting her daddy back. "It's okay now." And then quietly I murmur words that give me hope. Words that will finally set me free. "I... I forgive you."

The eyes that were glued to my hands climb to my face as more tears fall away, tiny droplets landing on his jacket. He takes me off guard by pulling me into an embrace, my arms remaining stiff at my sides, as uncertain as I am about what to do. But then I make the decision for them, and wrap them around his shoulders as the tears begin a helpless descent from my eyes, too.

It doesn't last long before he backs away, placing his hands on either side of my hair, holding me with eyes of blue that so closely resemble mine. "I'd like to be able to say that I raised you to be like this, caring and compassionate, but I can't. You did this all on your own. You've obviously grown into such a beautiful person. I'm proud to call you my daughter and thankful to be given a second chance."

I'm only able to respond with a single shake of the head. My mouth refuses to work, shock numbing my vocal cords, making them worthless. The rest of me isn't doing so hot either. It's hard to accept a change in the direction of your life when you were already resigned to it being one way. And while this is a welcome one, it doesn't make it any easier for me to digest.

"So what now?" I have to ask the question because I honestly don't know where we go from here. It's taken a long time to get where we are and I'm not sure how to turn back.

"I guess we start over." He gives me a small smile. "From here." A nervous pause interrupts his thoughts. "I've got to go back to Seattle early to try a case, but do you maybe want to get a quick bite to eat before I head to the airport?" he asks, his hands moving back into his own lap.

"I'd like to, but I really need to get to work." What I don't say, that the hitch in my chest says for me, is that this is too much all at once. "Plus, I guess I just need time to process everything, you know?"

"Yes, of course. I understand." He lowers his head in what I can only assume is disappointment. But this is a big step for me and I need do it at my own pace. "Well, I was thinking that I'd like to come in every so often for a visit, if it works for you, and maybe in the meantime, if it's okay, we can keep in touch via phone."

"Yes, I'd like that," I tell him, shifting from foot to foot. I'm not sure what to do now. But he takes care of that for me.

"I'll talk to you soon then, huh?" He looks at me with a tentative gaze and I offer him a reassuring smile.

"Yes."

After another brief hug, he clears his throat then steps away. "Goodbye, Vanessa, and... thank you."

I march across the lobby, pausing at the door for a quick wave, before disappearing into a swarm of people parading across the city street.

The sun is bursting through the clouds, hints of blue starting to peek out from behind them as I casually stroll back to my office. The sky has brightened, the darkness is no longer. And I feel it within me. I'm lighter, the anchor that weighed me down and held me back from truly living my life has been lifted. While I know I still have a long way to go, it's a fresh start. An opportunity to mold my life the way I want to. A shot at a different future—in more ways than one.

I'm almost to the office when I realize I need to get in touch with Olivia. I check my phone, smiling when I see texts from both her and Rex wanting to make sure that I'm okay. After responding to Olivia's text, I call Rex and leave him a quick message when it goes directly to voicemail.

I stride onto our floor with an enormous smile and a caramel latte, and within ten seconds, am accosted by Tillie.

"Boy," she cracks her gum, "I was about to send out the national guard." She looks me up and down in appraisal. "And don't you look happy. I guess that goes a long way to explaining what's going on in your office."

"What do you mean?" I peer around her tiny body and flowing red hair at my door.

"Beats me." She skips behind her desk, and I decide she's acting really unusual. Or more unusual than normal. "Here." She shoves a couple of pink slips into my hand. "That's it for messages, except Ryder called and wants to know if you still want to use him for the Taylor party next week."

"Okay, I'll call him," I say, anxious to move myself in the direction of my office so I can see what she's talking about. "Thanks, Tillie."

I open the door, my breath catching on a gasp, the coffee in my hand nearly spilling to the ground. My eyes blink on repeat, trying to make sure I'm not seeing things. An array of beautiful colors: brilliant reds, oranges, yellows, stunning pinks, purples are on every available surface. It's like I just stepped into a field of... wildflowers. My hand flies to my neck, unable to suppress the audible sob or the tears that are already coursing down my cheeks.

Rex.

The wall is the only thing holding me up as I collapse back against it, my limbs shaking, heart racing so fast it feels as if it might burst from my chest. I can't believe he did this for me.

Through my watery eyes and blurred vision, I spot a card on the corner of my desk and will my legs to take me there. Setting my coffee down, I take a seat on the chair, reaching for the envelope with trembling hands. Somehow I manage to tear it open and unfold the card.

*You see, Blondie, the flowers did grow.*
*All they needed was a little love.*

*ReX*

The card falls away and I cover my face with my hands, eyes flooding with happiness, a never-ending waterfall cascading down my skin. And I accept it. Embrace it. All the emotion that I was told never to feel, never to show, that's been buried beneath the surface, pushes past the pain, the fear, my mother's empty words—to what's real.

This is no longer a dream. This is my life. And *this* is as real as it gets.

My eyes roam from flower to flower, nose filling with the most wonderful fragrances, heart hypnotized by Rex and this unexpected yet beautiful gesture.

"I can't believe he did this for me," I voice out loud as though the field has ears, my head doing a continuous shake.

"Why not, he's fucking amazing," a sexy rasp says from behind me, and the wind gets knocked out of me once again when I turn my head to find Rex standing in the doorway with a roguish grin. He pushes off the wall and stalks over to me, his eyes never leaving mine. "Hi, baby." He takes my hand and helps me to my feet.

"Hi." My fingers attempt to erase the black smudges I know are staining my skin.

"You don't need to do that." He smiles. "You're beautiful."

"Are you trying to sweep me off my feet?" I wind my arms around his neck, his warm breath dancing across my skin.

He kisses the tip of my nose. "I don't know. Is it working?"

"I think it might be," I admit, my lips splitting into a grin.

"Well, don't get too used to it." His gentle hand pushes a wave of hair behind my ear. "I'm not a flowery type of a guy."

"Hmph. So you've said." I smirk, my mouth getting closer to his. "Thank you for this," I whisper. "You take my breath away."

"Oh, baby." His soft lips skim mine. "I think you got that backwards. Don't you get it? You've done something that no one else has been able to do."

"What do you mean?"

His thumb does a slow caress of my cheek and I lean into him. "You found a way into my heart. A heart that I didn't even think I had. A heart that every single fucking time it beats, I see your smile, I hear your laugh. I feel your touch. And now you fucking own it. You own me."

"Rex." I circle his nose with mine, smiling. "How could you not think you have a heart?" I press a hand to his chest, feeling the steady beat. "You have one of the most beautiful hearts I've ever known."

"*God*, I love you." His eyes hold me with their intensity as my own heart stops, hearing him say those three little words, words I never thought were possible for me. My lips part, and I try to grab for any available oxygen that will allow me to breathe.

"I love you... too," I stammer, tasting a salty tear as it lands on my smile.

"Thank fuck for that. Now shut up and kiss me, Blondie."

And so I do.

# EPILOGUE

## EIGHT MONTHS LATER

*Vanessa*

"I feel like we've come full circle," Rex says, the tattoo needle buzzing against my skin. I flinch, and he lifts it away, pausing in mid-air.

"You okay, baby? I'm almost done." He looks up at me with a reassuring smile and it instantly puts me at ease.

"Yes, I'm fine. Keep going." I haven't glanced down at it yet, and I won't until he's finished. "So are you excited about tomorrow?"

"A week in Hawaii with my baby. Hell yes. I can't fucking wait, you?"

"Hmph... let's see," I tease. "My string bikini, sandy beaches, a suite that I'm sure has a king-sized bed and a Jacuzzi tub, seeing you in nothing but your swim trunks the entire week. Yeah, I'm excited."

"Blondie," he rasps, "you're making me hard, and unless you want a lopsided heart, I'd stop talking like that."

"Okay, Okay," I concede. "I can't wait to see Olivia and Hunter get married though. Has that been the only thing Hunter's been talking about? Olivia eats, sleeps, and drinks their wedding."

"Yeah, my brother is stoked. He's been waiting a while and he deserves it. There." The vibration against my skin ceases and he sets the needle on the table. "Done." A cool cloth swipes across my skin just as my eyes settle on the tattoo.

I'm not sure where my smile is the brightest, my eyes or my mouth. "I love it, Rex!" I declare, glimpsing the inside of my wrist, where R ♥ V in bold, black letters sits with a red heart. Rex flips his hand over so I can see his—V ♥ R. "Now we match," I say as he covers mine up with a white bandage.

"You'll be able to take that off in about thirty minutes, and after any bleeding subsides, then you wash it." He starts cleaning up his station and I gather my things so I can head out.

"Wait," he spins around, "where do you think you're going?"

I search for my sunglasses then fling my purse over my shoulder. "I have some last minute things to get for our trip."

"Oh, you're not going anywhere," he says, his voice husky, strolling to the entrance of the deserted shop and locking the door. He stalks back over to me. The way his t-shirt hugs his abs and the thick bulge in his jeans tell me he's right. I'm not going anywhere.

"Hmmm...." My tongue darts out to wet my lips, hand rubbing over his erection. "I guess I could stay for a little while."

"God, I can't wait to have you all to myself in Hawaii." He licks at my top lip, drawing a moan from my mouth. "I predict a *lot* of beach sex."

"Hmph." I nip at his chin. "I don't know about the sand in my ass." My lower lip drops down in a pout and he sucks on it before letting it go with a pop... and one hell of a grin.

"Who said anything about sand?"

"Oh my God, Rex, it's so beautiful." I'm standing out on the deck of our hotel room, the Hawaiian breeze slapping against my skin, the dazzling sun warming my face. I look out on golden sand shimmering under its beams, a lazy sky watching over deep blue water speckled with green. The snow-capped waves lap against the shore while a distant chatter of birds welcomes us, all pointing toward one conclusion—this is paradise and I never want to leave.

Rex comes up behind me, snaking his arms around my waist, his warm breath fanning my neck. "It is beautiful here, baby. And I'm glad to be here with you." Soft lips find my skin and I angle my head so I can appreciate his mouth on any and all parts of me.

"What's that?" My gaze follows some words on the inside of his forearm, jutting out from the end of his sleeve. "Is that new?"

"Yes." He pulls his sleeve up. "Zeek did it for me yesterday."

"Carpe Diem... seize the day."

"You're smarter than you look," he teases, and I jab him with an elbow to the ribs.

"So why—"

There's a rhythmic knock on the door and Rex kisses my cheek before shuffling his sexy, bare feet to answer it. I'm still amazed that I get an entire week with him, away from the craziness of the city in, as far as I can tell, one of the most beautiful places on earth.

"I was wondering when you two would show up," I blurt out when Hunter and Olivia walk in. I give Olivia a big hug and Rex and Hunter do their hug and pat thing, which makes Olivia and I howl with laughter.

"What?" Rex and Hunter ask in unison, exchanging a quizzical stare.

"The whole guy hug thing cracks us up, that's all. It's like there's a timer or something on a guy hug and God forbid you go past when the buzzer sounds."

Rex chuckles and Hunter follows suit, latching onto Olivia's hand and holding her close. "So we need to go do some guy stuff, sweetheart." He smirks, tossing a look in her direction. "And besides, I know you really didn't want me seeing you before tonight."

"Yes, that's true." She winks at me. "Vanessa and I have some things we need to get done too, right, V?"

"Yup," I reply, and Rex's lips pull down in a frown.

He grips my t-shirt and pulls me to his side. "Wait, you're leaving?"

"For a little while." I run the back of my hand across his stubble. "I'll see you later, though."

"Oh." He draws his lip between his teeth. "I was hoping we could do some things together."

"We're going to do lots of things together." I edge closer and whisper in his ear, "Later."

Hunter stares at Rex, grinning, his eyes focused on a spot above his head.

Rex pats his hair, glancing behind us. "*What*?"

Hunter chuckles, his gaze full of humor. "Are those fairies I see dancing above your head?"

"Shut the fuck up," Rex retorts, giving him a playful smack on the arm.

"All right, come on. I need to take the bride-to-be out of here." I touch my lips to Rex's cheek and let them linger there. "Okay, I'll see you later."

"Yes, you will." He brings me in for one more kiss before Olivia and Hunter lock lips and I nearly have to drag her out of there.

I stop just outside the door once it closes. "Holy shit, Liv! You're getting married today!" I beam, and I find my own heart thundering in my chest as if it were me who was getting married. That's how much I love her. "I'm ecstatic for you."

Her blue eyes light up with her smile as she fans her hand in front of her face. "I'm sweating already. I'm so nervous, but Hunter doesn't seem nervous at all."

"Oh, I'm sure he's nervous. He just doesn't show it like you do. Gosh," I glance around, shaking my head, "I can't believe this." I wave my hand in the air, gesturing around us. "I can't believe Hunter put us up in The Four Seasons. My father was here a few months ago apparently, and he told me it was pretty spectacular."

"Speaking of which, how are things going with your dad?"

"They're good. I mean, it's slow going, you know. But we're both trying and that's what's important. Of course," I giggle, "Rex has already charmed him. He's even thinking about getting a tattoo."

"Why am I not surprised."

But there's something in her voice that makes me hesitate. I stop in front of a huge pastel painting of the ocean and shift to face her. "What is it? Are you upset about your family?"

"No, I mean...." She shuffles her feet along the floor. "Well, just disappointed. I know my father doesn't do well with planes, and my sisters had a hard time getting the time off. I understand. It just would've been nice for them to be here. But Hunter said in the next month or so we'll fly out to see them and have a big celebration."

"That will be great. Okay, come on now." I hook an arm over her shoulder as we continue to stroll through the lobby, exotic flowers at every turn. "I want to see that big, glowing smile on your face because *we* are about to get pampered for the biggest day of your life." A flower arrangement in the corner catches my eye. "Wait, hold on." I run over and plunge my nose into one of the petals, inhaling its fragrance.

She lodges a hand on her hip and shakes her head. "You are not seriously snorting those flowers are you? I can't take you anywhere." She giggles, throwing her hands up in the air and plodding off as I chase after her, our laughter echoing throughout the hotel.

The trellis is absolutely stunning, decorated with pink and yellow hibiscus, a scatter of white lilies, and Hawaiian fern. The sun is beginning to set, hints of orange streaking the sky unleashing a fiery glow on the ocean water beneath it. A glorious backdrop to the promises that are finally being exchanged, Hunter and Olivia pledging their love to one another in this romantic tropical paradise.

I'll admit, I haven't heard all of their vows. I'm trying to listen but Rex is very distracting. The black tux that is donning his perfect shape, the spike of his hair, the light shadow of stubble on his chin. I can hardly stand it. Speckles of gold dance in his russet-colored eyes as the departing sun casts a warm glow on his skin. And the way he's staring at me. The love shining in his gaze that I can't look away from—the one that makes my heart soar, my cheeks warm, my body come alive.

He pulls his cuff back, revealing the tattoo that matches mine, holding it up to me, smiling. I take in a silent breath of salty ocean air, my lips leaping at the corners, keeping time with my heart. How did I get so lucky? He is everything I could ever want, but never expected to have. And while I know he's not perfect, he's perfect for me, and I can finally say that I'm perfect for him, too.

"I now pronounce you husband and wife. You may kiss the bride." The judge's words bring my attention back to where it needs to be, albeit a little late.

Rex claps and whistles while I let out a squeal. Hunter and Olivia affirm their vows with a kiss to put all other kisses to shame. When they continue to lock lips, Rex comes over to me, pushing a ribbon of hair behind my shoulder.

"Now I can tell you how stunning you look."

"Well." I fist my hands in the lapels of his jacket, pulling him closer. "You look pretty stunning yourself," I murmur, my lips doing a soft brush against his. "Why aren't we kissing? Everyone else is."

"We are kissing, baby." He seals his lips over mine and I sigh into his mouth, relaxing against him as his arms come around my waist.

Someone clears their throat from behind us and I'm so lost in our kiss that I don't realize it's Hunter. "Who got married here?" he jokes, and I rush up to Olivia, throwing my arms around her while Rex embraces his brother.

"Congratulations, Mrs. Grayson." I squeeze her so tight, her happiness flowing right through me.

"Thanks, V," she replies, beaming when I let her go.

"Congrats, bro." Rex chimes in, hugging Hunter and lifting him off the ground. When he finally sets him down, I hug him, too.

"Congratulations, Hunter." I kiss him on the cheek and then step back. "So, what now? Isn't it time to party?"

"It sure is," Olivia agrees, her blue eyes twinkling, and I don't think I've ever seen her so happy.

I turn my head in Rex's direction and it looks like he's ready to party too. He removes his tux jacket, hanging it over the trellis, but I'm a bit puzzled when his hands lower to release buttons on his shirt.

The wrinkle that bubbles up whenever I'm confused makes an appearance. "What are you doing?" I ask, but am rewarded with nothing but silence.

Instead, he shoots me a mischievous grin before stopping midway down his shirt and popping the button on his pants. That's when I glance over at Hunter and Olivia, crinkling my nose, hands darting out from my sides.

"Hunter, will you do something about your brother, he's out of his mind!" I shout, but Hunter only shrugs in return, laughing with a huge smile on his face.

Rex continues to strip down, and I'm suddenly thankful we're on a private beach. I'm not interested in sharing him with anyone.

"What are you *doing*?" I ask again, and still he doesn't answer. Instead, I watch as his pants drop onto the sand, leaving him in a pair of swim trunks. When I look back to Olivia and Hunter for help again, they're locked in an embrace.

Buttons continue to be released on his shirt, all the while I'm shaking my head, doing my best to fight back the grin on my face. He's crazy, and this is exactly why I love him.

His shirt falls to the sand, and when my eyes drift back up to his sculptured abs, I blink them several times to make sure I'm not seeing things. Written across his chest in bold, black marker are the words **LOVE is Fucking Amazing**.

"What on earth are you doing?" I mouth, gesturing with my hands, and he ignores me, crooking his finger as he walks backward, urging me to follow. He continues toward the water until he spins around and I drop to my knees, stunned, the words **MARRY ME** splayed across the rippled muscles of his back in that same bold marker.

My entire body begins to shake, tears taking a furious roll down my cheeks. Rex finally turns around when he realizes I'm no longer behind him.

He walks over, crouching down on the sand in front of me. "If I knew this is all it would take to bring you to your knees, I would've done it a lot sooner."

"You're insane!" I cry out as he lifts a hand to cup my cheek, tears trailing over his thumb. And while I might be making a fuss, this is the single most amazing moment of my entire life.

"I'm insanely in love with you." He exhales a shaky breath. "You know, it wasn't until I met you that I started looking forward to the next day. And the next day after that." Sweat trickles down his skin as he takes a pause, meanwhile my head is spinning, my heart a wonderful jumble. Catching a tear from the corner of my eye with his finger, he continues, "I know that I may not always say the right thing, but I promise I'll do right by you. I'll jump over fucking hurdles for you, and I'll do anything to make you smile."

His other hand comes up to frame my face, his warm brown gaze holding mine. "I want you to know that you can be human with me and I'll be right by your side, that you can be imperfect and I'll love you no matter what. And that you never have to hide with me. I want to see how you feel, hear your thoughts, know your heart. I promise that I'll help you continue to bloom like those wildflowers that you loved so much."

With a loving smile on his lips, he presses a kiss to my forehead. "This is the real deal, baby. You and me. And," he hesitates, presenting me with a beautiful diamond ring that he seems to pull out of thin air, "I know this isn't a fancy restaurant, and the ring isn't sitting in a strawberry, but—"

"Rex." I refuse to let him go on. "It's you and I fucking love it. I love you so much. And I don't need anything else except what I have right here." I touch my palm to his cheek and he leans into me. "*You* are all I need." More tears spill down my cheeks and I feel as if I'm making up for lost time.

"I just wanted this to be perfect for you, you know?" The doubt in his stare makes my heart stumble, the need to reassure him the only thing that matters.

"*You* are perfect for me. So you need to stop talking now and just kiss me."

"Wait, is that a yes?" he asks over the screech of the overhead gulls. "You see," he grins, "even they want to know the answer."

"That's a hell yes. Now kiss me."

And so he does.

# EPILOGUE

She said yes.

I can't fucking believe it. But as our tongues move against one another, I taste it. Life. Hope. Love. And it's the best fucking thing I've ever tasted.

She leaves me, but stays close, her breath brushing my lips, both of us smiling against one another.

"So, this is what it's like," I murmur as she places gentle kisses around my mouth.

Her lips pause, a question in her gaze. "What what's like?"

"Happiness."

"Yes." She smiles, her blue eyes dancing with it. I love the way her eyes look now. Gone is that cold sadness from before, replaced by light and life.

My heart is running a marathon, thumping against my chest. A feeling that I'm getting used to, that I welcome. I'm not really one of those people that believe in fate but somehow it kind of feels like we belong together... like we were meant to be.

Standing up, I lift her under the arms and she wraps her legs around my waist. Her dress bunches around her hips, which doesn't concern her in the least bit. And it sure as hell doesn't concern me as I cup her ass, feeling the silk of her panties beneath my hands. Her hair sways with the gentle breeze, cheeks and lips pink from the sun. She smiles, arching a curious brow, but not bothering to ask me what I'm doing because she knows it won't make a difference.

My feet make contact with the cool, crisp water. All the while her eyes are on mine, gaze caressing me. "You're not attached to this dress, are you?" I ask as I continue to walk further into the ocean.

"Nope," she replies, not surprised when I set her down, knee deep in the clearest, bluest water I've ever seen.

"Give me your hand," I order, and she holds it out to me as I slip the engagement ring on her finger. It's a perfect fit.

"It's beautiful." She stares down at it, moving her hand from left to right, watching the sparkles as the sun continues to set behind us.

"So, I'm going to be Mrs. Rex Grayson." She lets out a happy sigh, still admiring the ring with a beaming smile on her lips.

"I like the sound of that. Actually, come to think of it, I like all your sounds," I tease, "and now I get to hear them for the rest of my life."

"And there's so many you've yet to hear." She weaves her arms back around my neck, resting her forehead against mine. "I love you, Rex."

"I love you too, baby."

Our heads both lift and turn at the same time, glancing up at the sky. The moon is beginning to make an appearance, casting a warm glow on the rippling water surrounding us.

"There's your moon, Rex. It looks so close, like it's finally within your reach."

My gaze slides to her, and I grasp her chin, slowly turning her face to mine. "You're right. It's in the palm of my hand now." I brush the backs of my fingers down her cheek. "And I don't have to run anymore."

"Rex."

"I really love you," I breathe out, "you're everything to me—my today, my tomorrow, my forever."

And then I kiss my future, finally saying goodbye to my past.

If you'd like to read about Hunter and Olivia's beginning, check out their story in
**_Finding Autumn_**

**_Lovely_**

## *Scarred Beautiful*

## *Love Love*

Want to hear about new books, giveaways, receive teasers or excerpts? Just sign up for my mailing list!

http://eepurl.com/Q1Ky1

# ACKNOWLEDGEMENTS

To my family, as always, for being so incredibly patient while I sat glued to my computer for hours on end to write this story. To Richard, for always listening and supporting me, even when I sound like a crazy person. To Isabella and Richie for being so patient when Mom had just one more thought to get out, and always running into the bathroom with paper and pen when inspiration hit me in the shower. The main reason I'm able to do what I do is because I have your support—and that means everything to me.

To Nikki Groom for, well, the list is endless. For your friendship, your support, for making me smile bigger when I'm already smiling, and lifting me up when my smile falters. Thank you for taking the time to read and provide your thoughts and feedback!

To Cheryl McIntyre. I feel so blessed that I discovered your books, that ultimately led me to you and our friendship. You are a treasure of a person and I am so happy to know you. Thank you for your unwavering support, for taking the time to read, and giving me invaluable suggestions.

To Dawn McIntyre. I'm happy to call you my friend. I so appreciate you reading through my work and taking the time to provide me with insight and lending me your critical eye. I honestly can't thank you enough!

To my pals Vi Keeland, Kristi Webster, Chris Carmilia, A.J. Warner, Cristina Arpin, Sunniva Dee, Natalie Catalano, Mary Tatar, Monica James, and Devon Herrera for your friendship, your laughter, your kindness, and your support. You all rock my entire existence!!

To my fellow authors, thank you for your support. You inspire me every day with your words and your stories, and I feel so blessed to be a part of this wonderful community.

To Lea Marika. What can I say, Lea? You are amazing. Thank you for being so in-tune with my thought process, my tireless pursuit of perfection, and my crazy mind. You are a wonderful editor and I appreciate all of your feedback and your support in helping me make my books the best they can be!

To Sommer Stein at Perfect Pear Creative for designing a unique and beautiful cover that fit so perfectly with my vision for REX.

To Golden Czermak at FuriousFotog for being so amazing to work with, and for the fabulous photograph that couldn't have been more perfect for my REX.

To Angela McLaurin at Fictional Formats for always turning my books into beautiful works of art. I am so appreciative of your creativity, your hard work, and your time.

To all of the bloggers who willingly take the time to read, review, share, and promote. There is no way that I could get the word out about my books without you. From blog tours, to reviews, to ARCs, to all the little messages I receive containing your enthusiasm and excitement for my novels. I can never thank you enough. Thank you to Love Between the Sheets for always doing such a wonderful job organizing my release blitz's, blog tours, and anything else that my mind conjures up!

Finally, to my readers. I honestly don't know how to express what it means to me that you take the time to read my work, send me messages, mention me in posts, and spread the word about my books. You always manage to put the biggest smile on my face. Knowing my writing has made a difference in your life is what makes a difference in mine. Thank you.

# ABOUT THE AUTHOR

Beth Michele is the author of *Love Love*, *Lovely*, *Scarred Beautiful*, *Finding Autumn*, and *Rex*. She is a Connecticut native who loves spending time with her husband and two children. If you can't find her, though, she's probably hiding out with her laptop or her kindle somewhere quiet, preferably a spot overlooking the ocean. She has an affinity for Twizzlers, is a hopeless romantic, and a happily ever after fanatic.

**I would love to hear from you, so please feel free to reach out to me:**

**Email:**
beth@bethmichele.com

**Website:**
http://www.bethmichele.com

**Twitter:**
http://www.twitter.com/bethmichele8

**Facebook:**
https://www.facebook.com/pages/Beth-Michele-Author/198619836947212

**Booktropolous Social:**
https://booktropoloussocial.com/index.php?do=/profile-2/

www.ingramcontent.com/pod-product-compliance
Lightning Source LLC
Chambersburg PA
CBHW031249170626
46807CB00001B/48